Dear Reader,

For centuries, British inheritance laws favored eldest sons to the detriment of younger sons, and daughters. It often created dire situations of wealthy eldest sons and younger children desperate for enough to live on, with the money and estate given to a sole inheritor. Even today, in other countries, not just England, inequities in an inheritance can cause desperation for some, and strife among siblings.

The Duchess was fascinating to write, because of both the history and the human dramas involved in unexpected situations and unorthodox solutions. A young girl is cast out of her safe, familiar, extremely comfortable world, even her adoring father unable to protect her from the laws of the land and her cruel older brother. What do you do when everything you know is lost to you, and you have nothing, and no one to help you? Where do you go when all the doors close resoundingly behind you? And then yet another door closes and the ledge you are standing on, delicately balanced, becomes even narrower. What do you do, faced by a family member who has all the power and chooses to use it against you? And when an employer falsely accuses you, and you have nowhere to turn, and lose the job you relied on? The young duchess loses everything and everyone she had to protect her.

The resourcefulness and courage of the human spirit have always fascinated me, and I love to write about it. The duchess chooses the most unfamiliar, unimaginable path and creates a world beyond her own imagining, and even ours. A fascinating world, full of powerful men and important people, and she moves among them, untouched, unharmed, in control of her own destiny, and even helping others. Where life leads her will intrigue you, I hope. And beneath it all is my belief that good triumphs over evil, and certainly should. The way is not clear at first, as it isn't for any of us, and the road to salvation can be a very bumpy one, but it is my hope that the good, the brave, the honest, and the strong prevail in the end. The story could be just as true in our modern day. I hope you enjoy reading it as much as I enjoyed writing it.

Love,
Danielle Steel

The Duchess

By Danielle Steel

DANIELLE STEEL

THE DUCHESS

A Novel

Delacorte Press | New York

Published in the United States by Delacorte Press, an imprint of Random House, a division of Penguin Random House LLC, New York.

DELACORTE PRESS and the HOUSE colophon are registered trademarks of Penguin Random House LLC.

LIBRARY OF CONGRESS CATALOGING-IN-PUBLICATION DATA

Names: Steel, Danielle, author.
Title: The duchess : a novel / Danielle Steel.
Description: New York : Delacorte Press, [2017]
Identifiers: LCCN 2016038517| ISBN 9780345531087 (print) | ISBN 9780425285367 (ebook)
Classification: LCC PS3569.T33828 D83 2017 | DDC 813/.54--dc23
LC record available at https://lccn.loc.gov/2016038517

Printed in the United States of America on acid-free paper

randomhousebooks.com

2 4 6 8 9 7 5 3 1

First Edition

Book design by Virginia Norey

To my beloved children,
Beatrix, Trevor, Todd, Nick,
Samantha, Victoria, Vanessa,
Maxx, and Zara,
Always fight for what you know
is right. Seek justice and all
that you deserve.
God and Destiny will do the rest.
I love you with all my heart and
every fiber of my being.

               With all my love,
               Mommy/ds

Courage is not the absence of fear or despair,
but the strength to conquer them.

THE DUCHESS

Chapter 1

Belgrave Castle sat in all its splendor in the heart of Hertford-shire, as it had for eleven generations and nearly three hundred years, since the sixteenth century. And aside from some more modern features that had been added, and a few decorative touches, very little had changed in its history. And its owners followed the same traditions they had for more than two hundred years, which was reassuring. It was the family seat of Phillip, Duke of Westerfield. The Latham family had built Belgrave Castle, it was one of the largest castles in England, and due to the duke's fortune, one of the most beautifully maintained.

The land around it was extensive and stretched as far as the eye could see, with forests, a large lake—which the groundsmen kept well stocked for fishing—and tenant farms, which were run by farmers whose ancestors had been serfs. The duke had overseen all of it since his youth, when his father died in a hunting accident on a neighboring estate. And under his diligent care, Belgrave and all its land

and properties had prospered. At seventy-four, he had been schooling his eldest son, Tristan, in the management of the estate for several years. Phillip felt that his son was ready to take it on, and handle it responsibly, but he had other concerns about him. Tristan was forty-five years old, married with two daughters. The duke's younger son, Edward, was forty-two years old, had never married, and had no legitimate children, though countless illegitimate ones. No one knew just how many, not even Edward himself. And he was given to strong drink and gambling, and every kind of indulgence one could imagine, preferably if it involved fast horses or women. It would have been a disaster if he had been the eldest, but fortunately he wasn't, although neither of Phillip's sons had produced a son and heir.

Both men were the sons of the duke's first wife, Arabella, the daughter of an earl, and Phillip's second cousin, with a handsome fortune of her own. She came from an irreproachable family, of aristocratic lineage, and she had been young when they married. It had been a union both families had approved of, Phillip had been twenty-eight, and Arabella barely seventeen, and strikingly pretty. She had been the star of her first London Season, where she had been expected to meet her future husband, and she had done so very successfully. But Phillip had discovered that she had a cold nature as she grew older, and she was far more interested in social pursuits, and enjoying the benefits of being a duchess, than she was in her husband, and she had even less interest in her children. She was a very self-centered woman, though greatly admired for her beauty. She had died of influenza when the boys were four and seven, and with the assistance of governesses, the large staff he employed, and his mother, the dowager duchess, who had still been alive at the time, Phillip had brought up his boys alone.

The young women of neighboring families, and the London hostesses who entertained him when he went to town, did their best to catch his interest in the ensuing years. But the boys were in their twenties before Phillip met the woman who enchanted him totally and became the love of his life the moment he met her. Marie-Isabelle was the daughter of a French marquis, first cousin of the late French king who had died in the French Revolution. She was a Bourbon on one side of her family and Orléans on the other, with royals on both sides. She had been born during the first year of the Revolution, and her parents had been killed shortly after, their château burned to the ground and all their possessions stolen or destroyed. Sensing what was coming, her father had sent her as an infant to stay with friends in England, with provisions made for her, should the worst he feared happen in France. She had grown up happily in the bosom of the English family who had agreed to take her in, and doted on her. She was an enchanting young girl of striking beauty, with almost-white blond hair, enormous blue eyes, an exquisite figure, and skin like fine porcelain. And she had been just as taken with the duke, when she met him, as he was with her. They were equally well born, both related to monarchs, and Marie-Isabelle had fallen in love with him immediately. They were married four months later, when she was eighteen, and for the first time in his life, Phillip knew true happiness, with a woman he adored. And they made a striking couple. He was tall, powerfully built, and elegant, and Marie-Isabelle combined the aristocratic habits of the English, among whom she had grown up, with the charm of the French, through her own ancestry. She proved to be a wonderful addition to his life, and loved Belgrave as much as he did, helping him to add beautiful decorative pieces to his existing heirlooms. The castle shone with her presence, and everyone loved her, with her bright sunny ways, and obvious adoration of her husband. He was fifty-five when they married, and felt like a boy again when he was with her.

Their life together was like a fairy tale, which ended all too quickly. She conceived a child during their first year of marriage, and died two days after giving birth to a daughter they named Angélique because she looked like an angel, with the same white-blond hair and sky-blue eyes as her mother. Bereft without Marie-Isabelle, Phillip devoted his life to his daughter, who was the joy of his existence. He took her everywhere with him, and taught her as much as her brothers knew about the estate, perhaps more. She had the same passion for their land and home that he did, and the same innate instincts for it. They spent many long winter nights talking about the running of Belgrave, and the farms, and in the summer they rode out on horseback together while he showed her changes and improvements he had made, explaining to her why they were important. She had a complete understanding about how the estate worked, and a good head for figures and finance, and gave him sound advice.

Angélique was tutored at home, and spoke fluent French, taught to her by a French governess Phillip had hired for her. He wanted her to speak her mother's language as well. Marie-Isabelle had spoken both too, thanks to the attentions of the family who had raised her.

And as Angélique grew older, she took perfect care of her father, watched him attentively, worried when he wasn't well, and nursed him herself through any illness. She was the perfect daughter, and Phillip felt guilty for not taking her to London more often. But it tired him to go there, and he had long since lost interest in attending balls and major social events, although he had taken Angélique to his cousin King George IV's coronation when she was twelve, at Westminster Abbey in 1821. She had been one of the few children there, but due to their close relationship, the king had allowed it. Angélique had been agog at all the pomp and circumstance, and the festivities afterward. Sixty-eight by then, and in failing health, Phillip had been relieved to return to the country but happy he had taken her. She said she would never forget it and talked about it for years afterward.

Since then, the duke had often thought about Angélique's first Season, the ball he should give her at their London home in Grosvenor Square, and the men she would meet there. But he couldn't bear the thought of exposing her to the world quite so soon, and losing her to a husband, who would surely take her away from him. She was too beautiful for that not to happen, and he dreaded it.

Several years earlier he had allowed Tristan and his wife and their two daughters to move into the London house, since he no longer went there. He was more comfortable and at ease at Belgrave, and he found London and the social whirl exhausting. And Angélique always insisted she was happy in Hertfordshire with him, and had no need to go to London. She preferred to be at home with her father.

Tristan's wife, Elizabeth, could easily have taken over the duties of escorting Angélique through her first Season, and even arranged a ball for her, which the duke would have paid for. But Tristan had been consumed with jealousy of Angélique from the day she was born, a feeling that had started with his hatred of her mother, and anger over his father's second marriage. Despite Marie-Isabelle's royal ancestry, Tristan and his younger brother had referred to her as "the French whore." It was not unknown to their father, and caused him untold grief. And their open hostility to their sister once she was born caused him greater concern with each passing year.

According to the law, the title, his estate, and the bulk of his fortune were entailed to Tristan, with some considerably lesser provision for Edward, as younger son. Edward was to inherit the Dower House on the estate, which was a handsome sprawling manor, occupied by his grandmother for many years until her death. And Phillip had settled an income on him, which would provide well for him, if he didn't indulge all his follies. But if he did, Phillip knew that his older brother would take care of him, as the two brothers had always been close, and Tristan would never allow him to be ruined. But Phillip could leave nothing to his only daughter, other than a dowry if she married. He had several times expressed the wish to Tristan that she live in the castle for as long as she wanted, and in a house on the estate they referred to as "the Cottage," when she grew older, if she chose to, even if she married.

The Cottage was almost as large as the Dower House, and similarly required a large staff to run it, and her father knew she would be comfortable there. But the ultimate decision would be up to Tristan, and how generous he wished to be with her. He was under no legal obligation to provide for his sister. Her father had also requested that Tristan support her financially, and settle a proper amount on her when she married, as befitting their position in the world, and her noble birth. He did not want Angélique to become penniless, or pushed to the side at his death, but according to the law, there was no way he could prevent it. She would be at the mercy of her brothers, and could not inherit from him directly. He had spoken of it to Angélique often, and she insisted he not worry. She didn't need a great deal to be happy, and as long as she could live at Belgrave forever, it was all she wanted and could imagine. But knowing the ways of the world better, the dangers of the estate being entailed to an oldest son, the hardness of Tristan's character, and the greed of his wife, Phillip spent many sleepless nights worrying about his daughter. And even more so recently, as he got older and his health continued to fail.

Phillip had been ill for the past month, with a lung infection that had been worsening steadily, and Angélique was very concerned. She had had the doctor in to see him several times, and for the past week he had been running a fever. It was November, it had been unusually cold, and she had had the maids keeping the fire bright in her father's bedroom to keep him warm. Belgrave had a tendency to be drafty in winter, and the weather had been bitter cold this year, with snows since October, and she could hear the wind howling outside as she sat at his bedside and read to him. He had drifted off to sleep several times that afternoon. Whenever he woke, he seemed agitated, and his cheeks were bright with fever. Mrs. White, the housekeeper, had been in to look at him while he was asleep, and she agreed with Angélique that they should send for the doctor again. His valet, John Markham, thought so too. Markham had served the duke since long before Angélique was born and was nearly as old as his employer, whom he was deeply devoted to. None of them liked the turn this illness was taking. The duke had a deep, racking cough, and he wished to neither eat nor drink, although Markham had brought several trays to his room.

A butler named Hobson ran the house, and often vied with Markham for the duke's attention, but for now, with the duke feeling so ill, Hobson allowed Markham to tend to him without interference. Angélique was grateful for their devotion to her father, who was well loved by all, and a kind man, who cared for each of them as an attentive and responsible employer. And he had taught Angélique to do the same.

She knew each of their footmen and housemaids by name, their histories and something about their origins, as well as the groundskeepers and grooms in the stables, and the tenant farmers and their families. She spoke to them as they crossed paths in the course of a day, as she went about her tasks around the castle, checking the linens with Mrs. White, or listening to problems in the kitchen. Their cook, Mrs. Williams, was a fierce but good-hearted woman who ran her kitchen with an iron hand, and ordered the kitchen maids around like an army sergeant, but the meals she produced were delicious, and worthy of any grand home. She was trying to tempt the duke with some of his favorite meals at the moment, and the trays had come back untouched for three days. She cried when she saw it, and feared it was an ominous sign, as did those who had seen him. He looked desperately sick, and Angélique had observed it too. At eighteen, she was mature for her age, knew how to run her father's home, and had nursed him many times in recent years. But this time was different. He'd been ill for a month, with no sign of improvement, and after nearly a week of fever, he was not responding to the care and good nursing being lavished on him. And all he wanted to do was sleep, which was very unlike him. Even at seventy-four, he was a vital man, and interested in everything until now.

The doctor came again when he was sent for, and said he wasn't pleased at the turn things were taking. And after he left, Angélique tried to coax her father to eat the broth Mrs. Williams had made him, with thin slices of poached chicken on the side, but he wanted none of it, and waved it away, as Angélique watched him with tears in her eyes.

"Papa, please . . . just try some of the soup. It's delicious, and you'll hurt Mrs. Williams's feelings if you don't at least take a little." He coughed for five minutes then, when he attempted to argue with her, and sank back against the pillows, looking exhausted. She noticed that he seemed to be shrinking, growing thinner, and losing strength, and there was no denying that he had become frail, although usually she tried to pretend otherwise. He drifted off to sleep then, as she held his hand, and sat watching him. Markham came and went several times, glancing in from the doorway, and then leaving on silent feet.

Hobson the butler saw Markham come downstairs to the kitchen, and spoke to him quietly. "How is His Grace?"

"About the same," Markham said with worried eyes, as Mrs. White hovered nearby to listen. The kitchen was bustling with activity, although neither Angélique nor her father was eating. They were going to send Angélique's supper up on a tray, but there were twenty-five servants still to feed in the house. Belgrave was a busy place, particularly below stairs.

"What's going to happen to the little one?" Mrs. White asked the butler when Markham went to join the others for supper. "She'll be at the mercy of her brothers if something happens to His Grace."

"It can't be helped," Hobson said, wishing he weren't as concerned as the housekeeper, but he was. He had come into service as a butler years before, when his wife and daughter died in an epidemic of influenza. He had discovered that a life of service suited him, and he had stayed. Now, he thought that the safest solution for Angélique would have been for her to be married by the time her father died, and under the protection of a husband, with a settlement from her father. But she was still young, she hadn't done the Season in London that summer, which was the first time she could have, and didn't really want to. And now if her father didn't recover, it would be too late, unless Tristan saw to it the following summer, and that didn't seem likely. Angélique's future was of no interest to him, and he had made that clear. He had two daughters of his own who were sixteen and seventeen, not nearly as pretty as their young aunt, who was only a year older. Angélique would have been the star of any London Season, in competition with their daughters, which was the last thing Tristan and his wife wanted.

Mrs. White and Hobson joined the others for supper, and shortly afterward Markham went upstairs to check on the duke again. He had been up and down stairs all day. When he got there, His Grace was sleeping, and Angélique only picked at the supper tray he brought her, and he could see that she'd been crying. She felt as though her father were slipping away from her. She had always known this day would happen, but she wasn't ready for it yet.

Her father hung on for three more days, neither worsening nor getting better. His eyes were bright with fever when he opened them and looked at her late one night, but as Angélique watched him, she could see that he was more alert, and seemed stronger.

"I want to go into my study," he said firmly, in a voice that sounded more like himself, and she hoped that it was a sign that the fever was finally breaking and he'd recover. She had been desperately worried about him and trying not to show him, and put on a brave face.

"Not tonight, Papa. It's too cold in there." The maids hadn't lit the fire in the small library next to his bedroom, where he often pored over the ledgers of accounts of the estate late at night. But since he hadn't been out of bed in over a week, Angélique had told them they didn't need to light the fire, and she didn't want him leaving the warmth of his bedroom.

"Don't argue with me," he said sternly. "There's something I want to give you." She wondered for a moment if he was delirious, but he seemed entirely lucid, and wide awake.

"We can do it tomorrow, Papa. Or tell me what it is, and I'll bring it to you." She was already on her feet when he pushed the bedcovers aside, got out of bed, and stood up with a look of determination. She rushed to his side, afraid he would fall after so many days in bed. Seeing that she couldn't stop him, she put an arm around him to support him, and he towered over her, as they walked toward his study, with Angélique trying to steady him with all her strength. Like her mother before her, she was a slip of a girl, and she would have had a hard time carrying his full weight if he had fallen.

They were in the small, book-lined study a moment later, and it was as icy cold as she had feared. Knowing exactly what he had come for, her father walked to the bookcase, removed a large leatherbound book, and sat down heavily in a chair. She left him to light a candle on the desk, and in the candlelight she saw him open the book, and noticed that it was hollowed out. He removed a leather pouch from it, and a letter, with a serious glance at his daughter. Then he rose again, and replaced the book, and still holding the contents, he turned back toward his bedroom, leaning on Angélique and exhausted from the effort.

Angélique quickly blew out the candle in the study, and helped him back into bed, as he held the papers in his hand and looked at the daughter he loved so much.

"I want you to put this in a safe place, Angélique, where no one else will find it. If something happens to me, I want you to have it. I put it aside for you some time ago. Do not tell anyone. You must keep this to yourself. I want to believe that I can rely on your brother to take care of you after I'm gone, but the law does not protect you. You may need this someday. Keep it, save it, do not use it unless you must. Do not use it now. It will provide for you later if something happens. You can buy a house with it when you're older, or use it to live comfortably, if you don't wish to stay at Belgrave, or find that you can't." He spoke with utter seriousness and clarity, of events she couldn't imagine and didn't want to think about, and never had. But he had thought of nothing else.

"Papa, don't say that," she said as tears sprang to her eyes. "Why would I not want to stay here, or have to buy a house on my own? Belgrave is our home." She was confused by what he was saying, and didn't like it. His words sent a shiver down her spine, and she looked like a frightened child, as he held the pouch out to her, with the letter.

"You don't need to read it now, my child. This is for when I'm gone. When that happens, this will be Tristan's home, and Elizabeth's. You must live on their generosity, and by their rules. They have two daughters to think of, almost as old as you are. Their first concern will not be you. But you are mine. There are twenty-five thousand pounds here, enough for you to live on for a long time, if you need to and use it wisely. You must save it for now. It's enough to bring to a respectable man who loves you, or to take care of yourself until you marry, should that be necessary, or even if you choose not to marry. I hope that Belgrave will be your home forever, my darling, or until you marry, but I cannot be sure. I've asked Tristan to let you live here, in the house or at the Cottage when you're older. It's as comfortable as the Dower House I've given Edward. And I'd prefer that you stay in this house until you're much older. But I will sleep more peacefully at night, knowing that you have this. I give it to you with all my love. The letter confirms that I gave this to you in my lifetime, and it is yours to do with as you wish." Tears spilled down her cheeks as she listened to him, but she could see that he looked calmer than he had before, and relieved to have given her the pouch and letter. It seemed like a vast fortune to her and was a very handsome sum. It had obviously been worrying him a great deal; concern for her future was preying on his mind. He settled back against the pillows with a tired smile once she took the pouch in her trembling hands.

"I don't want this, Papa. I won't need it. And you shouldn't give it to me now." It was a first step toward his leaving her forever, and she knew it, and didn't want to help him start on that path. But she didn't want to upset him either, although she couldn't imagine what she would do with twenty-five thousand pounds. It was an astounding amount of money, but in truth, it was all she had of her own. Should her older brother not give her enough money to support her, she would be less dependent on him. Her father had protected her with his generous gift. "Thank you, Papa," was all she could muster as she leaned over and kissed him, tears still rolling down her cheeks, as he closed his eyes.

"I'm going to sleep now," he said softly, and a moment later he was asleep, as Angélique sat beside him, and stared into the fire, with the pouch still in her lap. It was so like her father to think of everything and do whatever he could for her. If he got old or weak or infirm now, she would have enough to live comfortably, if not lavishly, for the rest of her life. But all she wanted, as she looked at him sleeping, was for her father to live for a long, long time. That meant more to her than anything he could give her. Her father was a generous, loving man.

She read his letter then, and it confirmed what he had said to her, and the gift, and that she could keep all the jewelry he had bought for her mother in the short time they had been married before her death. Angélique knew that if Tristan wished it, she would have to return to him any family heirlooms her father had given her, but the beautiful pieces Phillip had given his second wife were hers to keep. There was nothing more Phillip could do for her now, except pray that Tristan would be kind to her, and honor her as his sister, according to his wishes. Angélique was sure Tristan would, despite his resentment of her mother, they were blood relatives after all, and he would certainly respect their father's requests. Angélique was confident of that.

She slept at her father's bedside that night, with the letter and pouch in the deep pocket of her full skirt. She didn't want to leave him to put them in her room, and the money was safe where it was. She fell into a deep sleep, curled in the chair next to his bed. She was as comforted by his presence as he was by hers.

Chapter 2

In the morning, they sent for the doctor when Markham and Mrs. White agreed with Angélique that her father seemed worse. The duke had had a restful night, but his fever was higher when he woke up. He coughed so much he could hardly breathe, and was shivering beneath the blankets and covers Angélique put on him to keep him warm. Nothing seemed to help. He had a little tea for breakfast, but that was all.

The doctor examined him, and emerged from the duke's bedroom frowning, and said that clearly His Grace was worse. Angélique was terrified he might have caught a chill going into the study the night before, but the doctor explained that it was the infection in his lungs that was making him so ill. He would have bled him, but didn't think he was even strong enough for that. He was going to suggest sending for her brothers, but didn't want to frighten Angélique more than she already was. She was panicked at how poorly her father was doing, and left him with his valet only long enough to go to her room, hide the pouch in a locked drawer in her desk, bathe, change her clothes, and return to her father's bedroom as quickly as she could. He was sound asleep by then, and seemed even hotter to the touch than before. His lips were parched, but he wasn't drinking, and she noticed how thin and white his hands were, lying on the covers. He suddenly looked like a very, very old man. She didn't leave his room all day, and watched him closely as he struggled for breath.

He woke in the late afternoon, and talked to Angélique for a few minutes. He asked if she had put the pouch in a safe place, and she assured him she had, in a locked drawer, and then he closed his eyes with a smile, and drifted off to sleep again. It was almost midnight when he woke, opened his eyes, and smiled at her. He seemed better than he had before, although the fever hadn't changed, but he seemed comfortable as he took her hand in his own, kissed her fingers, and she leaned down to kiss his cheek.

"You have to get well, Papa. I need you." He nodded, closed his eyes, and slept again as she watched him long into the night. He never stirred, and with a peaceful expression on his face, as Angélique held his hand, he drifted away silently and stopped breathing. Angélique saw it immediately, kissed his forehead, and tried to gently rouse him and wake him, but he was gone, after seventy-four years, leading the life he had been born to, caring for those who depended on him, and the estate he had been entrusted with. He had been a wonderful father, husband, and lord of the estate he had been given, had left everything in good order for his older son, and had given Angélique an incredible gift at the end. And now he was gone, and Tristan was the Duke of Westerfield, even if he didn't know it yet.

Angélique sat with her father all through the night, and in the morning she went to tell Hobson what had happened. He sent one of the grooms for the doctor, on horseback, and he came a short while later to confirm that Phillip, Duke of Westerfield, had died during the night. He offered his condolences to Angélique and left, as word spread quietly through the house and into the servants' hall. Angélique felt as though she were living a bad dream, and then she went to help Markham bathe and dress her father. The footmen carried him into the library downstairs to lie in state, until his older son arrived. Another footman was dispatched to London in the carriage to advise Tristan of his father's death. Angélique sat with her father in the library through most of the day. The footman returned from London at nightfall to say that His Grace would arrive in the morning. It pained her to hear Tristan called "His Grace," but that was who he was now. He was the Duke of Westerfield and master of Belgrave Castle and the estate.

For most of the night, Angélique stayed with her father in the library, keeping him company, until Mrs. White came to encourage her to rest for a little while. She felt dazed as she followed her out of the library to eat some broth that Mrs. Williams had prepared. Angélique couldn't remember the last time she'd eaten and didn't care. The father she loved so much was gone. It didn't matter what happened now—she couldn't imagine life at Belgrave without him, or anywhere else. A thousand memories flooded her mind. She was an orphan now, and had lost her last surviving parent. She knew that no one would ever take his place. No brother, no husband, no man. Her world had suddenly become an empty place.

At Mrs. White's urging, she slept in her bed that night, for the first time in days, and she was so exhausted, she slept deeply until morning when she heard a carriage arrive, and shouting outside, as the grooms held the horses, and she heard the footmen calling to each other, and then her brother Tristan's voice. He had arrived. She peeked through her bedroom curtains and saw him just before he walked inside. He was dressed in solemn mourning, and she knew the servants had put a black wreath on the front door the day before. There was no sign of Elizabeth with him; he had come alone. Angélique hastened to dress and comb her hair to meet him properly downstairs. They shared the loss of a beloved parent, and she wanted to tell him how sorry she was.

Tristan was in the dining room quietly having breakfast, and he looked up when she walked in. She was wearing a somber black high-necked dress, which was proper mourning attire, but still showed off her tiny waist. Her face looked as ravaged as she felt. She approached him immediately, and hugged him, and he sat at the head of the table as though etched in stone. It shocked her that he was sitting in her father's chair, at his habitual place, and seemed totally at ease there, but she didn't comment. It was his rightful place now. He was the lord of Belgrave Castle and the entire estate.

"Good morning, Tristan," she said quietly as she sat down next to him. "Have you seen Papa yet?" He shook his head and then turned to look at her again.

"I'll go in after breakfast. I was ravenous when I arrived." She nodded, not knowing what to say. She could barely eat she was so bereft, and she was stunned that he hadn't gone first to see their father. "Elizabeth will be here tonight. I told Hobson to have Mrs. White get their rooms ready—the girls are coming with her. Edward will come tomorrow. I thought we'd have the funeral on Sunday." He said it matter-of-factly, like an ordinary dinner he was planning, not the burial of their father. He would be laid to rest in the family mausoleum, which was fortunate since the ground was frozen too hard to dig a grave. Her mother was in the mausoleum as well, along with Edward and Tristan's mother, and several generations of Lathams before them.

Angélique went upstairs after breakfast and was shocked to see several housemaids airing out her father's room, and putting clean linens on the bed. At first, she thought they were simply tidying up, and then she saw them bringing in vases of flowers from the hothouse, and lighting the fire, as though the room were going to be used that night. "Why are you doing all this?" she asked them. "There's no need." It made the room seem even sadder to keep it as though her father would be sleeping there that night, when he would never sleep there again.

"Mrs. White told us to get it ready for His Grace and the duchess," the head maid Margaret said, as Angélique's mind went blank, and she tried to comprehend what had just been said, and what it meant.

"They're sleeping in here tonight?" Angélique asked in a whisper, and Margaret nodded, feeling sorry for her. Her oldest brother was losing no time stepping into his father's shoes, even sleeping in his bed. The thought of it made Angélique shudder. She checked further and discovered that they were preparing one of the two best suites of rooms for her nieces, far nicer than the ones they usually stayed in when they came to Belgrave. The rooms were usually reserved for royal dignitaries who came to visit. They were losing no time making themselves at home.

She retired to her own suite then, and sat shaking in a chair for a little while, and reminded herself that she would have to make herself useful and assist them with whatever changes they wanted to make, but it all seemed so much too soon. Their father wasn't even buried yet, and was still lying in state in the library. He had been dead for only a day. She steeled herself to go back downstairs, and Angélique watched her brother, with a serious expression, leaving the library after he had seen their father.

"By the way," Tristan accosted her immediately with a chilly stare, "Elizabeth thought you might move to one of the smaller guest rooms. She wants the girls to feel at ease here, and Gwyneth has always liked the view from your suite." She couldn't believe what she was hearing. This was her home, or it had been. Now it was his, and belonged to him, Elizabeth, and their daughters. She was a guest now, literally overnight. The changes her father had feared had already begun to happen.

"Of course. I'll get it ready for her," Angélique said demurely. "And the yellow suite is for Louisa?" she confirmed. It was their finest one. He knew it well since he and Elizabeth had normally slept there on their brief, infrequent visits to his father. Elizabeth always said the country bored them. Apparently, that was about to change as well.

Angélique didn't ask him what room she was to sleep in, but chose a smaller room far down the hall from them, so as to have some privacy and not interfere. But before she could carry out the plan, Tristan spoke to her again. "Elizabeth thought you would be happier in one of the rooms upstairs." There was a whole floor of smaller guest rooms there, which were less beautifully appointed and had some of their older furniture. Despite a fireplace in each room, they were usually drafty and cold. She was beginning to see now what her fate was going to be like at their hands, and moving to the Cottage as her father had requested for her in later years, was beginning to seem like a wise plan. She would wait to see how

things worked once Elizabeth and the girls arrived, but keeping out
of harm's way in the Cottage might be better for everyone.

There was no way she could empty her room in a few hours, but
she set to work immediately, clearing some space for Gwyneth in
the hanging cupboards, emptying a chest of drawers, and putting
away some of her papers to leave room on the desk. And she took
the pouch with her fortune in it with her, and locked it in a drawer
in the room upstairs. It was a small, cramped space with depressing
furniture, and a view that overlooked the estate. The gardens were
just beneath her, and she could see the first of the tenant farms in
the distance, since the trees that ordinarily concealed it were bare.
And the lake was frozen over. She was going to suggest ice skating
to her nieces, the week after the funeral of course, if they were planning to stay. She wondered how soon she could move back to her
room. She was going to do whatever Elizabeth wanted while she
was there. There was no point getting on their wrong side so soon,
or at all. She had to respect that this was their home now, and adjust
to it as best she could.

After she put away her own things upstairs, with the help of one
of the maids, she went back downstairs to inspect the bedrooms
they'd be using. Mrs. White had seen to everything, and the rooms
were impeccable. She hesitated in the doorway of her father's room,
and couldn't bear to go in. She couldn't understand how Elizabeth
would want to sleep there, with her father-in-law so recently dead.
And every time one of the servants addressed Tristan as "Your
Grace," Angélique had to steel herself not to flinch. It was hard to
think of him as lord of everything now. But like it or not, he was. She
had always known it would happen someday, just not so soon.
Tristan was a dignified man, more than a little self-important, with

none of the kindness of her father; but it would have been a tragedy if Edward had inherited the title and estate. He would have run it into the ground.

Tristan was planning to spend the week after the funeral with their father's estate manager to better understand how it all worked. He had spent hours discussing it with his father, but he wanted to learn the nuts and bolts of it now, down to the last detail. He had every intention of running it responsibly, just differently than his father, whom he had always considered a soft touch, and too gentle and generous with his employees. Angélique had often noticed Tristan's harshness with the servants, and the way he spoke to them, so unlike their father, who had been revered. Tristan preferred to rule by fear. And he had already decided he would cut back on what they spent to run the estate, and had planned it for a long time. He thought his father had far too many servants, and paid them much too well.

With the new duke very much in evidence, there was an obvious sense of malaise downstairs. He poked his nose into every nook and cranny that day, and asked Hobson a lot of questions about running the house. Hobson tried his best not to appear to take umbrage, but Angélique could see that the devoted old butler's feathers were ruffled, though he hid it well from Tristan and was irreproachably polite.

It was the end of the afternoon when Elizabeth arrived in an enormous, very showy barouche-landau with the top down, drawn by four black horses, with two coachmen. She had both of her daughters with her, all of them wearing very grand dresses with large sweeping skirts, in somber black, with black gloves. Elizabeth was wearing a huge black hat with a veil, and a brace of black foxes around her shoulders. And the girls' black hats looked as though they'd been made in Paris. Elizabeth spared no expense on their clothes, and loved wearing the latest fashions.

She swept into the main hall, appearing very grand, as she glanced around her and made a face. All of the servants had lined up and stood at attention outside in their thin clothes in the freezing cold. She didn't seem to care, and left them standing there, when she walked in. And then she said loudly where Mrs. White could hear her, "I wonder how long it will take us to get the place clean." The house was immaculate, and Mrs. White was very proud of how meticulously they kept it.

Like the servants, Angélique had greeted the new mistress of Belgrave at the door, and Elizabeth brushed past her, without kissing her or offering her condolences, and Gwyneth and Louisa gave her a haughty glance, as if to say she was of no importance anymore. Angélique was beginning to feel that way herself.

She took Gwyneth up to her suite, and told her she hoped she'd enjoy staying there, and Gwyneth looked at her and laughed.

"I'm moving into these rooms now, you know. My mother said I could. You can take the rest of your things tomorrow." Angélique didn't say a word. She would speak to Elizabeth about it herself. It would be the ultimate humiliation if Elizabeth intended to keep her in the small, dreary room upstairs, which hadn't been redone in forty years, unlike her own suite of rooms, which had been completely redone three years before, on her fifteenth birthday, as a surprise from her father. They had gone to Italy to visit an old friend of his in Florence, and when they got back, everything was in place, and all her old girlhood furniture had been removed. It was a very elegant suite of rooms, all done in pink satin, with French furniture her father had bought for her in Paris.

Louisa walked into the room then, and gave her young aunt, only two years older than she was, another haughty look, full of disdain. Moving to the Cottage was becoming more appealing every minute. Elizabeth had brought her own maid with her, and another one for the girls, to tend to their clothes. And when Angélique went downstairs a little while later, Elizabeth was giving Mrs. White orders, and changing the menu for that night, which was going to be difficult for Mrs. Williams to conjure up so late in the day, although she was very creative. But she wasn't a magician, and everyone on the staff was still shaken and upset about her father, and not operating in top form. Elizabeth was indifferent to their feelings and wanted what she wanted, now! She explained that they all had delicate stomachs and couldn't eat country food, which made Mrs. Williams flush nearly purple when Elizabeth said it, since the cook prided herself on her sophisticated food, often learned from other cooks she knew, who worked in grand houses in London, or French recipes she copied down from magazines. She did not serve "country food."

It appeared as though the change was not going to be easy for the staff either, and there was nothing Angélique could do. As long as Tristan and his family were in residence, she felt she couldn't run the house and give orders. It was no longer her home. She was a barely tolerated guest, in what had been her domain only hours before.

Supper that night was a tense affair for Angélique, while Elizabeth talked openly about all the changes she was going to make, her plans for redecoration, and the furniture she wanted to move around. It gave Angélique the uncomfortable feeling that she was standing on shifting sands. And both her nieces were rude to the servants during the meal, and no one corrected them. After supper, the girls went upstairs to what had been Angélique's suite, without

even saying goodnight to her. And Tristan and Elizabeth retired to
the study, did not invite her to join them, and firmly closed the door
in her face, after saying they had private matters to discuss.

Angélique went into the library for a few minutes to sit with her
father, gently touched his hand, kissed his cold gray cheek, and
went upstairs to the room they'd assigned to her, where she burst
into tears, and lay sobbing on the bed until she heard someone knocking. It was Mrs. White, who had come to see how she was. There had
been much discussion at the servants' dining table about the changes
of rooms, and Mrs. White had discreetly warned the younger maids
to be careful when Sir Edward arrived the next day. They got her
meaning and several of them giggled. He had cornered more than
one of them on previous occasions, and had even caused one or two
to be dismissed after he left, for indulging his whims and giving in
to him. Despite his bad behavior, he was a handsome man. Mrs. White
did not tolerate that kind of behavior from the maids, although she
had never explained it to His Grace, and didn't need to.

"Are you all right?" Mrs. White asked Angélique, with deep concern. They both knew how difficult this was, losing her father, and
having to deal with Tristan and his wife and daughters, who so clearly
disrespected her, and resented her existence, and the favored position
she had had with the late duke. He could do nothing to protect her
now, any more than the servants could support her in any meaningful
way, except to feel sorry for her, which they did. She had been nothing
but kind to them all her life, like her father, and they were very fond
of her. They had all spoken openly in the servants' hall that night
about what an arrogant beast the new duchess was.

Angélique nodded, and tried to smile bravely through her tears.
Mrs. White had always been motherly to her, and had been at Bel-

grave even before the duke married Marie-Isabelle, and she had thought her a lovely girl. Mrs. White had been one of the first to hold Angélique in her arms after she was born, and had given her a warm hug whenever possible as a child.

"It's all so different," Angélique said cautiously, embarrassed to complain. She didn't want to seem rude.

"It was bound to be different," Mrs. White said, standing next to her bed and gently stroking her hair, "but not quite so soon. They're in an awful hurry to let us all know that Belgrave is theirs now." Angélique silently agreed with her, and looked up at the older woman, grateful for the visit. To Fiona White, Angélique was the child she'd never had. She had given up marriage and children for a life of service. She was the daughter of one of the tenant farmers, her family had served the Dukes of Westerfield for generations, and she was proud to do the same. Achieving the post of head housekeeper had been a major accomplishment for her, and one which meant a great deal to her. "They'll get tired of it soon enough, and go back to London," she said with a smile. "I can't see them staying in the country for long. They'll be bored." But from what the girls had said at supper, Angélique had the uncomfortable feeling that they were planning to stay.

"I hope you're right."

"I'm sure I am, and then everything will go back to normal." Except that Angélique knew her father would no longer be there, which altered everything for her, far more than it did for the servants. The new duke and his family needed the servants, but they had already made it clear that they didn't need or want Angélique. She was only Tristan's sister, by a wife he had hated from the first. All they wanted was to put her in the attic somewhere—they had lost no time commandeering her suite.

Mrs. White stayed for a few minutes and then went back downstairs. Hobson waylaid her as soon as he saw her. "How is she?" he asked about Angélique, his worry evident. He had felt fatherly toward her the moment he saw her as a baby.

"She's upset, and who can blame her?" Mrs. White answered. "Her father is barely cold in the library, and they're already treating her like one of us." He nodded his agreement. He was horrified that she'd been put out of her rooms, and even more so that Tristan and Elizabeth were planning to sleep in the late duke's room so soon.

"His Grace wouldn't like what's going on," Hobson said ominously, but the Grace he meant was gone, and the one who had taken his place seemed to have no heart, particularly where his half-sister was concerned.

Angélique lay in bed for hours that night, trying to absorb everything that had happened in the past two days. The room she was sleeping in was freezing cold, and the windows didn't close properly. An icy wind blew at her all night, and she was frozen stiff when she came down in the morning.

Angélique joined Tristan in the dining room for breakfast, and he said not a word to her as he read the newspaper. Elizabeth and her daughters were having breakfast in bed, something Angélique never did. She'd had breakfast in the dining room with her father every day, where they chatted and laughed, talked about the books they were reading, or world events, and their plans for the day. Tristan had nothing to say to her until after breakfast, when he reminded her to return any family jewels her father had given her, except for the ones he had bought for her mother. Angélique handed him the jewelry half an hour later with a stoic expression.

After that, she spent the morning quietly making sure that the house was running smoothly, and trying to stay out of Elizabeth and the girls' way, which she succeeded in doing until the midday meal, which they referred to as dinner. Elizabeth had ordered a complicated meal, which Mrs. Williams had managed to perfection. Angélique was pleased. They weren't the bumpkins Elizabeth thought.

Shortly after dinner, Edward arrived, in an elegant chariot, drawn by four fast horses, with two of his best horses following behind. He had a sword case on the back. He didn't trust his father's stables, the horses in it were always far too tame in his opinion, and he planned to do some riding while he was there. He disliked country life even more than his brother and sister-in-law. He found it intolerably boring, which was why he seldom came. He had more entertaining things to do in London.

He ignored Angélique entirely and was satisfied with the luxurious suite of rooms his sister-in-law had assigned to him. He spent the rest of the afternoon out riding while the locals continued to come to pay their respects in a steady stream. Two footmen stood at the front door, and two more were in the library, with the late duke, as people filed by to see him. The tenant farmers came in their Sunday best, to pay their respects. They stood beside Angélique's father for a long time, whispering in hushed tones, and many of them were crying when they left.

All in all it was another exhausting day, and Angélique retired to bed with several hot bricks wrapped in towels to warm her, covered the window with blankets, and made a blazing fire to keep herself warm, but the night was no better than the one before, and the next morning was her father's funeral in the chapel on the estate. The local vicar performed the service, and Phillip Latham, Duke of Westerfield, was laid to rest in the mausoleum, with his parents, grandparents, and both wives. Angélique stayed there for a few more minutes after the others went back to the house for something to eat. Several of Phillip's local friends had come for the service, and to share a meal with them. By the end of the meal, Angélique felt drained of every ounce of blood, and energy. And when the last guest left, and her female relatives went upstairs, Tristan asked her to join him in the library, where her father had lain only hours before. Edward was bantering with his nieces on their way upstairs after pointedly ignoring Angélique since he'd arrived, and snubbing her every chance he got, incredibly rudely. Elizabeth had called for Mrs. White about the next day's meals, the results of which were to be conveyed to Mrs. Williams. Elizabeth was still not satisfied with the cooking, and had already mentioned to Mrs. White that she might replace the cook and bring someone from London, although Mrs. Williams had worked there for twenty years.

"I wanted to speak to you for a moment," Tristan said casually, as Angélique tried not to remember her father lying in the room. She wondered what Tristan was going to say to her, and for a moment considered if he was going to suggest himself that she move into the Cottage. They had already given her the clear impression that they thought she was in the way. And moving her into the Cottage, even though earlier than her father had planned it, might be a plausible solution, for her too. She couldn't continue to sleep in the drafty upstairs bedroom for much longer, without getting sick, and there was no room for her things, and no place to put them. She had had to take over another of the smaller bedrooms for her clothes, since Gwyneth had insisted she empty the closets in her old suite, to make room for her elaborate gowns.

"Elizabeth and I have been talking," Tristan began. "I know what an awkward situation this must be for you, and to be honest, it's confusing for the servants as well. Father let you run the house for him, but there's no need for you to do that anymore. Elizabeth is going to reorganize everything and get it running smoothly." Just hearing him say it was something of a slap in the face, as though she didn't know what she was doing, because she was only eighteen. But she had done a fine job of it for several years, more than many young women her age who were married, and had never even seen a house or staff as big as this. "It will be embarrassing for you to find yourself with nothing to do here, and we don't want them confused in their loyalties."

"I'm sure they won't be," Angélique said nervously. "They are very clear that it's your house now, and Elizabeth is going to run it. They always expected this to happen. We all did. And Papa had been failing for a long time." Now that she thought about it, his death was heartbreaking but not really a surprise. She just hadn't wanted to see the end coming. "And of course I won't interfere."

"Precisely. That's what we have in mind too."

"Papa thought that eventually I should move into the Cottage. Maybe I should do that now," she suggested hesitantly, thinking it would be a relief for all of them, and Elizabeth and the girls would be pleased to get her out of the house.

"Of course not." Tristan dismissed the idea summarily. "A girl your age can't live alone in a house, and actually we have plans for it. Elizabeth's mother has been feeling poorly, and might benefit from some country air. Elizabeth wants to redo that house for her.

"In fact, we had another idea for you. As you know, Angélique, our father didn't provide for you. He couldn't. He suggested an amount that I might give you as an allowance, but quite honestly, I would be irresponsible if I did so. Father was getting old, and some of his ideas were the ramblings of an old man. I cannot dilute what I need to run the estate by giving you an allowance, and it would be unfair to my own daughters if I did. He set aside a sum for Edward, but in fact, he left nothing outright to you, and he couldn't. The entail on the estate doesn't allow for it—everything comes to me. And I feel sure that you don't want to become a burden to us."

"No, not at all," Angélique interjected, embarrassed, not sure where he was going, since he had ruled out the possibility of her living in the Cottage.

"The sad fact, my dear, is that young women in your position have no choice but to go to work. And there is very little you can do. You're not trained to be a teacher. And well-born young women with no means at their disposal become governesses, and live under the protection of the families they work for. You have no experience as a governess, but there's no reason why you can't be a nanny, and I'm sure in time, you could work your way up to being a governess, as you mature. Elizabeth and I want to help you. I spoke to some very nice people I know, when Father began to fall ill, seeing this eventuality looming toward us. And they are willing to do you a great favor. They have agreed to take you on as a nanny, for a small salary at first since you have no experience.

"They live in Hampshire, have four young children, and are very pleasant people. Her father was a baron, and her husband has no title, but they run a very respectable household. Not as large as this, of course, but they're willing to pay you a wage to take care of their children. And really, my dear, there's nothing else you can do. I've already told them you'd take it. I'm very pleased for you. I think this is an ideal solution for all of us. I know you'll be well cared for, you won't be a burden on us, and you won't have the awkwardness of staying on here now that Father is gone. I actually think you'll be very happy." He smiled at her as though he had just bestowed a wonderful gift on her, and she should be immensely grateful.

For a moment, Angélique thought she might faint, but she didn't want to give him the satisfaction. She steeled her spine and sat up straighter, although she was deathly pale. Her father had been right not to trust him to take care of her after he was gone. Tristan was a snake. He had promised their father he would provide for her, and instead he was turning her out of their home, to go and work as a nanny for strangers, people she had never even met. It was almost beyond belief, but not quite, knowing how much Tristan, Edward, and Elizabeth had always hated her, and resented the close relationship she had with her father. Now they had set on her like wolves.

"We have everything arranged," he assured her, and she was sure he did. "You won't need most of your things—you can leave them here. We'll put them in the attic for you. You can send for them if you find you want them, but I doubt you will. Elaborate gowns would be of no use to you—you'll be wearing a simple dress suitable for a nanny, and an apron, when you're on duty. We were going to tell you in a week or two, but apparently their nanny is leaving and they need you sooner. The timing is quite perfect, really. You don't have to stay, grieving over Father. You'll be busy at the Fergusons', and will have to think of other things." According to him, everything about it was perfect, except for the sad reality of what he was doing. He was betraying his own sister, and sending her out into the world without a penny as far as he knew, to be a nanny. It was the ultimate revenge for how much their father had loved her. He had finally gotten even, after resenting her all her life. His time had come, and he was simply getting rid of her, without giving her a second thought.

"When do they expect me to start?" she managed to choke out as she stared at him in horror.

"Tomorrow, actually. You'll leave in the morning. I'll send you to Hampshire in the small chaise—not Father's carriage, of course. You don't want to embarrass yourself by arriving in a formal carriage or the coach. You're a working woman now, Angélique. I'm sure you'll do a very good job, and wind up as a governess one day. You can teach the children French."

He had always hated the fact that she spoke another language, and he didn't, but he had never bothered to learn one either. He had been jealous of everything she had and was, and had waited all these years to take it all away from her, and now he had the power to do so. The entail played right into his hands since he had inherited everything, and had chosen to give her nothing. She understood now why her father had given her the pouch with the money before he died. He had been afraid something like this would happen, and it was the only way he could provide for her, and he hadn't trusted Tristan to do it. But even her father couldn't protect her now from having to be a nanny, a servant in someone else's home, and being forced from her own. He had told her not to use the money frivolously or until she truly had to, and for now, she wouldn't. She would keep it until she needed to provide a home for herself one day, or had no other form of income, which could happen too, if they sacked her or she left them. And she was much too young to buy a house now and would have no idea how to do so. They were sending her away in a matter of hours, with no time for her to prepare or make an alternate plan.

For now, thanks to her brother's machinations, she had a job as a nanny, and presumably she would be safe in her employers' home. She would do it for as long as she had to, and then find some other way to support herself. There had to be more to life, and her destiny, than this. It sounded like being forced into slavery to her.

"So, we're all set, then," he said, standing up to indicate that their meeting was over. "You'll have a lot to do tonight, packing. There's no need to say goodbye to Elizabeth and the girls—they told me to say goodbye to you. They won't be up in the morning when you leave." So they had banished her. She had been dismissed. Her life at Belgrave was over. It belonged to them now. And there was no room in their life or home for her. He had always thought that their father had spoiled her, and he had found a job as a nanny to put her in her place. She knew as she said goodnight to him that she would never be back here again. She would never see her home again. It would remain like a distant dream, with the memories of her father and the wonderful times they had shared. All of that was over now. Tristan and his evil wife had dispossessed her, and she had no choice but to try and survive in the world and life they had cast her into. Perhaps they thought that losing everything would destroy her, but she knew she couldn't let it. She had to fight for her survival, what- ever it took, in spite of them.

Tristan walked up the stairs to their father's bedroom, as she watched him. Elizabeth would be waiting for him, and he could tell her that he had "taken care of it." The matter of Angélique had been solved, with the end result they wanted. And Angélique had never hated anyone as she did her own brother that night.

Instead of going upstairs after Tristan left her, she went down- stairs to see Mrs. White. She was just locking her small office next

to Hobson's, and they were saying goodnight to each other, as Angélique came running down the stairs, her eyes wide, her face pale.
She had to tell them she was leaving, and Mrs. White could see instantly that something terrible had happened to her.

"What is it, child?" She didn't seem like Lady Angélique at that
moment, but like the little girl Mrs. White had known all her life.

"They're sending me away to work as a nanny," Angélique blurted
out, still shaking from everything she'd just heard. Mrs. White's eyes
were shocked, and Hobson couldn't help but overhear her.

"They're doing *what*? That's impossible! His Grace would never
allow such a thing!" he said in a horrified tone, but he and the housekeeper both knew what the entail meant, and all the implications of
it. She was truly at Tristan's mercy, and he had devised a clever plan
to simply get rid of her, rather than take care of her. He had waited
eighteen years for this moment. The two devoted servants couldn't
believe the cruelty of it, to lose her father who had loved her so
much, and her home only days after.

"They'll have to change their minds and bring you back at some
point," Mrs. White said hopefully, but even she didn't think it was
likely. Tristan was a bad man, and his wife was a hard-hearted, self-
ish, greedy woman.

Angélique melted into the older woman's arms then, as Hobson
turned so the two women wouldn't see the tears rolling down his
cheeks. He couldn't bear what Tristan and his wife were doing, but
there was no way to help this child who had never been out in the
world on her own. And somehow she would have to endure it.

"I'll be all right," she said bravely, thinking of the money her father had given her. But she wasn't going to touch it yet. Her father
had told her not to, although he couldn't have known what Tristan

had in store for her. Even he, in his worst fears, couldn't imagine treachery to this degree.

"You'll stay in touch, won't you?" Mrs. White asked her, looking desperately worried.

"Of course. I'll write to you as soon as I get there. Will you write to me?" Angélique asked her with pleading eyes.

"You know I will." They hugged again, and Angélique went upstairs to pack for her new life. She put all but a few of her beautiful dresses in trunks, along with her books, and a few favorite possessions she knew she couldn't take with her. In the bags she was planning to bring, she packed a small portrait of her father and a miniature of her mother, painted on ivory, a few treasured books, as many sensible dresses as she could put into her valises, with a hatbox full of sober bonnets, and a fan that had been her mother's that she had always loved as a child. Her mind was whirling as she finished packing, and she lay in bed all night in the freezing room, feeling like she was going to the guillotine like her mother's ancestors in the morning.

She had breakfast in the servants' dining room; only a few of them were up. And when she left, Hobson and Mrs. White saw her into the small chaise, like loving parents. They were the only ones she had left. And as the chaise pulled away from Belgrave Castle in the morning fog, she didn't see her older brother watching her from his bedroom window with a look of satisfaction. He had done it. The French whore's daughter was gone, and Belgrave and all its land was his now. He had waited a lifetime for it.

Angélique was looking at the outline of her home against the morning sky as she left, and both Hobson and Mrs. White cried after the chaise rolled away. They wondered how Tristan and Elizabeth would explain her sudden disappearance.

As Angélique bumped along toward Hampshire and the Fergusons, with a coachman and no footmen, the daughter of the last duke of Westerfield faced her future with fear, dignity, and courage. She had her father's money locked in a small trunk she had brought with her. And she thanked him silently yet again for the immeasurable gift he had given her. It would provide her with a home one day, and if she absolutely had to, and was frugal, she would live on it in her later years, and might have to. But not yet. For now, she would have the nanny job at the Fergusons' and a roof over her head.

She had no idea where the future would lead her or what it would look like, but whatever happened, she was determined to survive it.

Belgrave Castle was strangely silent that morning, as though the life and soul had gone out of it. Everyone working there knew that they had entered a very dark time, without their beloved duke and his daughter. And in answer to where she was, Hobson and Mrs. White said nothing except "She's gone." And Tristan Latham, the new Duke of Westerfield, said absolutely nothing. Only the servants of Belgrave Castle knew that they were mourning both the father and daughter as they went about their work, wearing their black armbands with heavy hearts and tears in their eyes. Their beloved Lady Angélique was gone, and they knew they would never see her again. Her brother had orchestrated it perfectly.

Chapter 3

Wilfred, the youngest coachman from Belgrave, had driven her on the journey from Hertfordshire to Hampshire, and they drove through St. Albans on the way. They stopped in Slough at a simple tavern and resumed the trip after a meal of sausages and cider. Angélique felt uncomfortable eating alone, while Wilfred ate with the stable boys in the barn. She sat quietly at a table in the corner. It was the first time in her life she had gone anywhere on her own, and she had much to think about. The death of her father, the sudden unexpected loss of her home, the betrayal of her brother, the money her father had given her, and the future that lay ahead of her, working as a nanny for strangers. Her brother had obviously planned that for some time, as a way to get rid of her. She had never expected something like this to happen, or to be cast out into the world without protection. And rather than living in the rarefied upstairs atmosphere of Belgrave Castle as the beloved daughter of a

duke, she was now to be part of the downstairs world. She was familiar with it from running her father's home, but she had never
remotely suspected that it would be her own life one day. Everything was going to be very different now. And all she could hope
was that the Fergusons were decent people, had a kind staff, and
would treat her well.

Angélique had never put on airs, but her breeding and lineage
were written all over her. She was every inch a lady of noble birth,
in her speech, in her manners, in the way she moved, no matter
what simple gown she wore. She had worn a plain black dress for
the journey, and had brought the plainest clothes she owned, but all
she had were the gowns of a lady, not a nanny. And the severity of
her black clothes said that she was in mourning for someone close
to her. She had lost not only her father, but her entire world, and she
cried more than once on the way to Hampshire. She knew she would
have to be brave once she got there, but as long as she was in the
simple carriage, she could hang on to the last shreds of all she had
known. It had come tumbling down all in a matter of days. It was
what Tristan and Elizabeth had wanted to happen to her, and she
knew that if her father could have known it, he would have been in
despair. And there was no one she could turn to now. She would
never contact her brothers again. She had barely seen Edward, but
was sure he was aware of the plan. She wondered if they were cel-
ebrating at Belgrave. And she knew that the only place where she
would be missed would be below stairs, where Hobson and Mrs. White
would be mourning her departure, along with Mrs. Williams and
the others who had known her all her life. They had lost the duke
and his daughter at one swoop, and would have to deal with Tristan

and Elizabeth now, who were cold, demanding, mean-spirited people with no heart, who loved to show off, and were always unkind
to the servants when they were there.

It was late afternoon and nearly nightfall when they reached
Alton in Hampshire. They had been traveling for eleven hours,
bumping along in the chaise. It had been a long trip for the horses
as well, but they had taken two strong sturdy ones that didn't need
to rest as often as their fine ones. And following the directions
Tristan had given Wilfred, they easily found the house. It was a
pretty manor house with well-tended grounds on a handsome estate, though by no means on the scale of Belgrave Castle. It was
clearly the home of wealthy people, and the house looked relatively
new, like the fortune of the man who had built it. Tristan had hinted
that Mrs. Ferguson had married her husband for his money, which
he lavished on her. She was from an aristocratic family, though her
father was only a life peer with no inheritable title, and he had
squandered his fortune on bad investments. So Ferguson had married her for her social position, and she for the life he could offer.

The house looked warm and inviting, as a footman came out and
directed them to go around the back to the servants' entrance. Wilfred had assumed that Lady Angélique would be going through the
front door with her bags. He had no idea why she was there, and
she didn't tell him. All he knew was that she would be staying there
for some time, and he thought they must be friends and she was
taking a holiday to recover from her father's death. He tried to explain that she was a guest, but the stern-faced footman continued to
direct him to the rear entrance of the large house.

"I'm sorry, Your Ladyship," Wilfred said in an undertone, looking
embarrassed. "This clod would have us go in through the servants'

entrance. I can walk you around to the front," he said as he pulled the chaise to a halt, and a groom held the horses' heads while he got down.

"This will be fine," she said just loud enough for him to hear her, and she saw another footman emerge and look them over, and he pointed inside.

"You can go in," he directed her. "Mrs. Allbright told us to expect you, she's the housekeeper here. We'll be eating supper in a few minutes." He made no attempt to help Wilfred with the bags, and was wearing immaculate livery. He appeared very smart, and told Wilfred to leave her things outside. "She can take them up later," he said, as Wilfred glanced at Angélique in confusion. She was being treated like a servant, not the lady she was. She smiled gently at him and nodded.

"It's all right. Someone will help me," she reassured him, but he was doubtful. They weren't being pleasant or welcoming, and he wasn't going to just abandon her there, with this surly, starched young footman treating her like a maid. "I'll be fine." She wanted him to leave as quickly as possible, without drawing attention to her.

"You're sure?" He didn't want Hobson berating him when he got back, for not doing his duty, and taking care of her properly. But she seemed anxious for him to drive away.

"Yes, I am sure. And thank you for getting me here." He was planning to stay at a pub nearby that night. Tristan had told him which one. He seemed to know the area well.

As she watched Wilfred get back on the seat of the carriage, turn it around, and roll in the direction from which they'd come, she felt the last evidence of Belgrave being torn from her, and she could feel a sob rising in her throat, which she used every bit of strength she had to control. It began snowing as she watched him, and an instant later, she followed the footman inside to a busy servants' hall teeming with people. The house was much smaller, but the staff appeared to be almost as big as the one she had grown up with. And their liveries all looked brand new and were fancier than the ones she was used to. They seemed almost French, and several of the footmen were wearing powdered wigs, which they never did at home, except when royalty visited. Angélique's eyes were wide as she took it all in. And a tall angular woman with gray hair approached her. She had the face of a large bird and looked like a prison warden, with her ring of keys jangling from her waist, which indicated her position.

"I'm Mrs. Allbright, the housekeeper," she introduced herself without a smile. "And you must be the new nanny, Angela Latham?"

"Angélique," she corrected her softly. She was terrified of the woman, but determined not to show it.

"Sounds foreign," she said disapprovingly.

"It's French," Angélique confirmed.

"Mrs. Ferguson will like that," she said through pursed lips, but she didn't look as if she approved. "We're sitting down to supper now. One of the maids will show you to your room later. It'll just be for tonight. Your room will be in the nursery with the children, but the present nanny isn't leaving until tomorrow. You can move into her room then. I hear you have a lot of bags," she said, frowning. "I don't know why you'd bring them here. You'll be wearing the dress Mrs. Ferguson has all the nannies wear. It's quite plain. You'll only be wearing your own clothes on your half-day off once a month, if the children aren't sick." There was no point trying to explain to this severe-looking woman why she had brought three bags and a small trunk. It was all she had left in the world. She had brought a few of her father's things, some of the books they had read together, and as many small personal mementoes as she could. And the locked trunk held her jewelry and money. She'd make room for all of it as best she could, no matter how tiny the room, and she suspected it wouldn't be large.

The servants' dining hall was clean and spacious, and the cook looked efficient and busy with three kitchen maids to help her. Angélique counted twenty indoor staff around the table. Someone pointed to an empty chair, and she sat down, watching them quietly as supper was served. The food was plentiful and everyone dug in. They looked busy, hungry, and rushed.

"They're having a house party this weekend. It's been quite mad. They went shooting today. They're having a big party tonight, with friends from the neighborhood invited. They entertain a lot, especially in London. But you won't be going there often. They usually leave the children here when they go to town," the maid sitting next to her explained. "I'm Sarah, by the way. I'm one of the upstairs maids. Watch out for Mrs. Allbright. She's a terror, and she'll sack you faster than you can wink," she warned her in a whisper.

"Was the nanny that's here now sacked?" Angélique asked, looking worried.

"No, she's going back to Ireland. And happy to leave here. The children are wild." Angélique nodded and introduced herself, and Sarah smiled and then introduced her to the others. The head butler, Mr. Gilhooley, presided over the head of the table, there was an underbutler too, next to him, and Mrs. Allbright sat at the other end of the table, observing the maids and house staff like the headmistress in a school. The atmosphere around the table was congenial although they had no time to linger over their food, and Angélique was too tense to eat. "Where was your last job?" Sarah asked her as they left the table, and Mrs. Ferguson's lady's maid flirted coyly with the underbutler, until Mr. Gilhooley intervened and made a disparaging comment. He and Mrs. Allbright appeared to be thick as thieves, and kept them all on a short leash. They ran a tight ship.

Angélique wondered for a moment what she should say to Sarah in response to the question about her last job, and decided on a modified version of the truth.

"I didn't have one. This is my first position," Angélique said shyly, and Sarah smiled.

"How old are you?"

"Eighteen," she admitted, and without her hair done up nicely, in the plain black dress, she looked even younger.

"That's sweet. I'm twenty-six," Sarah said ruefully, and then lowered her voice conspiratorially. "I've been doing this for ten years. One of the grooms and I have been walking out together. We're getting married when we have enough saved up. Maybe soon." She looked hopeful as she said it, and Angélique was touched. She suddenly got a glimpse of how difficult things were for some of them. Money was short, jobs were hard, and marriage and babies were not a given, but had to be earned and saved for, sometimes for years.

"You'll meet Nanny Ferguson tomorrow morning," Mrs. Allbright said to her as they left the dining hall, and the footmen and both butlers prepared to go upstairs to serve the party. As was customary, the nannies and ladies' maids were addressed by the surname of the family they worked for, not their own.

The maids were going to tend to the rooms after the guests and family dressed. A whole flock of them headed for the back stairs. "Please be down for breakfast at six," she said to Angélique, sounding like a schoolteacher again. "Sarah will show you to the room you'll use tonight, Nanny Latham." Angélique knew that when she assumed her duties the next morning, she would become Nanny Ferguson too, until the day she left. She quietly followed Sarah up several flights of stairs.

"He's all right," Sarah filled her in about the Fergusons in a whisper. "He's got a bit of a roving eye, but he's not too bad. In my last job, I had to lock my door to keep his lordship out every night. Watch out for her brother, though. He's a devil, but a handsome one, if you fancy a bit of that. But if you do, watch out for Mrs. Allbright. If she catches you, you'll be out on your ear without a character."

"No, no, I'd never do that," Angélique said, looking horrified. She didn't say that she had a brother like that too. "What's she like?" she asked, referring to their mistress.

"Very spoiled. He gives her whatever she wants. She's got some beautiful clothes and jewels. I don't know why she has children, though—she never sees them. You're meant to bring them down on Sunday for tea, but she usually finds some reason why she can't. She says they're always sick, and she's afraid of influenza. What about your parents? Where are they?" Sarah asked, curious about her, and Angélique caught her breath before she answered.

"I . . . my father just died . . . my mother died when I was born . . . I'm an orphan now." It pained her to say it, but it was true.

"Sorry to hear it," Sarah said sincerely, as they reached the room she'd be using for the night until she moved to the nursery. The room was tiny and spare with only a cot and a small dresser in it. There was a basin to wash in, and rough sheets, a blanket, and a single towel on the bed. The house might be new and modern, but the servants' quarters were not. The room was half the size of the smallest servants' room at Belgrave. Mrs. Ferguson had no interest in the comfort of her staff.

"The nanny's room in the nursery is a bit bigger," Sarah reassured her, "but not much. The children share rooms, but there's a nice nursery parlor you can sit in at night—if they go to sleep, that is. Bridget says the baby is up half the night, yowling with his teeth. She's not sorry to leave." Angélique nodded, wondering how she'd manage them. She knew nothing of caring for children. She had never been around any for all of her life, except for a few minutes when she visited the tenants' farms, but the children were kept away from her, so as not to disturb her ladyship, or soil her dress. This was going to be a whole new experience and a challenge. She had no idea what to expect. All she knew was that she would be caring for four young children, who according to Sarah were sadly misbehaved.

Angélique went back down to the servants' hall after Sarah showed her the room where she'd be staying, and brought her bags up the stairs. It took her three trips, and no one offered to help her. All she had the energy to do after that was wash in the basin in her room, after bringing in a pitcher of water, and go to bed. And she lay there for hours after that, wondering what the next day would bring. She just prayed that she'd be brave enough and strong enough to do her job, and would make a good impression on her employer. In her entire life, she had never expected to become a servant. She tried not to think about it as she drifted off to sleep. She woke with a start several times that night, afraid she'd oversleep in the morning. And she finally got up at five, washed and dressed and did her hair neatly in the freezing room, and was in the dining hall promptly at six, as the housekeeper had told her to do.

One of the kitchen maids made her a cup of tea, and before she could eat breakfast, one of the housemaids came in and told her she was expected in the nursery, and to follow her upstairs. They went up the servants' stairs to the third floor, and emerged just outside the nursery, where Angélique could hear a baby crying. The maid pointed to a heavy wooden door, as Angélique looked down a long, carpeted hall, with doors to several other servants' bedrooms. Mrs. Allbright's room was on that floor, as well as Mrs. Ferguson's lady's maid, the cook, and the senior housemaids. The nursery, a small sitting room, and bedrooms occupied most of the floor, and there was an elegant stairway that led down to the second floor, which the servants were not allowed to use, only the family if they chose to come upstairs.

Angélique knocked on the nursery door, and no one could hear her over the crying baby. She knocked again several times, and finally opened the door, and found herself looking at a freckled red-headed girl who was comforting the baby, while two other children were gathered around her, trying to get her attention, and a toddler was standing on a table, throwing toys. It looked like pandemonium, and for an instant Angélique was tempted to run. She was thinking that there must be some other job she could do that would be easier than this one.

"Hello, I'm Angélique!" she shouted over the din, as the baby screamed and pulled at his ears, and the pretty redhead in the simple nurse's uniform turned toward her.

"You're the new nanny?" she asked, looking hopeful.

"I am. What can I do to help?"

"Get Rupert off the table." She smiled gratefully, pointing to the two-year-old, then put the baby down in his crib, and the volume of his screaming intensified as she did. She walked toward Angélique, as she lifted Rupert in his nightshirt off the table. The moment she set him down, he ran unsteadily across the nursery, away from them, looking like a drunk, as both women laughed. The other two children had grown quiet and were looking up at Angélique. Simon looked to be about four years old, and Emma was three years old, with a head full of blond ringlets. Charles, the baby, was six months old.

"Welcome to the asylum," she said, laughing, as Angélique smiled and tried not to show how nervous she was. "Sarah came up to see me last night. She said this is your first job. You're a brave one—they only had two children when I came here. I never thought they'd have two more." She had a thick Irish brogue, and a friendly disposition, and she seemed undaunted by the constantly moving, busy children. "I'm the fifth nanny they've had. I come from a big family, so it doesn't bother me as much as some."

"I'm sorry you're leaving," Angélique said sincerely, sounding more like a lady than a servant than she realized.

"Don't be sorry I'm leaving—it got you the job," she said, and laughed again, and looked at her more closely. "You're a fancy one, aren't you?" In her years as a nanny, she had seen other girls whose families had lost their fortunes and had been forced to take jobs in other people's homes. But they were more like landed gentry, Angélique seemed like a cut above that, although she was friendly and open, and had obviously needed the job. Angélique didn't respond to her question about how fancy she was. She hoped she didn't look it. Only her demeanor and manner of speech suggested how well born she was. The girl would never have suspected that she was the daughter of a duke, and Angélique was determined not to tell anyone. It made no difference now, and would only make them resent her, which was the last thing she wanted. She wanted to blend in with the rest of the staff.

As Bridget poured her a cup of tea, the baby stopped crying, and she smiled. "Merciful God, thank you for that. The poor lad suffers with his teeth. Rupert"—she pointed to the toddler—"was that way too. So what madness brings you here, caring for four children in your first job?"

"A friend of the Fergusons recommended me. I have to work." Angélique said nothing of her brother's treachery or that he had gotten her the job.

"We all have to work," Bridget said with a smile. "I'm going home to Dublin to help my sister for a few months, with twins, but after that, I'll go back to London to find a job. The country is too quiet for me, and the family doesn't take us to town very often."

"I grew up in the country, I like it," Angélique said as they sat down for a minute and sipped their tea, before Bridget made their breakfast in the nursery pantry. The rest of their meals were sent up from the kitchen on trays.

"Then you'll be happy here," Bridget said confidently, "if you can get the little monsters to behave. There's Helen, the nurserymaid, but you really need another nanny to help you. Four of them is too much for one person. But Simon will be gone in a year, when he turns five, to Eton. It's the earliest they'll take them. She can't wait to send him. That might help you, if you can hold out for that long, providing she doesn't have another. You never know with her—it's Mr. Ferguson who wants them, though he doesn't come to see them either. And she doesn't seem to mind—she has them so easily, she drops them like a farmhand in a field." It was an interesting description of her new employer, who apparently preferred horses and social life to children but had them anyway. Bridget said that as long as she didn't have to see them or care for them, and had easy pregnancies, it didn't matter to her, and kept her husband happy and gratefully spoiling her for giving him sons. "You won't see her often up here. We take them downstairs on Sundays for tea. She puts up with them for about ten minutes, and then she'll send you away." It was not the vision Angélique had of motherhood, although it was familiar to her. Her sister-in-law, Elizabeth, hadn't been interested in her children either, until they were old enough to enter a more adult world. "I think we have a dress for you, if you look in the cupboard, although you're very small. You can stitch it to fit you. You can have my nurses' uniforms, but they'll be too big for you." She laughed— she had a generous figure, broad hips, and an ample bosom, and she was taller than Angélique. The nanny dress she offered her was gray with a long, starched white apron, which Bridget said she changed three times a day, with a starched cap trimmed with a pleated ruffle, and white cuffs to match. It was less austere than the black dresses worn by the housekeeper and ladies' maids, and slightly plainer. "I look like a rag bag by the end of the day, after chasing them. The nurserymaid helps me do all their laundry up here." She went on to explain their schedule to her then. They had naps morning and afternoon. She said they got up early, had dinner at noon, and a heavy teatime at five-thirty, and a bit of fruit before they went to bed. And they liked it when she read them stories. "I'm not much of a reader," she said honestly, "but I read well enough for them. And when I can't make something out, I just fake it. They're too young to know the difference." Angélique liked the thought of reading to them. She loved to read as a child, and still did, and it was something she knew she could do for them that seemed less complicated than all the rest.

"When are you leaving?" Angélique asked, still nervous.

"At dinnertime. I'll go when the dinner trays come up."

"They'll miss you," Angélique said sadly, remembering how bereft she had been when her own nanny had left. She had been like a mother to her, and after she went away, Angélique had gotten closer to Mrs. White, the housekeeper, who had always been kind to her.

"They'll only miss me for a day or two. They'll get used to you very quickly. They're too young to remember me for long. You'll be meeting Mrs. Ferguson tomorrow, for tea in the library with the children. Helen, the nurserymaid, will show you what they should wear. The Mrs. likes them looking pretty so she can show them off to her friends. And Mr. Ferguson loves Emma's ringlets. Be sure you brush them till they shine, even if she cries while you do it. There'll be hell to pay if you take them down with her hair all in knots."

She got up to make the children's breakfast then. They had a little stove to make oatmeal, and she buttered bread with marmalade and jam, and there was a jug of milk sitting on a block of ice. She set breakfast on the table, just as Helen walked in. She looked instantly suspicious of Angélique and was about her age. Like Bridget, she had worked there for two years. She had wanted to be the nanny, but had been told she'd been passed over for someone else the Fergusons had found through friends. So she considered Angélique a major threat, and she didn't look like she was inclined to help her. She and Bridget were friends, and she was sad that she was leaving. Helen had the same reaction as Bridget at first, and thought that

Angélique looked too aristocratic to be hiring out to work in a house, and wondered why she was there.

"You help her and tell her what she needs to know," Bridget admonished her. "No funny shenanigans to make her look bad. We all started out somewhere, and she'll need your help," Bridget said kindly, and Helen nodded, looking Angélique over again. Angélique was still feeling shy, as the little girl walked over to her, stared at her for a minute, and then climbed onto her lap, holding a doll. Her hair was a mass of soft blond curls.

Bridget showed her how to dress the children, after they'd had breakfast, and she washed their faces and hands. An hour after Angélique had arrived in the nursery, all was in good order. They'd eaten and were dressed, the beds were made, and the baby had woken up and was no longer crying. He smiled as he held his arms out to Bridget, and she picked him up, just as the toddler threw a wooden horse at Emma's head and missed her. She took toys out for them, and sat down with the baby in her lap to change and dress him. It seemed like an incredible amount of organizing and work, and good timing to be looking in four directions at once and keeping track of all of them. Helen did the laundry and washing up, but she didn't take care of the children, which was entirely the nanny's job. Angélique had no idea how Bridget did it—she was a magician with ten hands. Obviously growing up in a big family had helped.

"And watch out for Mrs. Ferguson's brother—he's a bad one," she said as Angélique smiled.

"So I've heard. Sarah warned me." He had quite a reputation in the house, apparently well deserved.

"He went after one of the maids last spring when he was here. He's a charmer. They sacked her when the Mrs. found out. She's having his baby in two months, but no one talks about it. Her parents work one of the farms, so she went home to them. He'll be a pretty baby, but she won't come back to work here again, and she won't get a reference from them. Remember that if he comes near you, and lock your door at night. Mr. Ferguson won't bother you, although they say he has some fancy pieces in town, when his wife is here. I don't think she minds—she's too busy spending his money to care. And she has a wandering eye herself when they have guests." Angélique was getting a vision of people with a lot of money, a spoiled, indulged woman who had married beneath her for her husband's fortune, both of whom were unfaithful to each other, and didn't care about their children. They were hardly people Angélique would admire, and it didn't surprise her that her brother and his wife were their friends. It all sounded very superficial, and like a wasted life to her. Her father had been a different kind of man, but her brother seemed to prefer this very empty life and everything that went with it. In some ways, Mrs. Ferguson seemed like a younger version of Elizabeth. Bridget said that Mr. Ferguson was thirty-four years old, and she was twenty-five. She was easy to work for, if you stayed on her good side, flattered her occasionally, and kept the children away from her. It didn't sound like a complicated job, just an exhausting one.

They chatted all through the morning, as Bridget explained things to her. The weather was poor so they stayed in the nursery, although she said they usually went to the gardens if the weather was fine. And after Angélique read the children a story, which only the older two listened to, Helen brought their trays in for dinner. Bridget, Helen, and Angélique ate with the children. It was a hearty meal of vegetables and chicken, with ice cream and fruit for dessert. "Mrs. Ferguson always says to feed Emma less than the boys. She doesn't want her to get fat, but I let her have pudding anyway. Poor little thing. We don't want to starve her, no matter what her mother says. She has a lovely figure, even after four children, but of course she's corseted to within an inch of her life. Her lady's maid said she faints sometimes when they lace her up. Her waist is about the size of my arm." Looking at Bridget, Angélique found that easy to believe, but she liked this friendly open girl, and hoped she'd do as well in the job, and manage it with equal ease. It was hard to imagine she would. And she felt a wave of panic wash over her as Bridget gathered up her things and got ready to leave. There was a tear in her eye when she said goodbye to the children and hugged each one of them, and then she looked at Angélique.

"Good luck to you, then. I hope it works out for you here. They're foolish at times, but they're not bad people, and it's a good job. If they spent more time in London with the children, I'd come back to them, but not here." It was what she had said before.

"Will you say goodbye to Mrs. Ferguson now?" Angélique asked, curious about her, more than ever after everything Bridget had said that morning.

"No, she said goodbye to me last week. She's not a sentimental woman. She's more interested in herself. She knows she can always find another nanny. We're easily replaced, you see, so remember that, and don't play fast and loose with the job, or she'll sack you and get someone else, just like she found you."

"I'll keep that in mind," Angélique said seriously, suddenly realizing that she was lucky to have this job if she had to work. Tristan could have sent her someplace worse, and wouldn't have cared, just so he got her out of the house.

Bridget hugged her and was gone a minute later, and Angélique put the children to bed for their naps, while Helen picked up the trays and sent them downstairs in the dumbwaiter. The baby was hardest to get down, but eventually he lay in his crib, holding the bottle his new nanny had given him, and within minutes he fell asleep.

She looked through the cupboard of nurses' uniforms the nannies wore, found the two smallest ones, and then asked Helen to listen for the children while she went downstairs to the laundry, and tried to alter the dresses to fit her. She hurried down the back stairs with the two dresses, and found Mrs. Ferguson's lady's maid chatting with the laundry maids while they washed their employer's clothes. They all looked at Angélique in surprise.

"I'm sorry to bother you," she said hesitantly, "I need to alter my dresses, if I can have some gray thread and a needle." Mildred, who was in charge of the laundry room, looked at her with a bright smile and took the dresses from her with ease.

"I'll do it for you. You're the new nanny, aren't you?"

"Yes, I am. Angélique."

Mildred shook her head with a scolding look, as she got out the needle and thread and a thimble, after Angélique explained where it was too large, and glanced up at Angélique. "The Mrs. won't want you being called by your first name around here. It's Nanny Ferguson now," she reminded her, as Angélique looked chastened, and Mildred smiled. "Happy to meet you, though," Mildred said, and stood up and held the gray dresses up to her slim figure to check them, and then put some pins in them to mark them, and promised to have the dresses for her in the morning. "How are you finding the nursery so far?" she asked with interest.

Angélique hesitated and then smiled cautiously. "A little scary," she admitted, "Bridget just left an hour ago. This is my first nanny job. I've never had to manage four children." She was breathless as she said it, and the other women laughed.

"I'm not sure I could either," Mrs. Ferguson's lady's maid said under her breath. Angélique heard one of the others call her Stella. "Not with that lot of little monsters," she chuckled. "They wear their mother out in five minutes. I'm glad I never had children." She was meticulously pressing a gown for that evening, and smiled at the new nanny. "Have you met Mrs. Ferguson yet?"

"No, I haven't. I just arrived last night."

"From London?" one of the other laundry maids asked her.

"Hertfordshire. The house and grounds look very pretty here."

"The London house is nicer," Stella said proudly. "I prefer it there, but it's better for the children to be in the country. She likes them to stay here. It's healthier for them than in the city." Angélique nodded, and thought she'd better get back to the nursery then. She said goodbye to the ladies, and went back upstairs. She was sorry she couldn't have her meals with them, and had to stay in the nursery with the children. It would have been nice to get to know the others, but she would be isolated most of the time with her charges, and Helen the nurserymaid. At least she had her to talk to.

Angélique went through the bookcase when she got upstairs and found some books she wanted to read to the children that she had loved herself as a child. After that, she went downstairs to get her things, and struggled up the stairs with her cases and small trunk. There was barely enough room for all of it in her bedroom in the nursery, but she piled them on top of each other, and slid the small trunk under her bed. It was still locked, and she left it that way, with her mother's jewelry and her father's money in it. Her entire future was concealed under her bed.

"What did you bring all those clothes for?" Helen asked her. "You'll never wear them." And Angélique had noticed there was no mirror in her bedroom. Helen said that Mrs. Ferguson felt that nannies didn't need them, nor kitchen staff.

"I might wear a nice dress one day," Angélique said wistfully, as Sarah peeked into the nursery for a quick visit on her break.

"You look like a proper nanny," Sarah commented, smiling at her, and Angélique was happy to see her. She felt as though she had at least one friend there. They chatted for a few minutes, and then Sarah left, and the children woke up, and they kept Angélique busy, while she read to them. She taught Simon and Emma to play a game she found in a cupboard, and then she bathed them in a tub she filled with water she had to carry herself, with Helen's help. And by the time she had finished the bath, Helen brought the tea trays in. The day had flown by, and when she put them to bed at seven, after reading them another story, she was ready for bed herself. And tomorrow was going to be a big day. She was going to take the children down to the library to see their parents, and meet the Fergusons. She was curious about them, and as she slipped between the sheets after reading by candlelight for a while in the nursery parlor, she wondered what the future held for her. The Duke of Westerfield's daughter had become Nanny Ferguson, and it was hard to guess what fate had in store for her next.

Chapter 4

It took Angélique longer than she'd expected to get the children ready to see their parents the following afternoon, even with Helen's help. She held the baby while Angélique dressed the others, and she brushed Emma's curls until they gleamed, and then tied a pink ribbon in her hair. The boys looked immaculate, and the baby was chuckling as she played with him and put on a delicate white infant's dress, and a little white sweater. He was a strapping boy, and heavy in her arms, as she carried him downstairs and held Emma's hand. The children were excited to go down—it had rained all day, and they had had to stay in again.

Angélique couldn't wait to explore the gardens and the park, and Helen told her there was a maze. She was anxious to see the grounds, although she knew that they were less extensive than where she'd grown up. But the Fergusons were said to have one of the prettiest gardens in Hampshire. And as they came through the servants' doors on the main floor, Angélique was suddenly dazzled by an enormous chandelier. All of the candles were lit. It was already dark outside, and the gleaming crystals were spectacular. She glanced around and saw that the décor was very grand, and she had been told by Sarah that there was a ballroom in the east wing.

The furniture was a mixture of English and French, and they had very important paintings. There was a long red runner in the main hall, and Angélique could see that it was a showplace more than a home. She could hear voices in the library, and she saw about twenty people there, talking and laughing and playing cards, as she stood in the doorway with the children, wondering which of the elegant women was their mother. Emma ran to her first, and an exquisite creature in a heavy blue-velvet gown walked toward them, as the two boys dove into her skirt while Eugenia Ferguson held her daughter's hand, and met Angélique's eyes with an icy blue gaze. Her dark auburn hair was piled in a mountain of curls on top of her head in a fashionable hairdo Stella had arranged for her. And she was wearing sapphires on her ears, with an enormous matching pin at her waist. The vision she presented took Angélique's breath away as she curtsied to her, and knew she was expected to, not because of her rank, which was insignificant, but because Angélique was now a servant and the woman was her employer. Angélique looked demure and played the role well, and each woman was struck by the other's beauty. The children's mother hadn't expected the new nanny to be so pretty.

"You're the Latham girl, are you?" she said haughtily as the children buzzed around her, and then deserted her to see their father and throw their arms around his legs. He was strikingly tall, and had straight blond hair. He was very handsome, and from the evidence, very rich. "Your cousin spoke highly of you," Eugenia said pleasantly. "He's been promising you to me for months." Angélique was stunned by everything she had just said.

"My cousin?" Angélique had no cousins, except distant ones, and King George, and she strongly doubted that His Majesty had recommended her to this woman. She looked at her employer blankly, with wide innocent eyes.

"His Grace, the Duke of Westerfield, of course, Tristan Latham. He said you're distant cousins and a charming girl." Angélique's mouth nearly fell open when she heard that her own brother had claimed that they were cousins, which of course sounded more respectable than pawning his sister off on her, which he didn't want to admit. And if he had been suggesting her for the position for months, then he had been lying in wait, as her father was failing, biding his time, until he could ship her off. It was why he had been able to send her away so quickly, as soon as their father died. He had been scheming for months. It stunned her to hear it. He was even worse than she thought.

"Oh . . . Tristan, of course . . ."

"His wife, the duchess, and I," she said, to impress the others around her, "are dear friends. We're constantly together in London." Angélique nodded, as she tried to keep her eye on her charges, who were wrapped around their father, and showing off for the guests. Visiting their parents was a huge treat for them.

"I'm very grateful for this opportunity, ma'am," Angélique said politely, although she wasn't grateful to her brother for plotting against her, in anticipation of their father's death, perhaps even hoping for it, so he could take over Belgrave, and at last inherit the title, the estate, and have an enormous fortune of his own. And Eugenia Ferguson liked having the impoverished cousin of a duke in her employ, and even better having the duke himself indebted to her for assisting his young relative. She had asked him why he didn't employ the girl himself, and he had responded that it would be too embarrassing for her, to work for her own family as a servant. He had assured Eugenia that she was both well educated and well behaved, and would even be able to teach the children French if Eugenia chose. He said that the girl's mother had been a lowborn French woman a distant cousin of his had married, and the girl had been left a penniless orphan. Angélique would have been horrified to hear her mother described as "lowborn" when she was related to the king of France, which meant that Angélique was related to the current one, Charles X, not to mention the British monarch, George IV, on her father's side. But even with the little she knew, Eugenia was pleased. She liked having an aristocratic nanny for her children, and thought it gave her more prestige. It had always bothered her that her father had been a mere baron, and a life peer, so her brother couldn't inherit the title. And Harry Ferguson had none at all. But his fortune more than made up for what he lacked in noble birth.

Eugenia thought Angélique looked very proper and dignified, and as the young woman crossed the room to the children, to rescue their father from them, Mrs. Ferguson whispered to a friend that she was a poor cousin of the Duke of Westerfield. It almost made Angélique want to spin around and correct her and explain that she was his sister, and not his cousin, and had been banished from their home only days after her father's death. But she said nothing, and got the two boys under control, while still holding the baby in her arms, and she saw that Emma had a mouth full of sweets she'd taken from a silver dish, unobserved by her mother.

"You can take them back up now," Harry Ferguson said with a look of relief. "You're the new girl, are you?" he asked, and she nodded and curtsied to him too.

Eugenia didn't object as Angélique led them out of the room and through the servants' door to the back stairs. The children didn't seem surprised by the short visit—they were used to it. They had been in the library for only slightly more than ten minutes, just as Bridget had predicted. And their parents wouldn't see them again for another week. Angélique knew that was the norm in most families, but thinking of the close relationship she had shared with her father, she felt sad for them. With parents who almost never saw them, they would be missing so much, and she felt a strange obligation to make it up to them, particularly Simon, who would be leaving home in less than a year, to go away to school. He still seemed like a baby to her at four. And leaving for boarding school at five seemed even worse than what had happened to her at eighteen. At least she had grown up in the warmth of her father's love. He would never have parted with her as a child, and she would have missed him far too much. And even little Rupert, who could barely talk, would follow his brother to Eton in three years. Angélique thought they were much too young to be sent away from home and felt sorry for them.

She read them a story when they got upstairs to help them settle down, after the excitement of seeing their parents and their guests. They seemed to like Angélique reading to them, particularly Emma, who cuddled close to her and asked where Bridget was, with a wistful look. She had taken care of them for two years, which was a long time in their lives. She was the only nanny they remembered and the person closest to them.

"She's going to visit her sister," Angélique explained. She didn't promise them that they would see her again, because she wasn't sure they would. Angélique didn't know if the Fergusons would let Bridget come back to visit; some parents didn't, and Angélique wondered if the Fergusons were among them. Angélique vowed to herself to try to make it up to her charges. Even if she didn't plan to stay forever, she wanted to do the best she could.

She got them all into their nightshirts, one by one, without Helen's help, and was proud of herself for doing so. She put Charles, the baby, down first, then Rupert, who climbed out of bed twice while she tucked Emma in, and Simon after that, and then she caught Rupert again, and put him back to bed. The two youngest boys shared a room, and Emma and Simon each had their own.

"Will you come in, if I have a bad dream?" Emma asked her, and Angélique promised she would, and kissed her goodnight. She left their doors open when they asked her to, and went to relax in the nursery parlor with a book. She was surprised by how well the day had gone, and they were sweet children despite their exuberance. She was thinking about how easy it had been, and the visit to their parents, when Sarah knocked softly and walked in.

"All finished? How did it go today?" She was happy to see her new friend, and sat down in one of the comfortable chairs across from her.

"Pretty well. We went down to the library for tea. She's very beautiful," she observed about their employer, and Sarah nodded.

"She's cold as ice and only thinks of herself," Sarah commented. "I think Mr. Ferguson is a very handsome man," she added, grinning. "He could have found a nicer one, but I think he's impressed that her father had a title. It doesn't do him much good, and she costs him a fortune. You should see the gowns Stella brings to the laundry to press and mend. She buys them in Paris. Wouldn't I love to wear a dress like that one day!" She changed the subject then. "They were all talking about you at supper tonight, downstairs. It's a shame you can't dine with us when the children are asleep. Maybe Helen would watch them for you one night, at least so you could join us for pudding and a cup of tea."

"I wish I could," Angélique said longingly. She was going to get lonely in the nursery with only Helen for adult company. They hadn't warmed up to each other yet, and Angélique wasn't sure they would. She had liked the bustling around the servants' dining room and kitchen. It reminded her of the kitchen at Belgrave and the staff there. It made her homesick, thinking about them, and she wondered how Hobson and Mrs. White, Mrs. Williams, and all the others were. She promised herself to write to Mrs. White the next day, to let her know how she was, and what she was doing in her job.

The two young women sat and talked for half an hour, and then Sarah got up and went to bed, and after reading for a little while, Angélique did the same. Bridget had warned her that the baby woke up every morning before six, and it would be a short night if she didn't get to bed soon. But it was nice to enjoy the peace in the nursery parlor at night. It gave her a respite from chasing the children all day. They were better behaved than she'd expected, and than the people downstairs had said. They were just children, and there were a lot of them. It made them seem worse than they really were.

The next day was sunny and cold, and Angélique explored the grounds with the children after breakfast. They ran in the garden, and she peeked into the maze but didn't risk it, in case she couldn't find her way out and got separated from the children. It was a beautiful park, as they strolled with the baby in the pram, and the children's cheeks were bright red from the cold when they came back through the kitchen. Everyone exclaimed over them, paying special attention to Emma, and the cook gave each of them a biscuit. The smells in the kitchen were delicious. The kitchen staff were preparing dinner, and they were baking several cakes to serve that night at supper. Their guests were leaving the next day, much to the staff's relief. Their hunting parties where the guests stayed for three or four days were a lot of work. Three of the female guests had brought their own maids; the others relied on the housemaids to dress them. But visiting staff were more work for the house staff too, and more mouths to feed. And one of Harry's close friends had brought his valet, who was very grand with the others, and had managed to annoy them all with his supercilious manner.

Angélique noticed the head butler, Mr. Gilhooley, staring at her, as they lingered in the kitchen for a few minutes, and then she ushered the children upstairs. She saw that the butler was still watching her when they left, although she couldn't imagine why. He looked fierce and unfriendly, but she knew that Hobson could look that way too, at Belgrave, when he wanted to impress the younger staff. But the Fergusons' butler seemed particularly unfriendly to her. It made her almost glad she couldn't eat downstairs, if he was going to glare at her. And the Fergusons' housekeeper, Mrs. Allbright, wasn't nearly as warm as Mrs. White. But Angélique also realized that she had never worked for her. And even among the staff at Belgrave, a new face in the crowd was always kept at a distance at first, until the staff got to know them. She was the new girl among the servants now. The whole idea of it was so absurd she almost laughed. She wondered what her father would say to see her there, in her uniform, other than to express his fury at Tristan, which Angélique could only imagine. She hoped he'd be proud of her, for dealing with it as gracefully as possible. And she knew for certain that what Tristan had done to her would have broken her father's heart.

The children had their naps, after the meal the cook sent up, and leaving Helen to listen for the children, she went back down to the kitchen for a cup of tea. As she walked by, she saw Mr. Gilhooley in his office, and he beckoned her to come in.

"Are you finding the nursery to your satisfaction?" he asked her formally. But he sounded as though he really cared, and then he lowered his voice conspiratorially, so no one would hear them. "Your Ladyship, I wanted you to know . . . I used to work for your father a long time ago, at Belgrave, and I wanted to tell you how sorry I am about your loss. He was a great man."

"Yes, he was," Angélique said sadly. "I miss him terribly. It only just happened."

"I don't know how it is that you came here, Your Ladyship," he said, as she cringed at how he had addressed her. It was precisely what she didn't want the staff here to know about her, that she had been born into the cream of aristocratic society, and had a title. She didn't want anything to set her apart from the others. If she had to live and work here, she wanted to be one of them, no matter how unlikely her presence there seemed. It still seemed improbable to her too, but at least she had met a few members of the staff, and she was touched by what the butler had said about her father.

"I think it would be best if you don't address me that way, Mr. Gilhooley. It will only make things more difficult for me with the others. They might even decide they don't like me for that reason alone. They needn't know who my father was—in fact, they shouldn't. That's all in the past now," she said seriously.

"Clearly there are reasons why you are here, and it must be very hard for you," he said, looking sympathetic and no longer fierce.

"Nothing surprises me anymore," she said honestly. "But now that I'm here, it's better than I thought. Everyone has been very kind to me."

"I'm happy to hear it. If there's anything I can do . . ." His eyes searched hers, and she shook her head. She didn't want to be singled out for special treatment. She had to get by, and do her job, like the others. She expected no favors from him, and he respected her for it. She was very young to be experiencing such a change. "Do the Fergusons know?" He was curious how she had come there.

Angélique shook her head. "No, they don't. My brother secured the position for me, and I believe he told them that we're cousins. It's probably best that way. Please don't tell anyone, Mr. Gilhooley." Her eyes pleaded with him and touched his heart.

"Certainly not, if that is your wish. I'm sure it would be a shock for the Fergusons too, to realize that they have the daughter of a duke under their roof, working in the nursery." But he suspected they'd like it.

"It doesn't make any difference now," she said, fighting back tears that threatened to overwhelm her. "My brother and his wife and daughters are at Belgrave. There is no place for me there." The butler looked tragic as he listened, and he suspected some foul play at work, particularly if the new duke was passing her off as his cousin and not his sister. But there was no way the duke could have explained to anyone that he had sent her away to become a nanny without looking like a cad. It was crystal clear now to Gilhooley.

"Life works in mysterious ways, Your Ladyship," he said softly. "I am certain you will go home again one day."

She nodded and couldn't speak as he patted her hand. At least she had a friend here, other than Sarah, and she was sure that Hobson at Belgrave would be pleased that a butler of the late duke had taken her under his wing and would protect her. And it was comforting for her that Gilhooley would be watching out for her. She stood up then—she had been away from the nursery longer than she'd planned.

"I should go back," she said quietly, and thanked him with a grateful look.

"Come and join us another time," he invited her, as she smiled at him.

"I will," she assured him, "although the children will keep me busy." He laughed at that.

"I'm certain they will, Your Ladyship. And I hope you'll be happy here and stay for a long time." Although what he really wished for her was that she would go home to Belgrave Castle where she belonged. He considered it nearly criminal for her brother to have sent her away to become a servant in someone's home. It had shocked him profoundly on her behalf. And a moment later Angélique hurried back upstairs to the nursery where Helen was waiting impatiently for her.

"What took you so long?" Helen was annoyed when she got there.

"I'm sorry. Mr. Gilhooley wanted to speak to me, and I couldn't get away."

"What did he want?" she asked suspiciously.

"As it turns out, he knew my father," she said, and then regretted it.

"Was your father a butler too? Or a footman?"

"No," Angélique said quietly, not sure what to say to her, "he wasn't. They just knew each other." And with that, the baby stirred, and Angélique went to get him, and the others woke up shortly after. They played games that afternoon, and took Simon to ride on his pony. His father walked past the stables while he did, and waved at him, but he didn't stop to speak to the children. He was going to ride himself, and it didn't even occur to him to visit with them. Eugenia was resting, and he wanted to get some air. And by the time he came back late that afternoon, the children were back in the house, being bathed by their nanny.

Life went on peacefully after that, as Angélique got accustomed to the children. Caring for four of them was something of a juggling act, but she was surprised to find she enjoyed it and felt useful, and it made the time pass quickly. They needed someone to care for them, and make life interesting. She started to teach them French, and was impressed to find that Emma picked it up easily, and Simon was learning too, although more slowly. And by the time she'd been there a month, they had made serious progress, and had learned many words and several songs in French. It was nearly Christmas by then, and the Fergusons had been in London all month going to parties, while their children waited for them in Hampshire. Their parents finally returned the day before Christmas Eve. An enormous Christmas tree had been put up in the main hall, and the children had helped decorate it, and were thrilled with the end result.

And when it had snowed hard the week before, Angélique had

made a snowman with them. She was full of ideas to entertain them, and was barely more than a child herself. But she had grown up fast in the last month. Working and living in someone else's home, taking care of their children, and having to get along with the staff had matured her as nothing ever had before. And when the Fergusons saw the children on Christmas morning to give them their presents, before a party they were giving, they had important news to share with them. They were going to have a new brother or sister in a few months, which came as startling news to Angélique too. When the new baby came, sometime in May, her employer told her in further detail, there would be a baby nurse for a month, and then Angélique would be taking care of five children instead of four, for a few months at least, until Simon left for Eton at the end of the summer. Mrs. Ferguson made it perfectly clear to her that she thought a second nanny unnecessary, since Simon would be going away so soon, and she said that Angélique managed so well with four. She had absolutely no idea what that entailed, nor did she want to know, since she had never spent more than a few minutes with her children at any time. She told Angélique that she was doing a splendid job of it, handed her a small Christmas gift, and then they were dismissed as guests started arriving. The children retreated to the nursery, where Eugenia said they belonged, and her husband agreed.

Once back in the nursery, Angélique helped them open their gifts. Simon received a game he wanted to play with her, Rupert a stuffed bear he carried around everywhere, Emma a new doll, and Charles a silver rattle, which he shoved into his mouth immediately. They were very pleased with their presents, and watched as Angélique opened hers. She had received a pair of gloves, which would be useful on their walks. They were gray leather to match her uniform, and looked very smart. They were a perfect fit when Emma made her try them on. Mrs. Ferguson had guessed well.

In January, the Fergusons decided exceptionally to take the children to London with them for two weeks, and Angélique was excited about it. There would be so much to do with the children there. They set out on a freezing-cold day, with the children, Helen, and Angélique traveling in the family's large coach, and Mrs. Ferguson in the barouche-landau, similar to Angélique's brother's, while Mr. Ferguson rode in his luxurious chariot. A carriage followed behind with their luggage. Simon was thrilled to be riding in the coach, and loved watching the horses, but Emma said she felt sick most of the way. The two little ones slept for several hours with the gentle rocking motion, with Angélique holding Charles in her arms. And when they got to London, the staff were happy to see them, and equally so to meet Angélique and show her around the house.

The Fergusons' London home was an enormous house on Curzon Street, filled with beautiful furniture and art, and they either entertained at home or went to parties every night. It was easy to see now why Eugenia found Hampshire boring. She had an enviable life in the city, surrounded by friends, evenings at the theater, the opera, and the ballet. And Harry seemed happy there too. He did business in the City, and went to his club frequently to meet his cronies to dine or gamble. They stayed out late every night.

One Sunday afternoon they had guests in for tea, and Angélique was asked to bring the children down at teatime, just as they did in the country. She dressed them in their finest clothes, two maids helped her, and when they arrived in the drawing room, Angélique got a shock. She found herself standing a few feet away from Tristan and Elizabeth, who looked right through her as though they didn't know her. She had been about to say hello to them, which was awkward enough, when Tristan walked away, and Elizabeth turned her back on her to talk to a woman she knew. And Angélique was sure they had seen her, although their faces revealed nothing.

It was Eugenia who finally pointed her out to them, in a most embarrassing way.

"Did you not recognize your cousin in her nurse's uniform?" she asked Tristan blandly. "And you were quite right about her—she's a wonderful nanny. She has Simon and Emma speaking French." Tristan feigned surprise then, and acknowledged his sister with a cool greeting, as though to give the impression that he barely knew her. His Grace, the Duke of Westerfield, was clearly not pleased to be associated with a nanny, who had been identified as his cousin.

"Indeed," he said in an icy tone, "I didn't see her." He nodded in Angélique's direction, and Elizabeth said nothing and just glared at her with hatred in her eyes. They clearly wanted her out of their lives forever. They had assumed she was in Hampshire when they accepted the Fergusons' invitation. Otherwise they might not have come. And Tristan didn't look in the least embarrassed to have claimed she was his cousin, rather than his sister. "Very distant cousin, I might add," he said to Eugenia. "I'm sure you've been very kind to her." He nodded at Angélique again then and walked away, and a few minutes later her mistress said she should take the children upstairs—they had been there long enough. The nearly fifteen minutes had given Angélique a chance to observe her brother and his wife.

Elizabeth was wearing a beautiful dress, although Eugenia was wearing a nicer one. And there was no sign of Tristan's daughters, who were really too young to be at a party for adults. She heard Elizabeth say that Gwyneth would be coming out in July, and presented at court at the same time. It was the Season Angélique had never had, nor wanted, and would never have now. All chance of meeting a husband from her own world had vanished when Tristan refused her his protection and sent her away. And he was relieved when she left the room and went back upstairs. He hoped not to see her again. It had been an unpleasant surprise for Elizabeth as well, who was pale and silent as Angélique walked by her.

Angélique was shaken by the experience, and upset when they got back to the nursery. She had wondered for the past two months if her brother had regretted what he'd done, or ever would. She had her answer now. He not only denied her as a sister, but he clearly wanted nothing to do with her. She was sure he would have been relieved if she died. It was a terrible feeling, and a shiver ran up her spine remembering his eyes when he had first seen her and pretended not to. She had ceased to exist for them. She was nothing more than a ghost from their past, and in their minds she was as dead as her father. It confirmed to her what she had feared since she left, that she would never see her home again. The first eighteen years of her life were nothing but memories now. He had reminded her of her worst fear that night. She was totally alone in the world.

Chapter 5

The Fergusons decided to stay in London until February, and make the best of the time to enjoy the social whirl before Eugenia's confinement, and the baby's birth in May. And most unusually, they kept the children in town with them, which Angélique enjoyed more than she'd expected.

It was an odd feeling knowing that it would have been her first winter properly out in Society, if she had come out the previous summer, as she should have if her father had been well. She would have been presented to all the important families in Society, and at court, and met all the eligible bachelors who could have pursued her. Her name and lineage would have been enough to satisfy many of them, even without her father's fortune. And she might have fallen in love with someone truly suitable. Instead she was unknown to many, had been sequestered in the country and disowned by her brother, and had become a servant. The world that should have belonged to her was out of her reach now, and always would be. Not being introduced to Society had made all the difference to her future. She was doomed now to become a governess, and probably spend the rest of her life unmarried. Tristan had condemned her to an unsuitable marriage, if any, and deprived her of the heritage she was born to. He had virtually destroyed not only her present life, but her future, by his actions.

Seeing him at the Fergusons' Curzon Street home, and hearing the lie he had told about her being merely a distant cousin, helped her to let go of any hope of returning to her old life and world one day, or even Belgrave, the home where she grew up. She knew her father would have been devastated by it, and she was even more grateful now for the money he had given her before he died. It would at least assure a comfortable future for her, even if she remained an old maid. She had vowed never to touch the money unless she was in dire need. There was no question in her mind, she could never turn to either of her brothers, no matter what happened to her. She tried to make the best of it, and focus on the life that was available to her now. She knew she would never have any other.

She was often pensive as she thought about her future, and wondered what would become of her. She could stay with the Fergusons, but it was unlikely she would stay forever. They weren't warm people, and felt none of the traditional responsibilities for their servants. Harry Ferguson was too nouveau riche to know the difference, and all he had was money. His wife considered those she employed as a convenience, but saw none of them as people, although her own parents had run a proper household, which she considered an enormous and unnecessary burden. Angélique knew that she couldn't count on them, and once the children got older, and the boys left for Eton, she would be dismissed, unless the new baby was a girl. But even that was time limited. At best she would have another five years with them, if they liked her well enough to keep her. But they had no particular allegiance to their nannies, and Eugenia had no great interest in her, except to be able to say that their nanny was distantly related to a duke. But that might not be enough for them to keep her, if they tired of her for some reason. After what her own brother had done to her, Angélique was well aware that nothing was sure in life, and her whole world could turn upside down in an instant. The only thing she could count on was her father's money in the locked trunk under her bed.

While in London, Angélique went to the park with the children every day, and she chatted with the other nannies she met there. Most of them were older than she was, and a few had as many charges, but in that case, they usually had an undernanny or nursery maid with them, while Angélique scrambled single-handedly after her four charges.

She discovered that there was a whole hierarchy among the nannies in the park, their importance dictated by that of the family they worked for, and their titles. Almost all of them used the surname of their employers to identify themselves. She had not only lost the life and world she had grown up with, but for the time being, even her family name as well. She had become an anonymous person. Tristan had stolen her identity as well.

She wrote to Mrs. White twice from London, and was excited to get several letters from her in return. They carried greetings from Hobson, Mrs. Williams, and several of the maids. Angélique had written to her about the children, the Fergusons, her duties, and how much she was enjoying London, and how splendid her employers' home was. Its newness struck some as vulgar—it had none of the dignity of centuries of tradition at Belgrave—but she liked the ease, comfort, and conveniences of a lavish modern home. Everything was new to her. And she told their housekeeper in her letters that she had seen her brother and Elizabeth, and that they had barely acknowledged her and said she was a distant cousin, which Mrs. White thought was a disgrace.

"The poor child is out in the world on her own," Mrs. White said in confidence to Hobson the night she got the letter. She told him about His Grace denying his own sister, and hearing it brought tears to the old man's eyes, thinking of how her father would have felt about it. They both agreed that it would have broken his heart, although Hobson suspected that he had feared it in the end. He knew his sons well, and their deep resentment of their sister.

Markham, the valet, had just handed in his notice, and said he was going to the Continent to retire. To Hobson, he had admitted that he could not bear serving the new duke, knowing what he had done to his half-sister, and felt he had to leave. And the head footman was going to be elevated to valet once he left. Tristan had not tried to detain Markham—he had been too devoted to his father, which annoyed him, and he preferred a younger man anyway.

And Mrs. White reported in her next letter that there had been a great many changes to the house since Angélique left. The new duchess had moved furniture from room to room, and had ordered several new pieces to be made in London. She was replacing draperies, re-covering existing furniture, and they had purchased a spectacular new chandelier in Vienna. She was spending her husband's new fortune very liberally, on making Belgrave grander than it had ever been. Mrs. White also mentioned that Elizabeth had taken her daughters to Paris, to order new gowns for them, and several for herself, befitting their new rank and position and the balls they intended to give at the castle in the spring. They were planning to lead a very grand life in their magnificent new home.

It made Angélique's heart ache to read the letters, and hear about how Tristan and Elizabeth were transforming her home. It made her miss her father even more, but she was happy to have news from Mrs. White and Hobson—they were the only family she had left. And the changes to the house they talked about sounded vulgar to her. Tristan had been waiting all his life for this, and was taking full advantage of it.

Eugenia saw even less of the children while they were in London— she was much too busy. And at last in mid-February, her husband insisted that she and the children return to Hampshire. She was six and a half months pregnant by then, and no matter how viciously she corseted herself, her condition was much too evident for her to stay in town and continue going out socially. She hated to leave, and begged him to let her stay. But he reminded her that it would become shockingly inappropriate soon, and people were already mentioning it to him. With great reluctance, Eugenia acceded to his wishes and went back to Hampshire in the third week of February, to sit out the rest of her pregnancy there, which she found intolerably boring. Angélique wondered if she would see more of the children then, with nothing else to do, but she didn't. She organized dinner parties for her women friends, and card parties. Eugenia's mother came to stay. She was a rather ordinary woman, the daughter of a wealthy merchant, who had married Eugenia's father for his title and fortune. And she was every bit as pretentious and arrogant as her daughter, and had as little interest in her grandchildren as their mother. They never came to the nursery to see them. And Angélique was left to her own devices to entertain them. They had grown very attached to her by then, and she was very fond of them. And Emma had become delightfully fluent in French.

Mr. Ferguson didn't return to Hampshire until six weeks after his wife's return, in early April, despite her complaints about it. He arrived with friends from London, and by then, Eugenia declared herself ready to go mad in the country, during her confinement. There had been rumors below stairs of the parties Harry had been giving in London, and the women who'd been seen there. Fortunately, Eugenia was unaware of her husband's escapades, which was just as well, since she had a fierce temper, and no one wanted to upset her now, right before the baby was due to be born.

Eugenia's mother left as soon as Harry arrived, since they were not fond of each other, and Harry took off with his friends a week after his return to make the rounds of the house parties nearby, while Eugenia spent the next month walking in the gardens, resting, and waiting for the baby to arrive. She was anxious for it to come, so she could get back to London, and was planning to be there for the summer Season, and debutante balls in June and July. She envied Harry the parties he was attending at neighboring country homes, while she languished at home alone.

"I wish this baby would hurry up and be born," she said to Angélique with a look of boredom and irritation, when she ran into her playing with the children in the park. They had just been to the small lake to see the ducks and swans.

"It won't be long, madame," Angélique said politely. Eugenia had gotten huge since they'd returned to Hampshire, and she was no longer corseting herself, and she said she couldn't sleep at night. The weather had been unusually warm, and the children were enjoying playing outside with their nanny every day. Simon had been riding his pony, and Charles had just learned to walk, so he was keeping Angélique busy, dashing after him from morning till night.

There was a baby nurse coming for the first month, due to arrive shortly, and a wet nurse, since Eugenia thought nursing babies was repulsive. And as soon as the baby nurse left, Angélique would take over. She was going to have her hands full until Simon left for Eton in September. The poor child was dreading it and had already told Angélique that he didn't want to go, but there was no choice. It was too important to their social status to do otherwise.

It was the end of April when Eugenia's brother Maynard showed up, and Angélique met him for the first time, after hearing about him for months. He told his sister he needed a rest from London, but he was in fact escaping the latest scandal. He'd been dallying with a young girl, a banker's daughter, and her father had found out. He was being talked about all over town. He had been pursuing her older sister, who had come out the previous year, and had switched his attentions to the younger girl, in secret, who was only fifteen. Her father was irate and had learned of their clandestine meetings from a maid. Her older sister was heartbroken, and their father had warned him that if he came near his younger daughter again, or in fact either of them, he would call for the police. Maynard had decided it was a good time to leave town. He was going on to visit friends in Derbyshire the following week, and stopped to see Eugenia in the meantime, and he planned to be back in London for the Season in June and July that his sister was also looking forward to.

"So what have you been up to?" Eugenia asked him as they sat in lounge chairs on the terrace, drinking lemonade. His was laced with rum. Eugenia had given up strong drink until the baby was born, and said it made her feel ill. She'd heard none of the gossip and rumors from London, of his latest bad behavior.

"Very little," he said, sipping his drink and looking out at the garden. "London's a bit tiresome at this time of year, so I decided to leave town."

"That sounds like you've been up to mischief," she responded, smiling at him. "Anyone I know?" He was two years younger than she was, and never tired of causing trouble.

"I hope not," he said, laughing, thinking of the recent object of his affections, who he knew was much too young, but it had been fun for a little while. "Nothing serious. Just a minor flirtation."

"With someone's wife?"

"Of course not," he said innocently. "A very pretty young girl."

"And?"

"Her father got a bit upset about it. She's rather young. It was quite harmless really."

"Maynard, you are a terror. Will you ever grow up?" she said, laughing at him.

"Certainly not. What fun would that be?"

"You're right—behaving oneself is dreadfully boring. I can't wait to go back to town after the baby. I won't stay here long." He was sure she wouldn't, and he always enjoyed running into her at parties, and exchanging gossip with her. In some ways, they were very much alike, although he would never have wanted all those children. He had no idea why she had them, and assumed it was his brother-in-law's idea, not his sister's. He knew her better.

They chatted about various people among their acquaintances in London, and he reported on the latest scandals and affairs, and then she went back up to her room for a rest, and he went for a stroll in the gardens, and was startled to run into Angélique coming out of the maze with the children. The youngest was strapped in a pram so he couldn't get out, and she wouldn't lose him in the maze or the garden. She had mastered the maze by then, and frequently led her charges through it. She literally crashed into him as they came out.

"Oh, I'm so sorry," she said, straightening her starched cap, as Maynard looked down at her in surprise. He thought he had never seen a woman so pretty, and she was very graceful as she sprang out of his way, and she blushed as the children gathered around her. Angélique had no idea who he was or that guests had arrived. No one had told her. And she was surprised that Eugenia was receiving, in such an advanced condition, with the birth only a few weeks away, if the baby came on time.

"Not at all," Maynard said politely, smiling, as he looked her over closely and liked everything he saw. She was obviously the new nanny and a strikingly pretty girl, with a delicate, perfectly chiseled face. And the moment she spoke, he could tell that she was from a family of rank, and not a simple girl. "I had no idea that my niece and nephews have such a charming new nanny. I must visit them more often," he said, teasing her, and she didn't smile. From what he said, she knew instantly who he was, and all the warnings she'd heard about him came rapidly to mind.

She dropped a formal curtsy to him and lowered her eyes. "It's very nice to meet you, sir," she responded, and rounded up her charges, ready to go inside for tea and their bath.

"Shall I come to visit you in the nursery?" he asked her, expecting a flirtatious answer, which she didn't give him. She gave him a serious one, with a cold expression, as she stood behind the pram, looking as though she would run him down.

"The children will be having tea and a bath shortly, and then it's their bedtime," she said firmly. And then she regretted what she'd said to him. It meant that the children would be in bed early, and if he showed up in the nursery, she wouldn't have them around to protect her. She looked flustered as she began rolling the pram away with the children following.

"See you later then," he said with a suggestive tone, and she didn't answer, but she told Helen about it when they were getting the tea tray ready.

"What am I going to do if he shows up here tonight?" Angélique was panicked. There had been lust in his eyes as he looked her over.

"He's a bad one," Helen said, shaking her head. "You've heard about the girl on the farm. Fifteen years old—she just had her baby last week. She broke her parents' hearts, and he'll never pay any attention to it or acknowledge it. It was a girl. She'll never see him again for sure." Helen said that Maynard had had several illegitimate children, and recognized none of them so far. And this one would be no different. He had no interest in the child or the mother, only in the fun he'd had with her for a brief time. The girl had heard nothing from him since their affair, when he'd spent a few days in Hampshire. And he knew there was a baby on the way. Her father had written to him in the fall, and Maynard never responded to the letter, and Mr. Ferguson had said there was nothing he could do about his brother-in-law. "Be sure you lock the nursery door tonight," Helen told her, and Angélique assured her that she would. The two had grown friendlier in the past five months, although Angélique was closer to Sarah, the maid who had taken her under her wing the first night. And occasionally Helen minded the children so Angélique could have dinner downstairs with the others. She always enjoyed it, and Mr. Gilhooley was happy to see her. He had heard from the housekeeper that she was doing well.

Angélique and Helen served tea to the children, and then Angélique gave them each a bath. She read stories to them afterward, and had even found a children's book for Simon and Emma in French, which they both liked. It was about a little boy and his dog. The dog gets lost, and the boy finds him again in the end.

It was still light, as it often was now, when she put them to bed. The air was cool, but the days were getting longer. She sat with Helen in the nursery parlor for a few minutes, and then Helen went to her own room, and Angélique locked the main nursery door, as she had said she would. They didn't want any surprise visitors that night, and the look that Eugenia's brother had given her that afternoon had suggested to her that he wouldn't hesitate to take what he wanted, and she was determined to make sure that didn't happen.

Maynard was downstairs in the dining room with his sister having an early supper when Angélique put the children to bed. Harry was still staying with friends for a few more days. He was close enough to return quickly if the baby came. And Eugenia was happy to have her brother's company for distraction.

"You didn't tell me that you have a very fetching new nanny," he scolded her. "When did she arrive?" His sister raised an eyebrow at his question, although there was no denying that Angélique was a very pretty girl. Others had noticed it too, but no one with the lascivious look she saw in her brother's eyes. It wasn't new to her.

"I don't remember, sometime before Christmas. But Maynard darling, please don't. She's very good with the children, and we don't need her leaving, right before the baby comes, or having one of her own in nine months. You'll have to entertain yourself with someone else." She looked at him sternly with a gleam in her eye. "She's a bit of an interesting one though. She's a distant cousin of Tristan Latham's. Her mother was French. She's an orphan."

"The Duke of Westerfield's cousin? How interesting. And if she's half French, she won't be nearly as prim as you think."

"Don't be so sure. She's very young. And he may not care much about her, but I'm sure Latham won't want her scattering bastards around the countryside. She's a very well-brought-up girl. Her mother may have been lowborn, as he says, but her aristocratic breeding shows. So do find someone else, another farm girl perhaps, but preferably not one of my maids. It causes such a ruckus when you do that. Harry gets upset." Maynard was tempted to tell her that her husband did a bit of that himself, but he thought it wiser not to, so he went back to talking about the nanny.

"How did you ever find her?"

"The duke and duchess sent her to me. They were very anxious to find her a job, and the Irish girl I had wanted to leave. It worked out perfectly. I already knew another baby was on the way when she arrived, but I didn't say anything."

"The cousin of a duke," he mused about Angélique. "That's really quite amusing . . . and very appealing, especially since she's so pretty. She almost ran me over today with the pram. Lovely girl." He smiled, and his sister gave him a mock-stern look.

"You'll have to answer to Harry if you frighten her away," Eugenia warned him, "and he won't be pleased. The business with the farm girl was rather awkward. She had it last week, you know."

"I neither know nor care," he said honestly with an indifferent look, as one of the footmen poured him more wine, and he'd already had more than enough. "This one is an entirely different story.

Too bad she wound up as a nanny. Girls like that never have a life, they're too good to marry one of the servants, and our kind don't want them if they're penniless and reduced to being maids. One can't marry a maid."

"Then don't, and don't seduce her either. And she's not a maid, she's a nanny. I suppose she'll be a governess one day. Maybe she'll stay with us. We'll see how it goes."

"Oh, it's all too boring. I'll have to go back to London soon to have some fun." He grinned at his sister.

"Yes, me too," she said enthusiastically. She couldn't wait. "I wish this wretched thing would hurry up. Harry wants another boy."

"Why? He already has three."

"He's building his own army. He wants them all to go into business with him one day. He says family are the only people you can trust."

"He's probably right," Maynard said thoughtfully. "I think Father thinks so too, except for me. I've got no head for business at all."

"Neither do I," Eugenia said with a sigh. "Harry always complains that I spend too much, but he's very sweet about it."

"You're a lucky girl," her brother said, looking around. "I'd like to find one just like him," he admitted to her, and she laughed.

"Then you'd better stop running after farm girls and nannies, even if they are related to dukes. Perhaps you'll meet a nice girl in London at someone's ball in July. Some sweet young thing in her first Season, just coming out, with an enormously rich father."

"I definitely need one of those. Father has been complaining that I spend too much too. It's such a bore." He finished his wine, and Eugenia got up, to leave him alone.

"I'll let you enjoy your cigar and a glass of port. I'm afraid the

cigar would make me ill. I'm going to bed. I'll see you in the morning, my darling brother, and do try to behave tonight." She kissed
him lightly on the cheek, and a moment later he was alone at the
table, smoking a cigar and enjoying a glass of Harry's very fine port.
It was a time of day he always enjoyed. He was sorry Harry wasn't
there to enjoy it with him, but it was pleasant anyway. And when he
left the table, he lingered in the drawing room for a few minutes,
trying to think of what to do, and then he laughed softly to himself
and headed up the stairs. He went past the second floor where he
was staying, and headed up another flight until he reached the third
floor and found himself in front of the nursery door. It was only
nine-thirty, and he was sure she was still awake.

Maynard gently tried the door handle and pushed, as Angélique
looked up from her book. She had heard a squeak, and she saw the
handle move as he worked it from the other side, but it was locked,
much to her relief. She watched him continue to move it to no avail,
and heard a gentle knock. She didn't stir from her chair so as not to
make a sound, and she knew that Helen was already asleep. But she
didn't need her help, she was safe.

He knocked again, and she didn't make a sound.

"Hello? Are you in there? I know you are. Open the door so we
can talk." She knew better than to fall for that. She sat glued to her
chair and didn't say a word.

"Don't be so silly," he tried again, "let's have some fun. I'm sure
the children are asleep, and you must be as bored as I am. Open the
door, come on, and let me in." He tried several more times for ten
minutes, and then he kicked the door and walked away. Angélique
still stayed in her seat, in case he was waiting to see what she would
do if she thought he'd gone downstairs. And then finally she heard

his footsteps on the stairs and knew he was gone. She exhaled slowly, and was so glad the others had warned her about him. She had no idea what he would have done if she had let him in, but she could guess. He might have forced her, or tried to cajole her into doing something she would regret. And she had no intention of falling for a cad like him. Even in all her innocence, she was far wiser than that. She found men like him repugnant, who took advantage of young girls, like a farm girl of fifteen.

Maynard was angry about Angélique by the time he got to his room. Who did she think she was, putting on airs and playing virtuous just because she was a distant cousin of a duke? He helped himself to another drink from the decanter in his room. He sat drinking for a while, staring into the fire. The silence of the room unnerved him, and the locked nursery door had angered him. He had two more drinks and fell asleep in the chair, thinking about what a bitch the nanny was. He would have taught her a lesson or two, to cut her down to size, if he could. But fortunately for her, he couldn't. She had been wise.

Chapter 6

Maynard left the next morning for more entertaining pursuits. "I'll see you in London in July," he promised his sister. "It's far too quiet for me here."

"For me too," she said miserably, sorry to see him leave. She didn't ask him what he'd done the night before, but his haste to leave suggested to her that he had not gone in pursuit of Angélique. If he had, he would have stayed at least another day or two. And she was relieved. She needed her nanny now, and didn't want her brother turning her life upside down, which he had done before. And she knew her husband would be pleased, not to return to one of Maynard's messes to clean up. But she was even more bored once he left, and anxious for Harry to come home, which he did several days later, with friends again. He promised they would only stay a few days, and Eugenia was annoyed that there were several very attractive women in the group. He told her it would be company for her, which it was. But she was in no condition to compete with them right now. Being confined at home in Hampshire felt like a prison sentence to her, and all she wanted was for it to end. While Harry's friends were there, they played cards in the evening, and went for walks in the afternoon, although Eugenia had trouble keeping up with them. She was the largest she'd ever been, and she was sure it was another boy.

Their friends stayed for a full week. Harry left with them to stay at friends' nearby, and by the time they moved on, Eugenia could barely get out of bed. Angélique came to check on her one afternoon when the children were asleep. She had been on her way downstairs to the laundry room to repair a dress she'd torn while running in the park with the children. She knocked on the door, and found Eugenia lying on her bed, propped up on pillows in tears. She was wearing a lace dressing gown, and she looked like she had an enormous ball hidden under it.

"How are you feeling, ma'am?" she asked in a gentle voice. "Is there anything I can do? Would you like a glass of cold tea?" She saw that Stella wasn't in the room, and she was happy to help in some way. Her employer looked miserable, as she had for weeks.

"No, I wouldn't," Eugenia said petulantly. "I want this thing out of me. I can't bear it anymore." She looked thoroughly uncomfortable, and utterly fed up. And she'd had enough, it was her fifth child in five years. "I don't care what Harry says, or how many he wants, I'm not going to have another one after this."

"Supposedly, one forgets all the discomforts afterward, and is ready to do it all again," Angélique said innocently.

"Well, I'm not." She frowned at Angélique. She had easy pregnancies, but they interfered with the things she wanted to do, and nothing fit. In the past few days, she'd gotten even bigger, and could only wear lace dressing gowns. Nothing she owned was large enough anymore, and when she complained to her husband about it, he had been amused and had gone off to visit friends again, while she was stuck at home.

"Would you like to see the children this afternoon?" she asked her, and Eugenia shook her head.

"No, I wouldn't. They make too much noise." Angélique nodded and didn't know what else to say. "Perhaps I'll take a walk down to the lake. There must be something I can wear. Help me get out of bed." Angélique assisted her, and Eugenia shuffled off to her dressing room, and then Angélique went downstairs. The maids in the laundry room were gossiping and exchanging local news, and Stella was ironing Mrs. Ferguson's nightgowns, which one of the maids commented unkindly was big enough to use as a garden party tent. But at least it was the first of May, and it wouldn't be long.

"She seems terribly uncomfortable," Angélique said sympathetically. She actually felt sorry for her, although ordinarily she wouldn't. She wasn't the kind of woman one felt sorry for, but she appeared so helpless at the moment and so unhappy. She didn't seem excited about the baby at all, just anxious for it to be born, so she could be free of it.

From the nursery window, Angélique saw Eugenia walking in the park that afternoon, lumbering along. She looked almost comical as she did. And she didn't stay out for long. Angélique got busy with the children then, and never stopped until that night when they were in bed, and then she went downstairs to have a cup of tea with Sarah, and saw one of the maids with a stack of sheets and towels going up the stairs. She said it had started, Mrs. Ferguson's water had broken an hour before, and the doctor had just come. But nothing else had happened yet.

"That's exciting," Angélique said to her, wondering if it would be a girl or a boy. "Tell her I'm thinking of her, and I hope everything goes well."

"I hope they don't ask me to stay," the maid said nervously. "I've never seen a baby born, and my mother wouldn't want me to, until I have my own." She was only sixteen.

"Did the doctor bring a nurse with him?"

"Two," she said, lingering on the stairs to talk to Angélique.

"Then they won't need you," she reassured her, and then the girl left to deliver the linens the nurse had asked for, and Angélique hurried down the stairs to meet Sarah in the servants' hall. Everyone was busy there. They were preparing a tea tray for the doctor, and something for the nurses to eat before they got too busy. They had said it would be a while before things got started, but they were getting ready. And the wet nurse had been called for. Mrs. Ferguson had said not to send for her husband, until the baby had been born. There was no point to his waiting around at home. It would just be tiresome for him, and she didn't want him with her. The doctor wouldn't let him anyway. It was too much for a man to see, and Harry hadn't been around for the others either.

"How is she?" Sarah asked her as they poured their tea and sat at the table. "Did you see her?"

"Not since this afternoon. I just saw one of the girls taking sheets and towels the nurses asked for. I can't wait to hear what it is. Poor thing, she looked miserable today. She'll be happy when it's over."

"Stella was with her last time, and said she just rolled the baby out like a bowling ball in a few minutes, without a squeak. She must have an easy time of it or she wouldn't have so many. But it looks like a hard thing to do. I'd be scared if it was me."

Several of the women at the table contributed birthing stories then, their own or others', and Angélique thought all of them sounded heroic. She was in no hurry to have children either. She had never even thought of it till now. She'd never been this close to a pregnant woman before, and it didn't look so simple to her.

Stella came downstairs a little while later, to get some tea for their mistress.

"The pains are starting and she's very thirsty." And the cook added a plate of freshly baked biscuits for her.

"That'll give her a bit of strength with the tea," she said pleasantly. "How is she?"

"Doing well. The doctor doesn't think it'll be born before morning, but one of the nurses told me she disagrees with him. She thinks it'll start to move quickly now since she's had so many. The last one didn't take long. We barely had time to get the sheets under her, and little Charlie was staring at us. She was very brave, but she's bigger this time. A lot bigger. It may not be so easy." The nurse had mentioned that to Stella too. "I'd better get back now, with her drink." Stella left the kitchen then, and hurried upstairs while the others went on talking, and after a second cup of tea, Angélique went upstairs to the nursery, and reported to Helen. It was exhilarating knowing that the baby was coming, and would be born by morning, or sooner.

"I think it's a boy again, she's so big," Helen commented, and Angélique agreed. "She was much smaller with Emma."

"Well, we'll know soon. I hope someone comes up here to tell us."

"I'm sure they will." And then Helen did some mending, and Angélique picked up a book. There were a number of women in the house who liked to read and they shared their books with her.

And in her bedroom, Eugenia was complaining that her back was hurting her. The pains had gotten stronger, and they were worse than she remembered with the other births. Or maybe she forgot from year to year. They had all been so easy, but Simon had come two weeks early, Emma had been smaller, and Rupert had come so fast she'd almost had him in the library, and Charles had been easy too. This one felt enormous and like it was wedged in so tight it seemed like it was breaking her back with every pain. The nurses had helped her alter her position to make her comfortable, which didn't change anything, and when the doctor examined her, she screamed during a pain. He looked concerned. The baby didn't seem to be moving down at all, although the pains had gotten strong very quickly. She'd only been in labor for two hours. And last time by then, Stella remembered, Charles had been born. This time the baby was going nowhere, and it was becoming obvious that the night would be long.

The doctor suggested she try to walk around the room with the assistance of the nurses, to get things moving, but she was in so much pain she couldn't get out of bed, and lay down again, screaming.

"It's tearing me apart," she said, sobbing piteously. "It's never been like this before."

"Each time is different," the doctor reassured her. "The baby is very large this time." The doctor listened to the heartbeat and seemed satisfied. He smiled at Eugenia then. "The baby's heart is strong."

"I don't care," she said, in agony, "just get it out."

"It's coming," he said calmly, as she was hit by a wave of contractions again, one after the other, and each one stronger, until she was gasping for breath and was deathly pale. Stella looked worried, and the nurses were watching closely as the doctor examined her again, and seemed pleased. "Things are moving along."

"I think I'm dying," she said with a look of panic. "What if this baby kills me?" she said, sounding frantic. She wanted to run away, and there was nowhere to hide from the pain. It was squeezing the life out of her, and she saw stars in front of her eyes now each time she was seized by another pain in its viselike grip.

"It won't kill you, Eugenia," the doctor said in a soothing tone. "We just have to work a little harder this time, both of us together." He was very intent as he examined her repeatedly, and she seemed dazed between the pains. No one in the room was speaking, and two hours went by with her intermittent screams and agonizingly slow progress, but the doctor assured them all that the baby was coming down. Stella was almost as pale as her employer while she watched. Even the nurses looked strained, and the doctor was concentrating on what he was doing. By midnight, Eugenia was sheet white, and after six hours of labor, he could see the baby's head. He told her the baby had dark hair, and told her to push.

Nothing happened then for another hour, except more pitiful screams, and little progress, while Eugenia worked desperately trying to push, and began throwing up while she did. One of the nurses held a bowl under her chin, while Stella and the other nurse held her legs, and the doctor watched as the baby came toward him with every push, and then retreated when she stopped. It was coming down excruciatingly slowly, and obviously having a hard time getting through, it was so large, but all they could do was wait and urge her to keep working. She gave up several times, crying that she couldn't, and with all of them encouraging her, she tried again. The doctor didn't like it taking this long, for the sake of mother and child, but there was nothing he could do to speed it along, except trust to nature to do its job along with her. And then finally, with the worst screams of all, the baby crowned, and the top of its head was nearly there, and Eugenia looked like she was going to faint and was still screaming about her back and saying it was breaking. The baby seemed to be causing its mother serious damage.

"We're almost there, Eugenia," the doctor urged her. "I need you to push harder now." He wanted the baby to be born as fast as possible, it had gone on for too long, and she was fading fast.

"I can't . . . I can't . . . just let me die . . ."

"Another push! Now!" The doctor was shouting at her as Eugenia cried, but roused herself for one last push, and this time the baby's head emerged and it gave a cry, but its mother was too weak to care, as she lay back against the pillows, crying, and threw up again, while the doctor told her to keep pushing, as he delivered the shoulders and gently turned it to deliver the rest. The baby was out, as Eugenia lay sobbing, and screamed again.

"My back . . . my back . . . ," she said again, as the doctor cut the cord, swaddled the baby, and handed it to the nurse. It was a big handsome boy who was crying loudly, as his mother continued to sob, and the doctor looked at her with concern. It had been a difficult birth, which was unusual for a fifth child.

"Eugenia, the baby is fine," he said gently. "He's a beautiful boy." But she screamed again, and lay back against her pillows, hysterical with the pain. Nothing like this had ever happened to her before. The doctor felt her still swollen belly, and examined her carefully, and then glanced at one of the nurses with surprise, and said in an undervoice, "This isn't over yet." He had been waiting to deliver the placenta, but what he could feel in the birth canal was another head, and the contractions were still strong. He tried to explain to Eugenia what was happening, and that he needed her help. "There's another baby—you're having twins." Both nurses looked at him in surprise, and Stella was visibly shocked. "We have to get the other baby out." He sounded as though it was urgent.

"No, I can't," Eugenia cried miserably, and started vomiting again. The contractions seemed worse with the second one, and Eugenia never stopped screaming again until it was out, but it was smaller than the first one, came down more quickly, and slid into the doctor's hands. It was a girl. Everyone in the room shouted victoriously when they saw her, except her mother, who was nearly unconscious from the pain and what she'd been through. She had stopped vomiting, but her eyes were closed and she was trembling all over. She was bleeding heavily, and her face was gray, as the doctor showed evident concern. He had never heard a second heartbeat and realized they must have been one behind the other, but it explained why she'd been so huge, and the delivery was so hard. She had done double the work that night, and the first baby, the boy, weighed nine pounds. The girl was smaller and weighed six.

The doctor watched her carefully after the nurses cleaned her up, and pressed down on her uterus to slow the bleeding, and both placentas appeared in due course. But Eugenia looked as though she'd been left for dead, as they sat at her bedside all night, and with the help of some drops the doctor gave her, she finally stopped crying and fell asleep. She wasn't peacefully asleep until nearly dawn. It had been a very long night. It allowed him to make some repairs where she'd been torn when the first twin was born. He had not expected the delivery to be this hard, and it had taken them all by surprise, particularly Eugenia.

The doctor was still there, and the nurses, as well as her maid, when she woke at nine. She said her back still hurt terribly, and she felt as though she'd been beaten all over, but the bleeding had slowed, her heart was normal, and she had no fever. Nothing had gone wrong, it had just been a difficult birth. She didn't even have the strength to sit up in bed, there were deep black circles under her eyes, which were bloodshot from popped veins, and her lips were gray. She had lost a lot of blood.

"Would you like to see your babies?" one of the nurses asked her when she woke up, still groggy from the drops. "They're beautiful."

"Not now," she said weakly, and closed her eyes again. She wasn't crying, but she was still shaking. She had never been through anything so terrible in her life, and promised herself as she lay there that she'd never do it again. She couldn't. She had thought she was dying all night, and at some points wished she would. The doctor had seen deliveries like it before, and they always took a toll on the mother. It would take her time to recover, but she was young and strong, and he was sure she would. She was in no danger now, although she could have been the night before, and they could have lost either or both twins from it taking so long. It was stressful for the babies too. His only concern now was infection, but there was no sign of it.

He left the drops with the nurses and told them when to administer them, and left Eugenia at ten. He had been there for sixteen hours, and looked tired too. Stella left the room with him, as Eugenia drifted off to sleep again. She hadn't seen the twins yet, but wasn't feeling up to it. And the wet nurse had been called to tend to them.

"You can send for Mr. Ferguson now. In fact, I think you should," the doctor told Stella, who looked as tired as he did.

"Is she in danger, Doctor?"

"No, she's not. We always worry about infection, especially after a difficult birth, but there's no reason why she should have a problem. She just needs to rest and get over the trauma of the birth. This wasn't easy for her." That had been obvious to everyone in the room. "I'll come back and see her this afternoon." And he knew the nurses would be checking her for signs of a fever. But failing that, he expected her to recover like the young, healthy woman she was. "It's often this way with twins," he reassured Stella, who was shaken by what she'd seen too. She felt desperately sorry for her mistress, but glad that she'd been there to do what she could to help. But nothing had brought Eugenia relief during the birth.

"Will her back be all right after this?" Stella asked, with concern, and he smiled.

"It's fine, there was no damage to it. The babies must have just been pressing on her spine as they came down. It's all very normal. I was never worried about her back, just the twins. And of course we don't want to lose the mother. I'm sure she's going to be fine. I want her in bed for the next two or three weeks. Longer, if she seems weak. And no visitors for a month." Stella nodded as she walked him downstairs, and let him out. A footman was standing nearby and opened the door. Stella had let one of the maids know about the twins after they were born, and the staff was jubilant, far more than their mother was upstairs. She didn't even want to see them after the excruciating pain they'd caused her.

Stella went to the servants' hall for a cup of tea then, knowing that Eugenia would sleep for several hours and that the nurses were with her. One of them was going to sleep on a cot they'd put in the dressing room, and the other was going to rest when she woke up. They would be taking turns tending to her for the next several days.

"How was it?" Mrs. Allbright asked her as soon as she came in.

"Terrible," Stella said honestly, and sat down in a chair, looking beaten. "The poor thing seemed like she was going to die."

"Let's hope she doesn't," one of the maids said somberly. "My cousin did, and my brother's wife." It was common.

"Mrs. Ferguson is not going to die," Mrs. Allbright said clearly, and Stella nodded. "She just gave birth to twins. It's normal for her to have had a hard time. We need to take good care of her now." They all chattered animatedly at the table, as Mrs. Allbright spoke to Stella quietly. "How is she? It must have been very difficult for her, to have two, not just one. She's always come through it easily before."

"She didn't this time," Stella said seriously. "I've never seen anything worse. She looks awful now."

"She'll perk up soon. She's young," Mrs. Allbright said confidently. "We sent for Mr. Ferguson. I'm sure he'll be here shortly." Stella nodded and went to her room to get some rest herself.

Harry Ferguson arrived after dinner, and was thrilled. The first thing he wanted to do was see his babies as he bounded up the stairs like an excited boy. The baby nurse and wet nurse and both babies had been put in a large guest bedroom near theirs. He strode into the room, and each of the women was holding one, and both babies were sound asleep. He peeked at them, beaming, gently touched their tiny fingers, and noticed instantly that the little girl had red hair and perfect features. Other than that, she resembled her older sister, and the boy had dark hair and was huge. He was the size of a three-month-old. They were beautiful children, and he was extremely pleased, with Eugenia, and himself. He had two daughters now, and four sons. They were a perfect family, and as he left the temporary nursery, all he wanted to do was see his wife. She was asleep and woke up groggily when she heard him enter the room and speak to the nurse. He approached her bed then with a broad smile, and was shocked at how she looked. They had cleaned her up, but her hair was tangled, her eyes were sunk into her face, and she was still deathly pale.

". . .'lo Harry . . . ," she said sleepily, ". . . it was awful . . . never do it again . . . never . . . no more babies . . ." It was all she could think of now. Just seeing her, he could tell how hard it had been. He felt momentarily guilty, but ecstatic over the twins at the same time.

"They're beautiful . . . I'm sorry . . . they're just wonderful, though. You did a terrific job." She nodded at him with glazed eyes.

"No more . . ."

"All right," he said gently, as the nurse left them alone. If she really meant it, he could live with it. Six children was enough. He had always wanted six children, and having twins made it perfect for him. "I love you very much," he added as she drifted off to sleep again. And after he left her, he went back to the nursery to take another peek at them. The little girl was just waking up, and seemed to stare at him with puzzled eyes, and then yawned. Her brother was sound asleep, and Harry left them a moment later, and went to pour himself a drink. He stood in the library, gazing out the window, over his land, thinking of their babies, grateful to Eugenia for having them, and all was well in his world.

Chapter 7

There was jubilation in the nursery the day the twins were born. Angélique and Helen were thrilled to hear the news when Sarah came to tell them, and when they told the children, they were very excited that they had a brother and a sister and wanted to see them. But Angélique explained that they had to give them a few days to rest.

"Why? Did they get tired getting here? Did they come from a long way?" Emma asked. They were all young enough not to have made the connection between a baby coming and their mother's growing girth. And it had not been explained to them, so they were surprised to hear that the babies were tired now.

Emma wanted to see her mother, but Angélique said she was exhausted and probably asleep. And Emma looked disappointed.

"Did they come from far away? Did Mommy go to fetch them?" It all seemed very confusing to them. And their father came to see them that afternoon while they were having tea. He said that their new brother and sister were being named George and Rose, and they could see them very soon. He said they were very small and were going to sleep for a few days. And their mother was fine, and had things to do. He didn't want to worry them, and there was no reason for them to know or see how battered she was by the birth. By the time they saw her again, he wanted her to be well and feeling better. There was no sense in frightening them, and had they seen her then, they would have been. He was worried about her too.

She looked better the next day, and sat up in bed to drink some tea. She hadn't eaten in two days. She was following the doctor's orders closely, and well tended by the nurses, and the doctor had told her that if she wanted to recover quickly, she had to rest. She had no trouble following his orders and said she felt so weak that she was sure that if she tried to get out of bed, she'd fall down. But she got stronger every day, and had better color. And when the babies were a week old, Angélique was allowed to bring all four children down from the nursery to see them. Both twins were wide awake, wearing little wool dresses and warm caps and matching booties, and were tightly wrapped in blankets as the wet nurse and baby nurse held them and warned the children not to touch them. Their four older siblings stared at them in awe, and Angélique was touched by how beautiful they were. They looked absolutely perfect.

"Can I hold one?" Emma asked with interest, as she hovered over Rose, and the nurse said she'd have to wait until the baby was stronger, and soon she'd be in the nursery with them. The baby stared at her big sister, listening to the sound of her voice.

"Why are there two of them?" Simon asked. "Why didn't we just get one, like we were supposed to?" It seemed mysterious to him and made no sense. Last time there was only one baby when Charles was born, and Rupert before that.

"They gave us an extra one," Angélique explained.

"Did no one want the other one, so they gave him to us?" he asked, frowning.

"Your mother and father wanted both of them," Angélique said, smiling, although it clearly seemed like unnecessary excess to him. "Now there are six of you." Simon nodded. That made sense.

They lingered in the temporary nursery for half an hour, and then they went outside to play, and they seemed pleased. Emma commented that Rose was very pretty.

"She looks just like you," Angélique told her, "except for her red hair."

"Will she get ringlets too?"

"We'll have to wait and see."

After that, they went to visit the babies every day. Simon got bored with it after a few days, they were always asleep, and Rupert and Charles were still too young to be interested. But Emma asked to see the twins every day, and Angélique took her to visit them. Emma was particularly enchanted with her new sister, and enthralled by the fact that there were two babies, although Simon still said it was silly. It seemed like a mistake to him. Like a delivery error from a shop, that had sent two babies instead of one. But Emma liked them, and talked about the babies constantly.

They were allowed to visit their mother for a few minutes, three weeks after the birth. She was lying on a daybed in her dressing room, and she still looked tired and pale, but they were happy to see her and said they liked their new brother and sister very much.

"Are you feeling better now after your trip?" Emma asked her politely, and Eugenia looked blank. "They said you were very tired after you went to fetch them. It must have been far away."

"Yes, it was," Eugenia said, smiling at her. "Very far away. But I'm better now." She and Angélique exchanged a smile and a look, and then their mother said they should go out to play. The weather had been glorious since the twins were born. Their visit with her lasted only five minutes, and for Eugenia, it was enough. She didn't want to exhaust herself with them, and was trying to regain her strength.

The twins were a month old when she came downstairs for the first time. She had dinner with her husband in the dining room, sat on the terrace for a little while to get some air afterward, and then went back to bed. He was leaving for London the next day, and she was planning to join him in a few weeks, and hoped she would be stronger then. The social Season was starting in a few weeks, and she didn't want to miss it. Gwyneth's ball was at the end of June, and she had promised Elizabeth she'd be there, and hoped to have gotten her figure back by then. She had begun having Stella lace her into her corsets, and felt more like herself once she did.

They had acquired a second pram, and both nurses took the twins out every day, to get fresh air. They slept peacefully while the two women wheeled them through the park, and the older children peeked at them whenever they could, as did the rest of the staff, who couldn't wait to see them.

Later in June, Eugenia's friends began coming to visit, excited to see the twins too. Eugenia had finally begun holding them. She had been so distraught after the birth that she hadn't seen them for the first two weeks, and didn't want them brought to her, but Harry had been so ecstatic about them that she eventually asked for them, and held each of them for a few minutes, and sent them away when they started to cry, saying that they needed to be fed. Newborn babies always made her uncomfortable, they were so small and delicate, she said she was afraid she'd break them, like porcelain dolls. But she was content to look in on the nursery and peek at them once in a while. Mostly, she was concerned with her figure. And as always, after a delivery, she was careful about what she ate. And the weight she had gained had already begun to slip away. She had no intention of losing her figure because of them. And by the end of June, when they were seven weeks old, she looked beautiful when she left for London. Her shape was still a little fuller, but she was voluptuous and lovely. And of course she left the twins in Hampshire, with the other children. She said that London was no place for newborns, with all the activity and noise. The staff at the house on Curzon Street were disappointed not to see them, but Harry had told them they weren't coming.

The moment Eugenia arrived in London, she felt like she'd been released from prison, after the last boring months at their country home, and her long recovery from the delivery. But just as the doctor had predicted, she was young and got her strength back quickly, and told all her friends that having them had been the worst experience of her life, and she wouldn't think of doing it again. Harry believed her, which made the twins seem even more special to him.

Once Eugenia left Hampshire, Angélique began spending more time with the babies. She wanted to get to know them, and get used to them, before they moved to the nursery in August, when they were weaned and the baby nurse went back to London. They had kept her longer than planned since they were twins. And Helen had been told that she would have to help Angélique care for them, since there would be six children in the nursery for a month, and five when Simon left for Eton. And Eugenia still insisted they didn't need a second nanny, which Sarah said was crazy. How was Angélique going to manage five children, and two of them brand-new babies?

"You'll have to be an octopus to manage that one," Sarah said wryly.

"The baby nurse said they're easy babies," Angélique said confidently. It was going to be a new experience for her, caring for such young infants. Mrs. Ferguson had assured her she could do it, and that she had total faith in her to do it well. Angélique loved holding them, and like Emma, although she didn't admit it, she had a marked preference for Rose. She even looked like a rosebud, while George looked like a sturdy little man. One of the Scottish housemaids called him a "bonny bairn."

Eugenia and Harry didn't return to Hampshire until they had gone to every ball they had been invited to, including Gwyneth's, and came home at the end of July, when the Season ended. And three days after they got back, they went to Bath for the month on holiday without the children and to enjoy the restorative waters, which Eugenia said she needed after all she'd been through.

When they returned at the end of August, they were busy every night right until the end of the first week of September, the night before Simon was leaving for Eton. He had cried about it for several days with Angélique, but he knew that he could not complain to his parents. Angélique had told him he had to be brave, and he promised he would be. She never let him know how sad she was for him to be leaving home so young, and she knew she would miss him.

The morning he left was a beautiful day, and Angélique got him up early. She had been packing for him for days, and included his favorite books, a blanket he loved, his pillow, and a beloved bear that he had slept with since he was born. He was far too young to give that up, especially if he was going to leave his parents. He had to have some small form of comfort. She just hoped the other boys didn't make fun of him or take it from him. But there had to be other boys with whom he would form lifelong friendships. And all the boys in the entering class were the same age he was, at five. Angélique thought to herself that it was really a class of babies. She hated the idea of sending him away at five, and thought his parents were doing it just because everyone else did and the school was legendary, famous, and their son going there was a sign of their social status.

Angélique had taken Simon to say goodbye to his parents the afternoon before he left. His father had shaken his hand and his mother had hugged him, and they had warned him to be good and study hard. He looked like a baby to Angélique as he stood before them. And then she took him back upstairs to the nursery, and had given him extra hugs that night herself.

The next morning when it was time to leave, she took him downstairs. His bags had been collected by the footmen the night before and had already been put in the carriage. His father was sending him with their best carriage and coachman for the trip to Windsor, which would take them five hours. And the cook had prepared a picnic basket to take with him for the journey. He had everything he needed, and before they handed him into the carriage, Angélique hugged him tight. Neither of his parents came to see him off. And as the coach pulled away, Angélique stood waving at him for as long as she could see him, and Simon sat silently in the coach with tears rolling relentlessly down his cheeks as though his heart would break.

Once Simon left, she went back to the nursery where Helen was tending to the others. They had two baskets for the twins, whom Angélique had been taking care of since August. It gave her little time for anything else, but she was managing nicely, and Helen was being extremely helpful. They ran their feet off all day, and except when they were sleeping, one of them was always holding one of the twins. The babies had adjusted well to nursery life, and Emma was thrilled to have them close at hand. She was four years old now, and loved her baby sister. She was never jealous of her and wanted to play with her like a doll. And Angélique constantly reminded her to be gentle with her. The two younger boys were still too young and too rough to hold a baby, but Angélique let Emma sit on the floor and hold one of them, wrapped in a blanket. That way, the baby was protected and wouldn't have far to fall, if Emma lost her grip when the baby squirmed, or got too heavy for her.

The nursery felt strange to her without Simon. He had been such a strong presence ever since her arrival, and had all the earmarks of an oldest son. He took care of his sister, was protective of the others, and in some ways was like a little man. He talked to Angélique as though they understood each other. And she found it very odd without him now, and very sad. She hoped he'd be happy at school, but she didn't see how he could be, being sent away so young. Angélique felt Simon's absence sharply for two months, and in November it was shocking to her to realize that she had been with the Fergusons for a year. In some ways, it seemed like only minutes, at other times it felt like a lifetime, and she had begun to wonder what she was going to do with the rest of her life. She was happy in the job and doing well, and even liked being a nanny. She had grown very attached to the children, and most recently the twins. She had no desire to live or work anywhere else, except Belgrave, but she knew that would never be possible. She wondered at times if she should be doing something more important with her life, or when she should use her father's money to buy a house. But it still felt much too soon for that, and she was safer under the Fergusons' protection. And it seemed like the right job. Who would hire her with no experience, except now as a nanny?

She liked working for the Fergusons, and they gave her a fair amount of leeway with the children. Eugenia didn't come upstairs to observe them or have tea with them. Whenever she wanted to see them, she had them brought downstairs to her but rarely for more than a few minutes and never more than once a week. Her absence left Angélique totally in charge and free to make decisions. If she was going to be a nanny, this was the best job she could think of, but she knew she didn't want to be a nanny all her life. It was a strange existence bringing up other people's children, and living in someone else's house, and she knew that as long as she did, she would never have a life of her own.

Most of the people she worked with had been brought up to a life of service. She never had been. She thought about it from time to time, and wondered what it would be like to run her own home the way she wanted, and make decisions about her life. The Fergusons offered her protection, but she gave up a great deal to be there as well. The years would so easily slip by, and one day she would be old, like many of the other servants. When her brother had banished her, he had not only stolen her home from her, but he had condemned her to a life that she hadn't been prepared for, and had never dreamed of, and she couldn't help wondering at times if this was now her destiny and she had no other choice.

She spent her second Christmas with the Fergusons, and it was all familiar to her now. And with Helen's help, she was managing five children, and she knew she loved them, more than their parents did at times. And she also knew them better. But they would always be someone else's children, and it would always be someone else's home. She wondered if the other servants ever thought about it, and questioned what they were doing, but she didn't dare to ask. She and Sarah talked about it at times, since she knew Sarah wanted to marry one day and have children, and was still secretly walking out with one of the grooms.

At nineteen, Angélique had no idea if this was meant to be her life forever, or if somewhere, someday, she would follow another path. She had no time to think about it, except sometimes at night when she lay in bed, and then one of the children would call out to her, or have a nightmare, and she would get up to comfort them, and when she did, or held the twins in her arms, she realized that this was the life she was meant to live for now. What she didn't know was if it was forever, or only for a time. And for now, maybe she didn't need to know.

Simon came home from boarding school for Christmas, and Angélique saw instantly that he had grown taller, and was very thin. She was worried they weren't feeding him enough, and his eyes were sad. He looked like an abandoned child. She poured all her love and energy into him while he was home. And one of the maids had taught her to knit a sweater for him, which she gave him for Christmas. She asked him where his bear was, and he told her that when he got to Eton, they had made him leave it in his trunk, and told him he was too old to have it, and a big boy now.

He looked thrilled to be home, and clung to her the entire time he was there. And he sobbed miserably in her arms the night before he had to go back. He begged her to let him stay home with her.

"I can't do that, Simon," she said, with a lump in her throat. "Your parents want you to be there. They won't listen to me."

"Tell them I'll be good for the rest of my life."

"They want you to get a fine education, and meet new friends."

"I don't want new friends. I have you. Will you stay here forever?" He was asking her the same questions she had asked herself, and she didn't have the answers for him either. And she couldn't lie to him—it wouldn't be fair.

"I don't know. That depends if your parents want me. And one day you'll all grow up." Sooner than he thought. His brothers would all go to school at the same age he had, and they might send the girls away to school as well, though not at five.

"Why can't we just stay here?" he asked her unhappily.

"Because boys like you go to schools like Eton, and it's a good thing to do." But she wasn't sure she was telling him the truth. She would have loved to keep him at home, and school him herself, or have tutors like she had. But his parents led a different life, and she was a girl. Her own brothers had gone to boarding school too, though not as young. Edward had hated it and done poorly. Tristan had loved going away to school.

Simon looked miserable when she put him in the carriage the next day, and his parents had said goodbye to him the night before.

She watched his small unhappy face in the window as the carriage pulled away, and felt as though she had failed him again.

She went back to the nursery with a heavy heart, and made breakfast for the children when they got up. She noticed that Emma seemed feverish and had a cough, and decided to keep her in that day. She had wanted to go skating on the pond, but she couldn't go if she was sick. Angélique promised to take them another day. Helen said she'd watch Emma, when she took the boys out for some air. And before she left, Angélique tucked her back into bed. She seemed happy to be there with her favorite doll next to her, and before Angélique left the nursery with Rupert and Charles, Emma was sound asleep.

"Send someone for me if she gets worse," Angélique told Helen as she left. Helen was holding both twins—it was too cold for them to go out too, but the two older boys needed a run. And as Angélique hurried down the back stairs after them, she hoped that Emma would be better when she woke up. Her mind was focused on Emma, as she tried not to think of Simon on his lonely ride back to school. It was more than Eugenia was thinking of. She was planning her menus, for friends arriving from London that night. Eugenia wasn't thinking of her son at all.

Chapter 8

When Angélique came back from the park with the boys, her face was tingling, and her hands were ice cold, but they'd had fun. The two little boys were tireless, but fortunately she had as much energy as they did. They had come in through the kitchen, and the cook had whispered to her, "I don't know how you do it, with six of them now." She had offered the two little boys a plate of biscuits as Angélique smiled.

"Helen helps," Angélique answered, as she took one of the delicious gingerbread biscuits, which had just come out of the oven. Mrs. Williams at Belgrave had made them for her too as a child, and it brought back memories of her childhood home as she ate it.

They went back upstairs then, and Angélique looked in on Emma, whom Helen said hadn't woken up since she left. But she felt even warmer to the touch than she had earlier, and Angélique was worried. She watched her for a few minutes, and went back to check on the boys playing in the nursery parlor, and picked up Rose to change her. She could feel that she was wet, and Helen was holding George, asleep in her arms after she'd given him his bottle. She said that Rose would be due for one soon. She was a happy, easy baby, and easier than her twin, who had recently become prone to colic, and woke more frequently at night. Angélique had been getting up with him three times a night, whereas his sister slept straight through without a peep, and a broad smile and giggle when she woke up. Angélique loved playing with her, but she was worried about Emma when she went to get the baby's bottle.

After she fed the baby, Angélique went to check on the little girl again. Emma had begun to stir in her bed, and started to cry the minute she opened her eyes and saw her nanny looking down at her.

"I hurt," she said in a hoarse whisper, and then gave a terrifying barking cough that nearly choked her. Angélique had her sit up and gave her a sip of water, and gently touched her forehead. She was blazing. She was crying, and the more she cried the more she coughed. It was a full five minutes before she could catch her breath and lie back down. Angélique told her she'd be back in a minute, went to the parlor, and told Helen to listen for her.

"Where are you going?"

"I want to send for the doctor," she whispered. She didn't like the sound of her cough, the look in her eyes, or the fever. She was no nurse, but it was easy to tell that the child was very sick, and it had come on very quickly since the night before, when she'd seemed fine when she went to bed.

Angélique hurried down the stairs to the second floor, and saw Stella leaving Eugenia's bedroom.

"I wouldn't go in now," Stella told her quickly, as she saw Angélique ready to move past her. "She's not in the best of spirits." She lowered her voice further. "She doesn't like the way I did her hair." She rolled her eyes as she said it.

"I have to," Angélique said with a worried look. "We need the doctor."

Stella nodded. "Do it at your own risk. She threw her slipper at me as I left." Eugenia was given to tantrums, although more frequently at her maid, when she didn't like the way a dress fit, thought her mending was clumsy, had pressed something wrong, or hadn't laced her corset tight enough. She was as beautiful as ever but she had thickened slightly in the waist since the twins and didn't want anyone to know. Stella had tried to tell her as diplomatically as possible that she could pull the corset strings only so far before they broke.

Angélique slipped quietly toward her employer's dressing room and knocked before she went in.

"Yes? Have you come back to do it right?" she said in a querulous voice, thinking it was her maid, and talking about her hair.

"I'm sorry, Mrs. Ferguson," Angélique said as she stepped through the door and saw her with an elaborate hairdo that looked fine to her. Eugenia looked surprised to see who it was.

"What are you doing down here?" She didn't look pleased to see her, and Angélique didn't care.

"It's Emma. She's not well. She has a fever and a nasty cough."

"Well, give her some tea with honey, and some of that syrup the doctor left for us when Rupert was sick. It's probably the same thing."

"He didn't have a fever, ma'am," she said politely. "I think she should see the doctor."

"Don't be silly. For a cold? They're always sick anyway. Just don't let her near the twins—they're too young to get sick." In fact, they were eight months old, and Angélique didn't want them to get sick either. But she wanted to convey to their mother, without alarming her unduly, that Emma seemed very ill to her.

"I think it's more than a cold, ma'am," Angélique said firmly.

"You're not a doctor. Where's Stella? I told her to come back and do my hair again. Where is she?"

"I'm sure she'll be back in a minute," Angélique said quietly. "I'd really like to send for Dr. Smith."

"We shouldn't trouble him with the children, unless we need to, or we'd be calling for him every time they sneeze."

"She has a high fever, ma'am, and she's barking like a seal."

"What an unattractive thing to say." She turned to glare at Angélique. "We'll see how she is in a few days. If she's worse tomorrow, tell me. The poor man can't run all over the county for every child with a cold. I'm sure she'll be fine tomorrow. You know how children are." And after fourteen months caring for them night and day, she did. Emma was never sick. She appeared delicate but was hardier than the boys, which made her feeling so ill seem even worse. This was a rarity for her, and by now Angélique had a good instinct for their ills. "Now go back upstairs and take care of her. How are the twins?" She hadn't seen them in weeks.

"They're very well, ma'am," Angélique said, distraught. Emma's mother clearly didn't understand how sick she was, and would never have considered coming to see for herself. She hated it when they were ill, and didn't want to catch whatever it was herself. "I'd really like to send for Dr. Smith," she tried one more time, and Eugenia looked like she might throw a shoe at her too.

"I told you not to bother him. Let's not discuss it again. Go and find Stella for me, and tell her to come back and do my hair. And don't annoy Dr. Smith for a child with a cold."

"Very well, ma'am," Angélique said through clenched teeth as Stella walked in on her own, still seeming tense. She knew what was in store for her—several more attempts to do her mistress's hair to her satisfaction, however many times it took.

"There you are," Eugenia said to Stella with an exasperated expression, dismissing the nanny, who withdrew quietly with a knot of panic in her stomach, as the lady's maid went to do her hair again. The two servants exchanged a pointed glance as Angélique left. She felt sorry for Stella, but she was much more worried about Emma, who had been denied the doctor's help. She wondered if the child's father would have been as cavalier, although she suspected he would be. And since he was in London, he had no idea Emma was ill. And when Angélique went back upstairs, the child was worse. The fever was higher, and she was whimpering in her bed.

Angélique sat down next to her, and told Helen to watch the others. Helen didn't like taking care of all four of them, but Angélique didn't want to leave Emma until she went back to sleep. She bathed her forehead in cool cloths and sang to her, after giving her a spoonful of the syrup her mother had suggested. It didn't help, but half an hour later, she went back to sleep. And Angélique emerged from her room and turned her attention to the boys. The twins were down for a nap before dinner. It was going to be a long day, juggling them all, with Emma sick.

"What did she say?" Helen asked her when they sat down together for a minute.

"She said not to send for him, it's just a cold."

"It looks like more than a cold to me," Helen said in a hushed tone. "She coughed the whole time you were gone."

Angélique wasn't surprised to hear it, and was distressed by Eugenia's denial of medical care for her child, although if she had been sick herself, she would have called for the doctor immediately. She seldom did for the children, and thought their maladies were either imaginary, transitory, or insignificant, and didn't require the services of a doctor, who should be kept in reserve for adults.

Helen brought the dinner trays in when they sent them up from downstairs. They had included more of the gingerbread biscuits, thick beef stew, and potatoes for each child. It was a hearty meal for a winter afternoon, and when the two boys woke up, they ate well. They were still eating when Angélique told Helen she was going downstairs to get some broth and toast, and tea with honey for Emma when she woke up. The twins were still asleep, and only drank milk and ate soft food, which had come up on the trays as well.

"I'll be back in a flash," Angélique promised, and hurried downstairs. She found the kitchen teeming with activity. Eugenia was having guests from a neighboring estate. They were having soup and fish followed by suckling pig, and an elaborate dessert. The cook was busy, as were all of her assistants and kitchen maids, so Angélique helped herself to what she needed.

"Didn't they like the stew?" the cook asked over her shoulder as she put the delicate sole on a platter.

"They devoured it. Emma's sick—I need a bit of broth for her. She's got a fever and is feeling very ill."

"Poor lamb. I'll send her up some of the pudding, and for the boys, after dinner." Angélique doubted that she'd eat it, as sick as she was, and she was panicked at not being able to call the doctor for her.

Emma ate soup and toast and some boiled potatoes they'd had on the stove, but threw up immediately after, and Angélique spent the rest of the day at her bedside, either watching her, or singing to her, holding her hand, or bathing her brow. And by nightfall she was in a deep sleep. Helen had managed the others all afternoon, and put them to bed, and then went to bed herself. She had far less energy with them than Angélique, and was less adept at keeping them busy. Since they had already been out once that day, Helen didn't want to take them to the park where she would have been afraid to lose them. They loved running away from her, which Angélique didn't allow. She had grown to be very capable with the children, much to her own surprise. They loved and respected her, and did what she said, most of the time.

She spent the night sitting in a chair at Emma's bedside, still in her clothes. She hadn't wanted to leave her long enough to change into her nightgown. Emma woke several times in the night. And in the morning she was no better, but at least she was no worse, and since that was the case, Angélique didn't dare approach her mother again. She was sure she would refuse to send for Dr. Smith.

They limped along for another day—it was raining, so the boys couldn't go out anyway. Angélique fed the babies, set up games for the boys, and sent Helen downstairs for more broth for Emma, and some rice, but by suppertime, she thought Emma was worse. The fever was higher, and Emma said her head and whole body hurt and she could hardly swallow it hurt so much, and she had a racking cough. Angélique was determined to tackle the child's mother again in the morning.

After a restless night, Emma seemed weaker, and as though she were fading away. At eight in the morning, Angélique went downstairs and knocked on her employer's door, which she knew was bold, but she didn't want to wait a moment longer. Emma had been too sick for too long. This was the third day, with no improvement.

She knocked softly at first, and then harder, and then finally Eugenia called out in her darkened room, while Angélique waited on the other side of the door.

"What is it?" She sounded sleepy and not pleased to be awakened.

"It's Angélique, ma'am. I really think we need the doctor for Emma."

"Is she worse?" she called out from her bed, through the door.

"No," Angélique said honestly, "but she's not better, and she's very, very sick." There was a long hesitation as Angélique waited for her to respond, and then finally she did.

"Wait till tomorrow. I'm sure she'll be fine." How could she know that? She hadn't even seen her. Angélique wanted to pound on the door and scream at her, but didn't dare.

"I really think we . . ." She was pleading her charge's case with tears in her eyes. What if the child died of influenza? Angélique loved her, perhaps more even than her own mother.

"That'll be all, Angélique!" Eugenia shouted, and with tears rolling down her cheeks, Angélique walked away. Her hands were tied. She couldn't send for the doctor without her mother's permission.

Angélique went back to the nursery and stayed with her again all that day, and by nightfall she was worse again. Emma was weak from the fever and couldn't get out of bed. The fever was higher, and she was delirious and not making sense. And by then, Angélique refused to wait a moment longer. She knew that Mr. Ferguson had arrived earlier that day from London. Maybe he would get his wife to listen to reason or be more concerned himself. She went downstairs when they were dining with guests. She stood outside the dining room with trembling knees, ready to ask a footman to go in and take them a message, when Gilhooley saw her, and asked what she was doing there. She explained the situation to him as he frowned.

"You can't go in," he said sternly to her.

"I know. Will you tell them? I want to send for the doctor now. It can't wait any longer."

The serious-looking butler nodded, and lowered his voice to answer Angélique. "I will send for him myself. If she gets angry, she can blame me. It sounds as though you believe the child is very ill, abnormally so."

"Yes, I do," she confirmed, grateful that he was willing to pay attention to her. No one else had for four days, least of all the child's mother, and Angélique was even more panicked after watching Emma waste away with the fever, and her cough getting worse every day.

"I will tell her after supper, and by then Dr. Smith will have seen her, and there will be nothing she can do except shout at me." He smiled at Angélique. "If she dares. I'll send one of the grooms for him immediately."

"Thank you, Mr. Gilhooley," she said in a whisper, with enormous gratitude. "I'll be waiting for him in the nursery."

"Good girl," he whispered back, and went downstairs to fulfill his mission, after sending the footmen in to serve.

Angélique hurried back upstairs, and hoped that the doctor would come soon. And much to her surprise, he was there half an hour later, and entered the nursery, carrying his bag. She had just come out of Emma's room when he walked in. She was so relieved to see him, thanked him for coming, and told him all of Emma's symptoms of the past few days.

"Why didn't you send for me earlier?" he asked unhappily. He didn't like what he'd just heard. He was concerned that it might be scarlet fever, or something even worse. He asked if she'd had seizures, but she hadn't. And he was worried for the other children if they came down with it too, especially the twins.

"Mrs. Ferguson thought it was just a cold," Angélique said softly. The doctor pursed his lips and didn't answer, thinking of the many times Eugenia had summoned him for herself for far less. And this was clearly more than a cold.

They walked into Emma's room together, and Angélique gently woke her up. She cried when she saw the doctor and said she hurt, and then gave her hideous racking cough and eventually threw up. She went through the full repertoire of symptoms in front of him, and finally when she settled down again, they left the room.

"It's not scarlet fever," he said, relieved, "but it's a very severe case of influenza, which can be fatal in children that age. You were wise to have them send for me. Mr. Gilhooley said to come at once. Fortunately I was free and not delivering a baby somewhere. We need to break the fever, and she needs strong medicine for that cough. And I'm going to give you some drops to make her sleep. I don't want her left alone, someone must sit with her at night. I want her closely watched, and if the fever rises, send for me at once." He looked concerned, and despite what he said of the risks of influenza to a child Emma's age, she was relieved. At least he was there to help, and tell her it wasn't something worse, and confirm that she'd been right to ask him to come. It would be worth facing Eugenia's wrath now when she found out what Angélique had done. She was sure that her employer would blame her and not the butler for calling the doctor, but she didn't care.

"I've been with her every night," Angélique told the doctor, "and most of the day. The nurserymaid has been helping me with the others."

"We don't need to quarantine her, but I don't want them in the same room." As he said it, Angélique prayed that Simon hadn't caught it from her before he left. It would be terrible if he were as sick as his sister, alone at school. But she had no way to know, since they couldn't contact him. And the school would never tell them unless he contracted a serious disease or died.

As they spoke in whispers, they could hear Emma's barking cough start again. He handed Angélique the syrup he wanted her to use, a bottle of the drops to make her sleep, and told her to keep Emma warm, but bathe her face in cool water, and he promised to return in the morning, and told her to send for him during the night if she thought it necessary. "Thank you, sir," she said gratefully, and he smiled. He was impressed by her diligence and by how obviously bright she was.

"They're lucky to have you," he said sincerely. "You'd make a good nurse one day if you decide not to remain in service. I'd be happy to have a nurse like you."

"Thank you," she said shyly. Nursing was a career she had never considered, and she wasn't sure she was suited to it, but she loved Emma, and had been desperately worried about her, which he could see.

"She'll be all right," he reassured her, "as long as she doesn't get any worse. The drops will help her sleep, so she can get her strength back. Children recover quickly." *Unless they die,* Angélique thought to herself. She wasn't sure if Emma's life had been in danger, but it had looked that way to her. "Things move like lightning when children are ill, either for the better or the worse. We'll get her going in the right direction now." He patted Angélique's shoulder with a fatherly gesture, and left a moment later, and went back down the stairs and out through the kitchen. He was told by Mrs. Allbright that the Fergusons were having a party, so he didn't ask to speak to them. And their very competent nanny had everything under control. She looked young, but she seemed resourceful and as though she knew what she was doing. The child was in good hands. He left, feeling hopeful that the little girl would improve soon.

Angélique gave Emma all her medicine after the doctor's visit, and bathed her face and hands, and a little while later she was asleep, and hardly coughed in the night. She had a more peaceful night than she'd had in days, and Angélique sat in the chair next to her and dozed, as she had since Emma got sick. Helen told Angélique in the morning that she didn't know how she was still on her feet. But there was no other choice.

The doctor returned at nine, right after the other children had had breakfast, and Emma was just waking up. Angélique looked tired and pale, but she was alert and busy, in a clean dress and apron when he arrived.

"How's our patient?" he asked, after greeting the children, and noticing that they all looked well, and had eaten a hearty breakfast.

"She had a much easier night, and I think the fever is a little lower. She's still hot, but she doesn't seem as dazed, and she didn't cry when she woke up, for the first time in days."

"Splendid." He went in to see Emma with Angélique, and to a new visitor to the nursery, she would have appeared frighteningly sick, but to both of them, she looked better than the night before, and Emma smiled, which was a major improvement. He saw Angélique hold her hand, and the child gaze lovingly up at her. "I think you're going to feel well again very soon, young lady," he said to Emma. "Now you have to take your medicine, and do everything Nanny tells you, and eat all the good things Cook sends up for you, and very soon you'll be right as rain and playing with your brothers and sister." It was obvious that her aches and pains had lessened since she hadn't complained, and she held her doll out to him as he talked to her.

"She's sick too. She needs medicine to make her better." Angélique and the doctor exchanged a smile across her bed. This was a definite improvement from the previous days.

"Really? Well, we'll have to have Nanny give her some medicine too. Has she been coughing?" Emma nodded with a grin. She liked the doctor and thought he was a nice man. "Then she'll need syrup," he said seriously to Angélique, "and drops. See to it that she takes them and doesn't spit them out," he said, pretending to be very stern as Emma giggled about her doll. "Good children always take their medicine and then they get well."

"Can I see Rose today?" she asked about her baby sister, which was a good sign too. All the evidence was pointing in the right direction, much to the adults' relief. But the doctor told her she still needed to rest until she was all better. She had missed playing with Rose. She loved her baby sister, and being with her whenever she could. She liked helping Angélique take care of her, and watching her feed her.

The doctor left the nursery a few minutes later, and promised to return the next day, unless she needed him before that, or for the others if they felt ill too. Angélique hoped they wouldn't and was so relieved that Emma was out of danger, she was smiling from ear to ear.

The doctor stopped on the second floor on the way down. He knew where Eugenia's room was, after being there many times, and delivering her babies, and he knocked on the door to her dressing room. Stella opened it immediately and panicked when she saw him, and her eyes grew wide in fear.

"Oh, no . . . is it . . . is something . . ."

"Not at all," he quieted her concern immediately. "She's doing better. But I wonder if I might have a word with Mrs. Ferguson for a moment."

"I'll tell her. Her hair's not done and she's just had breakfast, but I'll ask her immediately." Stella disappeared into the inner sanctum of the bedroom, and returned at once, and told the doctor he could go in. Eugenia was sitting up in bed, in her dressing gown, with her breakfast tray across her knees. She was surprised to see the doctor, and momentarily worried.

"Is someone ill?" Her eyes were blank. It never even occurred to her it could be Emma, since she had told Angélique not to bother the doctor with a cold.

The doctor understood the situation perfectly, and wanted to spare Angélique the grief of being scolded for calling for him, and Gilhooley hadn't had time to mention it to her the night before. "Of course I know you were concerned about Emma. But fortunately, no one else is ill, and I wanted to commend you on your caution, having the nanny send for me. Emma has had a very severe case of influenza, which can be so very dangerous, even fatal in children, but I believe she's on the mend. Wonderful nanny you have, she's a very bright girl, and so sensible with the children. What a wise thing you did, hiring her. She was quite right to send for me. The child took a turn for the worse last night during your party, and she was afraid to disturb you. Good level-headed girl," he said easily, as Eugenia stared at him, and realized she was getting credit for deeds she hadn't done. She hadn't even thought to ask about Emma for two days.

"Yes, we had a party here last night," she said vaguely. "I'm glad she called you if it was that serious." She sounded utterly amazed that the doctor had taken her condition so seriously.

"I won't have them come down for a week or so. You never know. Children always make one sick."

"She'll be fine in a few days or a week. I wouldn't worry." But Eugenia never went near her children when they were sick. And now that they knew Emma had influenza, she considered her a major threat. She had apparently been as sick as the nanny said. Eugenia had thought she was just a hysterical young girl, overly worried and making a fuss about a cold. "Well, your nanny is a gem, and you were so wise to let her call for me. Just let me know if any of the others get sick."

"Of course," she said, worrying about herself.

"I'll be back tomorrow, unless you need me before," he said with a smile.

"Thank you, Doctor," Eugenia said as he walked out of the room, and she stared into space for a moment. She would have berated Angélique for calling for him after all, except that apparently she'd been right to be worried, and he was praising them for sending for him, so she could hardly accuse Angélique for that. She didn't want to see anyone from the nursery for a while, if Emma had influenza. She told Stella about it when she came in.

"Apparently Emma became quite ill last night, and Nanny sent for the doctor. She has influenza. Whatever you do, don't go up to the third floor. I certainly don't want to, and you shouldn't either, if you're with me, and touching my hair."

"Yes, madame," Stella said politely. "Is Emma all right now?"

"Not yet, but he says she will be. I suppose it's a good thing Nanny sent for the doctor. He says that influenza can be very dangerous to children and even fatal. I always knew that, of course. I don't know how she got so sick. She took a turn for the worse during our party last night." Which wasn't true, she had been just as sick for four days, but her mother wouldn't listen and didn't care. And what she cared about now was not getting sick herself. "Tell Nanny that if she takes the others out, she's to go down the back stairs, and never come into the second-floor hall."

"Of course, ma'am," Stella said, curtsied, and left the room, and went to deliver the message to Angélique in the nursery. "How is she?" she asked about Emma, looking genuinely concerned.

"A little better. The poor thing was very sick."

"So I hear. Her mother is terrified to catch it now—she says you're not to come anywhere near the second-floor hall, and keep to the

back stairs. You won't be coming down to the drawing room anytime soon!" She laughed, and Angélique smiled. They both knew
their mistress well. Stella went back to Eugenia's dressing room
then, and assured Eugenia she hadn't touched anyone or anything.
And with that, she told Stella to pour a bath for her, and she could
do her hair afterward, she had friends coming to dinner. Stella went
to get the buckets of warm water from the pantry where they heated
them, and Eugenia sat down at her dressing table and looked at
herself in the mirror, wondering if she should try something different with her hair.

Chapter 9

The Fergusons spent most of February in London, and returned to their house in Hampshire in March. Eugenia had brought trunks of new gowns back from London, which were made of beautiful silks, and showed more of her bosom than the gowns she'd had before. Some of them were very daring. And Stella had learned some new styles for her hair. Eugenia was lovelier-looking than ever. She saw her children, for tea on Sunday, for the first time in almost two months, since she had avoided them for weeks after Emma had influenza, and didn't visit them before she left. She was surprised how much the twins had grown at ten months, and George had just started walking. Emma was deeply attached to Angélique by then, particularly after her illness, which had left her weak for longer than expected, but by March Emma was in good health again.

They were having a house party the week after they came home, and Gilhooley and Mrs. Allbright were busy planning it. The Fergusons had added some new acquaintances to their repertoire of houseguests, notably several handsome bachelors who had courted Eugenia openly, and flirted with her in London. And Harry didn't seem to mind. He had dalliances of his own, albeit discreetly. And flirting with others had always been somewhat their style, whether innocent or not. They were both good-looking people, and Harry kept her bejeweled and decked out in the latest fashions and denied her nothing. He had achieved the family he'd wanted from her, with six children. She'd been a good sport about it and a willing partner, until the twins, and he was grateful to her for that, and rewarded her handsomely for it.

Angélique had had two more letters from Mrs. White, with tales of what was going on at Belgrave, more remodeling, more decorating, new fabrics everywhere, constant parties and houseguests, and hordes of new staff. It sounded like Elizabeth was in competition with Eugenia, and had a far more important house in which to do it. It made Angélique homesick hearing about it, and long for the way things used to be. Her father had been gone for nearly a year and a half, and it was hard to believe she'd ever had a life other than as a servant on the Fergusons' staff. Her own days of grandeur, comfort, and ease were over. She was a working person now, unless she found a husband to support her, which seemed unlikely. The only men available to her were footmen, or grooms, or an underbutler, and she somehow couldn't imagine doing that. She was trapped in a no-man's-land as a servant, born into a higher social class than the rest of them, which would have made them uncomfortable about her if they'd known that she was in fact a duke's daughter. But her secret had been kept so far. She couldn't imagine marrying anyone, or having children of her own, in her new life, which made her charges even more precious to her, and made her more willing to stay in her job, although she thought Eugenia a terrible mother and didn't respect her. Her children hardly knew her. Even more than the rest of her peers, she spent as little time as possible with them.

Once the house party began, with twenty guests staying at Ferguson Manor, Angélique didn't expect her employers to see the children, and she devised entertainments for them that would keep them well away from their parents and guests. Visitors always delighted in the complicated maze and the beauties of the park, so she took them walking in the remoter areas, and down to the lake early in the morning to feed the ducks and swans. The weather was fine, so Rupert and Emma had their riding lesson on their ponies. She was pushing Rose back to the house in the pram, since she wasn't walking yet, and Helen had already gone back with Charles and George, when Angélique encountered a particularly handsome male guest out walking on his own. He looked surprised and pleased when he saw Angélique with Rose in her pram.

"My, my, what have we here," he said, laughing. "A sprite of the forest, and such a lovely one at that." He could easily see that she was a nanny, given her dress, the cape she wore over it, and her cap, with the baby with her. And she blushed at his comment. "Hello," he said, falling into step beside her. "Where have you been hiding?" He was very bold in his remarks, and Angélique continued on the path. Rupert and Emma were still at their riding lesson, and the guests weren't up yet. Or at least they weren't out walking—the men were probably in the dining room for breakfast. The women were served the first meal of the day on trays in their rooms, which they preferred.

"What's your name?" he asked, observing her closely. He was very tall, well built, and had dark hair and dark eyes. Angélique looked tiny beside him.

"Nanny Ferguson," she answered politely, hoping he'd go away before they reached the house. She didn't want him walking in with her and causing comment.

"Not that name, silly—your real one, your first name. Mary? Jane? Margaret?" He tried guessing, and wouldn't leave her alone, and they were still a long way from the house. She had strolled farther than she meant to with the pram.

"Angélique," she said quietly, not wanting to be rude to him, but not wanting to encourage him either. Some of their friends were fairly racy, and all were young, some not much older than she was, but they lived in a different world. And she had never been part of the group that surrounded Eugenia and Harry. They were more like her brothers' friends than anyone she had known in her father's home, who were all better behaved, older, and more dignified.

"What a pretty name," he commented when she told him, albeit reluctantly. "French, I assume. But you sound English." And something about her told him that she was not an ordinary servant. He knew from the way she walked, and her accent, that she was, or had been, of higher rank. She was more like one of the nannies from genteel families that had lost their money. "Why haven't I seen you at the house in London?" he questioned her, as she prayed he'd go away, but he showed no sign of it.

"They leave the children in Hampshire most of the time." The year before they'd spent a month there, but after Emma's illness, they hadn't taken them to London again.

"That must be boring for you," he said sympathetically.

"Not at all."

"Don't pretend to me that you like it here, my girl. You're much too pretty to waste your life in the country." She didn't answer, and hastened along, quickening her step, and he had no trouble following her with his long stride. "A girl like you should be in London."

"I'm very happy here, sir," she said politely, wishing him to perdition. She wasn't flattered by his attention, but unnerved by it. No guest had ever been this insistent with her before, or paid as much attention to her, in a way she didn't welcome or like. Even Eugenia's brother Maynard hadn't been as bold.

"I'm going to be coming down here a lot more this spring and summer, to visit"—he hesitated for a second—"your employers. You and I could be great friends, and have some fun." He was shameless in what he was suggesting. "Think about it," he said, as she kept her gaze on the pram, and didn't look at him, nor respond. "You're a shy one," he added. "You don't need to be shy with me. I won't tell anyone, you know. You can rely on me."

"Thank you, sir," she said as the house came mercifully into view, and she nearly ran toward it, trying to escape him. He laughed as she hurried away, and he watched her go in through the servants' entrance into the kitchen. He looked very pleased indeed. She had a waist he could have circled with both hands, a delicate bosom, exquisite white blond hair she wore in a tight knot he longed to loosen, and huge blue eyes. He guessed her to be somewhere between seventeen and twenty, and he had rarely seen a girl as pretty. She had none of the womanliness of Eugenia, nor the hardness, and he loved her modesty and shyness, which only made her more enticing. It gave him something to overcome and conquer. He went in the front door after that, whistling to himself. His visits to Hampshire were going to be much more fun now, and would keep him busy, with two women to amuse him, one upstairs and one down, which was often the way he liked it.

He strolled into the dining room and found Harry having breakfast with half a dozen men, reading the papers, and talking. Harry
looked up with a smile as soon as he saw him. They were recent
friends.

"Ho, Bertie! What have you been up to?"

"I was out walking. I like getting some exercise before breakfast.
Lovely scenery around here, beautiful grounds," he said, thinking of
the young nanny he'd met pushing the pram.

"We'll go for a ride after breakfast." Harry had some new horses
he wanted to show off, and had invited his guests to join him.

"I'd like that very much," Bertie said with a broad smile. "Will the
women ride with us?" he asked with interest.

"Probably not—most of them don't stir before noon. At least Eugenia doesn't. She likes to stay up late, and moves slowly in the
morning." Bertie helped himself to some eggs and fruit, and a footman poured him a cup of coffee. He picked up one of the newspa-
pers that had been left there for the guests, and looked perfectly
content as he glanced around the table at his new friends. It was
going to be a very pleasant spring and summer, with a bit of a dalli-
ance to spice things up.

The men went riding while the women dressed, and they all got
together for a sumptuous dinner in the dining room, at one o'clock.
Eugenia had organized a game of croquet for them afterward, and
everyone was in good spirits. Three of the guests were flirting with
her, with Bertie the least obvious one. He liked being the dark horse,
and he was still cultivating his friendship with Harry, and wanted to
gain his trust before he made any serious moves with Eugenia. And
he knew he had time. Because he appeared the least interested in
her, of her many suitors, he was the one she most desired, and did

everything in her power to charm him and catch his attention. It was a game he played well, and often. He had never married and had no wish to—he had much too much fun sleeping with the women who were willing, particularly other people's wives.

After croquet, they played cards until teatime, and a huge tea was laid out in the library. They all sat chatting until it was time to go upstairs to dress for supper.

The women came down in beautiful evening gowns, some of them wearing delicate tiaras. Women liked to show off at the Fergusons', although Eugenia's gowns were the richest and finest and her jewels the biggest. Harry was a grateful and generous man, and everyone lingered after the meal, long past midnight. Harry and Bertie were the last to go upstairs, just after Eugenia, who had stayed to talk to Bertie. He had told her in a sensuous whisper that she was enchanting and he was falling in love with her. She had blushed, but didn't deter him. She was wondering how to lure him to her room, without causing Harry to suspect it. She and her husband had separate rooms, so she was alone. That had begun the first time she got pregnant, and he'd never moved back to her room again, which was just as well since she'd been pregnant constantly for five years. She was adamant now about not letting it happen again, which was even more reason not to sleep with him. And it suited him too. He was no longer excited by Eugenia after all their babies, and he had other interests as well. And with some caution, Eugenia was more than willing to dally with others.

"There's no hurry," Bertie whispered to her. "I'll come back as often as you want me . . . the next time he goes to town." And after saying it, he got up and walked across the room to Harry, and Eugenia curtsied to both of them and retired, drunk on the words Bertie had just said to her, and the anticipation of what was in store for them. She still looked dreamy as Stella helped her undress.

"Did you have a nice evening, madame?" she asked her, as Eugenia beamed at her.

"Wonderful. We have such lovely guests this time." Stella had heard downstairs about the handsome men staying there that weekend. Her mistress had several to choose from, and Stella wondered which of them would be back again. Eugenia seemed ready for mischief these days and bored with her husband. Stella had seen situations like that before and nothing surprised her.

Angélique had said nothing to anyone about meeting Bertie that morning. She had been profoundly unnerved by it, and had found it very unpleasant. It reminded her of Eugenia's brother, except this one was far more direct and seemed more ominous. He hadn't hesitated to offer her "a bit of fun," and to suggest that it was what she really wanted, but didn't have the courage to admit. In fact, he was far off the mark. And she was grateful she hadn't run into him again.

She doubted he'd be foolish enough to come upstairs, particularly if he was one of the guests pursuing Eugenia, which she had heard downstairs as well. The lady of the house had been openly encouraging several of them, and Mr. Ferguson didn't seem to care, from what the footmen said. He had been equally intent talking to one of the women, a German baroness, a young widow they had recently met as well. The Fergusons were a well-suited pair. And with all of that going on, Angélique felt she was safe. The man on the path that morning would be much too busy pursuing the women in the bedrooms on the second floor, to bother coming upstairs to seduce her. She tidied up the parlor, blew out the candle, and walked into her bedroom. The nurserymaid and the children were sound asleep, and she went to get a drink of water before she went to bed. She was in her nightgown in bare feet, with her long hair in a braid down her back, as she saw a vision walk into the darkened room in white tie and tails. He looked spectacularly handsome as he smiled at her in the moonlight, and she could feel her heart beat in fear.

"What are you doing here?" she asked in a whisper, trying to sound stern instead of frightened.

"I thought we'd get to know each other better, after everyone went to bed," he whispered to her, as he took two steps, stood next to her, and grabbed her waist hard in his hands, and then ran one hand over her belly, and slipped it down between her legs. She wrenched free of him and ran across the room, to the door of Helen's room. She didn't want to scream and wake the children, but she had never been so terrified in her life. No man had ever done to her what he just did. He walked toward her quickly and grabbed her again, crushing his mouth down on hers, as he grabbed her breast. He tasted of strong drink, and she knew he had to be drunk to act like this. "Come on," he said roughly, "don't pretend to be shy. You know you want it too."

"No, I don't," she said, pulling away and circling the room. She wanted to run out the door and down the stairs but didn't want to leave him loose in the nursery. She didn't know what he would do, and she was responsible for the children. "I want you to leave," she said clearly. "I'm not going to do anything with you." He laughed at what she said.

"Yes, you are. If I want you to. Your mistress begged me to come to her bed. I'd rather be in yours." She was younger and prettier and fresher, and her resistance titillated him more. Eugenia was too willing, but he knew that in time he would take her too. This was what he did for sport—pursue other men's wives, or shy young girls.

"Please go away," Angélique said, pleading with her eyes, and they were still speaking in soft voices, so as not to wake anyone up.

"And if I won't?" he said, reaching out to grab her, and this time, he wouldn't let her go as he pulled her close to him and held her tight. "What will you do then?"

"Scream," she said in a tiny voice, as he kissed her again and shoved his tongue down her throat, while pressing her buttocks with both hands. And knowing she had to do something then, before he went even further, she bit him hard on the mouth and shoved him away from her, and he fell hard into one of the chairs, as blood dripped on his immaculately starched shirt and vest and he let out a cry of pain.

"You bitch!" he said, grabbing at her again, but she opened the nursery door, and stood shaking beside it.

"I'll scream," she said firmly, "and tomorrow I'll tell Mr. Ferguson. All of it," she said with an intent look, and she looked like she meant what she said. She was more trouble than she was worth. He had misjudged her, she was not the easy piece he had thought.

"You wouldn't dare," Bertie said, as he faced her in the doorway, but he didn't touch her again. He liked resistance, but not a brawl, and his lip was bleeding a lot, as he held a handkerchief to it, but his shirt was already covered in blood.

"I would," Angélique assured him, "if you ever come near me again."

"You're not worth the trouble," he spat at her, "and you'll be sorry if you mess with me, Miss Prim and Proper. Who are you giving it to here? One of the stable hands, so you don't want to give it up to me? Who do you think you are?"

"Not your whore," she said to him, as he walked through, and before he could turn or slap her, she slammed the door and locked it behind him. She was faster than he was, and she heard him go down the stairs a moment later. She was shaking from head to foot, and sat down in the chair where he had fallen. She saw that there was blood on it, and she wiped it off with a damp towel. It took her ten minutes to calm down and go back to her bedroom. She lay awake for hours thinking of what he had said, and tried to do to her. She had been terrified of him, but thank God, nothing had happened, and she had no intention of reporting it to her employers. He wouldn't be back again, of that she was sure. And if Mrs. Ferguson wanted him to come to her bedroom, she wouldn't like the idea of his trying to seduce the nanny. She had nothing to win by telling them.

She lay looking at the moon, through her bedroom window, and at last she fell asleep and felt groggy when she woke up in the morning. Her whole body ached as though it had been beaten, from wrestling with him, and her own tension as she tried to fight him off.

The children had woken early. And Helen asked her, "Was someone up here last night?" as they got the children dressed and ready for breakfast.

"No," Angélique said firmly. She had already unlocked the nursery door so Helen wouldn't suspect anything. She didn't want to tell her, or anyone. She was too shaken, and embarrassed, although she had done nothing wrong. She just wanted to forget the incident had happened.

"I thought I heard voices, but then I thought I was dreaming and went back to sleep." Angélique smiled at her and shrugged.

"Dreams can seem so real sometimes. I have dreams like that too." Helen went to get the breakfast trays off the dumbwaiter then and set the table for breakfast while Angélique washed and changed the twins. George was already running around with a wet diaper, and she had to catch him to change him after she put Rose in the high chair. Helen looked tired, as they all sat down to breakfast, and Angélique tried to push what had happened the night before from her mind.

Helen cleaned the rooms that morning, while Angélique took the children out and kept them closer to the house. Angélique managed all five of them with ease. Emma pushed Rose's pram, and Angélique chased George on his sturdy unsteady legs, as she kept an eye on Rupert and Charles. They had a good morning, and came back in time for dinner. She had just sat them down at the table, when she got a message that Mrs. Ferguson wanted to see her at once, in the library. Angélique couldn't imagine why, but she told Helen to serve them the hot meal that had come up, and she'd be back in a few minutes.

She hurried down the back stairs, and came out in the main hall. The guests were in the drawing room before dinner, and she could hear them, and was startled to see both her employers when she walked into the library, and Mr. Ferguson told her to close the door. This looked serious, and they were both staring at her in disapproval. They didn't invite her to sit down. Eugenia was sitting on the couch, looking furious, and Harry was standing behind his desk.

"Something very serious happened here last night," he said, looking straight at her, "and I want you to know how personally disappointed in you I am." She couldn't imagine what she'd done, and she hadn't complained about their guest coming to the nursery trying to rape her, and she could have. And she had done nothing wrong with the children. She waited to hear what it was. "I think you know what I'm talking about."

"No, sir, I don't," she said honestly, alarmed. She had never been in trouble with them before, and Eugenia was looking daggers at her. She wondered if someone had stolen something and blamed her.

"I'm particularly shocked, given your relations. The cousin of a duke, however impoverished, does not behave like a harlot. Although His Grace told us about your mother," Harry said with disgust.

"What about my mother?" Angélique looked dazed as she stood there, with the word "harlot" ringing in her ears.

"Never mind. Sir Bertram told us what happened last night."

"He did?" If so, why were they angry at her? "I wasn't going to tell you, sir. Nothing happened, and I didn't want to cause a problem with one of your guests. I think he'd probably had a lot to drink." Harry Ferguson stared right through her.

"He told us that you came to his room last night, and tried to seduce him. You offered him your body, and exposed yourself to him. He had to threaten you to make you leave, and before you left his room after he rejected you, you attacked him. He has the marks of it on his face this morning." Angélique's eyes flew open wide, and she stared at both of them. Eugenia was shaking with jealousy and rage, which her husband mistook for righteous indignation.

"No, sir," Angélique said, as tears sprang to her eyes. "He came to the nursery and attacked me. I saw him when I was out walking yesterday, and he approached me. I did nothing to encourage him. And he came up last night, after everyone went to bed. I was in my nightgown, and he tried to seduce me. He kept trying to grab me, and he wanted to have his way with me, and I wouldn't let him. So I bit him," she said as tears rolled down her cheeks. She could see they didn't believe her. Bertie had gotten to them first and convinced them that she had come to his room to seduce him, and attacked him when he refused her. He had gotten his full measure of revenge for her rejection. He didn't take her refusal lightly. And she remembered what he had said about Eugenia begging him to come to bed with her, but she didn't say it, and wouldn't. They believed his story and not hers. "I'm telling you the truth, sir . . . madame . . ." She turned to Eugenia, who glared at her in open hatred. This girl, this nobody, this servant, had tried to seduce the man she wanted. It was unthinkable.

"I suppose you would have seduced him in front of my children in the nursery, if you could have," Eugenia spat at her.

"Of course not, I would never do anything to hurt the children. And I wouldn't have seduced him anywhere. That was why I fought him off, and he didn't like it." The tears were continuing to roll down her cheeks as she told her story, but she could see she wouldn't be able to make them believe her, and she was panicked. What would happen to her now?

"Sir Bertram is a gentleman," Harry reminded her. "He would never do what you are suggesting."

"No, he isn't," she said in a stronger voice. "I thought he was going to rape me, and he's very powerful."

"Precisely, and you're barely bigger than a child. If he had wanted to take you, he would have. But it was you who threw yourself at him, not the reverse. We wanted you to know how outraged we are by your behavior. You will leave this house today, by suppertime, without a character. We don't want a whore caring for our children," he said harshly, and his wife looked pleased. Bertie had been vindicated, and the nanny who had resisted him was to be banished.

"Today, sir?" Angélique looked horrified. "But where will I go?"

"That's not our concern. What you do now is up to you. You'll get no reference from us. We'll have one of the grooms drop you at the pub. You can stay there and catch the next coach to London if that's where you're going, but we want you out of here by tonight." He was adamant, and Eugenia was delighted. She wanted no competition for Bertie. And it never occurred to her to wonder who would take care of her children, nor did she care. The Fergusons were presenting a united front against the nanny they had decided was a "whore," and no longer wanted in their home.

"And the children?" Angélique asked in a choked voice. It pained her to leave them. She had come to love them in the sixteen months she'd been there, particularly Emma, who needed her and she hated to abandon.

"The children are no longer your concern." They left no room for argument, and she wouldn't have argued anyway. She knew when she had lost, just as she had with Tristan. "You may go now," Harry said, dismissing her with a glance at his wife. She was pleased.

"I'm very sorry, Mr. and Mrs. Ferguson. But please believe me, what Sir Bertram has told you is not true. I hope that one day you will know it," she said simply, and then she turned and walked out of the room, with as much dignity as she could muster. As she crossed the hall to the back stairs, she could see Bertie standing in the drawing room. He glanced at her, with no sign of recognition, turned his back, and walked away, as she bolted to the stairs, and ran up to the nursery. She was breathless when she got there.

"Where were you?" Emma asked, looking worried. For a moment, Angélique didn't know what to say and Helen could see she'd been crying. "You missed dinner," Emma said, and handed Angélique a biscuit, which she had saved for her.

"I just found out that I have to leave tonight. Someone in my family is sick, and I must go to them." It was the only story she could think of.

"Will you come back when they get well? Do they have influenza?" Angélique didn't want to lie to her more than she had to, or promise to return when she knew she wouldn't.

"No, my darling girl, I won't. I can't. I will have to stay and take care of them. But I will always, always love you, all of you," she said, glancing around the table as Emma climbed into her lap and clung to her and began to cry. Angélique was crying too, and Helen was shocked.

"Who will take care of us?" Emma asked her.

"Helen for a while, and I'm sure your mummy and daddy will find a very nice nanny to take my place." But very few nannies would be willing to take on five young children—six, when Simon was home for holidays. Angélique sat there for a long time, and she put them all down for their naps. She promised Emma she'd still be there when she woke up, and then she went to talk to Helen in the pantry.

"Is that true?" Helen asked her in a whisper as Angélique shook her head. "You said you had no family, except a cousin who doesn't like you."

"That's true. I got sacked, without a character. The voices you heard here last night weren't a dream. One of their guests came up after dinner. I met him out walking yesterday. He's a fancy piece, and he offered 'a bit of fun,' and I let him know I wasn't interested. He came up here last night, in his cups, and surprised me. He grabbed me, and I fought him off. I didn't know what else to do, so I bit him on the lip when he kissed me, and he left. He told them that I came to his room and tried to seduce him, and they believed him, and not me when I told them the real story. He's a liar. He has an eye to Mrs. Ferguson, and I suppose he doesn't want me interfering, but I wasn't going to tell anyone. I was just glad nothing happened. Mr. Ferguson called me a harlot and a whore," she said, as tears rolled down her cheeks. "They want me gone by suppertime. One of the stableboys will drop me off at the pub, and they don't care what happens to me after that."

"Do you have somewhere to go?" Helen asked, sorry for her and worried about her.

"No, I don't. I don't know where to go. Maybe London."

"There's a woman I know in London you could see to try to find another nanny job. She was a housekeeper years ago, and now she helps girls find jobs with families she knows. She's very discreet, but no one will hire you without a reference."

"I know. Maybe I can get some other kind of job, mending clothes or something." She had come straight from Belgrave to the Fergusons, and had never been out in the world alone. The two women hugged then, and Angélique went to pack, although she had unpacked very little of what she had brought with her. All she really needed to put in her bags were a few of her personal things, and the two portraits of her parents. She had just put in the last of it, when Helen appeared in the doorway.

"I want you to know that I believe you. They get some bad people here sometimes. Her brother is one of them, but I've seen others. Be careful, Angélique. Find a good job where they'll take care of you. I hear stories like that from the maids all the time. Don't go to a house where the husband is after you, or someone's brother. You were luckier than most last night. He could have forced you, and no one would have believed you then either. Not even if you got pregnant. Take care now." Angélique had just turned twenty years old, and was not yet wise to the ways of the world. But she once again was faced with a bitter lesson about how ephemeral life was, and how easily she could lose everything and have to start all over again.

"Thank you. I'll be all right," she said softly. "I'll miss you and the children." Especially the children. She loved them more than their mother.

"We'll miss you too. And God knows who she'll get here now."

"I hope it's someone who'll be good to the children," Angélique said sadly.

"So do I," Helen agreed, upset for her.

Angélique went down to see Sarah then and told her what had happened. It was a familiar story to her too. Maids got fired all the time, when guests lied about them, or accused them of stealing, or they got seduced by some guest who took a fancy to them, like the farm girl who'd had Mrs. Ferguson's brother's baby. Sarah hugged her and told her to write to them, and Angélique promised she would. And then she went back to the nursery in time for the children to wake up. She played games and read to them all afternoon. Her bags were packed, and just after teatime, she changed into her own plain black dress, and hung her nanny dresses and aprons in the cupboard. Emma was watching her with wide eyes.

After she bathed the children and put them in their nightclothes, Angélique left the nursery and took her bags downstairs one by one, while Emma sobbed uncontrollably. Finally, she carried the small trunk with her fortune and treasures and turned to hug Helen and the children. The three oldest ones clung to her, and she kissed Emma for the last time, and kissed the twins, and then she silently closed the door to the nursery with tears rolling down her face.

Eugenia was dressing for supper by then, when Harry walked in from his dressing room and said he wanted to speak to her. She told Stella to leave them alone for a moment.

"What is it?" She was still upset about the story of the night before. How dare that girl set her cap at Bertie! She was saving him for herself.

"You don't suppose the nanny's story is true, do you? I've been thinking about it all day. She seemed very honest about it, and we don't know him all that well. It wouldn't be right to send her away if she's telling the truth."

"Of course not," Eugenia said, irritated. "The girl's a liar. Can't you tell? She went after him, and he didn't want her. She's an ambitious little piece, trying to land a husband among our guests. You're such an innocent. I saw right through her."

"I'm not as innocent as you think," he said, looking her dead in the eye. "He's an arrogant man. Be careful he doesn't go after you," he warned her. There was a limit to even his patience if she embarrassed him. And there was something about Bertie he didn't like, especially after hearing Angélique's story.

"Harry, don't be silly. And I would never do that to you." He nodded and didn't comment, and went back to his dressing room, as Stella came back to do her hair. She was even more relieved now that Angélique was leaving. She was a complication Eugenia just didn't need, and an obstacle she wanted to remove.

"I'm sorry to hear about Nanny Latham, ma'am," Stella said as she arranged her hair in an elaborate coiffure. "She was a nice girl and a good nanny."

"Not as nice as any of us thought, apparently. I don't want a whore chasing my guests or caring for my children." Stella didn't answer. She had heard the real story from Sarah that afternoon. But they all knew that no one would believe a servant over a guest. And Eugenia's motives were clear to them, even if her husband could be duped.

Downstairs, Angélique was saying goodbye to Mr. Gilhooley.

"Please believe me. I did nothing wrong," she said quietly.

"I do believe you. Please take good care of yourself, Your Lady-ship. Be careful." She nodded and went out to the cart one of the grooms had saddled up for her with her bags in the back, to take her to the pub. Mr. Gilhooley came out and stood watching with tears in his eyes as they drove away.

It took them a short time to get to the pub, which was full of rowdy men drinking. It was noisy and smelled of ale, and they had three rooms to let. She asked when the next coach was leaving for London, and they told her there was one leaving at midnight, if she wanted to be on it. She preferred that to spending the night in the pub, full of drunks downstairs. She paid for a room for a few hours, and a stableboy took her bags and trunk upstairs, where she could wait for the coach.

"Will you be wanting something to eat?" the boy asked her.

"No, thank you," she said softly, thinking of the children she had left, and the journey ahead to the city. She had nowhere to stay, and no connections now in London. And worst of all, she knew she would never see the children again. Her heart ached at the thought of them.

She sat quietly in the room until the coach arrived, and then went downstairs and asked the stableboy to load her bags onto it. She climbed in and kept the small trunk on her knees. There was one man traveling with her, and he fell asleep as soon as he got in. He smelled like he'd had a lot to drink. And a few minutes later, the coach left for London with Angélique bouncing around inside on the rutted roads. She finally fell asleep just before they reached London. And when she woke up and looked out, she saw the sun come up over the city. She remembered a small respectable hotel near her father's house in Grosvenor Square. And as she thought of it, she was grateful for her father's money again. At least she would never starve, and would have a roof over her head. Without it, she might have been destitute in the streets. She could see now how that could happen.

She knew staying at a decent hotel would be expensive, but at least there she'd be safe. She'd been thinking about it all night. She was going to tell people she was a widow. And she would go to visit the old housekeeper Helen knew and try to get a job. And somewhere, somehow, with God's help, and some luck, she would start all over again.

Chapter 10

When the coach from Hampshire dropped her off, Angélique hired a carriage to take her to the small hotel she remembered near her former home. She didn't want to risk being in a bad neighborhood, or with frightening people. And she willingly spent the wages Gilhooley had paid her to stay in a safe place. She checked in as Mrs. Latham, had breakfast in the dining room, and walked around London for a while. Sarah had given her the name and address of Mrs. McCarthy, the old housekeeper in London. She helped housemaids, housekeepers, and nannies if she thought they were respectable, came to her through friends, and had references.

She let Angélique into her small, tidy home cautiously, and asked to wait for a few minutes. She was a serious-looking woman with gray hair, and she then offered Angélique a cup of tea, and showed her into the kitchen, where they sat down. Angélique was wearing a simple black dress, with her hair pulled back in a bun, and explained that she needed a position as a nanny, and that she had worked for the Fergusons in Hampshire for sixteen months, taking care of six children, although one was in boarding school since September.

"Sole-charge nanny for six children?" She looked surprised.

"Yes, with a nurserymaid to help me." She told her the ages of the children, including twins, and the gray-haired woman was impressed.

"How old are you?" She looked very young to her, too young to handle that many children. She had heard of the Fergusons and was surprised they didn't have two nannies, since their homes were very grand.

"I just turned twenty," Angélique said with wide eyes, and the woman smiled.

"You're still very young. Where did you work before that?"

"I didn't. I lived with my father in Hertfordshire. I helped run his house." She didn't say how large it was, though Mrs. McCarthy could tell from the way she spoke, and her demeanor, that she was educated and well brought up. "My father died a year and a half ago, almost. My brother inherited everything, so I went to work." She didn't say that her brother had sold her into slavery to the Fergusons. It made no difference now, and she didn't want to complain. She thought it would make a bad impression, and others had been in similar circumstances to hers.

"The Fergusons gave you a reference, I assume," she said, as Angélique gazed at her, and didn't answer, and then shook her head.

"No, they didn't." She told her exactly what had happened, and then sat back in her chair and sighed.

"You have no idea how common that is. I hear these stories all the time. That's why I try to help young girls find new jobs. It's usually the husband who does something like it, not a guest. He sounds like a nasty piece of work," she said sympathetically.

"He was. I wasn't going to tell them. But he lied about me. And they believed him."

"Men like that often do lie. He was probably afraid you'd tell them, so he told them his story to protect himself. Sad about the children, though. That's a bad way to leave. I'm sure they were very upset." Angélique nodded, trying not to think of Emma with tears running down her cheeks, and her own. The woman looked regretful as she met Angélique's eyes. "I'm sure you're a very good nanny. Any girl as young as you who can manage six children that age has a knack for it. And it sounds like you enjoyed it."

"I did," she said with a small smile, although she hadn't expected to at first.

"The problem is that without a character, I can't help you find a job. People will be afraid that you did something to the children, or dropped the baby, or got drunk, or stole, or slept with the husband. They assume the worst if you have no letter of recommendation, and you've had no other jobs. We could explain it as a mad employer, if you had earlier references. But I can't even suggest you as a housemaid with no character at all. They'll think you were stealing, or worse. I'm sorry, I'd like to assist you, but there's no way I can."

"What should I do?" Angélique asked her, looking desperate. She had no idea where to go next, and she trusted this woman's advice.

"You can answer newspaper ads, but they'll turn you away. Without a letter to recommend you, there are no jobs. No one wants to take that risk, which one can understand. Particularly where there are children involved." She looked at her thoughtfully then. "Do you speak any languages? German? Italian? French? The Italians are a bit easier about references, but you have to speak the language. I knew a very nice family in Florence a few years ago. The wife was English, of course. But the children are too old now anyway."

"I speak French," Angélique said quietly. "I'm half French. I speak it fluently. I taught the Ferguson children. The little girl speaks it very well." Mrs. McCarthy was impressed again.

"You are quite amazing for someone who's never been a nanny before. They were very foolish to let you go, on the strength of that man's story. They'll regret it one day, maybe sooner than later. You might try France," she said, thinking about it. "Most of them will want a character too, but they're a bit less strict than we are. And they might give you a chance. You could offer to teach the children English. I know the name of one woman there who does what I do. We worked together years ago." She wrote down her friend's name on a piece of paper and handed it to Angélique. "I'm afraid that's the best I can do. There will be nothing for you here. If their houseguest meant to get even with you for rejecting him, he certainly did."

"I think Mrs. Ferguson wanted me to go too," Angélique said quietly.

"Oh?" There was a sharply raised eyebrow across the table, as she wondered if Angélique had committed some unpardonable sin after all.

"He said something about her wanting him. Maybe that was true. But he wanted me more, or that's what he said." Mrs. McCarthy nearly groaned at what she said.

"My dear, you were doomed. If there was something going on between them, and he claimed you tried to seduce him, she was sure to get rid of you. I think he knew exactly what he was doing when he told the story. You're the victim in all this, but it won't change anything now. Without a letter of recommendation, no one will hire you as a nanny, or any other job. I think the only answer is for you to go to France, and try there. Or perhaps America, New York. But that's a bit extreme. Try France first, since you speak French." She stood up then, shook Angélique's hand, and wished her luck, and Angélique left her house in a daze. She couldn't get a job, and had to leave England. She had been to Paris with her father, but not in many years. And it would be very different, looking for a job in a foreign country. It was hard enough here, in a city she knew. But she realized that the woman was right. She had no other choice. And America sounded terrifying to her. At least France was close, and she could always come back.

When she got back to the hotel, she asked about taking a boat across the channel, and they explained that she would have to take a boat from Dover to Calais, and hire a coach from there to Paris. They said they'd be happy to make the arrangements for her, and she asked them to. There was no point staying in London if she couldn't find work, and she said she'd like to go the next day. And at least she could sleep in a clean room tonight, after spending the night in the filthy coach from Hampshire the night before.

She walked past her father's house in Grosvenor Square that afternoon, and half-expected to see Tristan or Elizabeth stepping out, but the house looked closed, and she wandered slowly back to the hotel, feeling low. She had no idea what she'd find in Paris, or what to do. What if she couldn't find work there either? Without a character or a letter of some kind, no one would want her. Sir Bertram and the Fergusons had put her in a terrible position. All she could hope now was that someone would hire her as a nanny in Paris and give her a chance. And why should they? She could be a murderer for all they knew. She didn't look like one, but that didn't occur to her. She looked like a well-brought-up young woman visiting London, in one of her older, discreet dresses. But someone had to want to hire her, and she was afraid no one would.

She spent the night at the hotel, and asked for a tray in her room. She wanted to be alone, and didn't want to meet people in the dining room. She didn't know what to say to them. Her story about being a widow sounded thin even to her. She slept badly that night, thinking about the people she had left at the Fergusons', and the children, and worried about what she would find in Paris. She felt totally alone in the world. She sat looking at the small portrait of her father for a long time that night, and had never missed him more.

She got up before dawn the next morning, and dressed in travel clothes. The hotel had hired a coach for her, to take her to Dover, and the coachman put her bags on top after she paid the bill at the hotel, and what she owed the coachman for the trip. And they bumped along for eleven hours after they left London. It was a pleasant ride at first, but she was too worried to enjoy it. And she was tired after the long bumpy trip when they reached Dover in the late afternoon, and she paid for passage on the small paddle steamer to cross the channel. It was a short journey, but she knew it was often rough, and a strong wind had come up. She boarded the small boat as it pitched and rolled. She had reserved a small cabin and sat alone, waiting to reach the French shore. It was very choppy, but she wasn't sick, and she went out on deck for a few minutes to take the air. She watched England shrinking behind them, as she thought about Paris. The hotel in London had given her the name of a small respectable hotel, which they said wasn't too expensive, but was in a good neighborhood. And she was planning to go to visit Mrs. McCarthy's friend the next day, to ask her if she knew of a job.

After her long day's journey and the brief boat trip, she was feeling refreshed when they got to Calais. The sea air had done her good. Her head was clear, and she booked a coach with two other passengers, both of them French, bound for Paris, and she had no problem speaking to anyone or paying her fare. Her French was as good as it always had been. They had checked her identity papers and found them in order, and a few minutes after they arrived, after just enough time for a cup of tea in a nearby restaurant, they left for Paris. Angélique had her small locked trunk on her lap and fell asleep on the bumpy drive. She slept most of the way, and woke up when they got to Paris in the early morning hours. She had to hire another carriage then, to take her to the hotel in the sixth arrondissement, bordering the seventh, on the Left Bank.

She had been traveling for more than twenty-four hours by the time they got there, and she was pleasantly surprised by the pretty little hotel, the Hôtel des Saints Pères in Saint Germain des Prés. The lobby was well decorated, and her room was bright and sunny, and she had a lovely view from her windows, of a garden, a church, and a small park. She could see women pushing prams, or walking dogs. It was a beautiful city, and she was suddenly glad to be there, in a whole new place where she could start a new life, far from the Fergusons and her brother, and all the pain and disappointment of the past year and a half. She'd have to take a job in service again, but for now she was free.

She left her bags and her locked trunk in the room, and then went out for a walk, and listened to people speaking French around her. She watched the carriages roll by, some very grand, and some very sporty looking, others making deliveries. It was a bustling city, and she walked past several small parks with statues in them, and lovely trees, before she finally headed back to the hotel. She went up to her room with a feeling of peace and hope for the next day when she would ask Mme. Bardaud if she knew of a job.

She thought about going to the Louvre in the morning, or for a walk on the Faubourg Saint Honoré, past the handsome houses there, but decided she should go to meet Mme. Bardaud first, and then walk around Paris. It brought back memories of being with her father there. She had had some wonderful times with him, staying at the Hôtel Meurice on the rue Saint Honoré, and visiting friends. She felt some strange, inexplicable tie to the city, as if part of her knew she was half French, and was glad to be home. She wished she could have known her mother and her family before they all died. Their château had been rebuilt after the Revolution, and belonged to someone else now, although she didn't know who. The monarchy had been restored fifteen years before, after Napoleon, and now Charles X was on the throne. He was a Bourbon, and she knew she was distantly related to him through her mother, but it did her no good now. What she needed was a job, and her noble ancestry wouldn't help her get one, any more than it had in England, where she was related to King George IV, through her father.

Related to kings in two countries, and daughter of a duke, banished by her brother, she was reduced to working as a domestic, and at the mercy of anyone who would hire her. The only thing that saved her from total ruin was the pouch in her locked trunk. Without that, she would literally be a penniless pauper in the streets.

And she was well aware of it when she went to bed that night. She had dipped slightly into her father's money to pay for the hotel in Paris, and the travel between the two cities. She had spent most of her wages on the hotels, the coaches, and the boat. Her father's money allowed her to stay in respectable places where she felt safe, which was important to her, and the blessing he had bestowed on her with the money he gave her before he died. But she knew she had to find work soon.

She couldn't live on his money forever, and wanted to save as much as she could so that one day when she was older she could buy a home of her own and stop working at menial jobs. But it was too soon now. She didn't know how to buy a house on her own, and the responsibility was too great for a girl her age. She needed to work now. And she wasn't sure where she wanted to live, in England or France. She had no current ties to either one. She was drifting between her lost world and one she hadn't found yet. It was like traveling through the sky, with nothing to tie her down. She had to land somewhere but had no idea where yet. All the bonds that had once held her securely had been cut, when her father died and Tristan set her adrift.

She fell asleep that night, thinking about all of it, and woke late the next morning, trying to figure out where she was, in the unfamiliar room at the hotel. And then she remembered as she glanced out the window, and also recalled what she had to do that day. She was going to meet Mme. Bardaud to ask about work. And soon she would be in a life of service again. She wanted to enjoy her freedom while she could. And hopefully, it wouldn't be for long.

She dressed in another sober gown—she had brought very few frivolous ones with her when she left Belgrave. She had croissants and café au lait in the small dining room at her hotel, and asked the desk clerk for directions to the address she'd been given. She decided to walk there—it was a beautiful spring day, and she was happy as she walked along. She missed the Ferguson children, but she had to concentrate on her own life now.

Mme. Bardaud lived in a narrow building in the second arrondissement on the Right Bank, on the third floor. She walked upstairs, knocked, and a grandmotherly-looking woman peeked out at her, and Angélique explained that Mrs. McCarthy had sent her. Mme. Bardaud had been a governess in London before she married. She invited Angélique to sit down.

"What can I do to help you?" she asked kindly. Angélique explained to the woman in flawless French that she was looking for a job as a nanny, or a governess, and could teach the children English if the parents wished. And as the woman had in London, she asked about Angélique's last job.

She told her she had cared for six children, their ages, and what she had done, how long she'd been there, and that it had been her first job.

"And the reason why you left?" she asked, and Angélique told her honestly what had happened, and that she had no reference to show for sixteen months of work, although she promised that she had done a good job.

"I'm sure you did," the woman said gently, "and these stories are not unusual. I believe you, my dear. But no employer will hire someone without a reference. They don't know if you stole from your last employer, or did something far worse than refuse to be seduced by one of their guests. And there is no one to corroborate your story." It was no different here than it had been in London. Mme. Bardaud

told her that without a character, there was no way she would find
work, except perhaps washing dishes somewhere, or scrubbing floors,
but not in a decent home. And she knew of no one who would employ her.

"What am I going to do?" she said out loud, putting a voice to her
thoughts. She was fighting back tears and felt completely lost.

"I can't help you. You need some proof that you're a responsible,
honest person, and without a reference from your previous employer,
they won't hire you," she said wisely. Angélique thanked her, looking
dazed, and left a few minutes later, and went back downstairs to the
street. There was nothing she could do, nowhere to go. She thought
of Mrs. McCarthy's suggestion that she go to America, but what if
they wanted a reference there? Then what would she do?

She walked away slowly, and wandered all the way to the Jardin
des Tuileries, after passing through the Place Louis XVI. Paris was
so beautiful, but she had no friends and no protection there either.
It was another city where she had nowhere to go. She was trying
not to panic, but she was frightened of what would become of her
now. She wondered what her father would say and advise her to do.
And how could he even have imagined a situation like the one she
was in?

She sat on a park bench for a while, and thought about all of it,
trying to formulate a plan, with no success, and then she walked
back to the hotel, and went to her room. She took out a book and
read for a while, trying to escape her worries. She wondered if the
hotel would let her work for them as a maid, but she was too embarrassed to ask.

She stayed in her room until after dark, and then walked through
the streets of Paris again, and stopped for something to eat, but she

felt awkward being in a restaurant alone. She had never done that before, and it made her uncomfortable. She saw men staring at her, and couples. She was a young, pretty girl on her own. Her lie about being a widow meant nothing to them. She didn't belong out on the streets alone, and as soon as she finished eating, she walked back toward her hotel. She took a different route and went down a narrow street, and was suddenly confused about which way to go. She doubled back and found herself in another narrow street, and then knew she was lost. She was frightened and it was dark, and then she heard a moan, and jumped as she looked around. She wondered if it was a cat or a dog—it wasn't a human sound. All she wanted to do was run. And as she started to hurry away, she saw a crumpled figure in the gutter, and heard the same moan again. She stopped to look, and thought it might be an injured child. She walked slowly toward the form on the pavement, and without thinking, bent down, and saw that it was a young girl with a gash on her forehead, and blood on her face. Her eyes were closed, and one of them was swollen shut. Angélique thought she was unconscious at first, and then the girl opened her eyes and stared into Angélique's.

"Go away," she groaned, "leave me alone." Angélique could hardly understand her through the battered lips.

"You're hurt," she said gently, "let me help you." She needed to go to a hospital, but Angélique didn't know how to get her there. The girl was wearing a red satin dress, and no coat, and she had a black bow in her hair. Someone had attacked the girl viciously. "Do you want me to call for the police?" The girl's eyes flew open again as she said it, and she shook her head and groaned.

"No police. Go away," she said again.

"I'm not leaving you here," Angélique said firmly. "I'll take you

home, or to a hospital if you like." The girl started to cry when
Angélique said it. She looked like a rag doll in the gutter where she
had been dumped, and she had dirt all over her dress. "You can't
stay here all night, or the police will find you," she said in a stronger
voice. "Can you stand up?" She didn't seem as though she could, or
walk. "I'll come back," Angélique said then, and hurried away. She
had seen carriages to hire in the street she had come from, and she
was determined to find one and bring it back to where the young
woman lay. She didn't appear as though she was able to go anywhere on her own.

It took her a few minutes to find a carriage to hire, and direct him
to the narrow street where she had found the young woman, but a
few minutes later, she recognized the street, and she told him to
stop and wait for her, as she hurried back to where the girl had
been. She was still there and seemed like she was asleep. There was
no sound from her as Angélique shook her gently, and she stirred.
She tried to protest at first when Angélique lifted her up, but she
didn't have the strength to resist. Angélique supported her and half-
carried her, back to the carriage, and the coachman lifted her in.

"She looks like something very bad happened to her," the coachman said with concern for the young woman Angélique had carried
to the coach.

"She fell down the stairs," Angélique said matter-of-factly, gave
him the address of her hotel, and hopped in beside the girl slumped
on the seat. Angélique took off her black cape and wrapped it around
her, as the girl opened her eyes and gazed at her.

"The hospital or my hotel?" Angélique asked her simply, as the
girl stared at her in disbelief.

"Your hotel." She didn't have the strength to argue with her, and she couldn't go anywhere under her own steam. Her whole body had been battered, she had broken ribs, and it hurt to breathe. "You should have left me there," she said miserably.

"Certainly not," Angélique said firmly as though to a child, and a moment later, they reached her hotel. She paid the coachman, and he helped get the injured passenger down. Wearing Angélique's cape, the girl leaned heavily against her and they walked into the hotel. The desk clerk was busy and paid no attention to them. He recognized Angélique and continued what he was doing as she assisted her guest up the stairs to her room. The girl looked like she was about to faint, as Angélique unlocked the door, nearly dragged her to the bed, and lifted her onto it, as the young woman observed Angélique gratefully through her tears.

"I'm sorry," she said, and closed her eyes with the pain, as Angélique went to get some towels and a nightgown. She gently washed her face, and took off her clothes. The dress was cheap, and she was wearing strong perfume, but all Angélique could see as she ministered to her were the cuts and bruises and dried blood on her face. It took her a while to clean the girl up. She took off the bow and smoothed down her hair, and the injured young woman appeared a little more human once she was cleaned up and tucked into the bed. Angélique gave her some water to drink, and she took a sip, and lay back on the pillows with a groan.

"What's your name?" Angélique asked her.

"Fabienne," she whispered.

"Do you know the person who did this to you?" She shook her head, and closed her eyes again, and a little while later, she fell asleep. Angélique sat in a chair next to her, and dozed off, and she woke several hours later when the girl cried out in her sleep and then woke up. "Sshhh . . . it's all right. You're safe," she said gently, as Fabienne stared at her, and remembered how she got there.

"Why did you help me?" She couldn't understand what had happened to her. She was in an unfamiliar room, in a comfortable bed, with clean sheets. It was all very surreal, after being beaten and dumped in the street.

"I couldn't leave you there," Angélique said simply. She took her own clothes off then, and put on her nightgown and a dressing gown. "How do you feel?"

"Terrible." Fabienne smiled through swollen lips, as Angélique observed the bruises on her face. The cut on her forehead wasn't as bad as she had feared, although it might leave a scar. "But I'm glad to be here. You must be an angel of some kind."

"No." Angélique smiled at her. "Not at all. I just happened by at the right time. Are you sure you don't want to go to a hospital? I could ask the hotel for a doctor if you like." Fabienne shook her head and looked frightened again. Her fear of any kind of authority made Angélique wonder about what she was hiding.

"Did you do something bad to get hurt like this?" She spoke to her as though to a child, and Fabienne shrugged and didn't answer as she averted her eyes. Whatever she had done, she didn't deserve to be beaten. Angélique remembered the red satin dress and bow in her hair, and the strong perfume she could smell on the dress and guessed at what she was, but she didn't care. The girl was badly hurt and needed help. Fabienne could see understanding in her eyes.

"How old are you?" With her face clean, she seemed very young.

"Seventeen," Fabienne answered.

"Do you have a family?" She shook her head in answer. "Neither do I." Angélique smiled at her. "So maybe it's a good thing that I helped you."

"It's very nice of you," Fabienne said gratefully. Angélique settled into the chair again, lowered the lamp, and Fabienne drifted off to sleep.

Fabienne was sitting up in bed when Angélique woke the next morning, and Fabienne was staring at her as she opened her eyes. She looked a little better but not much.

"I should go soon," she said when Angélique was fully awake.

"Do you have somewhere to go?" Fabienne took a long time to answer, shook her head, and then explained.

"I ran away."

"Is that why they beat you up? Did someone find you?" She shook her head again.

"I left home when I was fifteen. My parents died and I went to live with my aunt and uncle. He was a very bad person, and he . . . he . . . used me . . . all the time. My aunt didn't say anything. He was always drunk, so was she . . . so I ran away from them. It was in Marseilles, and I came to Paris to find work. I tried to find a job in a restaurant or a store, or at a hotel. I got a job cleaning in a hospital, but they fired me when they found out how old I was. I couldn't find work, and I had no money to eat. I was starving and cold all the time. Sometimes I hid and slept outside.

"And then I met a woman, and she said she would help me. She said she had other girls living at her house, and they were like a family. I didn't know what else to do so I went with her, and then I found out what they were. It was just like my uncle, except with strangers. We had to work for her all the time. There were five of us, and they paid her to use us. She kept the money, and she hardly ever fed us.

Everyone was young, except one girl was older, and none of us could find jobs. She said she would pay us, but she gave us very little, and she didn't give us clothes, so we couldn't go out. We sat around in our undergarments all the time, waiting for the men to come.

"I've been there for two years, and I couldn't stand it anymore. So I ran away, and I thought if I did the same thing on my own, I could keep all the money. But she protected us. She wasn't a good person, but she didn't let the men hurt us, at least not much. Some of them were rough, but if she heard any of us screaming, she stopped them, and sent them away. And she registered all of us with the Gendarmerie Royale, so her house is legal. But the girls on the street aren't. And once I was on my own, I had no one to protect me. Some of them are very bad men. This is the third time I've been beaten, this time was the worst. He took all my money, beat me, and ran away. I know other girls on the street—one of them was stabbed and killed last month. She was sixteen. I suppose I'll have to go back to Madame Albin's house, if she'll take me. She protects us and registers us properly. But on the streets, we have no papers. A policeman stopped me last month. He said he'd let me go if I took care of him, and he was very rough. Madame Albin runs the house correctly. I can't do this on my own." Angélique tried not to look shocked at what she'd heard. It was a tragic story of misery and despair and young girls who had nowhere to turn, and were exploited by people like Madame Albin, and abused by the men they served, like the one who had beaten and robbed Fabienne.

Angélique suspected she was pretty, but it was hard to tell with all the bruises and swelling on her face. She knew she should have been shocked, but she could see now how easily it could happen. Girls who couldn't find jobs, had no money, and nowhere to turn fell prey to the only thing they could do. She could understand it now. Without a reference, she couldn't get a job either, and if she didn't have her father's money, she might have been desperate too. Angélique couldn't envision the life that Fabienne had led almost since her childhood. All she could do was sell her body, for lack of anything else.

"What do you do?" Fabienne asked her. "You must be rich to stay in a place like this."

"No, I'm not," Angélique said honestly. "I'm a nanny. Or at least I was until a few days ago. I got fired, and they sent me away, without a reference. It was in England. I couldn't get a job in London, so I came here."

"You speak good French." Fabienne was impressed.

"I learned it as a child. My father had me taught because my mother was French. She died when I was born." Fabienne nodded, interested in her story too. "So now I'm looking for a job, without a reference, and I can't find one here either."

"I could introduce you to Madame Albin." Fabienne was teasing her, but she could see that Angélique wasn't that kind of girl. She seemed smart and educated, and there was something very distinguished about her. "I guess I'll go back to her, if she'll take me." She sounded sad as she said it. She wanted to get away from her, and now she knew she never would.

"Why don't you stay here for a few days until you feel better and make up your mind then? I'm not going anywhere, at least not for a while. I have to look for work. You can stay in bed and rest."

"I don't want to take advantage of your kindness. Madame Albin will give me a few days to rest before she puts me back to work. No one would want me now anyway." Although she knew that some would and wouldn't care what condition she was in. Madame Albin's customers weren't very particular. It wasn't a high-class house like some. But she had a lot of clients and did well, not that the girls ever saw much of the money.

It had been an amazing story for Angélique to hear. She never thought about women like her, and what got them into the life they led, the desperation and lack of opportunities to do anything else, except starve. And once they were trapped in that life, there was nowhere to go, and no escape for them.

"You don't hate me for what I told you?" she asked Angélique nervously.

"How could I hate you? I'm sad for you, and wish there were a better way for you to make a living, without getting beaten up or cheated by Madame Albin."

"She's not so bad really. She used to do it too, so she knows. She's too old now, except for one or two old customers, but they just come to talk. They're too old now too." She smiled. "She likes having very young girls for the men. They like that better. The oldest one in our house was eighteen. The youngest one was fourteen, but she looks older." Angélique was getting a rapid education in a world she had never seen or known, and hoped she never would. She felt sorry for all of them, and especially Fabienne. She seemed like a sweet girl, who could have had a decent life if she'd had a chance. But she hadn't, from her uncle to Madame Albin. They had all used her, and she couldn't find her way out.

"Some of the girls like what they do," she admitted, "especially if they make money at it. And some of the ones who work alone, and not in a house, have a pimp. But they beat them up and take all their money too. The only ones who make money at this are the madams, like Madame Albin, and the pimps. The girls never do, or not enough. They just use us like cows, or sheep, and take our money. She said it cost a lot to feed us and run the house. But none of us ate that much, we didn't have time. We were always working from morning till night. The men show up all the time, in the morning on the way to work, at dinnertime, when they can leave their office, at night on the way home, or they don't go home and say they're out with friends, or after their wife is asleep. Some of them aren't even married, they say it's just easier than finding women who'll do it. Or their wives don't want to do it with them anymore, or they're expecting a baby. There are a lot of reasons why men come to us. And a few of them just come to have someone to talk to. Some of them are very nice men, but most of them aren't." The whole story saddened Angélique for her. But Fabienne was very matter-of-fact about her life, and work. To her, it was a job, like Angélique was a nanny. She wondered what her brother would have said if she'd become a prostitute instead.

"Do you think you'll stay here, in Paris?" Fabienne asked her.

"I don't know. It depends if I find a job. They suggested in London that I try here, or go to America, but that seems so far away, and what if I don't find work when I get there?"

"It would scare me to go so far away," Fabienne admitted, and Angélique agreed. She liked talking to her. She felt as though she had a new friend, even though their lives were completely different. And their histories certainly were.

"Are you hungry?" Angélique asked her, and Fabienne nodded hesitantly. She didn't want to impose more than she already had. "I'll go and get something to eat. They have croissants and coffee downstairs."

Angélique put on some clothes and went downstairs to get breakfast for both of them. She brought it back on a tray and set it on the bed next to Fabienne. She was well aware that she had left her purse in the room, but she had very little in it. Her real money was in the locked trunk, and she trusted Fabienne with her purse. She didn't seem like the kind of girl who would steal from her, and she hoped she was right. And she could tell when she came back that it hadn't been touched.

They ate their croissants and drank the café au lait, and a little while later, Angélique put on a different dress. Fabienne tried to get up, but her ribs caused her too much pain, and she sank back onto the bed.

"Maybe I'll stay for another day," she said, looking pale.

"I want to go for a walk," Angélique said. "I'll bring back some food."

"Thank you," she said gratefully. No one had ever been this nice to her, not even when her parents were alive. And even the girls she worked with argued with each other at times. She could see that Angélique was a good person, and was of a cut far, far above anyone she'd ever known. Yet she was perfectly willing to share her hotel room with her, in the nicest place Fabienne had ever been.

She went out a little while later, and as promised, came back with cheese and some salami, pâté and a baguette, and some apples. It was simple but delicious, and Fabienne ate voraciously. She was starving.

"I'm sorry, I haven't eaten in two days," she apologized.

"It's all right," Angélique reassured her, and on the way back in, she had told the hotel her cousin was staying with her, so they didn't think she was trying to cheat them. They charged a small fee for an additional person in the room, and she was happy to pay it for Fabienne, and didn't mention it to her. She had no money anyway.

Angélique spoke to the housekeeper of the hotel that afternoon, and she said the same thing as the others, that with no reference she wouldn't find a job, and surely not as a nanny in a good home, or even as a hotel maid. She would have to take whatever she got, cleaning floors somewhere, or washing dishes in a restaurant, but not working for people of high caliber in a fine home, or a decent hotel. By not giving her a character, the Fergusons had destroyed her ability to work. Or Bertie had, and they believed him. Together, they had robbed her of any respectable future job, unless someone was willing to risk it and give her a chance, and everyone assured her that would never happen. She was discouraged when she got back to the room, and found Fabienne asleep in the bed. She looked better when she woke up. She knew Angélique was going to talk to the housekeeper about finding a job.

"What did she say?" she asked Angélique.

"That with no reference, there's no hope of a job. Maybe I will have to go to America after all. Maybe I can get a job sewing," she said, depressed.

"You'll go blind. And they pay almost nothing. I tried that when I came to Paris. And you have to sew really well. Can you cook?" Angélique hesitated before she answered and then shook her head.

"Not really. But I'd probably need a recommendation for that too. In a home anyway." She thought of all the staff at Belgrave, and the Fergusons, and all the things they knew how to do. But they had been in service all their lives, and all had had recommendations like her brother's when she arrived. There were keys to open the right doors, and she had none. She felt desperation starting to creep up on her.

Angélique went out to get supper for them that night, and brought back some roast chicken from a small restaurant nearby, carrots, potatoes, and a baguette. They shared it while they talked about their lives. Fabienne knew a great deal more about men than she did. All she knew about were the children she had just cared for, and the life she'd had growing up, which she didn't explain in detail to Fabienne, nor who her father was.

"I'd like to get married one day," Fabienne said innocently, sounding like any girl her age, as they finished their meal, "if anyone would have me. I'd love to have children."

"They're a lot of work." Angélique smiled. "The woman I worked for had twins last time. They were very sweet."

"That must have hurt a lot when she had them," Fabienne said practically.

"I'm sure it did. She didn't want any more after that."

"Neither would I. One of the girls I worked with got pregnant last year, and she decided to keep it. She went home to her parents and left it there when she came back to work. But it's nice when she goes home and sees it. Madame Albin doesn't let girls go home very often, and most of them have no home anyway, or their parents won't let them come back. The girl who had the baby told her parents she's a dressmaker in Paris, and they believe her. I never went back to Marseilles, and I never will. I hate them," she said, referring to her aunt and uncle. Angélique could understand why, after what her uncle had done to her.

They were both tired and went to bed early that night, and in the

morning, Angélique woke up first, and lay in bed, thinking. Fabienne had opened her eyes to a whole other way of life. It sounded
sordid and tawdry, but she had heard of women like that before.
They were badly thought of and shunned by polite society, but she
remembered hearing stories below stairs of houses where important
men went, almost like clubs, where the women were shocking and
unacceptable, but highly sought after privately by men. They were
courtesans. It was a dark side of life she knew nothing about, but
was suddenly intrigued by. And she mentioned it to Fabienne when
she woke up, and they chatted over their morning café au lait and
croissants from downstairs.

"Aren't there some very fancy houses that do what Madame Albin
does? I heard of it talked about in whispers. I think some very powerful men go there, to meet glamorous women away from their
wives."

"Of course," Fabienne said knowingly, "but not like Madame Albin's. Men like that don't go to her. They have very elegant women,
and the madams charge a huge amount of money. It's all very secret,
and very grand. I've heard about those houses too, but never been
there." Angélique was looking at her intently—they were like two
young girls up to mischief. Angélique sat lost in thought for a minute.

"What would it take to put together a house like that?" Angélique
said after a few minutes.

Fabienne laughed in answer. "A lot of money. A beautiful house,
or a very nice one, beautiful clothes, gorgeous women, wonderful
food and wine, probably servants. It would cost a fortune. And you'd
have to make it like a secret club that everyone would want to come
to, so important men feel comfortable there. You'd have to be very

rich and know a lot of important people to do something like that."
She'd heard of a luxurious house like that near the Palais Royal, but
had never met anyone who had worked there. It was a world away
from Madame Albin's.

"Have you ever known girls who worked in those places, not like
Madame Albin's?"

"I met one once. She said she used to work in one of the best
houses in Paris, but she drank a lot, and got fat, and I think she stole
money and they threw her out. She was very pretty though. And I
heard about two others who went into business together, and had
important clients. They made a lot of money, and retired to the
South. Why?"

"What if we started a house of our own? I know it sounds crazy,
but one of those really fancy ones, with a nice house, and some
really beautiful girls, and important men would want to come there.
Like a meeting place for those men, with girls. Do you think you
could meet some girls like that?"

"I could try. I could ask around. They're probably all in other
houses, though. But if the house is nice enough, they might come,
and they could bring their regular clients. But you'd need a lot of
money to do it."

"I might be able to get some, if it's not too much. And it would
have to be a safe place for the girls to work. Where they would be
protected, and never treated badly, and they'd get a fair share of the
money they make for the house."

"Are you talking about a hotel or a bordel?" Fabienne teased her,
but she could see a spark of excitement in Angélique's eyes. She was
thinking. It certainly wasn't what her father had intended her to do
with his money, but maybe if they did it for a few years, she could

make some money, and then they'd all retire. And it would be a lot better for those women than working on the streets on their own, or in bad houses where they were exploited. She couldn't think of what else to do now—she was never going to get a decent job, and her father's money would buy her a home one day, but she couldn't live on it forever. She still needed to work. And all respectable doors for good jobs were closed to her now. This seemed like a creative solution to the situation she was in, and a chance to make money to add to what her father had left her, so she wouldn't have to be a nanny.

"I'm serious," Angélique said. "What if we created the best bordel in Paris? One of the really luxurious ones, with the most beautiful women, where all the best men wanted to come? If I find the house, do you think you could find the girls, with good connections and important clients?"

"I could try. Do you really mean it?" Fabienne was stunned.

"I do."

"How many girls do you want?" Fabienne was looking at her with admiration.

"How many do we need?" Angélique was learning a new business.

"Six would be good. Eight would be better. And what about you? Would you work too?" Fabienne was shocked that she'd consider it. Angélique didn't look the type, but you never knew. Some of the most famous prostitutes in Paris looked like respectable women, and weren't. Fabienne had heard of them. And they usually had important protectors.

Angélique shook her head at her question. "No, I wouldn't. I would run it, and protect the women, and I'd even talk to the clients. But they can't have me. That's my one condition."

"Most madams just run it, and some only have a few clients," Fabienne said thoughtfully.

"Not even a few," Angélique said with a look of steel in her eyes.

"All right then. It's your house, your rules."

"Find the girls, and not too young. They have to be interesting and experienced, and good to talk to." Fabienne nodded—she was beginning to understand Angélique's vision. It was far beyond anything she'd ever seen, but she liked the idea, and it was much better than going back to Madame Albin, or risking her life on the streets alone, being beaten up, and fleeing the police. "I'll look for the house," Angélique said. "Now you have to get well, so you can start looking for the girls."

"Do you think you can really do it?" Fabienne asked her with a look of amazement. It sounded like a dream to her.

"I don't know. Let's try." She didn't want to squander her father's money, she wanted it to work. "I want to have the best bordel in Paris." And as they started to make a list of what they needed to make it happen, Angélique knew that destiny had just opened a door, and showed her a new path. It suddenly felt fated that she and Fabienne had met. Angélique looked over at her and smiled. A whole new life for both of them had just begun.

Chapter 11

Angélique began laying the groundwork for her plan that day. She took out her dresses to examine them. She wanted to look like a respectable widow when she went to search for a house to rent, and Fabienne could pose as her lady's maid. She wasn't going to buy a house, but rent in a good neighborhood, and not one where they would be too closely observed.

She took out a dark navy silk dress with a slim waist, wide skirt, and lace collar, with a matching coat over it, which she had worn to dinner at Belgrave with her father, a deep red gown with a matching shawl and a high neck, and two simple black dresses that she had worn when she was in mourning, both of which would be service-able in her role as genteel young widow, and her very bearing showed that she was an aristocrat, as well as the way she spoke. She had brought gloves with her, and a fan of her mother's, and a small purse from Paris. She had what she needed to be convincing as a woman who wanted to rent a house in a proper neighborhood in

Paris. And she had a very simple black wool gown she'd worn at the Fergusons'. She could add a bit of lace at the neck for Fabienne for her outfits as lady's maid in the coming days while they set things up. All of the clothes that Angélique had were obviously of quality. But when she pulled her hats out, they looked sadly squashed after two years packed away. She held each gown up and studied it carefully. The fashions for respectable young women hadn't changed much in two years, and she had always worn sober gowns, and not flashy ones like Eugenia Ferguson, in her case, more suited to her age and station as a duke's daughter.

"Where did you get those clothes?" Fabienne asked as she watched her. They were the prettiest gowns she'd ever seen, in velvets and silks, with exquisite lace collars.

"I had them from before I was a nanny," she said quietly.

"What were you? A queen?" she asked, only partly joking, and her new friend didn't answer—she obviously had secrets of her own.

"Of course not." She wished she had the rest of her clothes from Belgrave, but she had no way to get them. She wouldn't dare ask Mrs. White, who would want to know what she was up to. She hadn't written to her yet to tell her she had left the Fergusons, and wanted to find a new situation first, so she didn't worry. And Tristan would never want to release her clothes or send her other trunks. He had probably thrown them all away by now, hoping never to lay eyes on her again.

"Can you stand up?" she asked Fabienne, whose ribs were still painful, but she did as she was told. She was a few inches taller than Angélique, but other than that their figures were similar, although Fabienne's bust was slightly larger. Angélique held the simple black dresses up to her, and narrowed her eyes. "I can lower the hems. And with a bit of lace at the collar and cuffs, you'll look like a very proper lady's maid, and quite an elegant one at that." She smiled at her.

"I'm going to be a lady's maid?" Fabienne was shocked for a minute. That hadn't been part of the plan.

"While we search for a house to rent. I'm a widow, you're my lady's maid, or my young cousin. We've just come from Lyon, to be near relatives here. How old do I look?"

Fabienne studied her intensely. "About fifteen," she said honestly. She was lithe and small, and her pale blond hair somehow made her look younger than Fabienne's dark mass of hair.

"That won't do. Do you suppose I could look twenty-five or twenty-six?"

"Maybe with more elaborate dresses, with your bosom showing."

"That'll do when we're at the house. I don't want the clients to know I'm twenty. It's all right for you to be young, but the clients and the girls won't respect me if they think I am. I think I'll be twenty-six. That's a good age for a young widow."

"What did your husband die of?" Fabienne grinned. She liked the part they were playing. She had never had so much fun in her life as with this enterprising young girl who had pulled her out of the gutter and nursed her at her hotel. Angélique was the angel of mercy in her life, and they were about to become two young devils together, if they followed Angélique's plan.

"I killed him," Angélique said matter-of-factly, and Fabienne laughed. "Oh, I don't know, cholera, malaria, something dreadful. I'm quite heartbroken over it, or I will be when we rent the house. I'll be a happy widow when we receive clients. But one who loved her husband deeply and won't betray his memory, so that I'm untouchable to the clients. How does that sound?"

"Fascinating. I'm not sure if you're crazy, or very, very smart." Fabienne was sincere, and meant it.

"Let's hope I'm a little bit of both," she said seriously. "Crazy enough to do it, and smart enough to pull it off." It was a wild stretch of the imagination. She had to acquire and set up a home, one that men would be drawn to, and run a business, selling the flesh of beautiful young women, who might be challenging to control. And she wanted it to work so that they would all make money, and could eventually go away pleased, and richer for what they'd done. She just wanted to make some money at it, to add to her father's gift, and then retire. Fabienne said she wanted to make money and then leave Paris and get married and have children. She wanted to go back to the South, but not back home. Angélique had no idea where she'd go afterward. She had no home to go back to either, and no wish to marry, and be subjugated by a man. That seemed dangerous to her, and so many of them were dishonest. Her brothers were, and she had heard all the stories and backstairs gossip about Harry Ferguson. And Sir Bertie had wanted to have an affair with her and her employer. They all seemed like a bad lot, except her father, who had been a wonderful, honest man, and truly loved his wife.

"We'll need new bonnets. My hats are a mess now. Something simple for you, and perhaps a big one for me to make me look older."

"Won't that be expensive?" Fabienne was worried.

"Probably. And we'll need clothes for all the girls. Beautiful gowns. We don't have to buy very expensive ones at first, but they'll have to be elegant, for the kind of men we want as clients. You can't all sit around in your underclothes like at Madame Albin's. We'll need to have a proper drawing room to entertain them like the gentlemen they are, and then you can show them the rest when you go upstairs."

"How do you know all this?" Fabienne looked at her in fascination. Until then, Angélique had never met a prostitute in her life. Now she was ready to run a high-class brothel for the men who were the cream of Paris.

"I'm just making it up as I go along." She grinned like a delighted child. "Do you feel well enough to go out today?" Fabienne's face looked better, but she still had some bruises. The cut on her forehead was healing nicely, and her lips were no longer swollen. Her ribs were painful, but she could move around better, although she wouldn't have wanted to wear a corset, and Angélique said she didn't have to. It would make her look more like a lady's maid not to highlight her youthful figure.

"And how old am I in this fairyland you're inventing?" Fabienne asked her new madam. Fabienne already had great respect for Angélique, and what she'd done for her, and was intending to do. She had said several times that she would protect the girls and pay them well, which would be a strong selling point for all of them if it was true, and Fabienne believed her.

"Eighteen, I think. That sounds old enough," Angélique said, laying their clothes out on the bed, and discarding the somber dress she had worn hoping to have interviews as a nanny. Her nanny life had just ended, possibly forever. Although if she had to, she thought she might be a governess one day. She liked the idea of teaching older children, well-born young ladies who wanted to learn. She was adept at languages, read voraciously, and had a good head for numbers, which would serve her well in her new business. She had often looked over the estate ledgers with her father and understood them.

Just from listening to her, and watching her, and seeing the clothes she had with her, Fabienne had guessed that she must have come from an aristocratic background and something had gone very wrong, but she didn't want to pry, and thought that Angélique might tell her one day, when they knew each other better.

They dressed carefully then, after Angélique went downstairs to the laundry, to press their gowns. Angélique added a bit of lace to the neck of Fabienne's dress, helped her arrange her hair simply, since she couldn't raise her arms, and they left the hotel like two proper young ladies, hired a carriage, and went to a milliner the hotel had recommended, in the first arrondissement. When they got there, it was run by a very pretty older woman, and some of the hats were fabulous. Fabienne wanted to try them all. Angélique indulged her with one exceptionally pretty light blue one that framed her face, bought one small simple black one to go with her imaginary role as a lady's maid, and bought three very elegant ones for herself that went with the gowns she had with her. They could share most of their clothes with a little adjustment here and there.

They had dinner at a respectable restaurant, with Fabienne's eyes agog. She had never been in a place like it before. And with Fabienne with her, Angélique no longer looked questionable being alone.

After dinner, they went to meet with a "notaire" who handled real estate transactions, including the rental and sale of houses. Fabienne nearly choked when Angélique told him when they got there that she needed quite a lot of bedrooms, as her six children would be joining them.

"*Six* children?" Fabienne whispered when the notaire, who was like a lawyer, went into another room to get some files to show them. "Are we running an orphanage?" Angélique just smiled, and the man returned a moment later to describe three houses to them, all of them for rent. One of them was fearsomely expensive, and Angélique could tell he was testing the waters and how far she would go. She said demurely that it was a little out of her budget and the pension her late husband had left her. But the other two were possible. Both had handsome gardens, and one of them seemed crowded from the drawings, with all of the bedrooms crammed together. The other had a large reception room, a drawing room, a dining room, and a small parlor on the main floor. A kitchen and four maids' rooms were in the basement, and ten bedrooms divided five to a floor on the two top floors, plus a very handsome master suite, and some additional smaller rooms in the attic. The notaire said it was in good condition, the owners had moved to Limoges, but wanted to keep the house and rent it. The husband was a wealthy factory owner, and the rental price was more or less what Angélique had hoped it would be. It was across the street from a small park, and around the corner from another. The only less attractive feature of the house, he admitted, was that it was in an alley on its own, on the fringes of an excellent neighborhood but not exactly in it, and the kind of people who wanted a house as large and fine as that wanted to be in the heart of one of the best areas, not simply on the outer reaches of it, which for Angélique's purposes was absolutely perfect. They did not want to be surrounded by respectable households, outraged by male traffic in and out of the house, particularly if they were successful, and anyone was observing them closely. The alley and borderline location couldn't have been better suited to them, if they had designed it themselves.

"Is it safe?" Angélique asked, looking slightly worried, for the no-taire's benefit. "My children are very young, and we're a household of women. My servants are all women. We can't be in a dangerous area."

"Of course," he said grandly, "I assure you it's quite safe for women and children." The house had been available for rent for six months, and the families that had looked at it had been disappointed by the location and looked for a better one. But he realized this young widow didn't seem to mind, since the rental price was right. He said she could rent it for a year, or two, whatever she preferred, and renew it if the arrangement worked well for her.

"I think a year to start," she said without batting an eye, as Fabi-enne watched her, admiring how easily she pulled it off. "With an option to renew of course, if my children are happy there."

"I'm sure they will be, and the park nearby is very nice. Will they be going to school?" he inquired.

"They're tutored at home," she said demurely. "They're all girls." At least that much was true, since nothing else was. He told them there was a carriage house for two carriages around the corner, and she was pleased, since she didn't know how their clients would come. "With a room for your coachman," he added. And the four small rooms in the basement, next to the kitchen, were adequate for servants. It was a very fine house, he assured her.

"When may we see it?" she asked him.

"It's a little late in the day to see it now. I'd rather you see it in morning sunlight. I could take you there tomorrow." And he had an-other appointment that afternoon anyway. They made an appoint-ment for noon the next day, and after shaking hands, both young women left his office, and took a carriage for hire back to the hotel.

"My God, you're serious about this, aren't you?" Fabienne asked her, stunned by the hour they had just spent with the notaire. "I keep thinking I just dreamed it and I'm going to wake up." But Angélique was determined, with Fabienne's help, if she could find the right girls, which remained to be seen. But Angélique thought the house sounded like a gift from Heaven, or Hell, depending on how she looked at it, given what they were planning to do there. It sounded perfect for them.

"Of course I'm serious," Angélique said with a gleam in her eye.

"What are we going to do for furniture?"

"Buy it. That's the least of our worries. Now you have to find the girls, and the right ones. The kind of men we want as clients won't want girls off the streets. We have to find beautiful, intelligent girls who will fascinate them." She laughed to herself, thinking that Eugenia Ferguson would have been perfect. She was a beautiful woman of loose morals who liked men. But she was also tiresome and spoiled. They needed better girls than Eugenia. Angélique sensed that her clients would want women who enjoyed catering to men, and pleasing them. It was a life of service of a different kind— they had to be beautiful and elegant in the drawing room, and exotic when they went upstairs. She guessed it from some of the novels she enjoyed reading, and added the rest from her imagination. "Do you know where to start searching for them?" Angélique asked her as they got to the hotel.

"I'll need to go and talk to some people. I know one girl from Madame Albin's who's a sweet girl. She's young and pretty, and appears very innocent, but she isn't. The men who come to Madame Albin's love her. She makes all her clients feel important, and nothing seems to frighten her. And she isn't ruined by drink or drugs, she says she just likes what she's doing, and does it well."

"Remember, we'll need some other girls, slightly older, more sophisticated ones. These men will want to talk to them too. They have to be good listeners, playful, beautiful, elegant." She had exactly the kind of girl she wanted in mind. Fabienne could be one of the young sweet girls, but she wanted some enticing, mysterious women too. They walked into the hotel, talking about the house again, with their new bonnets in several large hatboxes. As soon as they got to the room, Fabienne put on her big beautiful pale blue one and pranced around the room, looking ecstatic, and thanked Angélique again.

"Thank you for being so good to me." She beamed at her new friend, and future employer.

"We're partners in crime now," Angélique told her, and put on one of her new hats too. They were like little girls playing dress-up with their mothers' clothes. But Angélique was taking her new role very seriously. She was going to establish the best bordel in town. Houses of its kind were legal, as was prostitution, as long as the prostitutes were registered with the gendarmerie, although the practice was frowned on by respectable citizens. But brothels had existed for hundreds of years, and the police paid no attention to them. All they would have to do was use discretion, and keep all their activities invisible behind their walls. And word would travel like wildfire if it was a good house and men wanted to come there. Angélique was determined to maintain high standards and make it more appealing to their clients than their clubs or homes. Angélique and Fabienne both knew that their clients were out there, just waiting for them. Now they needed to set up the house and locate the girls who would attract them like bees to honey.

Chapter 12

The next day, when the two girls went to see the house that had been described by the notaire, it was as perfect as Angélique had hoped, and she could envision just how it would be set up. It was referred to as an "hôtel particulier," a private home. The owners had left three chandeliers in the dining room, largest reception room, and front hall, and the rest of the house had to be decorated. Angélique had some experience with that from Belgrave, and what she'd seen at the Fergusons' two homes, but she wanted this to be warmer and more inviting, while still elegant, without spending a fortune on it. Entering the house had to be like a warm embrace, and so comfortable that the men wouldn't want to leave it, and would be anxious to return as soon as possible. Everything at the house had to go smoothly, and be set up for their clients' ultimate happiness.

Angélique told the notaire that they'd take it, once they had toured the entire house. It was clean and in good order, and as sunny as he had promised. Fabienne said they would put screens in each room, where the girls could do whatever they needed to with washbasins, out of sight. Angélique really didn't want to know those details. She preferred to take care of the grander scheme of things and the decorating project, while Fabienne found their "staff."

She told the notaire that she would return to his office with the money that afternoon. She preferred to pay in cash, and didn't tell him that she had to exchange British pounds for French francs. He wanted the first month's rent, which was quite reasonable. She went back to the hotel to get it, went to the bank with Fabienne, and their first month's rent was paid by that afternoon, and she had signed a lease for a year. In sympathy for her as a widow, he allowed her to do so on her own, and he asked for no proof of her status. She appeared to be entirely above reproach, and made no fuss over the money. He liked doing business that way, and said that the owner would be pleased to have rented it to such a nice family. A widow with six daughters.

Both girls were almost shaking with excitement when they left the notaire's office after paying for it and signing the lease. It was happening! The dream was becoming real, and very quickly. But they had so much to do now before they opened. They needed to buy furniture, and find servants. Two maids and a cook, Angélique decided, and they couldn't be shocked at what went on at the house. And a man to help, and protect them, and do the heavy work. And above all, Fabienne needed to find the girls they needed. That was key. The rest would be easy. But the women whose charms they would be offering had to be impeccably selected, and Angélique wanted to meet each of them and make the final decision. Fabienne knew women of the streets, and young girls, but Angélique knew far better the kind of men they'd be serving.

Fabienne began the search two days later. She sent a message to Juliette, the girl she'd mentioned at Madame Albin's, and asked to meet her somewhere. It took her five more days to get away on a pretext, and meet at a café, where she was surprised to see Fabienne look far more elegant than she had during her time at Madame Albin's. Juliette was stunned, as Fabienne described Angélique and her plan. She was eager to join them, and Fabienne arranged a meeting for her with Angélique. She found her a sweet girl, with an angelic innocence about her, who appeared younger than her eighteen years. But she could see the sensual woman under the surface too, and thought she had qualities that would appeal to some of their clients. Fabienne and Juliette could be the angelic young girls of the group, with greater knowledge of how to please a man than it appeared. But after that, she wanted racier women, and was counting on Fabienne to find them, which was no easy task. They told Juliette to bide her time at Madame Albin's, say nothing, and they would let her know when they were ready, they hoped in a month or two. Angélique wanted to do it right, and not hurry, although she was anxious to open their doors too.

Meanwhile she spent her days buying furniture and having it delivered to the house they'd rented. She bought ten large canopied beds in different places, and miles of fabric to cover them, which she did herself, and a smaller bed for herself. She bought nightstands, dressers, comfortable chairs in silks and satins, rugs for every room, including the reception rooms, oil lamps, a handsome English dining table and chairs, and divinely comfortable couches and Egyptian benches to recline on for the drawing room, where she could imagine the girls lounging as they talked to their clients before they went upstairs. She bought two card tables for the drawing room, and beautiful heavy damask curtains. The house was coming together nicely, and she was spending her father's money, but keeping good track of it, and staying within the budget she had set for herself. And the house was starting to look beautiful, warm, and opulent, as the pieces arrived, and she wanted the lighting to be just right at night, so that it would be romantic and flattering. And she bought a multitude of mirrors for the drawing room and bedrooms. And Fabienne showed her how to place them strategically in the bedrooms. They were doing all the work themselves, and as the furniture began arriving, even for the maids' bedrooms, the two women agreed that they needed a man to help them. The furniture was heavy, the curtains hard for them to hang, and they couldn't do it all alone, although Angélique was working magic. She had even found a few pieces she loved for her own rooms, which reminded her of her bedroom in Belgrave, the one Gwyneth had stolen from her when she arrived, with her parents' blessing. This time Angélique was in the attic by choice, but in a lovely suite of rooms no one would ever see but herself, away from the girls. And she bought a few simple paintings that she loved, by unknown French artists, which cost almost nothing.

They looked in the newspaper for a man to hire, and interviewed several. It was a delicate business telling each prospect that he would be protecting a houseful of women, but not telling him what they'd be doing. Several asked if it was a school, or a boardinghouse, but the last one they saw asked them nothing, and he and Fabienne instantly liked each other. He had broad shoulders and a strong back, came from the South as she did, and spoke the same patois. He said he had grown up on a farm and had four sisters and no brothers. His father had died when he was young, and he was used to being the only man in the house with a flock of women. His name was Jacques, and when they showed him the house, he followed Fabienne like a puppy. He didn't mind the small spare room in the carriage house, and Angélique explained to him that he would need to be discreet about whatever went on in the main house. She tried to feel him out for his values, and was relieved when he said he wasn't religious. One of his sisters was a nun, and he thought she was misguided. The others were married and had children.

"There will be men here, not just women," Angélique said, watching him intently. "Perhaps many men. And some very beautiful women." He asked if it was going to be a hotel, and she said no. And as he looked at her, she saw the light dawn in his eyes, and he said he understood. He was not as innocent as he appeared. He seemed worried for a minute and then nodded, and then asked her a question.

"Fabienne too?" He had a decided soft spot for her, which Angélique was not sure was a good idea, if he fell in love with her, and was jealous. It was a complication they didn't need.

"Yes, Fabienne too," she said definitely, and he nodded.

"I understand. It's a job like any other. We all have to make a living," he said seriously, and she could see that he meant it. They hired him immediately, and he was an enormous help, moving furniture, carrying things that arrived, hanging curtains and paintings, and assisting Angélique as she set up the bedrooms, while Fabienne conducted her search for the women.

The first few Fabienne met, through other women she knew,

weren't interested. They liked the arrangements they had, and didn't want to join a house so recently set up by women who weren't experienced at running a brothel. Fabienne told them they would be properly registered at the gendarmerie, and protected and paid fairly, but it wasn't enough to entice them. But they referred her to some others who were dissatisfied with their pimps or madams. And two girls seemed like good possibilities to her, and intrigued Angélique.

One was obviously from a good French family, and for whatever reason had chosen a very different path from her bourgeois sisters and parents. At twenty-four, she had been a prostitute for seven years, looked like a lady and apparently wasn't. And she made it clear that some of the more "exotic" requests of her clients appealed to her. She said casually that she used a small whip, and was an expert at bondage. She never injured her clients or allowed them to hurt her, but she was more than willing to experiment with new "techniques," and said she had a large collection of sexual aids. Angélique tried to look nonchalant about it, although she was somewhat unnerved by her. But she was a beautiful woman, and she was very erotic and appealing in a subtle, sensual way. Her name was Ambre, and she had worn a very elegant dress to the meeting, which showed that she knew how to dress well. Ambre had jet black hair and smoldering eyes, and was a tall woman with long legs and big breasts. She had been working alone for a while near the Palais Royal, and said she preferred a house, and hadn't found one she liked. What Angélique was doing had piqued her interest, and she could see that Angélique was intelligent, and liked that about her. She wanted to be in a house that was run like a business. She charged a fairly high rate because of her unusual specialties. And she had none of the seeming innocence of Fabienne and Juliette. She said she enjoyed her work, and was said to be skilled at her trade. Angélique told her she would be welcome to join them, and Fabienne approved when they talked about it later.

"She scares me a little," Fabienne admitted. "She's very cold. But I think some men like that."

"Apparently," Angélique said, feeling a little overwhelmed by the meeting, but pleased with their decision.

The other girl Fabienne thought was a possibility was a slightly round, very jovial girl with a great sense of humor and a quick wit, who had fled the convent in Bordeaux her parents had sent her to, and come to Paris on her own. She was twenty-two, had a warm personality, and seemed like everyone's favorite sister. Her name was Philippine, and Angélique enjoyed meeting her. She was a pretty blonde with a lovely face, slim legs, and a huge bosom, which Fabienne said men would want to dive into, and she was intelligent too.

"I didn't know if she looked fancy enough for you," Fabienne said, worried. There was a straightforward, open quality to her that Angélique liked.

"She's fun to talk to. Some men will really love that. And we can dress her up elegantly. She's very pretty. It's not a problem." They had laughed through the whole interview, and she had a lovely singing voice, could play the piano, and had sung in the convent choir. It reminded Angélique that she needed to buy a piano for the drawing room. They hired Philippine too, which left them four more women to find. They had half the number they needed now.

The next girl Fabienne located was an Ethiopian woman, with coffee-colored skin, delicate features, and huge green eyes. She had been sold into slavery by her father at a young age, brought to Paris by the family who bought her, and abandoned, and had been fending for herself ever since. She was nineteen, and the most exquisite girl of all. Her name was Yaba, and she added another kind of exoticism to the group they were trying to form. With Yaba, they now had five.

Angélique and Fabienne agreed that they could open the house with six women, but they both preferred the idea of eight, to give the men more choices, and the girls could linger with them longer that way, without rushing to the next client. And ultimately, since they had enough bedrooms, Angélique thought they could have ten. But eight was her goal for now.

It took several weeks for Fabienne to meet two more girls. One of them was suggested by Philippine. She was a beautiful flaming redhead named Agathe, she was a little older than the others, more sophisticated, and she'd had a patron who recently died, so she wanted to join a house again. He had been a politician, and she had interesting connections with the men around him, and said she would bring several clients with her. She was a true courtesan. They invited her to join them too.

Agathe recommended a friend to them, who also had the potential to bring them many clients. She had started as an actress on the stage, and found prostitution more lucrative. She had a star quality about her, and like Agathe was twenty-five years old, and had a strong self-assured presence, while remaining accessible. Her name was Camille, and she was a blonde with big blue eyes. She was every inch a star.

They were just debating if seven girls were enough, when Ambre, who preferred exotic practices and whips, contacted them to say she had met someone they might be interested in hiring. She was Japanese, had gotten stranded in Paris, when jilted by a man she'd been engaged to, and was too ashamed to go back to Japan to her relatives. She had disappeared into the underworld in Paris, but had been trained as a geisha before she left Japan. She sounded intriguing, and when Angélique met her, she looked like a little doll, and was even smaller than Angélique. She wore a traditional kimono, and spoke adequate French. She was a shy woman, but a long conversation about the art of being a geisha fascinated Angélique. She would be the last touch of exoticism they needed. She was twenty-two, and her name was Hiroko. They had someone for every male taste now, Asian, African, European, tall, small, bold, shy, Philippine with her sense of humor, and Ambre with her fondness for bondage. They had everyone they needed.

And with Jacques's help, the house was finally ready to move into. Fabienne and Angélique contacted all seven women and invited them to arrive as soon as possible to settle into their rooms. And Angélique wanted to take them to buy clothes and have some made. She wanted them to have fabulous lingerie, and the kind of evening gowns worthy of their clients. Agathe said she already had several, but Angélique wanted them all exquisitely dressed, their hair done perfectly. She wanted all eight of them to be a vision of beauty the moment a man stepped through the door. She had told Hiroko that for now she could wear her kimonos, which would be exciting too.

Over a span of a week, the women arrived with bags and trunks and boxes, and at last they had all moved in. Fabienne and Angélique had moved out of the hotel several weeks before. Fabienne had been allowed to pick the room she wanted, and Angélique was upstairs in the attic. And the others selected their rooms as they arrived, and each of them added little personal touches to their rooms. Juliette had a little stuffed bear on her bed, and Ambre had a small whip and riding crop hanging next to hers. Everyone seemed happy with the setup and loved the house. And Angélique had hired a young cook and two maids to serve them.

"I feel like I died and went to Heaven," Philippine said the first time they all had supper together in the dining room, at the handsome new table, which seated twenty. The girls and their clients could even dine there. Jacques ate his meals in the kitchen with the cook and maids. And everyone seemed comfortable with the kind of business they were going to run there. It was no longer a secret, except outside the house. But within it, the employees they had hired were clear.

After the meal, Philippine and Camille sang for them at the new piano, and the girls all joined in, and Angélique informed them that they were going shopping the next day, and there was excited conversation among them. It was like a boarding school full of girls. Everyone was in great spirits and couldn't wait to begin receiving their clients.

Fabienne and Angélique smiled at each other. "We did it," Angélique said to Fabienne, as she admired the women they'd chosen, chatting with each other between songs.

"No, *you* did it," Fabienne said gratefully, still amazed at how smoothly it had all gone, with Angélique's impeccable organization and boundless energy.

"All I did was the decorating. We'd have an empty house if you hadn't found the girls."

"You did a lot more than decorate." She had fronted all the money, and the girls had agreed to their rates, and the amount they would be paid. Angélique was going to pay them half of what they earned, which they all agreed was extremely generous. No one had ever done that for them before.

"We're going to be the talk of Paris," Agathe said pleasantly. She had already contacted her late patron's friends, and invited them to join her there when they opened, even if just to look around and share a meal. Angélique wanted them to feel welcome and comfortable, and said she didn't mind if they didn't go upstairs at first, until they met and liked the girls. She hoped it would be more than just a brothel—she envisioned it almost like a salon, until they got upstairs, where it was so much more. Camille and Ambre had contacted their regulars as well, and had much to contribute. They all did, each in her special way.

"And you, Angélique, will you be entertaining clients?" Ambre asked her in her very direct way, as Angélique shook her head.

"No, I won't. I'll talk to the men in the drawing room, and entertain them with you, but I'll be running the place, and working in other ways." Ambre nodded, and none of the girls seemed to mind. She wasn't exploiting them like most madams, she was opening doors to them to better clients than they'd ever had—at least that was Ambre's hope.

"What are we calling the house?" Yaba asked her. There was a flurry of conversation after that, with assorted suggestions, and the one they all liked best was "Le Boudoir," which had a sensual intimate ring to it, without being bawdy. And Angélique liked it too.

She took them shopping the next day, with all of them in two carriages Jacques hired for them for the afternoon. There was an old one in the carriage house, which was serviceable but not elegant enough to use. And Angélique was shocked when they arrived at a dressmaker's shop she had been told about and the woman who ran it refused to serve them and asked them to leave. She knew exactly what they were and wanted no part of it. It reminded Angélique that the polite world would not be amused by her new business, no matter how well she ran it, or how pretty the girls were. They had all dressed respectably for the outing, but they were a little too beautiful, a little exotic, and a little too exuberant. They didn't have the pinched look of bourgeois housewives, and even women in the street looked at them with disapproval while men stared.

They went to another shop then that she and Fabienne had been to before. They had some very pretty things, and even though the woman who ran it understood who and what she was dealing with, she was happy to serve them, and thanked them for their business. She was very polite, and gracious to the girls. And after that, they went to a store for corsets and lacy underwear, where they all went wild. As much as they were excited by the evening gowns they would be wearing in the drawing room, and one or two day dresses to wear, they needed what went under them far more. They came away with fabulous things in silks and satins, some with exotic openings, lace, garters, tiny corsets, and every kind of item to enhance their already beautiful bodies, and Philippine convinced Angélique to buy one set of satin and lace underthings for herself.

"No one will ever see it," Angélique said practically, laughing.

"Oh, don't be such a nun," Philippine teased her. "You could be run over by a carriage, and think how exciting it will be when you go to the hospital and they see your underthings! Come on, be one of us." She was so funny about it that Angélique bought it along with all the rest, and claimed it when they got back to the house, and the girls each took their pile of treasures.

The girls all modeled their new finery for each other, and they decided to have a dress rehearsal that night for supper, and wear their new evening gowns.

When they came downstairs for supper, Angélique thought she had never seen a more spectacular-looking group of women and knew she had made the right choices. She was relieved to see that all of them had good table manners. All eight of them behaved like ladies, no matter what profession they had decided on for whatever reason. And she was proud of them.

She had worn the one truly fine evening gown she had brought from Belgrave, in a rich blue velvet, with her mother's sapphires at her ears and around her throat, and all the women told her how beautiful she was, and were impressed. They were proud of her too.

"You look like a princess," Camille said generously, and meant it, and Angélique corrected her, laughing, before she could stop the words.

"No, just a duchess." And as soon as she said it, she was shocked at herself and regretted the words.

"What do you mean?" Agathe asked her pointedly.

"Nothing. I was just being silly."

"No, you weren't," they persisted. They had all sensed some mystery about her from the first. "Tell us the truth. Are you a duchess?" She hesitated for a moment, but she knew all of their stories, about where they came from, why they were there, and how they had come to this way of life. They might as well know hers.

"No, I'm not a duchess," she said honestly. "I'm only a lady. But my father was a duke. My brother inherited the title and the estate, according to British law, and the family fortune, all of it, except for a small house on the estate that went to my other brother. As a woman in England, I inherited nothing, neither the property, nor the title, nor the money. My mother was a duchess, married to my father, and her father was a French marquis. And when my father died, my brother sent me away to people he knew, to work as a nanny, and pretended that we were only distant cousins. So I have nothing, and I am nothing. My brother's wife is the Duchess of Westerfield. I am not," she said humbly.

"So how did you pay for all this?" Juliette asked her shyly, which the others had wondered too.

"My father gave me a gift before he died, which was meant to last me for the rest of my life, if I ever needed it. This is not what he intended me to do with it, to say the least. But hopefully we will all make money at it, and can eventually retire. In the meantime, thanks to my father we're all here."

"Le Boudoir de la Duchesse!" Philippine shouted enthusiastically, renaming the house as the others added their approval. "And to hell with your sister-in-law. You will be the Duchess to us. You really should be a princess, but Duchess will do." They all looked pleased, and Angélique was amused.

"When do we open?" Ambre wanted to know. They had their costumes now, the house looked impeccable, and all the girls were there. Angélique had registered all of them at the gendarmerie. There was no reason to wait.

"Why don't you all rest tomorrow?" Angélique suggested to them. "And we'll open the next day." It had taken two months for the entire process. "You can send messages to your clients tomorrow, and ask them to bring their friends to have a look. They're not obliged to do anything when they get here except meet all of you and get to know the place. We will open officially the day after tomorrow," she announced, having just decided it. And she raised her glass to all of them. "To you, ladies! Thank you for being here." She smiled at them, grateful that they believed in her.

"To the Duchess!" they said in unison, and raised their glasses to her.

Chapter 13

As promised, the girls who had clients alerted them that the house was now open, and for three terrifying weeks, no one came. The girls put on evening gowns every night, draped themselves on the furniture in the drawing room, in gentle candlelight, while Jacques stood at the door in livery, waiting to admit their guests, and not a single one of their clients showed up. Angélique was panicking, and by the end of the second week, the girls were depressed.

Not knowing what else to do, she took them all to the Louvre one afternoon, and for a walk in the park. She took them all to dinner at a restaurant called Maison Catherine on the Place du Tertre in Montmartre, where proper women stared them down, and people glanced at them with icy expressions, guessing what they were, no matter how well dressed they were, or perhaps because of it. And the nights continued to be painfully long with no men in the room. The girls played cards, Philippine entertained them with jokes, Camille played the piano, and Angélique tried to calm everyone down and assure them that the men would come in time, and prayed that she was right. The men they wanted as clients were busy people and had careers to pursue and lives to arrange. And then, finally, miraculously after three endless weeks, in the first week of June, one of Agathe's contacts arrived, and brought a friend. They were acquaintances of her late patron, and high-up political men. And when they walked into the drawing room of Le Boudoir, they were astounded by what they saw. Nine spectacularly beautiful women in elegant gowns, one of them wearing handsome jewels, and all of them with smiles that welcomed them.

"My, my," Alphonse Cardin said, looking around, happy to see Agathe again. They had come only out of curiosity, but were enchanted by the ladies in the drawing room. They drank and played cards with them, smoked cigars as they were welcome to do, and since no one else came that night, Angélique quietly mentioned to Mr. Cardin that he was welcome to take as many girls upstairs with him as he liked, or try them all, as a gift from her this first time. He looked thrilled, and he and his friend each chose four, and Angélique found herself alone in the drawing room, looking pleased. Both gentlemen stayed until six in the morning. She had gone to bed by then, but Cardin was kind enough to send her a note the next day with a magnum of champagne. The note said, "Bravo, ma chèrie! Merci. A.C." His night had apparently been a great success, as had his friend's, who had a preference for the exotic, and had been with Ambre, once her specialties were explained to him, as well as Yaba, Hiroko, and Agathe. He had enjoyed them all so much that he told Cardin he had no idea which, or how many, he would select again, although he wanted to try the girls Alphonse had been with too, who he said had been sublime. They were younger and more light-hearted, and didn't take things quite as seriously as the other group. It had been his friend's first experience being expertly and deliciously whipped, and he wanted to come back for more.

Alphonse had discreetly asked Angélique if she would be joining them—she would have been his first choice. And with a demurely sensual look, she told him that no, she wouldn't, which only made him more determined to convince her otherwise in the future. Fabienne complimented her the next day that she had done that very well. "They're all going to want you," she said, "because you refuse them." Angélique laughed in response, but she was delighted the night had gone well, and pleased with herself that she had thought to offer it to them as a gift. The girls reported to Angélique that the men had been extremely pleased and promised to return soon. Now they would be able to tell their friends how good the girls were, since between them they had been with them all, and sampled the wares of Le Boudoir lavishly.

Both men came back the following night, and every night for a week, taking two or three of the girls upstairs with them, or one by one. By the end of the week, other men had come, having heard from Cardin and his friend how terrific the house was, how elegant the madam, and how pleasant the furnishings, and what an interesting assortment the women were. Their friends and acquaintances wanted to see for themselves, and within two weeks, the house was crowded every night. Their guests were paying handsomely for the girls' services, and Angélique was keeping close track of the books. They were making a lot of money, serving light meals in the dining room, some played cards with the girls for a while, getting to know them, others wanted to talk, and a great many of them went directly upstairs with the girl of their choice. And a surprising number of their clients had a marked preference for Ambre and her specialties, which she apparently did extremely well, sometimes wearing nothing but a pair of riding boots.

The men who began frequenting Le Boudoir were exactly what Angélique had wanted right from the beginning. Political figures whose names were well known, bankers, lawyers, aristocrats, men with enormous fortunes willing to pay almost any price for the right women who could arouse them. The evenings began like an elegant party with impressive men and beautiful women, and thinned out quickly, as their guests disappeared with the girls. Some stayed for a short time, others longer. Several said immediately that they wanted to spend the night, though not many were able to do that with wives they had to go home to, unless they were at their country homes with the children. But the house was alive until five and six every morning, and the girls slept until one o'clock the next day. And every Sunday afternoon, Angélique paid out to them their half of what they had made the previous week, with meticulous lists of which clients they had been with on what night. All the girls agreed they had never made as much in their lives, as quickly and easily, and been paid so handsomely. Angélique had set her fees high, in anticipation of who would be coming. They wanted no paupers among their guests but only men with fortunes, and not one of them balked at her prices, or complained about the value of what they got. They came back again and again for more.

And as their wives left for the seaside or the country, or their châteaux in Périgord and Dordogne in July, and the men stayed in the city, allegedly to work, and dally, the house was more crowded than

ever, and business was booming. Angélique even mentioned to Fabienne that she thought they should get two more girls. The women
they had were constantly in demand, and some of the men had to
wait an hour or two in the drawing room for the girl they wanted to
be free. And while they did, Angélique entertained them, and became acquainted with many of them. Much to her own amazement,
she had found a profession that suited her. She didn't want to think
of what her father would have thought of it, but necessity had driven
her to it, with the Fergusons firing her without a character unjustly,
and the disastrous situation her brother had put her in. At least she
was not one of the women working in the bedrooms, she was the
madam, which was slightly more respectable, and her virginity was
intact. And there was no question in anyone's mind, the girls' or the
clients', she was a lady of distinction, and an aristocrat to the core.
The girls called her the Duchess, and some of the clients had picked
it up, while many wondered if it was true, and she denied it, since
she wasn't, despite her noble lineage, but only the daughter and
sister of a duke, and the granddaughter of a marquis on her mother's
side in France, which she didn't explain to their clients, but she had
the grace and demeanor of a duchess, no matter how often she
claimed not to be one. And none of the clients suspected how young
she was. She stuck to her invented story that she was twenty-six,
and they believed her. No one would have imagined her to be a girl
of twenty, given the enterprise she was running so smoothly. Even
the girls who worked for her didn't know her real age, except Fabienne, who kept it a secret.

Fabienne had continued to flirt with Jacques, when she had the
opportunity, but now that she was working constantly, she was too

busy to pursue it. He was her willing slave and did whatever she wished, and Angélique kept a watchful eye on them to make sure it went no further, and so far it hadn't.

The names of many of the men in the drawing room were familiar to Angélique. They were men of power, many of them part of the current Bourbon government that had followed Bonaparte, when Charles X took the throne and restored the monarchy. The heads of several banks were there, and she enjoyed talking finance with them, and learning from them. And in the first week of August, an imposing man arrived one night with a group of friends. He looked familiar to her, and she couldn't place his face. It was Agathe, with her political connections, who told her who he was. She knew many of the politicians through her previous patron, and they came for her at first, and then discovered the others whom they liked as well.

"Do you know who that is?" she whispered to Angélique, impressed herself for once, as they played cards. Angélique admitted she didn't know, and couldn't place the face. He had piercing eyes, an almost military bearing, and was strikingly handsome, with a chiseled face. "He's the minister of the interior," Agathe told her. "It's a big statement that he's here. He's very careful where he goes. He doesn't like anyone to know what he's up to." He had identified himself only as Thomas, by first name only, which was an invented alias. But everyone knew who he was. He didn't need to use his real name and was known to be a secretive person, which went with his job.

"Do you know him?" Angélique asked, impressed.

"We've met," Agathe said softly, "but I didn't invite him here. I don't know him well enough for that. Someone must have told him about us." Both women noticed him carefully looking around the room, observing who was there, while smoking a cigar.

Angélique watched him circle the room and chat with some of the men. He smiled at the women, but didn't engage them in conversation, and then she saw him watching her, and she nodded her head in acknowledgment, and he smiled. And a little while later, after Agathe had gone upstairs with one of her clients, he came over to sit next to her.

"So you are the Duchess all of Paris is talking about," he said softly, his eyes drinking her in. "Is the title real?"

"It is, but never destined to be mine," she told him honestly, as their eyes met and held. She could feel him near her, with an almost electric charge.

"Whose then?"

"My father's, and now my brother's."

"Ah," he said, even more intrigued. "You're British," he guessed, although one couldn't hear it in her flawless French.

"Half. My mother was French."

"And on her side, equally blue blood?" He was fascinated by her, and could see how highborn she was. He couldn't imagine what she was doing here, running the house. For a girl of her birth to be running a brothel seemed unthinkable, but she ran it with the grace of a dinner party.

"Bourbon and Orléans," she answered, which were both of the royal houses of France.

"I've been hearing about you," he said, mesmerized by her.

"Good things, I hope," she said demurely, her eyes never leaving his. She didn't try to avoid his intense gaze, and he liked that about her too.

"Only good things. I'm told that you don't go upstairs with the clients, and have the best girls in the city."

"I tried to put together an interesting group, in a pleasant atmosphere," she said modestly, and he smiled at her warmly.

"I'd say you've succeeded. I like it here, and so do my friends. Everyone feels at home here."

"That was my goal. I hope you'll come to see us often." She smiled invitingly at him, but not so much as to mislead him. She was exquisitely elegant and well bred in her manner as well as dress, and yet gentle and warm at the same time. He had never met a woman who intrigued him more.

"And if I do, will you come upstairs with me? As a special arrangement?" He was asking her to be his mistress in no uncertain terms, and she understood it perfectly. She had learned a lot in the past three months that she had never dreamed of before. And she could tell he was serious by the way he spoke to her.

"It would spoil our friendship if I did," she said quietly, with obvious respect.

"Are we to be friends then?" he asked, raising an eyebrow, hopeful and disappointed all at the same time. She was setting limits in advance.

"That's up to you, but I hope so. You are always welcome here," she said graciously. He looked satisfied for the moment, but not entirely. She wondered if he would actually have gone upstairs with her if she'd allowed it, but knew instinctively she would have been a fool to do so. He was much too dangerous and powerful to toy with, or be dependent on. He was far more valuable to her as an ally, protector, and friend, if he became that. And Agathe had told her he went to the best brothels often, but never went upstairs with the girls. But Angélique had a strong sense that he would have made an exception for her, and perhaps would have come back after hours, if she'd let him. "Thomas" was thoroughly enthralled and enchanted by her, and sat talking to her for a long time. He eventually bade her goodnight politely with a deep bow, and left, promising to return soon.

He appeared again a week later, and had supper in the dining room with her. The crowd had thinned by then, as everyone left Paris for summer holidays, and he said he had stayed in town to work.

"You're welcome to join me for supper anytime," Angélique reiterated her earlier invitation to him, and after that, he took her up on it, and came to dine with her, or visit her, or simply sit in the drawing room with her for a while several times a week, sometimes as often as four or five. He couldn't stay away from her, and they loved talking to each other. He described what they shared as an "amitié amoureuse," a "romantic friendship," or a loving one. It involved the meshing of their minds in their exchanges, with a constant aura of flirtation and romance that she allowed to go nowhere except the drawing room. He respected her for that. Their admiration of each other was mutual, and richer for its limitations. He treated her like the lady she was, and not a madam.

"Why this?" he asked her one day about the house and how it had come about.

"It's a long story, the usual sad tale about a property and title entailed in England, a jealous half-brother who was determined to get rid of me and succeeded, and sent me off to be a servant in someone's home."

"And you'd rather die than become a servant?" he teased her as she shook her head.

"Not at all. I was shocked at first, but I came to enjoy it. I was a nanny to six young children, and would have stayed, but one of their friends tried to take advantage of me. I rebuffed him, so he lied to them and said I tried to seduce him, which wasn't true. I bit him when he tried. They sent me away the next day without a character, and I could get no domestic job in London, or Paris when I came here. I met Fabienne then, one of the girls here, who had been beaten and dumped in a gutter, and I took her in and nursed her. And when she told me about her life, I got the idea of a house where women are protected, respected, and well paid, serving exciting, interesting, powerful men who deserve to be with charming, beautiful women"—she smiled at him—"and treat them well. I pay the girls half of everything we make, and use the rest to run the house, and put money aside for the future," she said wisely. "It's working very nicely." She looked pleased, and he was visibly impressed.

"And you preside over all of it, and engage in none of it, and don't judge them, or any of us." He had noticed that about her. She was kind to everyone, but had eyes of steel that saw all. She had that in common with him, nothing escaped his intense gaze, no matter how relaxed he seemed. "You're a remarkable woman." And then he thought of something. "How old are you, really?"

"I told you, I'm twenty-six," she said, smiling.

"Why is it that I don't believe you?" he said in a low tone so no one would hear him, as he watched her gently.

"Because it's not true," she lowered her voice to match his, and hesitated only for the fraction of an instant. She trusted him—they were indeed becoming friends. "I'm twenty, but even the girls here don't know that, except Fabienne."

"You are an amazing, amazing girl," he said admiringly. "And you must be very careful that no one ever tries to hurt you, or destroy you. If they do, I want you to come to me immediately. Paris is a dangerous place these days. Many people are unhappy with the government, they think that Charles is weak and doesn't understand his subjects. Prices are high, and so is unemployment. Finances are poor. There will be trouble at some point, but not for a while. I will warn you," he promised. "And there are some who will be jealous of you, if you succeed too well at this." He gestured around the room. And then he thought of something else. "Would you meet me for a midday meal sometime, in a discreet place?" He liked keeping his personal activities private, to a reasonable degree.

"I'd love to," she said, smiling at him. She knew that he was married, but was never seen with his wife publicly, like so many of the men she knew now. Someone had mentioned to her that his wife had been ill for years.

Thomas stood up to leave then, and smiled down at her. "I always enjoy talking to you."

"And I with you," she said honestly. He was more than twice her age, but by far the most exciting man who came there. And he never went upstairs. And she knew now he never would.

She didn't see him again after that for a while, and heard he had gone on holiday in Brittany, but she knew he would be back. Of that, she was sure.

Chapter 14

In September, when everyone came back from their vacations, Le Boudoir had been open and business had been booming for four months. They had had a regular stream of clients even over the summer, and their reputation was firmly established by then. Her friend "Thomas," the minister of the interior, had been telling the truth when he said that the Duchess was the talk of Paris. People didn't know who she was or where she had come from, but they said she was a breathtaking young woman, and every important man had been to Le Boudoir, and once they'd been, they went frequently, and couldn't stay away from the cozy, intimate atmosphere she had created and the outstanding women who worked there. She had chosen well.

Angélique had been hoping to find two more girls but hadn't seen any so far that she wanted to join them, although they had spoken to several. Her standards were high, and she wanted the approval of the other women to make sure that they were comfortable with them too. All the women in the house liked each other and got along, which was important to her.

She interviewed a girl on a September afternoon, who worked at a well-known house that had been the most popular one until Le Boudoir opened and Angélique appeared on the scene. It was run by a madam who was said to be a dragon. She no longer served the clients herself, but was said to have been very skilled in her time. And the girl Angélique interviewed that afternoon had sought her out, and said she wanted to get away from her house and madam. She said they paid her next to nothing, and the caliber of the men who went there had slipped. All the great men were at Le Boudoir now. But Angélique didn't like the girl. She thought she had a vulgar quality to her, and was common, which was the last thing she wanted in the house. Not with the kind of men they entertained there.

The usual party in the drawing room was in full swing that night, when there was a heavy knocking on the door. Angélique didn't hear it, with someone playing the piano, but Jacques did and opened the door, as four heavyset men pushed past him. They looked like thugs off the street, and an extremely blowzy, strident woman strode into the drawing room right behind them.

"Where is she?" she shouted, as the music stopped. "Where is this Duchess you're all talking about?" She looked at the men in white tie and tails in the drawing room, and recognized only a few of them. The cream of le tout Paris had never gone to her, but mostly the nouveau riche, men with fortunes, but not of noble birth. Angélique had all of the elite. The moment they saw her, they knew she was the real thing, whether her title was real or not. They neither knew nor cared about that, but she seemed genuine to them, and very charming.

"I believe you're asking for me," Angélique said quietly as she stepped forward, a tiny figure in a beautiful gray evening gown with her back straight and her head held high. She looked more like a queen. The minister of the interior was watching—he had just been talking to her—and waited to see what would happen. He was like a tiger ready to spring. Angélique didn't notice as she addressed the woman. "Who are you, and why are you here?"

"You know who I am. Antoinette Alençon. Madame Antoinette. You tried to steal one of my girls today," she said, sounding vulgar, as Angélique faced her with courteous disdain.

"Not at all," Angélique said coolly. "I told her to go back to you. I have no wish to hire her. Now please remove yourself from my drawing room. There is a private party under way." The thugs around the older woman coiled as though ready to strike, but weren't sure at whom. And Jacques was no match for them. Angélique prayed that they would attack no one in the drawing room, or cause them to send for the police. She wanted no notoriety of that kind for the house.

"She told me you offered to pay her more, and tried to get me to increase her wage."

"That is neither true nor of any interest to me. Goodnight, madame. Please take your friends and leave." She stood staring the woman down, as no one moved in the room. No one wanted to be involved in a scandal, or even worse, a brawl. And turning on her heel, Madame Antoinette gave a signal to her henchmen, and they followed her out the door, which Jacques closed and locked behind them, as everyone in the room heaved a sigh of relief.

"Good lord, what an awful woman," Angélique said, laughing, to conceal her trembling knees. She whispered to one of the maids to pour champagne for everyone, and more for those already drinking it. She then went on as though nothing had happened, and everyone relaxed, as her powerful friend came to stand next to her.

"Well done, my dear," Thomas whispered, and they exchanged a warm, affectionate look. They had had dinner several times by then and had gotten to know each other better. He had told her of his wife's long illness in an asylum, and she sensed his loneliness. He lived only for his work. She was flattered by his confidences, and loved his explanations of politics. And had he been single, and their lives different, she would have been happy to be more than his friend. But she had made it clear to him that could not be. She didn't want to be any man's mistress, and he accepted that from her. He loved being with her, and they went for long walks together in the Tuileries Gardens, with her small hand tucked into his arm. She was always exquisitely dressed when she had dinner with him, and was truly the most beautiful woman he knew. She already had a reputation for wearing the most fashionable clothes, and she dressed her girls well too. There was none of the vulgarity of other women of their kind. There was nothing shocking about them except upstairs, where it belonged, which had been her intention all along. "Are you all right?" he asked after the intrusion, and she nodded, but he could tell she had been frightened and covered it well. It reminded him of how brave she was. The four men Madame Antoinette had brought with her had looked dangerous to all of them, and probably were. And she clearly hadn't expected the reception she'd gotten, and had no bone to pick there.

"Of course, I'm fine." Angélique brushed it off to him. She didn't want her other clients upset.

"I want you to get a second man. The one you have isn't enough.

Something like that could happen again, or worse. You never know. We're all gentlemen here, but you can't predict when the wrong sort will wander in. I don't want anything to happen to you." His concern for her and affection showed in his eyes.

"I know everyone here," she reassured him, looking around.

"So do I." He smiled at her. "But please get a second man."

"I will," she promised. He left shortly after, he rarely stayed too long, but he came only to see her, and talk to her. He always had work he had to attend to, and secret missions he couldn't tell her about, and she knew not to ask.

As promised, she had Jacques find another man to work with him, which he thought was sensible too. They shared the room in the carriage house, and Jacques didn't mind. He was always kind and willing to do anything he could to help. And the appearance of the four tough men in the drawing room had worried him too. He agreed that it would be better with two. Luc, the man they hired, was young, barely more than a boy, but he was huge. He was a blacksmith's son, so he was good with the horses, but more than anything, he was an imposing figure with Jacques at the door, which made everyone, clients and girls alike, feel more secure, as well as Angélique.

As it turned out, the protection they needed was not outside, but upstairs. A school friend of one of their favorite clients, a regular of Yaba's, came with him one night for the first time, after his friend had raved about Le Boudoir. And the new client was particularly intrigued by the services of Ambre, when he heard that she was well versed with her small whip, and willing to tie him to the bed. He had been very pleasant in the drawing room, and rather meek, and had gone upstairs with her. They were absent for a long time, which no one thought unusual, until Ambre crawled out of her room on all fours, barely conscious and dripping blood. It was the first time one of the girls had gotten hurt, and they were horrified, as were the clients in the hall who saw it and rushed to help her. One of the men in the drawing room was a doctor and came upstairs to care for her. Apparently before she could apply a flick of the whip or use any of her tantalizing toys, he had beaten her to within an inch of her life with his fists, and punished her in every way he could. Before he could say a word, the other clients, who'd seen the condition Ambre was in, dragged him down the stairs and threw him into the street. They were appalled at what had happened. Many of them knew who he was. The friend who had brought him apologized profusely to Angélique and left a huge sum of money especially for Ambre. It was a very bad night.

Angélique went out of her way to reassure everyone the next day. And she and the girls discussed installing some kind of alarm system that would ring a bell, or a whistle they could keep, to use if any of them were in trouble, but nothing like it had ever happened before, and was unlikely to again. They knew who all of their clients were, and all of them were so kind. It took Ambre two weeks to recover, and everyone cheered when they saw her in the drawing room again. She knew she was among friends. All of the girls had taken care of her, just as Angélique had done for Fabienne when they first met.

To reward and cheer them up after Ambre's incident, Angélique took them shopping again. She wanted to keep their wardrobes fresh, and the house had a reputation for being fashionable, which she wanted to maintain. And this time, when they went to some of the best shops, there were no snubs or slights. Shopkeepers recognized Angélique, from having sold expensive gowns to her, and they welcomed her patronage and that of the girls. She spent a huge sum of money on their clothes and her own. But the house had become extremely profitable in a short time. Mountains of boxes arrived at the house after their shopping spree, and they were thrilled with their new gowns, and even more new lingerie. And they had selected a pile of gifts for Ambre as well. Angélique had become known as the most generous madam in town, and girls were clamoring to work for her, but she was extremely careful about who she hired. She still wanted two more girls, but hadn't found the right ones.

Despite their caution about who they let into the house, an unfamiliar American appeared in late September, referred by one of their best clients. He said he was in Paris on business, and had been told about Le Boudoir by his friend. He was an older, distinguished-looking, white-haired man, and appeared to be a man of substance. He said his name was John Carson, which the letter confirmed. But Angélique had an odd feeling about him. And he seemed to feel uncomfortable being there, as Americans sometimes were. Angélique had noticed that before—many of them were far more puritanical than the French. He looked nervous at first, and Angélique spent time putting him at ease. He finally relaxed and chatted with her. They talked mostly about politics and business, and avoided personal subjects, but she had seen immediately that he was wearing a wedding ring. After an hour in his company, she casually introduced him to some of the girls, but by then he only wanted to talk to Angélique. He made his interest in her clear when he lowered his voice, averted his eyes, and asked if she would go upstairs with him. And then he added in barely more than a whisper that he had never

been to a brothel before, and she believed him. He had looked nervous and guilty from the moment he walked in.

"I'm sorry, John," she said in a kind voice, wishing she could reassure him. "I don't go upstairs. I love talking to our clients, but I don't
entertain them personally." She could see that he understood what
she meant. "I'm better in the drawing room," she said lightly, and he
smiled.

"My friend told me about you. You're even more wonderful than
he said. I love talking to you."

"Thank you, John. You might enjoy some of the young ladies
too." She always referred to them as ladies, not women or girls.

"I would have gone upstairs with you," he said with a look of regret. "My wife and I . . . we haven't . . . we . . . we married a long
time ago. We're very different, we're not close." It was a story she
was familiar with, and she nodded.

"I understand," she said sympathetically, wanting to free him of
his inhibitions so he could enjoy the full services of the house. She
thought he might like Agathe, who had other clients like him, but he
showed no interest in her when she walked by. He only had eyes for
Angélique, and left at last after two hours with her, and promised to
return the next day. Angélique assured him she would be delighted
to see him when he returned. And after he was gone, one of their
clients had recognized him and mentioned to her that he was a very
important financier in the States. And he clearly wasn't a habitué of
brothels, he had looked uncomfortable all night, except while in
deep conversation with Angélique. He had told her that he frequently did business in Europe, though more often in London. They
had talked about England for a while, and he'd been startled when
he first talked to her to discover that she was British. And the mo-

ment he heard her very upper-class accent, it was obvious to him that she was no woman of the streets. Like everyone else, he was fascinated by her. He came to the house every night for a week after that, to talk to Angélique, and he took none of the girls upstairs, he just sat with Angélique and talked to her for hours. And on the last night he told her how much he enjoyed meeting her and that he was leaving the next day.

"I'll come back to see you the next time I'm in Paris, probably in a few months. I come several times a year," he said wistfully. "Perhaps you'll change your mind about going upstairs with me next time," he said with a determined expression. He was obviously used to getting his way.

"I won't do that," she said firmly with a warm look in her eyes, to soften the blow of rejection. "But I'll be very happy to see you. Have a safe journey home." When he left she thought about him for a while afterward. He seemed like an unhappy man, but his eyes lit up when he talked to her. She could sense that he was used to being in command, and was unfamiliar with not getting what he wanted, but if what he wanted was Angélique in a bedroom upstairs, he would be disappointed again. And he left a surprisingly large amount of money for the time he'd taken talking to her. Angélique had never expected to be paid for the time she spent in the drawing room conversing with their clients, and she put the money away to split later among the girls. And she had the strong feeling when he left that she'd be seeing him again.

Le Boudoir was becoming more and more well known, and their business was increasing. In October and November, she finally had to take on two more girls. Both were extremely pretty. One was a Swedish girl named Sigrid, who spoke English, French, and German. And the other was a striking Spanish girl named Carmen, who had been a flamenco dancer and had grown up as a gypsy in Seville. There was something very wild about her, and the men loved her as soon as she started to work. Both women were great additions to the group. Carmen was rarely in the drawing room for five minutes before she was taken upstairs again. She was playful and loved to tease and taunt the men, and they loved it.

They gave a party in December a few days before Christmas, which was lavish and elegant. The champagne flowed, they served caviar, and two hundred men crowded into the house. All their regular clients brought friends. Thomas came to wish her a merry Christmas, and as usual, didn't stay for long, but she was touched that he'd made the time to come. And the day after the party, Angélique was chatting with several of their regulars about how much fun it had been. She had worn a spectacular white satin gown to the party, which showed off more of her body than she usually did, tantalizing their clients more than ever, since they all knew they couldn't have her. For the madam of a brothel, she was unwaveringly chaste, much to the men's dismay.

She was wearing an elegant black dress the night after the party, with a handsome pearl choker around her neck that had been her mother's, when she heard two Englishmen walk in, and explain that they had been sent by friends. She recognized one of the voices immediately. Glancing into the hallway as he took off his coat, she saw her brother Edward, swaying unsteadily. He was drunk and saying that he wanted to meet the girls. Without hesitating, she excused herself to the man she was talking to, disappeared into the kitchen, and sent for Fabienne, who came to find her a minute later to discover what was wrong.

"The drunken Englishman in the drawing room by now is the younger of my brothers," she whispered. "He can't see me, or he'll tell all of England. Give him one of the girls, and send him upstairs quickly. I'm going to my room. Tell everyone I have a headache."

"I'll take him myself," Fabienne reassured her. She could do at least that for her, and she didn't have a client at the moment. "Don't worry, it will be fine."

"Thank you," Angélique said gratefully, and disappeared up the back stairs, as Fabienne went back to the drawing room, and nearly threw herself at Angélique's brother, oozing charm. He was very drunk, and quite flattered.

"Do I get a choice?" he asked, weaving. "Our friends say all the girls are terrific, and some are pretty exotic. There's an African girl I want to meet." He was emphatic about it, and fortunately Yaba was nowhere to be seen—she was upstairs with a client.

"She's with a regular client," Fabienne told him. "She won't be back down tonight." And then Fabienne pouted at him and looked like an innocent cherub. "My feelings will be hurt if you don't pick me."

"Oh, all right then," he said, lurching at her, as she took his hand and led him toward the stairs. "Who's the phony duchess, by the way? That's pretty funny, a whore calling herself a duchess. You know, my brother is a duke."

"Really?" Fabienne cooed at him as they headed toward her room, wishing she could slap him for what he'd said about Angélique. "I'm sure he's not nearly as exciting as you are, and only half the man."

"Well said," Edward answered as they walked into her room, and she closed the door as he lurched unsteadily toward the bed, lay down, and unbuttoned his pants. He was anything but exciting, or imaginative. He told her what he wanted, and with the amount he'd had to drink, it was over in five minutes, and he passed out and lay unconscious on her bed. She went to find his friend a little while later to come and get him, and Jacques helped carry him downstairs. Edward had been anything but charming or fun. His friend paid what they owed, and Fabienne was relieved when they left, and went to tell Angélique they were gone. She looked shaken from having seen him for the first time in two years. But at least it wasn't Tristan, which would have been even worse. She was still dressed and went back downstairs with Fabienne, to say goodnight to the other guests.

But seeing Edward had upset her. She lay in bed that night, thinking of him and their older brother, how terrible they had been to her, the home she would never see again, and the life she had chosen now. She hadn't had the courage to write to Mrs. White since she'd come to Paris nine months before. She felt terrible about it, but she hated to lie to her, and she couldn't admit what she was really doing. She decided then to write her a letter and tell her she had taken a job in Paris as a nanny, and had been very busy. There was no way she could tell her the truth. And as she fell asleep that night, tears rolled into her pillow. She was the most successful madam in Paris, and she was so homesick for her childhood home and her father that she was crying like a child.

Chapter 15

Angélique and the girls at Le Boudoir spent a quiet Christmas Day at the house. Most of their clients were at home with their families or away, so they assumed they'd have the day off. But they hadn't told anyone officially that they'd be closed, in case one or two of their clients were lonely or alone and wanted to come by. They kept their doors open to their customers at all times.

But on Christmas Day, much to the ladies' relief, no one came, and they set the table for what they called a "Boudoir Family Dinner." Their off time together always had a family feeling, like a group of loving sisters who got along. They wore whatever they wanted, with no makeup, no fancy hairdos, no elaborate gowns. It was the first time any of them had relaxed in a long time. They were never closed, and one or another of their clients was always dropping in unannounced. The men loved that they always felt welcome at any time, and the girls were happy to see them. They could talk or relax or play cards or play the piano, or just read a newspaper, almost like a club. They didn't have to go upstairs if they didn't want to. And if they wanted glamour, they could arrive in the evening, and find the girls beautifully dressed and waiting for them as the maids served champagne.

The girls all exchanged gifts with each other, and had bought or made lovely, thoughtful gifts. Angélique gave each of them a new purse or blouse or bonnet, something to wear when they weren't working, and a large bonus to each girl.

"I've never had so much money in my life," Philippine said happily. "I've been saving it for something special."

"I'm saving mine for a trip to Italy in the spring, if we get a holiday," Camille said. "I want to go to Florence or Venice. I've never been there." Angélique had opened doors for them that they'd never had access to before, with a steady stream of income. With the sophisticated, educated men they were dealing with, they had grown into more polished women, and many of them were more interesting than the men's wives, and certainly more exciting. Everyone had benefited from Le Boudoir. And Angélique found herself thinking of the Ferguson children and wondered how they were. She would have liked to send them all Christmas presents, but she didn't dare, and was sure their parents wouldn't have allowed them to have them. Even less so if they knew what she was doing now, but fortunately they had no way of knowing. In the end, they had done her an enormous favor by firing her. She had already been able to replace the money she had used from her father's pouch, and had even more now. She was building a sizable nest egg for herself.

She had also finally written to Mrs. White at Belgrave, and told her about a nanny job in Paris with two lovely children that she made up as she went along. Mrs. White was relieved to hear it and responded immediately. They were still redecorating, and had hired more staff for the big parties her brother and Elizabeth were giving. And she said they were redoing the house in Grosvenor Square and modernizing it completely, which was extremely costly.

Jacques came in after dinner and sat with the girls for a while. He and Fabienne played cards in the drawing room after that, and eventually they all gathered around the piano while Camille and Philippine took turns playing, and everyone sang Christmas carols. It was a tender day of shared memories, talking about the families they had left and most of them no longer had. They had become family to each other now. And in the late afternoon, Angélique noticed Jacques and Fabienne walking in the garden and kissing, and she wondered what would become of that. Some of the girls had formed close attachments to their clients, but most of them maintained superficial relationships with the men who came there. It was simpler that way, although almost all of them, except Angélique, talked about getting married one day. It was a dream she no longer shared. She had never fallen in love and didn't want to now. Her life was simpler alone than with a man. And she knew too much now. Almost all of their clients were married, and some had established mistresses as well as making visits to the house. She preferred not to be the wife a man cheated on, or a couple like the Fergusons, where each of them had a roving eye and affairs on the side. She was sure her father hadn't been that way, but most of the men she knew now saw no reason to resist a pretty woman, whether married or not.

The girls shared an easy, pleasant day, and a few of their clients wandered in that night for a quiet evening. And the day ended on a warm note.

And on New Year's Eve they gave another grand party that went on until the next morning, and all of their clients had too much to drink and had to be helped into their carriages by Luc and Jacques. And there were some very heavy heads when they came back the next day.

It was a week after that that John Carson, the older American financier, returned to the house, looking for Angélique, and seemed delighted when he saw her as soon as he walked in. She was surrounded by admirers in the drawing room, who all hoped that she would relent one day and give in to their pleas to spend a night with them. She was a challenge for them all, but she was staunch in her resistance to their entreaties and enjoyed playing with them. John sat at the edge of the group, admiring her, with a glass of scotch in his hand. He was a very prosperous-looking man, and he waited until the others had drifted off to speak to her quietly. There was something very strong and determined in his eyes, and he wasn't as uncomfortable being there as he had been before.

"I've been thinking about you a great deal since the last time I saw you." He looked deep into her eyes, and she smiled, but he didn't see there what he hoped to, or obviously felt for her.

"Thank you, John," she said quietly. She had thought of him occasionally too, and wondered if he'd return. He hadn't been to Paris in several months and said he'd been busy in New York. He told her the economy was booming, and he had his finger in many pies, and exciting new ventures. But he hadn't come here to talk business with her, and had been planning what he had to say for months. He said he was leaving for London in a few days for meetings there to assist the government, as the king was seriously in debt. The king had spent a fortune rebuilding Buckingham Palace and Windsor

Castle, and a number of other important buildings, and his advisers had been unable to discourage him from his excessive spending, which went hand in hand with his heavy drinking. He had become a most unpopular monarch by then. And they wanted John to help set things to rights, and advise the king, which was a great honor for him.

"I wanted to speak to you about an idea I had," John said quietly. "You're young, Angélique, and you're having a fine time here, and I can see your business is going well, and you're surrounded by the most interesting people in Paris. I daresay every man of means and power turns up here at some point, even frequently, but this isn't a profession you can stay in forever. One day it will become a heavy burden for you, and at any point something could go awry and everything you've built could disappear. It's a house built on sand," he said seriously. "I'd like to offer you something more solid." He paused for a moment as she looked at him in surprise, not sure where he was going with his carefully planned speech. She could tell he had put a great deal of thought into it, and she was right, he had. "I'd like to offer you a fine house in New York, a home just for you, with all the servants you want. You can decorate it as lavishly as you like, and have anything you desire. You can entertain, travel with me, lead the life of a respectable woman, to the degree that I can make that available to you, since I am married. I suppose there is no proper way to say this to you, but I would like you to be my mistress, with anything you want, and me at your feet." He smiled at her, certain that she'd be impressed, and she was. It was an extraordinarily generous offer, and for most women it would have been an alluring one, but not for her. She didn't love him, and she didn't want to be his woman on the side, or even his main one. And she knew that if she were to ever ally herself with a man, it would have to be respectable, and for love. "I would spend a great deal of time with you. My wife has been ill." He paused then. "And it's been an ill-fated marriage since the beginning. We have a wonderful son, but other than that we have nothing in common and never did. Even when she was well, we led separate lives and have for nearly thirty years." She guessed him to be about sixty, and he was a handsome man, but there was something missing. She had the strange feeling that he wanted to own her, not love her. She was sure that he would give her everything he promised, and would have kept his word. She knew that many women would have leaped at the chance he was offering her, but she couldn't. She had no desire to sell herself into slavery, to him or anyone else, or to be a bird in a gilded cage, and someone's mistress. She had given up a respectable life when she opened Le Boudoir, but she had acquired independence, and the ability to make her own decisions and do what she wanted, and she didn't want to give that up now, and wasn't even certain she could. The taste of freedom was too sweet. She didn't have a husband or employer, a benefactor, or brother or man to answer to and tell her what she could and couldn't do and make decisions for her. She would be turning twenty-one in a few months, and it seemed much too soon to give up all she had achieved. And she considered what she was doing temporary. Being his mistress would be forever, like being his wife, only worse. No matter how kind or intelligent he was, Angélique had no wish to be owned, and a man's possession.

"I'm very touched by your offer," she said, looking at him, trying to guess at what he felt for her. She couldn't tell if his ego was involved or his heart. And she could sense that her refusal would be a blow. "But I can't do that. I want to stay in Paris, and I'm not ready to give up Le Boudoir. I like running my own business. I don't want to be any man's mistress, no matter how tempting or kind the offer, and I doubt I ever will."

"I can't marry you, Angélique," he said sadly. "I couldn't do that to my wife after all this time. Particularly now that she's ill." He respected her even if he didn't love her and hadn't in years.

"I don't want marriage. I want to be free to make my own choices and decisions. I couldn't do that if you were supporting me lavishly. All the decisions would be yours, as though we were married. And the house and everything in it would be yours."

"I would give it to you as a gift, of course. Every gift I gave you would belong to you." He wondered for a moment if she was negotiating from strength and bargaining with him, but he could see that she wasn't. She was a woman of conviction, who didn't sacrifice her values or beliefs or what she wanted, for anyone or anything.

"And I'm happy in Paris. I'm not at all sure I would be happy in New York. And one day I might want to go back to England." Although she couldn't see how. For the moment, and perhaps forever, there was nothing left for her there except memories and heartbreak and loss. But it was still her country, more than France. She had grown up there and felt more English. But she had no tie at all to America, and couldn't envision herself there.

"I think you'd like it very much, especially with a grand home of your own." He tried to entice her, to no avail. And the look in his eyes was one of steely determination. He did not want to lose. But he was not going to win with her.

"Perhaps," she said quietly, but he could see that he hadn't convinced her, and he seemed angry for a minute and then sad.

"Will you think about it?" he urged her, and she shook her head.

"I don't want to mislead you and give you false hopes," she said honestly. She didn't want to lie to him. "I don't think I have the temperament to be a mistress. A courtesan perhaps, but not a mistress." It sounded much too confining to her. Her friends were the most powerful men in the city and the country, and increasingly men were coming to Le Boudoir from all over Europe, including her own brother, who was only a pathetic drunk and a second son. But others were more important and more interesting. And John was certainly one of those. He was a very important man in the States, from what she knew of him. "It's a very, very flattering offer, but I can't accept it." He nodded. He could see he was getting nowhere, and he left her with regret that night. He came back again the next day, and told her he was leaving for London, and promised to come to see her again the next time he was in Paris.

"Think about my offer. Maybe you'll change your mind," he said in the tone he used in business, to try and close a deal. She could tell that he meant it, although it didn't sound like love to her.

"Take good care of yourself," she said kindly. He didn't look like a happy man. "And go save the finances of our king." She smiled at him. "He's a cousin of my father's. I went to his coronation when I was a little girl."

"You're a most unusual woman," he said with longing. He kissed her on the cheek then and left. His mission to convince her to be his mistress had failed, and he felt the sting of it, as he went back to his hotel. It only made him want her more.

Things went well at Le Boudoir all through the spring. Their clients came regularly and frequently, and people had heard of them in other cities in Europe. They'd had several new British visitors, Ital-

ian princes and counts, a Spanish duke. Nobles and aristocrats
crowded into the drawing room along with their familiar clients,
and the girls who worked there were treated well, and often received beautiful gifts and generous tips from their clients.

In May, they celebrated their one-year anniversary of the opening
of the house. Angélique had already replaced and refurbished several things, and the house was slowly becoming more opulent and
luxurious, and the girls more elegant when they were dressed. And
Angélique's wardrobe was one of the most fashionable in Paris. She
was twenty-one years old and more beautiful than ever, and the
girls were infinitely more polished than they had been in the beginning. They were worthy of the men they served. And other girls
frequently contacted Angélique to ask to work for her, but she was
content with the number they had. It was a small, exclusive group
of people, both the men and the women who came together at Le
Boudoir. None of them had expected it to be the success it became.

A few days after their anniversary, another group of Englishmen
came to the house one night. They were rowdy and jovial, very well
dressed, and more than a little drunk. Angélique noticed them when
they arrived. And she heard them tell Jacques they had been sent by
friends. Jacques looked at her, and she nodded. They seemed fine to
her, and then she saw a familiar face in the group. It was Harry Ferguson, her employer when she was a nanny, and she discreetly disappeared, as she had when her brother Edward had turned up. She
whispered to Fabienne that she was going upstairs and left.

"Your brother again?" Fabienne asked as Angélique slipped by,
and she shook her head.

"I'll tell you later. Take care of them," she whispered, and was
gone up the stairs to her room in the attic. It was already late, and

she didn't intend to come down again, so she undressed and went to bed. She wasn't really surprised to see Harry at Le Boudoir. And she was sure he would never make the connection between the Duchess and the nanny he had sacked fourteen months before. He had done her the favor of a lifetime, and it no longer mattered to her that they hadn't believed her, and had listened to the lies of their friend. She was infinitely happier now, although she still missed Emma and thought of her at times.

Fabienne asked her who he was when they met at breakfast the next morning.

"He was the man I worked for as a nanny, that my brother sent me to, when they disposed of me like so much baggage."

"The one who fired you?"

"Yes," Angélique said with a smile. "Was he with you last night?"

"No, he wanted Ambre. He had heard about her. He wanted Yaba too, but she was busy. They stayed a long time, and paid very well. He seems to have a lot of money to spend." Angélique nodded, and read the newspaper. Harry Ferguson meant nothing to her, nor his wife, nor their money.

She saw that there was unrest in Paris again over the French king. He was threatening to dissolve the cabinet, and people were angry about it. She had discussed it at length with Thomas, who as minister knew a great deal. Politics always intrigued her. Thomas had told her he was worried that things would take a bad turn. There were rumors about trying to overthrow King Charles, and fear of another revolution, but he didn't think it would come to that. He had promised to warn her if it looked that way, but for now, all seemed to be in control. And none of their other clients in government seemed worried.

She was saddened in June to read of the death of King George IV in England, her father's cousin. He'd had a heart attack at Windsor Castle and died suddenly. He had been obese for many years, and given to excesses of all kinds. She wondered if John had solved some of his financial problems when he'd gone to England. King George was only sixty-seven years old, ten years younger than her father. And he was being succeeded by his younger brother William, who was to be King William IV. The newspaper said that the date for the coronation had not been set, and was not imminent. George had only had a daughter and several illegitimate children, so his brother William succeeded him, although he was only three years younger. And his succession would eventually become a problem as well, since none of his legitimate children survived infancy, and he had ten illegitimate children by an Irish actress, Dorothea Jordan, whom he had never married. The vagaries and misbehavior of the British monarchy were complicated to follow, but Angélique was familiar with them.

And in July, a month after King George's death, Thomas came to visit her quietly, as he often did, to spend a little while with her. He was a familiar figure at the house, and the girls always wondered if more would come of it, but Angélique insisted they were just friends. He said he was extremely concerned for her safety when he arrived that day. King Charles had dissolved the parliament, which he considered too liberal, and had censored the press. Outraged citizens were gathering, and barricades were going to be erected in the coming hours, and there was likely to be fighting in the streets. The people were tired of the Bourbons, and a dangerous clash was likely to occur, or even lead to another revolution.

"You and the girls must leave the city immediately, by tonight," he told her.

"But to where?" Angélique looked panicked. She was frightened at the thought of another revolution like the one that had killed her grandparents and most of her relatives, and had sent her mother to England as a baby.

"I strongly suggest a holiday at the seaside until things calm down." She could see that he was serious, and her mind was racing. She didn't want to leave the house, but she didn't want to risk their lives and safety either, and she was responsible for the ten women who lived there with her, and worked for her. "Can you be ready to leave in a few hours?" he asked, gravely concerned, and she knew he had enough inside information that if he told her to leave Paris, she'd be a fool not to. She trusted him completely and knew his concern for her was genuine.

"We will if we have to. I'll organize it at once," she said, as she tried to figure out what to do.

"Don't come back until it's safe," he warned her, and left a few minutes later with a gentle kiss on her cheek.

She sent Jacques and Luc out immediately to hire three carriages for them, and went from room to room to tell the girls to pack their bags. They would be leaving for Normandy in an hour, and would stay at an inn if she was able to get enough rooms for them. She wasn't sure if others would be fleeing the city, and fill the local inns. She was grateful that Thomas had warned her.

The girls hurried to pack their bags, and an hour later climbed into the three carriages the boys had found on short notice, and they used the old coach they had for their luggage. The carriages were less than elegant, but serviceable, and the horses looked strong. And two hours after the minister's visit they were on the road to Normandy and had left the city. They arrived that night, and she was able to secure rooms for all of them at a comfortable inn with a view of the sea. And they settled in to wait for news of the city. Angélique had brought her small trunk with her, with her fortune and jewelry in it, and she had brought enough clothes to stay for a month, and a large box of bonnets, and the other girls had done the same at her direction. Jacques and Luc had stayed to protect the house and the two maids, and assured her they would take good care of them.

The news for the next few days was alarming. They were calling the uprising a revolution, and forced King Charles to abdicate. But the small-scale revolution was over in three days, and a week later, the throne was offered to Charles's cousin, Louis-Philippe, of the house of Orléans, and they had a new king. Ten days later, as Angélique and the girls walked along country lanes amid wildflowers, far from Paris, Charles abdicated and left for England peacefully, and by then order had been restored in the city. In theory, they could go back. But Angélique thought it best to wait at least another week, to be sure that all was in fact peaceful again, and nothing further would happen. They had already been there for three weeks and could wait a few more. They were hardly suffering in the country, which had provided them with a pleasant and unexpected vacation, and had kept them far from the chaos in the city, thanks to Thomas's warning. She was very glad they had avoided it all and left in time, and the girls were having fun at the seaside, and enjoying the break from Paris life.

They had gotten several fierce stares from country women who saw them in their elegant dresses, all of them beauties, and the fact that there were eleven of them caught people's attention wherever they went, and women scolded their husbands for looking at them.

Angélique took the girls back to the city at the beginning of September, after Jacques sent them a message that all was peaceful and safe again. They had been gone for six weeks, and came back to the house energized and refreshed and in high spirits, ready to receive their clients again. The minister was their first visitor, wanting to be sure that they were well.

"Thank you for the warning," Angélique said when he came to see her. "It must have been very unpleasant here."

"Only for a few days. It was over very quickly. And we'll see how the new king does. I hope he'll be more reasonable than the last one."

"The girls loved their little holiday," she admitted, smiling at him, happy to see him again.

Their clients rushed to see them the moment they came home, delighted they were back. They had missed the girls in August, but many of the men had been away too, at their country homes and châteaux, as they were every year. But everyone had returned, and September was busy, and the weather unseasonably warm, even more so than it had been in Normandy, where there was always a pleasant breeze.

The week after they came back from Normandy, Angélique was surprised to see John return to Paris. He said he had business there, and had an appointment in London with the new king, but he said he had something to tell her that might make her see things differently. A significant change had occurred in his life since his last visit in January. His wife had passed away in June, and he said he would be in mourning for the next several months, but he wanted Angé-lique to know that after his period of formal mourning, he was prepared to marry her. He was no longer limited to offering her to be his mistress—he could make an honest woman of her. His eyes, as he spoke to her, begged her to accept. But the simple fact was that she didn't love him. He was forty years older than she was, and she liked him, and enjoyed talking to him in the drawing room, but she had no desire to marry him, no matter how generous he was prepared to be. And she was shocked by his unexpected proposal.

"John, I can't," she said, looking unhappy. "I told you before, my life is here. I don't want to go to New York. And I don't want to get married. We barely know each other. And what if someone finds out how we met? That you met me here? I'm a madam in a brothel. How would that fit into your life if someone should find out?"

"Why would they?" he asked confidently. "No one ever needs to know how or where we met. You're from an extremely dignified family. And I'm old enough to do what I want. I'm too old for it to hurt my career. And no one will find out." And even if they did, he didn't care. He wanted her desperately, and had thought of nothing else since June, and he had believed her when she'd said she would never be any man's mistress. He was willing to risk it, and deny this piece of her history if anyone recognized her. He wanted her to the point of it being an obsession. She didn't know if he loved her, although he said he did, but he wanted her more than anything on earth. He *had* to have her. Reason no longer entered into it, except for her.

"I cannot accept your offer," she said gently. "Not as a mistress, nor as your wife. I am deeply sorry about your wife's death. Even if you weren't happy with her, I'm sure that you're very sad about it.

But I can't marry you." He stood up then and looked down at her, and for a moment he seemed furious. He was distraught, and seemed unable to believe she had refused him, even with a proposal of marriage. He was willing to put everything on the line for her. But Angélique was adamant. She didn't want to be pressured by him into something she had told him repeatedly she didn't want. She didn't love him, didn't want to leave Paris. And she didn't say it to him, but she thought he was too old for her—he could have been her grandfather. But whatever his age, she didn't love him, which was essential to her.

"I won't come back to bother you again," he said, and with a last ravaged look at her, he strode across the room, and walked out the door without looking back. And this time she was certain she would not see him again.

Chapter 16

The fall was off to a pleasant start with old clients and new ones. After the three-day revolution in July and change of monarch, Paris had settled down again, and people were hopeful that the new king would rule better than the old one. And their clients were busy adjusting to the shift of power. New deals and laws and policies were being made. It added both to the tension and to the excitement of the hour, and Angélique and the girls could feel it in the house. A surge of fresh energy had occurred.

"They're lively right now, aren't they?" Philippine commented to the other girls one night after the last guest left. Ambre had been constantly busy, and Camille, Agathe, and Fabienne had been in great demand too. It was as though the men had too much energy and didn't know what to do with it. And Angélique also thought the political discussions had been more heated than usual in the drawing room. The hot weather contributed to it, but so did politics, and they were anxious to relieve their tension upstairs. The girls looked tired that night, and Angélique was too. They had several clients come in late, and some had had a lot to drink, which made them more excitable. And since none of them discussed politics with their wives, they all wanted to talk about the new changes with Angélique, who was so intelligent, and well informed about political events.

And the next night, in a similar atmosphere, in the dense heat that hung in the air, tempers flared. A debate began about the Bourbon kings versus the Orléans, and several men expressed the opinion that Louis-Philippe would be no better than his predecessor, and other clients disagreed. And before anyone could stop them, two men, who'd had too much to drink before they came to the house that night, began shouting at each other in the drawing room. One pushed the other, and others tried to intervene, a punch was thrown, and at a signal from Angélique, Jacques and Luc crossed the room. It was the first time a fight had broken out between her aristocratic clients, and before they hurt each other, she wanted them both removed. They were in no condition to stay, nor did she want them to. Le Boudoir was meant to be a haven for important men, not a boxing ring. And as Jacques grabbed one by the shoulder, before Luc could reach the other, the main aggressor in the argument pulled a pearl-handled pistol out of his pocket and shot his opponent in the chest, and a red flower of blood grew across his immaculately starched white vest. The man who'd been shot wore a look of surprise as he slumped to the floor at Jacques's feet, and the man holding the pistol attempted to lurch out of the room, as Luc reached out and stopped him with a powerful grip.

Angélique knew the shooter slightly, and his victim was one of their best clients. She bent down to him immediately as he gasped for air, and a dozen men joined Luc to stop the shooter from leaving, as Angélique looked up at them. "Get a doctor," she said to Luc, just as Thomas emerged from the crowd. For an instant she had forgotten he was there, and she was immensely grateful to see him. She had no idea what to do next. The situation seemed dire to her, and would lead to scandal for all of them. She couldn't imagine what Thomas could do now. The man who'd done the shooting had slumped into a chair with a dazed look, and was no longer attempting to leave, as Thomas surveyed the scene intently.

Angélique grabbed a cushion and put it under the head of the man who'd been shot. She didn't know what else to do, and one of the girls came running down the stairs with a stack of towels to stanch the blood—it was all over him by then, and on Angélique's dress, and his entire vest had turned bright red. He was obviously in extremis, and the pressure she and Agathe put on the wound did nothing to slow the bleeding. His eyes had rolled back in his head, and he could no longer speak. The damage from the bullet had been severe. They had only been a foot apart when his attacker fired the shot. As the men watched, there was a murmur in the room. Many of them knew the victim. He was one of the most respected bankers in Paris, and the shooter was a member of the parliament that had been dissolved by King Charles in July, and he was bitter about it.

The man on the floor gave a terrible rattling sound then, as Thomas knelt beside him with Angélique, and a rush of blood gurgled to his lips and ran down his chin. Angélique held him, hoping to help him breathe, as he gave a last gasp and died in her arms, while they all stared at him in horror. He had been murdered in her drawing room. She gently laid him back down as Thomas checked his pulse. The victim lay with open eyes, no longer breathing. There was a look of panic around the room, and conversations in low voices as they discussed what to do. No one had had time to send for the police or even think of it—everything had happened so quickly. Angélique looked at Thomas expectantly. There were at least thirty men standing in the room, as Thomas took control of the situation. He knew many or even most of them. The shooter sat, dazed at what he'd done, and knew that life as he knew it was about to end. Someone had taken the pistol from him after he shot the fatal bullet, and Angélique had no idea where it was, as Thomas spoke in a strong calm voice.

"Gentlemen, I suggest you all leave immediately. None of you were here tonight. We have not seen each other. Is that correct?" They all nodded with a look of relief, with no desire to be part of the inevitable scandal that would result if they admitted to being there that night. They filed out quickly, as he told Angélique to tell the girls upstairs to have the other guests leave. The clients in rooms with the girls had no idea what had happened, or that a man had been killed. She sent Agathe to tell them, and within minutes, the remaining men in the house hurried down the stairs, and the minister told them to leave, with the same instructions he had given the others. No one was likely to volunteer that they'd been in a brothel and seen a man murdered in a drunken argument. And as the last clients left, they could see the dead man on the floor in plain view. They left as quickly as the others, and the man who had taken the pistol passed it discreetly to Jacques on the way out. He was still holding it in his hand, as the shooter swayed to his feet, and gazed from Angélique to the minister. He was slightly more sober than when he'd pulled the trigger, but he was still very drunk.

Thomas quietly told Agathe to take him upstairs and let him sleep until he sobered up. He was afraid to send him home now for fear of what he'd say.

"I must go to the police," he said loudly.

"I am the police," the minister said angrily. "Go upstairs, and do as you're told."

"I killed him," he said as Agathe led him up the stairs to her room. The shooter was crying as Thomas turned to look at Angélique. She was frightened but trying valiantly to appear calm.

"What do we do now?" Angélique asked Thomas. She was almost as pale as the dead man still lying at their feet.

"We must get him somewhere near his home, where he'll be found. His wife doesn't need to suffer the indignity of knowing he was killed here. No one will talk." It wasn't the first time a man had died in a brothel. And what Thomas wanted now was to avoid scandal for all of them, and particularly Angélique, even more than the shooter.

"I'll take Dumas to the police tomorrow when he sobers up, and he'll confess to shooting him in an argument on the street, and leaving him there in his own drunken stupor. Do you have a carriage?" he asked her quickly.

"Yes."

"Send one of your men to bring it around. They can drop Vincent in a quiet street near his home, where he'll be found." He instructed Luc and Jacques to wrap the victim in a blanket, so they could put him in the carriage, and a minute later, Luc went to get the carriage, as Jacques handed Thomas the gun. Angélique was infinitely grateful he was there.

Luc was back with the carriage in a few minutes, rolled up to the door. Fortunately, there were no other houses around them, and Luc and Jacques quickly carried the dead man out, wrapped in the blanket, and laid him on the floor of the carriage.

Thomas told them the area where the man lived, and they left shortly after on their grisly mission to spare her and the house from the notoriety Thomas was trying to avoid. He knew that someone would find the victim soon enough and call the police. Luc and Jacques left without saying a word, as Angélique called one of the maids to clean the carpet, but most of the dead man's blood was on her dress.

The girls had all come downstairs by then, murmuring over what had happened, and were waiting to hear what should be done next. They all looked desperately afraid. "None of you saw anything tonight," the minister told them firmly. "Nothing happened. It was an ordinary evening. No one will ask you anything. He wasn't shot here. He will be found in the street." He sent the girls back to their rooms then and looked seriously at Angélique, as they went to sit in the dining room. She poured a glass of brandy and handed it to him. He hated what he had to tell her. But there was no other choice.

"You have to leave, Angélique. Not forever, but for now, for six months or a year, to avoid any hint of this touching you. And your clients will be too afraid to come here for a while. They will want no part in this, and neither should you. You can open again, in another house. But not for a while. Things like this have happened before, but you need to give it time for the cloud to dispel before you open again." She'd been afraid he would say that from the moment it happened, and she knew he was right. She didn't argue with him, and nodded with tears in her eyes as he took her hand in his and held it. Just as she did, he wished the murder hadn't happened. Once again fate had intervened to change her life, just when things were going so well. And now a man was dead, she had to close the house, and she had no idea where to go.

"How soon do I have to leave?" she asked sadly. His heart ached looking at her, and it pained him to say the words.

"As soon as possible. This has to cool down before you can come back." Listening to him, she appeared to be in shock. But she had a powerful protector in Thomas. Without him, the situation would have been infinitely worse.

"What will happen to the girls? Where will they go?"

"They've made a lot of money since you opened. They can go somewhere else for a while, or go home. You can all come back— you just can't be here now. What about you? Where will you go?"

"I don't know," she said, and closed her eyes for a moment, and then opened them again and stared sadly at him. She hated to hear it, but she knew he was right. "There's nothing left for me in England. I have nowhere to go." As she said it, she wondered why she was always at the mercy of other people's follies: her brother's, Bertie's, and now this.

"New York?" he suggested as she thought about it and nodded.

"Maybe. I have nothing and no one there either."

"You can have a fresh start and get away from this for a while. It might do you good. This isn't a life for a girl like you, the daughter of a duke. La Duchesse." She smiled at the girls' nickname for her— it sounded foolish on his lips. "You should book your passage tomorrow. Your clients have a lot at risk. They won't talk. And none of them want to explain why they were here. If you leave now, you won't be involved." She nodded and knew he was right again. They sat talking for a long time, until at last the sun came up. Jacques and Luc were back by then, and reported that they had accomplished their mission. They had even placed the dead man's top hat beside him on the street where they left him. There was no evidence remaining in the house, except Angélique's bloody dress and two towels, which she would dispose of.

At nine o'clock Thomas went to wake Dumas in Agathe's room. It was the first time he'd ever been upstairs. Dumas was still slightly drunk when they woke him, and Angélique sent the maid to bring him strong coffee. Thomas informed him that he was going to tell the police that he had shot the victim during a drunken argument in self-defense, and had wandered the streets all night, and then went to find Thomas at home and confessed to him. There was no mention of Le Boudoir in the story, which was what Thomas wanted, and Dumas was more than willing. He didn't want it known that he'd been in a brothel either. He left with Thomas shortly after, and Angélique went to wake the girls, to tell them what had to happen. Thomas had promised to come back later, and had told her she had to book her passage to New York that day.

She was still wearing her bloodstained dress when the girls came to the kitchen one by one, and waited to hear what she had to say. They were gathered around the table, looking worried, and she gave them the bad news.

"We all have to go. I have to close the house. I'll put the furniture in storage, and we can open again in six months or a year, but not before that." She was echoing Thomas's instructions.

"Six months or a year? What will we do until then?" Ambre asked her, and Fabienne started to cry. She had guessed as much last night, and there was no way she was going back to Madame Albin's or anyplace like it, nor work the streets alone. This was the only kind of job she'd ever had, and she didn't know how to do anything else. She had saved her money for the past sixteen months. It had been a wonderful dream and now it was over. Le Boudoir was as dead as the man who had been shot. Angélique might revive it one day, but not for a long time. But all the girls had money now, more than they'd ever had before, thanks to Angélique. It gave them choices they never would have had otherwise. Some or most of them could afford to take a year off. And so could Angélique, with ease.

"I'm not going back to the convent," Philippine said with a wry smile.

"Some of us could take an apartment and work together while we wait for Angélique to come back," Agathe suggested, and several of the others liked that idea, if they continued to work. Hiroko said she might go back to Japan and had the money to do so now. Camille said she might go back to the theater. The two new girls, Sigrid and Carmen, both said they would go home with the money they had earned. Because Angélique had paid them fairly, none of them would be destitute when she closed, or be forced into situations they didn't want. They all were in far better shape financially than they'd ever been before or ever hoped to be. Le Boudoir de la Duchesse had been a huge success, and profitable beyond their hopes in the beginning.

"What about you?" Fabienne asked Angélique. She was worried about her too.

"I'm going to book passage on a ship to New York." She was sad as she said it, and tears filled her eyes.

"And work there?" They looked shocked.

"No, I think I'll sit it out. I have nothing to sell without you"— she smiled—"and I can't be a nanny without a character. I'm past all that anyway. I wasn't meant for a life of service." They nodded and knew that was true. But she had an amazing head for business, which had served them all well. It had been magical while it lasted, and hopefully would be again.

They all had much to do that morning, to pack and make their plans. She told them that the clothes she had given to each of them were theirs as a gift from her. She had given them beautiful gowns and accessories to go with them. She had been generous, not just with the money, but all the caring details she'd seen to, to be fair and treat them with respect and kindness, for the first time in their lives. For most, this was the only safe haven they'd ever had, and they were heartbroken to leave Le Boudoir, and the tiny brave woman who had created it.

She went to the notaire who represented the house's owner that morning and told him that she was leaving, and taking her family to New York. She paid them three months' rent, which was what she owed once she gave notice. And he was satisfied. He said the owners would be sorry she was leaving, she had been an excellent tenant and paid her rent on time. No one had ever suspected what really went on in the house, not the neighbors, not the notaire, and not the owners.

She went to a storage company and arranged to have the contents of the house packed up and put into storage, and then she went to the office of the Second Line and booked passage on the packet boat *Desdemona* to New York. It was the "palace" of the Second Line. And in a moment of madness, she bought a first-class ticket, and a steerage ticket for one of the maids, whichever one was willing to go with her. The ship was leaving in four days, and she had a lot to do till then.

And when she got back to the house, Fabienne said she had something to tell her. She and Jacques had been talking. They were going to get married and move to Provence, and even when Le Boudoir reopened, she would not come back to work.

"I want to have babies." She smiled at her friend and employer, and Angélique hugged her. She knew their plan was right for her.

"I'm glad for you," she said sincerely, and as she went to start packing, she thought about John Carson's proposal only a week before, but she didn't regret her refusal. It wasn't what she wanted, no matter how upset he was, and she wondered if she would run into him in New York. But she was sure of her decision. If she ever married, she knew it had to be for love.

Thomas came back to see her that afternoon when she returned from the shipping line with her ticket, and he said Dumas's confession had gone as expected. He was in jail and would remain there while he awaited trial. No one had questioned the story he told them, and the subject of Le Boudoir never came up. Thomas had saved them from scandal, and orchestrated the aftermath perfectly. And then he asked her when she was leaving.

"In four days," she said looking tragic. She was leaving behind women she had come to love, the life they had created there, a thriving business, however improper, and a dear friend in him. He had been unfailingly kind and respectful of her since they'd met, and he felt the impending loss as acutely as she did. And he looked as devastated as she did when he left a little while later. He was re-

lieved that she was leaving, but he knew he would never meet another woman like her. As beautiful and exceptional as she was, he
suspected she would meet a man in New York and never return to
France.

In two days, as hastily as they could arrange it, the girls all left for
their destinations. Some stayed in Paris, some went to the cities they
came from, and a few of the girls moved in together. And all of them
said, as they bade her tearful farewells, that they would wait for her
return and come back to work for her. It made Angélique's heart
ache to say goodbye, and disband the family of loving sisters they
had become.

By the third day after the murder, the house was empty. She
and Fabienne cried as they said goodbye that morning, when she
and Jacques left for Provence, and Angélique wished them well.
She was happy that Fabienne was going to a better life, of marriage
and babies.

Angélique walked around the house one last time before she left
it. They had had good times there and done well, beyond her imagination. It had been a glittering dream for a moment, but now it was
over. She went to the hotel with her mountains of trunks, and the
maid who had agreed to join her, Claire. She was staying at the
Meurice, which would have been impossible for her when she came
to Paris. Now she could afford it with ease, without touching her
father's money. She was taking all her clothes with her, and after
sending Thomas a message, he came to see her there the night before she left.

"You're leaving tomorrow?" he asked softly when he came to her suite, and she nodded sadly. "I hope it's a smooth passage. And I hope you come back one day. I have the feeling that you won't."

"Where else would I go?" she asked simply.

"Anywhere. Argentina. Brazil. Rome, Florence, back to England. There are a lot of possibilities you haven't explored." She hadn't even thought of them, and didn't want to. She didn't want to leave at all, but knew she had to. He was right about that.

"I want to come back here and start again," she said firmly, with her strength and spirit in her eyes.

"Sometimes that's not as easy as we think. But I hope you do," he said, and meant it, with a tender look. And then, without a sound, he bent to kiss her, and she wished that things had been different, that he wasn't married, and she wasn't leaving, and he wasn't who he was. It could never work between them, and she had always known that, but he had been a remarkable friend, the best one she'd ever had. And he had cleaned up a disaster for her, and given her excellent advice. She knew that if she stayed, somehow, sometime, somewhere, the truth of what happened would come out, of who had done it, and where, and that Le Boudoir was hers. But thanks to him, for now it had been silenced. She couldn't have asked for more. "Will you write to me?" he asked her. She nodded, but he wasn't sure he believed her. It would be delicate writing to him. And who knew what life had in store for her in New York? He wished her only good things and hated to see her go. If life had been different and more fair, he knew he would have married her. He had never known a woman like her or loved anyone as much.

"Thank you," she said before he left her. The words were much too small for what he'd done.

"Don't thank me, Angélique. Just come back. I hope I see you again." She nodded as tears ran down her cheeks. She felt like she was leaving home again, without her friends, with no parents and no plan. She was stepping out into empty space into thin air, bereft and alone again, without the people she loved. And all she could hope was that once again, she would land on her feet. Thomas hoped so too, and was sure she would, as he kissed her for the last time, whispered, *"Au revoir, mon amour,"* and hurried down the stairs of her hotel and sped off in his carriage. Angélique stood at the window and watched him go, crying silently, and la Duchesse of Le Boudoir disappeared with him.

Chapter 17

The morning Angélique left, after a year and a half in Paris, she rose at dawn to get ready, after a sleepless night, and wondered if she'd ever see Paris again. She wore a very elegant dark gray silk suit with a huge hat and a veil that concealed her face, as she got in the carriage for the ride to Le Havre with Claire, who was to become her lady's maid. Their other maid had gone home to her parents in the South.

Angélique was thinking of Thomas, as they rode along. He couldn't come to see her off, it would have been much too visible, and awkward if he were recognized. They had said all they needed to say the day before. There were no words left, only memories between them.

She watched Paris and the outskirts slip away as they traveled into the countryside toward the port. The journey took many hours, and the packet boat looked large to her as she boarded, and was painted black. She had never traveled so far before, and she had adopted the story of being a young widow once again. It still seemed more respectable than being a very young woman traveling alone, even with a maid. Claire was excited to board the ship too and to go to America with her. It seemed like an adventure to her, but Angélique had a heavy heart as she looked around her cabin. It was spacious, well-lit, and airy, and the mattress seemed comfortable. Well-wishers had come to see the other passengers off. It was still hard for her to believe that a whole new life had ended with a single bullet five days before. She and Fabienne had burned her dress and the towels, and she was sure that, just as Thomas said, none of the men who had seen the murder would talk. They had far more at risk than she did. But she had paid a high price for one client's hot temper and a disagreement about politics. One man had lost his life, and now she was losing hers.

She watched the ship slip away from the dock with her hat pulled low, and her veil over her face, and felt the pleasant sea breeze as they set sail. Several people had already noticed her, a small, elegant, fashionable woman, who looked mysterious, and was traveling alone. She took a short walk around the deck after they were under way. There were pens for sheep and goats, a cow house, and a space for hens, chickens, ducks, and geese. Then she went back to her cabin, and read for a while. She had written to Mrs. White from the hotel, and told her that the family she worked for was moving to New York, and she was going with them to settle them in, she didn't know for how long. She hoped not too long. And she promised to let her know where she was. She wondered if the old housekeeper would believe her, but there was no reason why she shouldn't. Angélique hated lying to her, but there was no way to tell her the truth about her reason for leaving France. She was sure that in her wildest dreams Mrs. White couldn't possibly imagine that Angélique had run the best brothel in Paris for the last sixteen months. Nor could anyone watching her on the ship. She looked like a distinguished, well-born lady, and the young widow she claimed to be.

She had dinner in her cabin, and then took a long walk around the deck, and explored the ship. There was a handsome saloon with wood paneling and gilt decoration. Her fellow passengers passed the time reading and playing cards. And she'd been told that tea was served in the afternoon. The luxury of the appointments made her think of the Fergusons. She thought wistfully of Emma and wished she could see her again. She remembered then too seeing Harry Ferguson at Le Boudoir, and wondered what other lascivious mischief he was up to, and whether his wife was almost as busy as he was, pursuing other men.

Angélique had learned a great deal about the human race during her time in Paris: the people who were unexpectedly far nicer than you expected, those who pretended to be and weren't, the strength, values, and principles of the women who had worked for her despite what they did for a living, and the lack of those same values in others who claimed to have them, how easily people betrayed each other, and how strong one had to become to survive. She had been learning that lesson for three years since her father's death. It was impossible to imagine what his reaction would be to what her life had become, and if he would be proud of her for surviving, or deeply ashamed. She hoped more of the former, but there were things she wasn't proud of either. She had done the best she could in the circumstances she had, and hoped that if he was watching over her, he'd understand.

She was thinking about it with a look of longing and regret as she stared out to sea under the billowing sails, and then closed her eyes, and a moment later she heard a voice beside her and glanced up. It was a tall man with a pleasant face.

"It can't be as bad as all that," he said sympathetically.

"Sorry, I was just thinking." She smiled shyly at him through her veil.

"Of something not very happy, I'm afraid." He had seen her twice on deck, and didn't intend to speak to her, but she had looked so heartbroken, as she gazed out to sea, that he felt he must. No one deserved to be that sad.

"I've lost my husband, and I'm leaving home," she said, grasping at a rapid explanation for her situation and grief. It seemed the right thing to say and all she could think of just then.

"Which proves that there is always someone with worse troubles than one's own. I just lost my fiancée. To another man," he added openly. "I came to Europe for a change of scene, from all the gossip in New York. It turns out that running away doesn't really work. So I'm going home, after a month of solitary pursuits and feeling sorry for myself," he said ruefully, and smiled. She wondered what he'd say if she told him she had lost the brothel she'd built and was grieving for her business and clients and the wonderful women who worked for her. It made her smile to think of it. Her honesty would have been so absurd and would have shocked him profoundly.

"I'm sorry to hear about your fiancée," she said sympathetically, surprised and touched by how honest he had been, which was very different from the European men she knew, who were always more hidden about their feelings.

"And I about your husband. Do you have children?" He hadn't seen any when she boarded the ship, and he had first noticed her then. He had seen her only with a maid. Their cabins weren't far apart, on the same deck, although hers was larger—he could tell from where it was placed. But his was pleasant too. She shook her head in answer to his question.

"No, I don't." *And probably never will,* she almost added. She would never have children now. Who would marry her if she was honest with him? She had chosen her destiny in Paris when she opened Le Boudoir. Some of the girls might marry eventually, like Fabienne, but in her world she couldn't. The man she was talking to on the deck of the ship had no idea what she was or where she'd been. She was sure he wouldn't have spoken to her publicly if he did—only in a house like the one she'd run, if he was inclined to those pursuits. And the fact that she'd never engaged upstairs with her clients made no difference. She was tainted forever, and she knew it. All she could do now would be the same thing again when the time was right, and open another, similar house. All the girls were hoping she would. And her clients would be delighted to return, and grateful for her having spared them from the scandal of the murder. And in the meantime, she had enhanced the gift from her father by a healthy amount. She and the girls had benefited handsomely from the success of Le Boudoir.

"Will you be visiting New York for long?" he asked politely, and she looked vague.

"I don't know. A few months, perhaps a year. I have no reason to hurry back." He had realized by then that she wasn't French, but English, although he had heard her speak French to the deck stewards when she declined a deck chair and a blanket they had offered, and said she didn't need them. He spoke enough French to understand, and she sounded fluent to him.

"Do you live in England, or Paris?" he asked, curious about her, and the correct answer was "nowhere," which was why she looked so sad.

"We moved to Paris from England a year ago, and then my husband died. I thought I'd go to New York while I decide what to do now. It's all rather a big change." He liked the aristocratic sound of her voice, and she was friendlier and more accessible than most of the English women he'd met, and she seemed comfortable speaking to a man, which wasn't always the case for a woman of high rank alone. It was a practiced art she'd learned, and had overcome most of her initial shyness in Paris, which he had no way to know.

"Do you have friends in New York?" he asked her.

She hesitated before she answered. "Not many." And those she did know, she couldn't look up and wouldn't have known how to find them anyway. It would have been most inappropriate to contact them, given where they'd met. They'd had several American clients in the past year, mostly from New York, and a few from Boston. His question made her think of John Carson, and their difficult final exchange, when he'd been so unhappy over her turning down his proposal. She had no regrets about it, even now. She wasn't going to marry a man she didn't love, for money. She simply didn't love him and was sure she never could. There was something about him that was wrong for her, despite his generous offers, first to be his mistress, then his wife, after his previous wife died. She still remembered something hard in him, and anger when he didn't get his way.

The man Angélique was speaking to thought she was brave to go to New York, with few friends. It was an unusual thing for a woman to do, and he admired the courage it showed.

"My name is Andrew Hanson, by the way," he said, extending a

hand, which she shook with her delicate black-gloved one. He noticed how small her hands were, and she had tiny feet in elegant
black shoes.

"Angélique Latham," she introduced herself, praying he didn't
know her brother Tristan or who he was, or even worse, Edward. He
had been as repulsive as ever when she saw him in Paris.

"That's a very pretty name," Andrew commented, and she was a
beautiful woman. And he liked talking to her. They stood in silence
for a while, looking out to sea, each lost in their own thoughts, and
then she made a move as though to leave.

"I'm going to read in my cabin for a while," she said quietly, and
he smiled at her. He was a great deal taller than she, and appeared
to be about ten years older. He had guessed her age to be about
twenty-four or -five—she seemed older than she was because of the
elegant wardrobe, which was her intention. She loved pretty clothes,
and had developed a taste for them in Paris, and indulged it whenever possible. He didn't ask to see her again. There was no need to.
They would meet often on the ship in the next weeks. It was a long
trip. They had the luxury of time to get to know each other better, if
they chose. They might make it to New York in three weeks in good
weather, or four if conditions were less favorable or the wind was
poor.

He didn't want to intrude on her mourning, particularly not
knowing how recently her husband had died, and he didn't want to
ask. He had been jilted nearly at the altar, two days before the wedding, in early August. And the wound inflicted by his fiancée had
finally begun to heal six weeks later, enough so to be content talking
to a pretty woman on a ship. As she walked away he smiled and
then he went for a long walk alone on the deck.

Angélique fell asleep on her bed reading her book, in the gentle movement of the ship, and never appeared for tea. Claire came to check on her, found her asleep, and left her alone. She woke in time for supper, but decided to eat in her stateroom. She didn't emerge again until the next day in a striking white wool suit and another enormous hat, which this time showed more of her face. She noticed Andrew again when she came onto the deck, and he looked pleased to see her as he approached. She was far more beautifully dressed than any woman on the ship, and the other women stared in envy at what she wore.

"I didn't see you at tea or supper yesterday," he commented. "Were you all right?"

"Yes, just tired. The book I was reading was very boring, and I fell asleep." She smiled at him, and he laughed.

"I always fall asleep when I read. And that's not a good thing. I'm a lawyer, and I have to read a lot." They fell into step together, as they walked along, while others read or dozed, the women under parasols to avoid the sun. He noticed that Angélique didn't seem to mind the sun and didn't carry a parasol of her own.

"What sort of law do you practice?" she asked, seeming to care about what he did. She was an expert at drawing men out about themselves—it was second nature to her now, and she enjoyed it. He seemed like an intelligent, interesting man, even though he was young.

"I've been practicing general law, and some constitutional law, which is very dull. I want to go into politics. I'm hoping to run for Congress or the Senate in a year or two."

"Maybe you'll be president one day," she teased him, but she had no idea who he was, or what his connections were. Perhaps he really would. America was so different from England, where you had to be born to the ruling class. For Americans, everything was possible, for anyone.

"Maybe," he said cautiously, "although that is my father's dream for me more than my own," he added honestly. "I'd be content to be a congressman or senator. I think that was one of the things that frightened my fiancée. She didn't like the idea at all. She thought being a politician would be 'vulgar' and a very unpleasant life. She tried to talk me out of it several times." He smiled ruefully at Angélique again and was surprised himself by the things he told her.

"I feel the same way about being king," Angélique said with a straight face. "So vulgar and so much work." And then she laughed, and he did too. He noticed that she looked very young when she laughed.

"Have you ever met the king?" he asked. He had the impression it might be possible, but she shook her head.

"Not this one." She didn't say she was related to him, and to the new king of France. It was interesting that both countries had new monarchs in the same year.

They walked along for a while longer, and he introduced her to some people he knew, who looked intrigued by her. And then they sat down on two deck chairs and ordered tea. It came with delicate biscuits, which were delicious.

They talked about American politics then, and the election of Andrew Jackson two years before, who seemed like an impressive person to her. And Andrew explained some things that she didn't understand and found confusing about American elections. It was all unfamiliar to her, but she found his explanations to her easy to understand as they talked.

"What did you do in Paris to keep busy?" he asked her, and she thought about it for a minute, trying to decide how to translate it palatably for him.

"Some charitable work, helping young women who had grown up disadvantaged, and many of them had been seriously abused and exploited. I did what I could to help them improve their lot in life." She made it sound like a noble cause, and in some ways it was, and was the truth, although she didn't try to change what they did for a living and had benefited from it herself. But she had seen to it that they were paid handsomely, and the money they earned made it possible for them to follow a different path now if they wished.

"And did you succeed?"

"I think so."

"That's a little bit like politics, trying to help the masses and get them a fair deal."

"I never thought of it that way. Sometimes I think our kings just eat a lot and drink too much, and indulge themselves at our expense." It had certainly been true of the previous kings of England and France, both of whom were obese, drank excessively, and had lost touch with their subjects, with dire results. And the economies of their countries had suffered because of it.

"Are you interested in politics, Angélique?"

"Sometimes. The brief revolution in Paris in July was very unnerving."

"Were you in the city?"

"No, I was a coward, and took refuge in Normandy with friends."

"That sounds sensible," he approved. "And the monarchy in England certainly seems more solid than the one in France."

"They haven't had a revolution in England. My French relatives were all killed in the last one, except my mother, who was sent to England as a baby, which is how she met my father later. She was French." Hence her name, he surmised.

"Are your parents still alive?" She shook her head, looking sad for a moment.

"No, they're not. Both of them are dead. I have two brothers, but we're not on good terms." *To say the least,* she thought.

"I'm an only child, and I lost my mother too. And I have a father I don't always get along with, and sometimes try not to see. He's very ambitious about my political career, more so than I am, so we frequently don't agree. I see politics as a chance to make a difference, which is important to me. I'm not content to just accept things as they are. I want to have a voice in how the country's run." She looked fascinated as he said it. She would have liked to do something like that too, which was impossible for a woman.

"You're lucky to be a man. Women don't get that opportunity."

"Maybe they will one day. Things change."

"Very slowly. That probably won't happen in your lifetime or mine."

"Sometimes things happen faster than we expect," he said hopefully. He had a lot of ideals and exciting ideas, some of them too early for his time. But he believed that someone had to take the first step. "Would you like to join me for dinner?" he asked cautiously, not sure if she would think it proper, and she nodded and smiled. She went to change a short while later, and met him in the saloon, where tables were set up. She was wearing a black taffeta dress, with a diamond pin on her shoulder that caught his eye, and he complimented her on it.

"It was my mother's," she said simply, and had been in her locked trunk for a while, although she'd worn it once or twice at Le Boudoir on special nights, where it had been admired too. "My father gave it to her." She didn't tell him that her brother's wife, Elizabeth, had gotten most of the jewels. There were many things he didn't need to know. He was curious to know who her father was, but not enough so to ask, and he didn't want to be rude.

They had a very pleasant time during the meal, and she dined in her stateroom again that night. Claire came to visit her, and said she was having a good time with the people in steerage, there was a very nice Irish girl in her cabin, going to meet her relatives in the States, and they had made friends. She hoped to see her in New York. Angélique felt the same way about Andrew, and hoped they'd meet again. And for now, a comfortable friendship was developing. It made the trip more agreeable for them both, as they nursed their respective wounds and losses, although hers were different than he thought.

On the third day of the trip, when they met on deck, she noticed several people watching them as they walked along. They made a striking couple, and the women admired her clothes and watched to see what she wore each day, and they thought there was something mysterious about her. Andrew had noticed their attention too, and the admiring gazes of other men. He liked being with her, and being the lucky one she was talking to. And she looked deeply intent on everything he said, as though he was the only man in the world she wanted to be walking and having a conversation with. She made him feel important and special, which was how he was coming to feel about her. When she listened to him, she was fully engaged, unlike so many women he knew who seemed bored, or were overly interested for all the wrong reasons. There was none of that with

Angélique. She was a straightforward person, who was comfortable talking to a man, with no ulterior motives behind it, other than the pleasure of his company.

On the fourth day, she agreed to have supper with him, and he was delighted. She wore a spectacular, simple black evening gown with a discreetly bell-shaped skirt, and a low-cut neck, diamonds at her ears, a string of pearls, and long white gloves, which she only removed when she ate. And they both enjoyed listening to the musicians play for the entertainment of the guests. And after a while, Andrew suggested they go out on deck for some air. The sea was very calm and the boat steady, as he helped her put a small fox wrap on her shoulders, and they stepped outside. They had met the captain, and he was very pleasant to both of them, as they passed him leaving the saloon, where he had been visiting some of the passengers. And he greeted Mrs. Latham like the lady that she was. He didn't address her as Her Ladyship, because he didn't know, and it didn't occur to Andrew that she had a title. As an American, he didn't think in those terms.

They dined together many nights thereafter, when she didn't dine in her cabin. By day they walked on deck, talked for hours about a multitude of subjects, and played cards. The weather had been perfect, and the trip went faster than expected under cameo blue skies.

They got to know each other during the voyage, and felt like old friends by the last day, after just over three weeks on the ship, seeing each other night and day. Andrew had had a wonderful time with her, and told her so as they sat in the saloon sipping champagne on the last night.

"I'd like to see you again in New York, if that would be all right." He hoped that she'd agree, and she had enjoyed the voyage as much as he. She hadn't expected to meet anyone, and didn't want to. She had been intending to mourn her lost life and prepare for a new one, and instead he had swept her off her feet like a fairy tale, and it made the prospect of New York much more exciting.

"I'd like that very much too," she said demurely, lowering her eyes. It was hard to look at him sometimes. His gaze was so direct, and his infatuation with her so obvious. He was the first man she had ever met that she genuinely wanted to spend time with, and where it was even a serious possibility. The others were all either unsuitable, too much older, or married. Andrew was none of those, although Angélique knew full well that she was the unsuitable one, and she wasn't sure what to do about it, but she knew she didn't want the fantasy to end. She had become accustomed to him, and didn't want to lose that now.

"Where will you be staying?" he asked quietly.

"I have a reservation at the City Hotel." It was the best hotel in New York, and supposedly quite large, with a hundred and forty rooms, a ballroom, shops, a library, a dining room, and several large suites, one of which she had written to reserve. "I thought I'd stay there for a while, and perhaps find a house to let for a few months, perhaps six months, or longer, until I go back." He nodded thoughtfully.

"I can help you find one, if you like. I know New York better than you do, and you'll want to be in the right neighborhood."

"Yes, I would," she agreed, as they smiled at each other. New York was going to be so much more fun now because of him.

"I'd like to show you around the city," he offered, and she looked pleased, and then they went back inside for a last glass of champagne. He left her at her cabin with regret that night. He liked having her to himself and not having to compete with all the men he knew would pursue her in New York. He had been well aware too that there were several who would have liked to do so on the ship, but he had happily monopolized her for the entire three weeks, and she didn't seem to mind. On the contrary, she seemed to be as delighted as he was to spend time together.

They stood side by side on deck as the ship docked the next day. Claire had packed all her trunks and bags, and they were waiting in Angélique's stateroom to be removed. She was wearing a dove-gray satin dress and matching coat, with a hat made of the same fabric by her favorite milliner in Paris, with a small silver fox around her neck. She looked like a picture in a magazine, as the other women stared at her in envy one last time. They had been watching her wardrobe for the entire trip and so had he.

"Is anyone meeting you?" Andrew asked with a look of concern, and she shook her head.

"I asked for the purser to arrange for a carriage to take me to the hotel." He nodded, satisfied.

"I'll come to check on you at the hotel later, to make sure that everything is all right."

"I'll be fine," she assured him, but she appreciated his help. This was a turn of events she had never expected. She would have managed without him, and had been determined to do so on her own, but his appearance in her life was a gift she was grateful for now. And she had had fun with him, and could tell that he had enjoyed it too. It had been healing for them both. "Will you be very busy?" she asked him, and he nodded, as they watched the dockworkers secure the ship with enormous ropes.

"I have to go back to work. I've been dodging my responsibilities for two months. That's about as long as you can get away with for a broken heart." He smiled as he said it, and looked as though it wasn't troubling him anymore. He turned to Angélique seriously then. "You've changed everything for me in the past few weeks. I never expected this to happen," he said in a gentle voice. He wanted her to know how he felt before they parted and went on to their lives in New York.

"Neither did I. I thought I'd cry for the entire trip." She smiled at him. "I had a wonderful time with you, Andrew. Thank you." He didn't answer her, and slipped her small gloved hand into his until the disembarkation was announced, and then he walked her to her cabin and left her with Claire, and went to check on his own bags, and then returned to escort her off the ship and see her to her carriage. They walked off the ship together, both of them beaming, and when he handed her into the carriage, she turned, and he kissed her on the cheek. He could barely tear himself away. He could no longer imagine not being with her every day.

"I'll see you later," he said gently. He had given her his address, and told her to send a message if she had any problem. And she waved as they rolled away, with a separate carriage behind them for her bags. Claire was riding with her, and seemed sad to leave the ship and her new friends. They had both had an unexpectedly happy voyage, and exchanged a smile as they rode to the hotel.

Chapter 18

The City Hotel was grander than she had expected, but it was at a price she could afford, with her father's money and her own. She was always careful with it, and knew that what she had would have to last her forever. She could expect no one's help, and didn't. And despite her fondness for fashion and expensive gowns, she wasn't extravagant. But her suite of rooms at the hotel was beautiful, and the decorating excellent, and Claire said she had a very nice room too, on the top floor with the other maids.

Two hours after they'd arrived, as Claire was unpacking her many trunks, and seeing what needed pressing, and Angélique ordered a light meal, an enormous arrangement of flowers arrived for her. It looked like an entire rose garden. It was from Andrew, and the card said "Welcome to New York. I miss you already. Fondly, A.H." They set it on a table, and Angélique was admiring it when an assistant manager came to tell her that Mr. Hanson was in the lobby and wished to come up.

"Send him up," Angélique said, and gave the man some coins, and a moment later, Andrew strode into the room, looking energetic and happy to see her as he kissed her on the cheek. The time on the boat, with so much opportunity to be together, had brought them closer faster, and in greater intimacy than might have happened otherwise. She felt as though she had known him for months, or even years.

"How would you like to look around New York?" he offered. His carriage was downstairs. It was a beautiful fall afternoon, and he had decided not to go to work until the next day. "One more day of shirking my duties can't hurt." He looked young and mischievous as he said it.

"You'll never become president this way," she scolded him, but she was pleased, picked up a wrap, and followed him out of the suite. And a moment later they were rolling through the streets of New York in his very handsomely appointed carriage. It wasn't showy, but it was extremely fine and appropriate for a man. And she enjoyed sitting next to him while he pointed out the sights, and instructed his coachman where to take them next. By late afternoon, she had seen all the important landmarks. They drove past Niblo's Garden, with its theater, Vauxhall Gardens, the National Theater, and the Morris-Jumel mansion, the James Watson home, and Gracie Mansion, as well as Castle Garden, City Hall, and St. Patrick's Cathedral on Mott and Prince streets. It was an extensive tour, and they were back at the hotel for a late tea.

They had it in the dining room, where they could watch guests and visitors going in and out, and she could observe what they were wearing, and the different styles of dress. Women seemed more conservatively dressed in New York than they were in Paris, although there were some beautiful coats and gowns, and a few very pretty hats, though none as elaborate or elegant as her own. Andrew loved the way she looked with every change. He had never known a woman as fashionable as she. His lost fiancée had been very plain compared to her, and far less sophisticated and interested in the world. He was beginning to feel that their broken engagement had been a blessing in disguise. He could never have guessed that Angélique would come along and steal his heart.

He left her to settle in that night, but invited her to supper and the theater at the Sans Souci the next day, the opera at the National Theater two days later, and for supper and dancing at Delmonico's and Niblo's Garden after that. She barely had time to catch her breath, between evenings with him, and discovering the city on her own by day.

By the end of two weeks, she hadn't met any of his friends, and he openly admitted that he wanted her to himself, although they ran into his acquaintances at the theater and in restaurants and he introduced her proudly. His male friends were struck by her beauty, and even the women were impressed and liked her easy, sunny ways. She didn't put on airs, and didn't seem taken with herself. She was happy to meet them, and seemed ecstatic at Andrew's side.

They looked at a few houses for her to move into, but she saw nothing she liked, and said she was happy at the hotel for now. And three weeks after they'd arrived, Andrew kissed her firmly and passionately one night. After six weeks constantly in each other's company, he could no longer stop himself and settle for a kiss on the cheek. And she didn't object, she was as in love with him as he was with her. It was the beginning of November by then, and he said he wanted to introduce her to his father, but he was very busy at the moment with some important deals, and traveling back and forth to Boston. Andrew was happy to spend all his time with her when he wasn't working himself, and they spent Thanksgiving together at the hotel, since his father was away with friends. Andrew explained the holiday to her, and she liked the idea of a day, spent with friends and family, based on gratitude.

It was nearly Christmas, three months after they'd met, when they came back from a walk in the snow one afternoon, when he took both her hands in his to warm them, and then as she took off her hat and put down her fur muff in the parlor of her suite, he stunned her by dropping to one knee.

"Andrew, what are you doing?" she asked him gently, her eyes bright with all she felt for him, and her cheeks pink from the cold.

"Angélique Latham," he said with tears of emotion shining in his eyes, "will you do me the honor of marrying me?" She hadn't expected it, although anyone else would have, watching them. Marriage wasn't the outcome she'd anticipated, and she had had no expectations or designs on him. She sincerely loved him, and tears filled her eyes then as she nodded.

"OhmyGod . . . yes . . . yes . . . oh my darling, I love you," she said, as he stood up and took her in his arms and held her. All he could envision was their bright future together, and all their dreams come true. And as he held her, she knew that there were things she should say to him, but she didn't want to lose him. She wondered if she should tell him about Paris, and Le Boudoir, but perhaps he didn't need to know. She didn't want to hurt him, nor lie to him, and she was troubled by it, and all she knew was how much she loved him and wanted to be his wife. She had never felt that way before. "I love you so much" was all she could say. He didn't know about her being a nanny, or her brother abandoning her either. There was so much he didn't know, and he accepted her as she was. How much more could she ask, and how could she risk losing him now if she told him everything? But what if he found out? New York seemed so far away from all that had happened to her in the past three years. She clung to him like a lost child, as he began to make plans for the future.

"We have to find a house," he said, looking excited, "and I want to get married soon. We don't have to wait." And then he thought of something. "Should I write to your brother and ask him for your hand? I know you said you don't get along, but I don't want to offend him, or do something improperly."

"He won't be offended," she said quietly, brought to earth by what Andrew said. "He won't care. He hates me. You don't need to ask anyone."

"Should we invite him to the wedding, and your other brother?"

"Certainly not. If you do, I won't come," she teased him, and he laughed.

"I want you to meet my father as soon as he gets back from Boston. He's been insanely busy for the past few months. I know he'll love you," Andrew said happily.

Three days later, he gave her an engagement ring that was far bigger than anything she'd expected, with an intricate setting and a large diamond in the center. She would have been happy with a tiny ring or none at all. It was Andrew that she loved, not what he could give her. She had never been as happy in her life, thinking of their future, and the days ahead of them. And now he wanted to introduce her to his friends as his future wife. But he thought it best to introduce her to his father first, who was a stickler about tradition and form and very old-fashioned. Andrew warned her that he was very conservative in his beliefs, but he was sure he would be enchanted by her. He knew that everyone would be, and he was most of all.

He wanted to plan for their wedding and didn't see why they should wait long. They both knew what they wanted, and were of a reasonable age, and as he said it, she admitted to him that she was younger than she'd said at first. She said it seemed more respectable to her than her proper age. "I'm really twenty-one," she said shyly. It was the only truth she was willing to admit to him of the lies she'd told. And he laughed at her confession and was pleased. He was thirty, and he thought their ages right together. He thought everything about their union was perfect, and he was certain his father would think so too. Angélique hoped that would be the case and was nervous about meeting him. Andrew made him sound daunting and a little stiff, but she was sure he loved his only son, and wanted him to be happy, and they were.

"Let's get married in February, on Saint Valentine's Day," Andrew suggested, and she loved the idea too.

"It doesn't give us much time to plan," she said thoughtfully. "Do you want a big wedding?" She wasn't sure how to arrange it, especially in New York. She could have done so in Paris or London, but not here. The city was too new to her.

"Not really," he said honestly. "You have no friends here, and if you don't want your family to come from England, it would feel wrong to have hundreds of my acquaintances whom you don't know. Why don't we try to keep it small?" And he didn't say it, but since she was a recent widow, he didn't think they should have a showy wedding, and he was sure his father would think so too. Andrew thought an intimate wedding would be more appropriate, with only his father and closest friends. He didn't care how they got married, as long as they did, and the sooner the better. And he couldn't wait to start a family with her, and she liked that idea too. All she wanted now was to be his wife and have his babies. And she wanted to write to the girls from Le Boudoir and tell them, so they wouldn't expect her to come back and open the house again. She knew Fabienne would be happy for her. Angélique had written to her when she got to New York, and Fabienne had responded that she and Jacques had gotten married in October and a baby was already on the way. Their lives had changed so much.

She was planning to sell the furniture from Le Boudoir that she had put in storage. She didn't want the furniture from her brothel in their new home. She had written to them as well and the storage company was going to sell it for her.

Angélique could hardly absorb it all as she and Andrew made plans, and he told her that they were having supper with his father the night before Christmas Eve, and he was very excited to meet her, and pleased for his son. From everything Andrew had described to him, she sounded like the perfect girl, and Andrew knew she was.

The night they went to supper with his father, she wore a simple black velvet gown, with just enough bosom showing, but not too much, her mother's pearls, and a small tiara in her hair that had been her maternal grandmother's when she was a young girl. It was something Angélique had always treasured and had only worn once before when she went to a ball in London with her father, and after that he got sick, they stopped going to town, and she never wore it again. It seemed appropriate to wear tonight, with the beautiful engagement ring Andrew had given her. His breath caught when he picked her up at the hotel. She looked exquisite, and he had never been so proud in his life. He couldn't wait for his father to meet her.

Angélique was a little startled when the carriage pulled up to an enormous mansion on Pearl Street. She hadn't expected it to be quite so grand, and was a little daunted for a moment, but she had been in bigger houses before, she reminded herself. And Belgrave, where she had grown up, was many times larger than this. She had never told Andrew anything about it, there was no reason to, since it was no longer hers and she couldn't go there anymore. There was no point crying about the past with the future so bright.

Two footmen and a butler let them into the house, which reminded her of Belgrave again, but everything here seemed newer, and smaller of course, than their vast ancestral home in England. The front hall of Andrew's father's house was all done in marble, with an enormous chandelier of candles to light the room. She took off her wrap and left it with one of the footmen, as Andrew led her into the large drawing room, where his father was waiting for them. He had his back to them, and was looking out at the garden with a drink in his hand, wearing white tie and tails, as Andrew was. His father turned, and the two men exchanged a warm glance, and he then turned his gaze to his future daughter-in-law with a welcoming smile, and as he did, Angélique nearly fainted, and so did he, as they stared at each other in disbelief.

It was John Carson, the American financier, who had proposed to her only three months before at Le Boudoir, and whom she had refused. He had clearly used "Carson" as an alias for his visits to Le Boudoir, and not his real name. Neither of them said anything for a minute, as his face hardened and Angélique tried to cover her shock at seeing him and went deathly pale. It was a final cruel turn of fate in too many recent years of them. He had been deeply infatuated with her, and first offered to make her his mistress, and then was determined to marry her once he was widowed, despite her running a brothel. He had been willing to do almost anything to marry her and had been shocked and angry when she declined, and now she was marrying his son. It was almost too ironic to be true. He knew about her past in Paris, and she was terrified that he would tell Andrew now.

"I . . . how do you do . . . ," she said, curtsying to him in deep respect, with tears glittering in her eyes. She prayed that he would be able to get over what had happened, and accept her as Andrew's future wife, but the look in his eyes was one of pure fury, and Andrew saw it too.

"Is something wrong?" he asked his father, glancing from him to Angélique, unable to understand the expression on his father's face.

"Not at all," John said to his son. "Happy to meet you," he said to Angélique, finished his drink, and signaled a footman for another, and sat down in the drawing room with them with an unpleasant expression. All he wanted to do was get through the evening, and get her out of his house and his son's life. There was no way he would allow Andrew to marry her, although he had been willing to himself, had wanted to very much, and had done everything he could to convince her. He hadn't recovered from her refusal yet. And now this cruel turn of fate as they met again.

Supper was agonizingly painful and silent, as John continued to drink heavily, said not a word to her, never even glanced at her, and spoke to his son about business matters as though she wasn't there.

Andrew had no idea what was going on, but Angélique looked ill all night and barely ate. And as soon as the meal was over, his father stood up and asked to have a word with him alone. He walked into the library, and acted like a raging bull the moment Andrew closed the door and turned to him.

"What is going on?" He had never seen his father look that way before, like an animal in a cage.

"You cannot marry that woman!" his father shouted at him. "I won't allow it! You must break it off at once!"

"Why? I don't understand. You've been acting like a maniac all night."

"I know things about her that you don't. She's a whore, Andrew, and nothing more. She's after you for your money, and mine." If that had been true, she would have accepted his offer in Paris, and she had turned him down flat, but the last thing he wanted was for his son to marry the woman he had wanted, and what's more one who had been the madam of a Paris brothel. He considered himself old enough to make a choice like that, but not his son. Andrew's mother had been a respectable woman, from one of the finest families in New York, no matter how much they had come to dislike each other. This girl was anything but respectable, no matter how distinguished she seemed. In John's opinion, it was an act, convincing but certainly not enough to warrant her marrying his son. "I will do everything I can to stand in the way of your marriage, Andrew. You must stop this travesty at once."

"It's not a travesty, I love her. She's a wonderful person. Have you ever met her before?"

"No!" his father shouted at him, lying to him, but he could hardly admit the truth, that he had met her in a bordel, and proposed to her himself. But he was worried now that Angélique would tell An-drew, if she told him the truth about the rest. It was a risk for him, a serious one. He would never want his son to know something like that about him. Had she agreed to marry him, he would have in-vented a proper history for her, just as she herself had done to marry his son. "You know nothing of her history. I do. I've never met her," he lied again, "but I've heard about her from others. She's quite fa-mous in Paris. What did she tell you about herself?"

"That she has two brothers who don't like her and whom she hates. Her parents are dead. She was married in Paris, her husband died, and she came here for a change of scene. And I met her on the ship. Why? What do you know different from that?" Andrew looked worried, but not very. He was far more upset by how badly his fa-ther had behaved, and what he was saying now, all of which sounded like lies to him. "Are you upset because she's European, and not an American girl from a family you know?" He was such a snob that it was possible. Andrew felt sure his father would never have gotten involved with a European woman himself. Little did he know of what his father did.

"That has nothing to do with it, although you don't need to go abroad to find a wife. There are plenty of nice girls here. She'll de-stroy your political career and your chance to be important in poli-tics. And I can tell you one thing—I will do everything in my power to prevent you marrying that girl!" He was still shouting, and his eyes and a vein in his forehead were bulging, he was so crazed. "Tell her to tell you the truth about herself, and let's see if she does! I can assure you it has nothing to do with the story you know." He was pacing the room as he spoke. Andrew hadn't moved as he watched him.

"She's an honest person, and I will ask her. We all have secrets we don't want others to know. If she has any, I'm sure she'll tell me the truth. But I'm thirty years old, Father. You can't tell me who to marry, or forbid me to marry a woman I love. I won't end up like you and Mother, hating each other for thirty years, lonely and miserable, because you married someone from the 'right' family. I'd rather be married to someone from the wrong family, than the wrong woman, which is what you did. And you can't dictate to me how to live my life. I was just engaged to a girl you considered the right one, and she ran off with my best friend after cheating on me." He was angry now too. He had never seen such appalling behavior from his father before, and he was deeply sorry for Angélique, who had lived through an evening of torture and been dignified and polite about it, although she looked like she was about to burst into tears.

"I'm sure this one will cheat on you too, very quickly. And my marriage to your mother and the reasons for it are none of your business."

"I watched the two of you loathe each other all my life, barely able to stand being in the same room. I don't want that for myself." They both knew he was right, but John said nothing as he stared at his son miserably.

"Get rid of her," he said bluntly. "You'll regret it if you don't. And I will never have her in my house again. If you stay with her out of some folly, or because she lies to you, don't expect me to receive her or ever see her again."

"I don't know why she'd want to after the way you behaved to-night," Andrew said, as he strode to the door and yanked it open. "Goodnight, Father. Thank you for supper." And with that, he walked out and slammed the door behind him, as John looked at it, sank heavily into a chair, and suddenly felt a hundred years old. She had rejected him, and now she was marrying Andrew. He had wanted to own her, possess her, and give her everything he had. He had done everything he could to lure her and convince her. He had been obsessed with her, and still was, and now Andrew had won. And at that exact moment, he didn't know who he hated more, Angélique or his son, for having her.

Chapter 19

Andrew and Angélique rode back to the hotel in silence. He was stone-faced, thinking about his father, and what he'd said, and Angélique was sure he was furious with her, and she was deathly afraid of what his father had told him behind closed doors after supper. Her face was ashen in the darkened carriage as she sat up straight in her seat. She expected never to see Andrew again. He wouldn't marry her now after what his father must have told him, and she was prepared to give him back the ring when they got back to the hotel. She didn't want to give it to him in the carriage and risk dropping it on the floor. But she had no doubt that their engagement was over as she fought tears. She just wanted to be alone now to grieve what they had had so briefly. It was yet another loss in her life, an important one.

The doorman helped her down from the carriage, and Andrew looked at her seriously. "May I come upstairs?" She nodded. She would give him the ring there. He didn't have to ask for it. She understood. She didn't deserve it, and she hadn't told him the truth about her life. It had been an incredibly cruel turn of fate that the man who had proposed to her in Paris under an assumed name, and whom she had refused, had turned out to be Andrew's father. She couldn't imagine anything worse except if she had slept with him. Thank God she hadn't. She truly couldn't have faced Andrew then.

The moment they were in the parlor of her suite, Andrew gently took her shoulders in his hands and spoke to her kindly. "I want you to sit down, and we're going to talk. My father says that there are things about you I don't know. I want you to tell me everything now, no matter how bad you think it is. I love you, and it won't make a difference to me. But I should know, so something like this doesn't happen again. If I'm to be your husband, I want to know everything about you. Love is about loving not just the good parts, but the bad parts too." Tears rolled down her cheeks as he said it, and they sat down.

"I don't deserve you," she said in a choked voice, as he held her hand. "Would you like your ring back now?" She began to take it off, and he stopped her.

"No, I wouldn't. Now start at the beginning. We can skip diapers and your first nanny, but I want to hear the rest, so I understand things better." He could vaguely guess what his father had been hinting at, but he wasn't sure. And now he wanted to know. "I want the whole truth, all of it. There should be no secrets between us."

"My mother died when I was born, she was French. You already know that. She was a Bourbon and an Orléans, and her family was killed in the Revolution. My father was Phillip, Duke of Westerfield, also related to the king. And he loved me very much. He was wonderful to me." Her eyes filled with tears as she said it, especially after tonight. "We lived in a very big house called Belgrave Castle, in Hertfordshire. It's a beautiful house. And my father was married before. He had two sons by his first marriage, and they hated my mother, and me even more, and were jealous of me all my life. We had a house in Grosvenor Square too, where my oldest brother lived for the last few years, before my father died. Tristan, my oldest brother, has a dreadful wife named Elizabeth, and two daughters. They all hate me too." Andrew was listening to her quietly, and could imagine the scene; first marriage, jealous sons, Angélique the apple of her father's eye.

"Because of the laws in England," she went on, "my oldest brother had to inherit everything. The title, my father's fortune, Belgrave Castle, Grosvenor Square, all of it. My father couldn't leave me anything, not legally anyway. He wanted Tristan to let me live in a large cottage on the estate when he died, but Tristan wouldn't allow it, nor let me stay at home. I was eighteen when my father died, and he gave me some money and my mother's jewelry the night before he died, and that's all I was entitled to, unless my brother wanted to be more generous with me.

"Tristan and his family, and my brother Edward, arrived as soon as Papa died, and the night of the funeral, Tristan told me that I would be a burden to him, I no longer had a right to be there. And they arranged to have me hired as a nanny by people they knew in Hampshire, and I would be leaving the next day. They claimed I was a distant cousin, and sent me to some very spoiled rich people, where I was the nanny to their six children and became a servant." Andrew made no comment, but his heart began to ache for her as he listened, at the vision of a young girl sent away from her home to become a servant after her father's death. It was a terrible story.

"I loved the children I took care of. They were very nice, although their parents were spoiled and dreadful. I was there for sixteen months." And then she told him about Bertie, defending herself, biting him, and the lies he told the next day as revenge. "So I was sacked, and sent away that day without a reference. At first I didn't understand what that meant. It meant I could not get any kind of job when I went to London. No one would hire me without a character." Andrew could guess what came next, or thought he could. "They suggested I try France and I might have better luck. I didn't. No one would hire me there either, not as a nanny, a maid, or to scrub floors. With no reference, I couldn't get a job."

"You don't need to tell me the rest," he said gently, not wanting to put her through further agony and confession, and humiliate her totally. He already felt desperately sorry for her.

"Yes, I do. You said you wanted to know it all. I stayed at a hotel in Paris, trying to figure out what to do. A woman I met said I should try to come to America, but I was afraid to." She told him about finding Fabienne then, injured in the gutter, beaten by a "client." And all the things she had told her, and how sorry she felt for girls like her. "And I couldn't get a job myself, and I didn't want to end up like them. They were being exploited by everyone, their madams, their pimps, the clients, and getting beaten up, and making nothing. The madams and pimps make all the money," she informed him, looking very young, and he smiled.

"So I've been told," he said with a tender look at her. It seemed incredible that she would even know that, given her background and upbringing.

"So I decided to use some of my father's money to set up an establishment, a 'house.' I set out to buy furniture, find girls with Fabienne's help, pay them fairly, and set up the best house in Paris, with the best girls, for the best men." This time Andrew stared at her in disbelief.

"You set up a brothel?" She had finally shocked him, not with the immorality of it, but with the courage, guts, and spirit of enterprise that had led her to do it.

"Yes," she said in a small voice, "I did. And it was wonderful. The house was beautiful. It worked perfectly. The men loved it, the girls were happy, and we made a lot of money, which I shared equally with them. It was the best house in Paris," she said proudly, and Andrew shook his head and laughed. He would never in a million years have guessed that about her, or that she could do it. She was so demure and aristocratic, and so young.

"And you were twenty when you did all this?"

"Yes. It went perfectly for a year and a half." And then she told him about the murder on their last night in business. "All the most powerful men in Paris came to us, and I knew some important people. The minister of the interior was sort of a patron, and a friend. He helped arrange everything that night." She told him about that too. "And he said we had to close. He told me to go away for a while, six months or a year, and then I could come back and set it up again, but there was too much risk for scandal if I stayed open. He told me to book passage on a ship and go to America, so I did. I thought I'd come here for six months and then go back. But then I met you on the boat, and we fell in love and got engaged. I wrote to Fabienne and all the girls to tell them I'm not coming back now. I thought they should know." She looked at him with wide innocent eyes, and he smiled at her. "You know it all now. There is nothing else." Except one last detail, and he wanted to know that too, just for himself.

"I have no right to ask you this, Angélique, but I'd rather know and hear it from you. Did you serve the clients too? . . . the way the girls did?" She shook her head emphatically.

"No, that was part of our agreement from the beginning. I ran the house. I was the madam, but I never had sex with anyone. I'm still a virgin," she said quietly. "Some of the men called me the Ice Queen. I spoke to them in the drawing room, I played cards with them, I knew them well, but it never went any further, and I think they respected it." And so did he.

"That's quite a story, of courage and resourcefulness." And he could tell that she had been honest with him about it. He had trusted her completely, and he wasn't wrong. And he loved her all the more for everything she'd been through. His father was right, she had lied to him, but he respected her more, not less, after what he'd heard. And in her shoes, he realized he might have lied too.

"I'm sorry I was afraid to tell you. I thought about it, but I didn't know how. What about your political career? Won't that hurt you one day? If your father heard about it, I suppose people know, even here," she said, although she knew this wasn't true. She knew that John had met her at the brothel. No one had "told" him in New York.

"It could. But I'm not worried. People have done worse things here in politics and gotten away with it. This is America—there are some very rough people both in business here and in government. They're not all gentlemen. And who would believe this anyway? It's an amazing story." She nodded, grateful that he hadn't gotten up and walked out of the room halfway through it. She started to take his ring off then, and he stopped her again. "I love you, Angélique. Thank you for being honest with me. I want to marry you. This doesn't change anything for me. I just want you to promise me that you'll never be afraid to tell me the truth again."

And then he stopped for a moment and thought about something else he wanted to ask her, just to be sure. "Did you ever see my father there, at the house? Did he ever go there?" She gazed into Andrew's eyes, and agonized over her answer. She felt she had no right to destroy their relationship, even if John hated her. She didn't need to damn him to clear herself, and who they saw at the brothel was like a sacred trust they never admitted to anyone. Even a man like John had a right to secrets from his son. She vowed to herself before she answered that it was the last lie she'd ever tell Andrew. He didn't need to know. It was a generous decision on her part, to protect Andrew's illusions about his father, more than John.

"No, I never saw him there," she said simply, and Andrew nodded.

"I just wondered. I didn't think he would, but you never know. He was so outraged. I'll speak to him tomorrow." He kissed her then, and she looked at him with eyes wide with surprise and gratitude.

"You're sure?" she asked him softly. "I promise you, I will never lie to you again." And she meant it with her heart and soul.

"I'm totally sure. I love you." And then he couldn't help laughing. "It's quite exotic. I'm going to be married to a madam, and a duchess."

"I'm not a duchess," she said primly. "My brother's wife is. But I was a madam." And then she laughed too. "It really was the best house in Paris. I wish you could have seen it," she said, sounding like a child again, and then he kissed her hard as he held her. All he wanted was to marry her as soon as he could. Saint Valentine's Day, or sooner, even now that he knew the truth.

* * *

He strode into his father's office the next day shortly after his father got there, and stood across the desk from him.

"She told me everything," he said, his eyes digging into his father's.

"Did she?" He stared back at his son just as hard. "And what would that be?" He was terrified she had told Andrew about him.

"Being sent away by her brother when her father died, working as a nanny, arriving in London and then Paris without a reference, and setting up a brothel in Paris. It sounds like quite a place." His father's eyes grew even harder, and then he looked away, afraid to meet his son's gaze.

"I wouldn't know, and I don't want to." He didn't dare ask his son if she had said she had met him there, or about his two proposals, first as his mistress, then his wife. But Andrew said nothing about it, which led him to hope that by some miracle she had spared him. He thought Andrew would have said something if he knew. "What about your political ambitions? What happens to all that if someone finds out you're married to a whore?"

"She's not a whore," Andrew said angrily. "She was a madam. And for a girl of twenty, daughter of a duke, in a crazy way, I think that's pretty damn impressive."

"You're out of your mind." He could understand it all too well. He had been out of his mind over her too, and still was. She was that kind of woman, who drove men to wanting her desperately, especially when they couldn't have her. "And I'm not sure the world will care about the distinction between a whore and a madam. To most people, it's the same thing."

"Apparently, it isn't. She ran a business."

"Let's not whitewash this, Andrew. She ran a Paris whorehouse, whether or not she slept with the clients. That's not going to help you become senator, or president one day, if that's what you want. If anyone finds out, the scandal will blow you right out of whatever seat you're in."

"Maybe I don't care about that as much as you do. And I'll take the risk. She's worth it, and I love her. I'm going to marry her, whether you approve or not." John Hanson was silent for a long time, and then slumped in his seat. He didn't want to lose his son, but he would never forgive Angélique either, for loving Andrew and not him. John Hanson was a man who never forgave once he was injured, and held on to enemies for life. She had become one by refusing him in Paris, which he might have forgiven her. But he would never forgive her for preferring his son.

"Do what you want. But never bring her to my home. Never speak to me of her. I think you're a fool to marry her, and I want nothing to do with her. I don't consort with women like that," he lied to Andrew. "And you shouldn't either, let alone marry them. And I am begging you to reconsider." He wouldn't admit to his son that he would have married her himself if he had the chance, whatever sort of woman she was. She was like a beautiful jewel he had wanted to own. Andrew truly loved her, no matter what she had done in the past.

"I would ask the same of you, to reconsider. She's going to be your daughter-in-law, and the mother of your grandchildren one day." The thought of it made John sick, and he didn't comment.

Andrew left then, and had dinner with Angélique at the hotel.

"How was your father?" she asked in a nervous tone. She was afraid that he might have confessed to meeting her, and then Andrew would know she had lied, although it was her only lie to him now, and one she thought best for him. But apparently John had said nothing, and she suspected now that he never would. And she didn't intend to tell Andrew either. It made no difference now.

"He's an unreasonable man sometimes," Andrew said quietly. "And if he's going to be difficult about it, I don't want to wait to get married. Let's get married now, in the next week or two. I want to live with you." She loved that idea too, and they arranged a tiny intimate wedding for New Year's Eve, with two of his close friends as witnesses. Angélique met them a few days later and loved them, and they were crazy about her. They were looking for a house and hadn't found one yet. And his bachelor apartment was too small for both of them.

She and Andrew spent Christmas quietly at the hotel. He went to see his father for a drink, but did not have dinner with him, and neither of them spoke of Angélique.

And on New Year's Eve, in a white satin gown she had brought with her, that she had worn once at Le Boudoir on Christmas, she and Andrew were married in a private ceremony at St. Mark's Church in-the-Bowery, modeled after St. Martin-in-the-Fields Church in London, and he spent the night with her at her hotel.

They left the next day on a wedding trip for two weeks at the luxurious Greenbrier in Virginia. When they returned, she rapidly became known as one of the most beautiful, elegant women in New York.

Andrew hadn't met with his father since before the wedding, and he was in no hurry to see him. He and Angélique were in the papers constantly, as the golden couple. And a month after they returned from their honeymoon, Angélique realized that she was pregnant. Their new life had begun, their dreams were coming true, and Andrew told her every day how much he loved her and that they deserved it. And she believed him.

Chapter 20

Angélique wrote to Mrs. White to tell her that she and Andrew had gotten married, how happy she was, how much she liked New York, and then she wrote to her again when she knew she was pregnant. Mrs. White told Hobson all about it, and he was pleased. He was relieved to know that Her Ladyship was happy, had married a nice man, and was in good hands.

And a letter from Mrs. White in the spring gave her the news that her brother Edward had been killed in a hunting accident. She said the funeral had been at Belgrave, and he was buried in the mausoleum with her parents. She thought about writing to Tristan about it to offer her sympathy, but decided not to after discussing it with Andrew. She had heard nothing from her brother since the last time she had seen him at the Fergusons' and he had denied her as a sister.

"He doesn't deserve the time of day from you," Andrew told her, and she decided he was right.

They had just found a house on Washington Square, and she was busy decorating it, and getting it ready. They planned to move in, in May, and the baby was due at the beginning of October. She had been feeling well, and Andrew thought she was more beautiful than ever, with his baby growing in her gently swelling belly.

She had never seen his father again, although Andrew saw him for dinner from time to time, and had told him about the baby, which only made him angrier. He reminded Andrew that he wanted to hear nothing about her, nor their future offspring. The only relationship he wanted was with his son.

Andrew's political ambitions were going well, and he was planning to run for a congressional seat in November, in a special election to replace a congressman who had died. It was an excellent opportunity for him. It was his first big step into politics, and Angélique was excited for him too. She hoped to be able to be at his side for the final weeks before the election, after the baby was born.

And when they moved into their new home, it was beautiful and everything they hoped it would be, and she was four months pregnant. They entertained friends frequently, and Andrew knew he was a lucky man. He had a wonderful wife he adored.

She had a letter from Fabienne in June, from Provence. Their baby had been born, a son they named Étienne, and they were over the moon about it. And Angélique promised to let her know as soon as their baby was born. She could hardly wait. The nursery she had prepared for it looked like a child's dream. The only argument she and Andrew had was that she wanted to take care of it herself, and he insisted she have a baby nurse. He wanted to be able to go out with her, and said she couldn't do it all alone. They compromised on her having a young girl to help her, but she didn't plan to be a mother like Eugenia Ferguson, or even some of their friends in New

York, who never saw their children. And Andrew said he wanted many, and Angélique was willing. She was excited about becoming a mother. And it was surely going to be easier than taking care of Eugenia's twins. The doctor said it was just going to be one baby. They were hoping for a boy, but Andrew assured her he would be satisfied with a girl too, and they could try for a boy soon after, if that was the case.

They rented a house in Saratoga Springs for the summer, and stayed there for July and August until Labor Day. Andrew made occasional trips to the city for work and his campaign, and in September he got fiercely busy, with dinners, appearances, meetings, and shaking hands with voters everywhere he could, while Angélique stayed home and waited for the baby. She was too big to go out now, was expected to remain out of sight, and had almost nothing to wear that fit her. She complained that she was bored, but she was more tired than she wanted to admit, and she was going to have the baby at home. Everything was ready, and Andrew was more in love with her every day, and she with him.

On the first of October, she was folding tiny shirts in the nursery, with Claire's help, when her water broke and the first pains started. A baby nurse had been hired and was due to arrive from Boston in the next few days. She had been working for a family there.

Angélique went back to their bedroom, to lie down and wait. Claire and their new housekeeper, Mrs. Partridge, brought in stacks of sheets and towels, as she had seen done for Eugenia when she had the twins, and they sent a message to the doctor. He arrived an hour later and said that everything was going well. She was progressing slowly and not in too much pain. And Andrew was at an important dinner with his supporters, and not expected home until that evening. The doctor didn't think the baby would come before midnight, and promised to come back at suppertime. He expected things to move along at a faster pace by then, and he sent a nurse to watch her, as Angélique lay nervously on her bed, timing pains. And nothing much had happened when Andrew got home and said the dinner had gone well.

"It's so tiresome waiting for something to happen," she complained to him when the nurse went down to supper, and he kept her company. He was anxious for the baby to come too, although he was grateful she wasn't in too much pain. And when the doctor arrived to see her again, things were moving more slowly than he'd expected, and he didn't think she'd have the baby until the next day. And they both looked disappointed when he left.

"Maybe if I get up and walk around a little bit," she said to Andrew, and he looked nervous.

"I don't think that's a good idea. You should stay in bed." And just as he said it, the first big pain hit, a whole succession of them one after the other, as she clutched his hand and couldn't catch her breath. It had hit her much harder than she expected, and she lay back against the pillows. Andrew said he'd get the nurse, who was sitting downstairs having tea with Mrs. Partridge.

"No, don't leave me," she gasped as another wave of pain hit her like a tidal wave, and she clung to him for dear life. She felt as though a train were roaring through her and she couldn't stop it. "This is worse than I thought," she admitted to him, and he looked panicked.

"Let me get the nurse." He tried to get away, and she wouldn't let go of his arm.

"No, Andrew, no—" She cried out as pain after pain rolled through her, and she looked dazed when she got a moment's break, just as the nurse walked in, and she could see what was happening. She smiled and told Andrew he could leave.

"No," Angélique begged him, "don't leave me." And they both saw the nurse frown when she saw a pool of blood in the bed.

"Is that unusual?" Andrew asked her, as she shook her head and assured him Mrs. Hanson was fine, and then she discreetly left and asked Mrs. Partridge to send the coachman for the doctor. She said they needed him there at once.

"Is something wrong?" the housekeeper asked her, looking worried.

"Some women just bleed more than others. She looks like a bleeder" was all the nurse would say and went back upstairs where Angélique was starting to scream with the pain, and felt like her back was breaking. She said she could feel the baby coming down, and Andrew and the nurse could see that she was bleeding more.

"My mother died when she had me. What if I die too?" she said to Andrew in a hoarse voice, and he tried to sound calmer than he was. He was worried about all the blood, no one had warned him, and they were going through stacks of sheets and towels. Claire had just brought more. And by then, Angélique couldn't stop crying, and she seemed weaker. The nurse was telling her to push, and she couldn't, and each time she tried, a gush of blood would splash across the bed.

"You're not going to die," he reassured his wife, and prayed it was true, just as the doctor walked in.

"Well, I see we're getting busy. I guess I was wrong, and we're going to have a beautiful baby here tonight." But he frowned when he saw the blood, and Andrew noticed a silent exchange and nod to the nurse, and he knew with a sick feeling in the pit of his stomach that something was wrong. "My dear, let's try and get the baby out quickly," he said to Angélique. "There's no point wasting time, when you can have the baby in your arms. I'm going to need you to push as hard as you can." But she was already too weak and had lost too much blood. She couldn't push hard enough to get the baby out—all she could do was scream and cry with the pain. The doctor looked at Andrew then with an intense expression. "I need you to help her. When I tell you to, I want you to press the baby downward toward me. Don't be afraid to push." Andrew nodded just as another pain hit. The nurse held her legs, Andrew pressed, and Angélique did her best, as the doctor watched what was happening and tried to stanch the flow of blood. They kept at it for another five minutes, and then a tiny face emerged, and then the whole head, and the shoulders, and their little boy was born as Andrew watched him and cried. The baby gave a lusty cry, as his mother picked up her head, smiled at him, and slipped into unconsciousness. There was a pool of blood on the bed, her face was gray, and Andrew couldn't stop crying. He was terrified he was losing her, and the doctor was working hard as the nurse held the baby and took him away to clean him and wrap him in a blanket. He had been born covered in his mother's blood.

"Doctor—" Andrew said in a choked voice, gripped by panic.

"She's lost a lot of blood," the doctor said, and then miraculously it slowed. He watched her for a few minutes, and then put smelling salts under her nose, and Angélique regained consciousness. She was deathly pale and weak, but she was breathing and awake.

"Is the baby all right?" she asked Andrew and the doctor.

"He's fine," Andrew told her. She had given him the fright of his life, and he suspected that she wasn't out of the woods yet. But two

hours later, the doctor seemed satisfied, and after giving her laudanum drops to help her sleep and for the pain, and instructions to the
nurse to give her more in a few hours, he left and spoke to Andrew
on the way out.

"She had a condition called placenta previa," he explained. "Some
women hemorrhage to death from it. I think she'll be all right now,
but she can't get out of bed for a while. And it will take her time to
recover." And then he looked seriously at Andrew. "I wouldn't let
her try again. You could lose her next time or the baby. She was
lucky this time." Andrew nodded, feeling dazed by what he'd just
heard and all he'd seen for the past few hours. He had correctly
sensed that she could have died from the way things were going and
all the bleeding. And all he cared about now was that she was alive,
and so was their son. He walked back into their bedroom and looked
down at her. She was sleeping from the laudanum drops they'd
given her. And sensing him next to her, she looked up groggily and
smiled at him.

"I love you . . . ," she said, drifting off to sleep again.

"I love you too," he said, and meant it with every fiber of his
being. He didn't care if they never had any other children. They had
one now. And he wanted her safe and alive and at his side for the
rest of his life. They had been lucky that night, but he didn't want to
try their luck again. She meant too much to him to take the risk.

They had already agreed to name him Phillip Andrew Hanson,
after her father and Andrew. And her brother Tristan didn't know it,
but the next heir to Belgrave Castle, the estate, and the title, had
just been born. With her brother Edward gone, and Tristan having
only two daughters—unless he had a son before he died, which
seemed unlikely—the baby Angélique had given birth to that night

was Tristan's heir, and her father's. She had explained it all to Andrew in case they had a boy and something happened to her. She wanted him to inherit what was his right. Tristan would have to be told at some point, but there was no hurry. The future Duke of Westerfield had been born that night in New York.

Andrew smiled to himself as he thought about it. It was an antiquated system that cheated people who didn't deserve it, especially women, like his wife. But it was an odd feeling knowing that his son would be a duke one day. And it pleased him to know that the man who had been so cruel to Angélique would get his just deserts in the most natural way, by the same rules and laws he had used to hurt her. The title meant nothing to Andrew, or very little, but Angélique meant everything to him, and now so did their son. His Grace Phillip Andrew, Duke of Westerfield, had arrived.

Chapter 21

A ndrew won his congressional seat in the special election, six weeks after his son was born. Angélique was still too weak to be at his side on election night, but she was at his swearing-in, and so proud of him. He was ecstatic and had won by a wide margin.

The only disappointment in his life was that his father had refused to see the baby, and said he never would. He hated Angélique with an unabating, unrelenting passion, and said that he disapproved of her, which angered Andrew, but there was nothing he could do. His father remained adamant about her. Their life was happy otherwise.

They christened the baby, in January, when Angélique had regained her strength. She looked beautiful, and they gave a party at their home to celebrate the baby. They had been married for a year. And she had sent Tristan a letter from Andrew's attorney in New York, informing him that the heir and next duke had been born, and as they both knew, the estate would be entailed to him one day, and the title. She would have loved to see her brother's face when he got the letter, but just sending it was enough to satisfy her. Tristan had banished her, but her son would inherit the title and whatever was left at the time of Tristan's death, not her brother Edward, if he'd still been alive, or Tristan's daughters, who couldn't inherit any more than she could. They would have had to look for a male cousin if her son hadn't been born. Instead, her father's grandson would step into his shoes one day. Justice would finally be served.

The time passed easily after that. Andrew won his congressional seat the following year in a landslide reelection. They spent time in Washington whenever Andrew had to be there, and she took the baby and nanny with them. She hated to be away from him. They had wisely followed the doctor's advice not to have another baby. Andrew was emphatic about not risking her life again.

She had never seen Andrew's father since before they were married, and she was used to it by now. It was easier this way. She had never told Andrew about meeting him in Paris, and his proposals, and didn't intend to, out of respect for both of them, however little John deserved it.

Three years after he won the special election, at the end of Andrew's second term in Congress, he ran for the Senate. Andrew fought hard for the senatorial seat against a fierce candidate, and three weeks before the election, John Hanson's prediction before their marriage came true. They never knew who unearthed it, but a zealous reporter researched it, and found someone who recognized Angélique and had met her in Paris, at Le Boudoir, and exposed the whole story to the press. She wondered if Andrew's father had tipped off the newspaper, but she didn't think he'd go that far, and hurt his son. But the story was out there, the election was as good as lost, and Andrew withdrew from the race, with a dignified statement about his extraordinary, devoted, loving wife. He retired quietly from political life, while his father reminded him bitterly that he had warned him it would happen one day.

Andrew insisted to Angélique he didn't care. They were happy. She was twenty-five years old, and a happily married woman, Andrew was thirty-four, and their son was three. He had had three years in Congress, and after he withdrew from the election he went back to practice law. She felt terrible about costing him the election.

"It doesn't matter," he promised her, although they both wondered who had exposed her. Andrew had tried to do some investigating, but the journalist wouldn't reveal his source. And so many people had come to Le Boudoir, either once on their travels, or regularly, and had talked to others about the alleged "Duchess" who ran it. She had been famous in Paris, sotto voce, for a short time. And her life was far from all that now. It seemed like a dream when she thought about it. She thought of Thomas, her mentor and protector, occasionally, and wondered how he was, but she could never communicate with him without putting him at risk for some kind of scandal, so she just thought about him and wished him well. She had sent him a note when she got married and nothing since. And he had responded formally with his best wishes, although her note had confirmed what he had feared. That some lucky man would marry her and she would never return to Paris. He had no way of telling her but loved her as much as ever and knew he would to his grave.

She was still in touch with some of the girls. Ambre had married, quite remarkably, and had two children, which seemed unlike her. Fabienne had had one every year and now had four. Philippine had begun a career on the stage, Camille had gone back to her old one. Agathe had a new protector. And she had lost track of the others.

Mrs. White still kept her abreast of what was happening at Belgrave. Both of Tristan's daughters had gotten married to men with minor titles and small fortunes. Hobson was aging and getting frail but was still alive and the head butler at Belgrave, and Mrs. Williams was planning to retire. And some of the old staff she'd grown up with was still there. Markham, her father's devoted valet, had retired years before. And Angélique had been amused to hear that Harry Ferguson had discovered his wife's infidelities, matched only by his own, and had left her for another woman and shocked everyone. He had run off to Italy with a countess, and Eugenia was beside herself. Angélique had heard it all at a party in New York, from people who knew them.

Andrew was incredibly kind to Angélique, as always, about his blighted political career because of her and told her that in some ways it was a relief. And they spent the following summer in Sarasota Springs, as always, and little Phillip turned four in the fall. Angélique would have loved to show him Belgrave, which he would inherit one day, but that still was not possible. Tristan and his attorneys had never responded to the letter about Phillip's birth, but the reality of the entail was there, and where it would lead one day when Tristan died.

And then, just before Christmas, Angélique had a letter from Mrs. White, saying that Tristan was running into serious money troubles, and they were letting go a lot of the staff, but she was still there, and they needed her too much to sack her or force her to retire.

She meant to tell Andrew about it, but he was busy at work, a year after the failed senatorial campaign, and then it was Christmas, and she was busy buying gifts for everyone, and planning a huge party on New Year's Eve, to celebrate their fifth anniversary.

She had had a gown made specially and couldn't wait for Andrew to see it. She had hired an orchestra and they were going to dance after supper. They had invited a hundred guests to celebrate both their anniversary and the New Year with them.

She was dressing that night and waiting for Andrew to come home. He was late, as he often was, and had promised he'd be home in time to dress for their party and guests. She had just slipped into her gown, with Claire's help, and was putting her diamond earrings on that Andrew had bought for her for their fourth anniversary the year before, when Mrs. Partridge came into her dressing room with her face ashen. Instantly, Angélique thought of her son, and feared something had happened to him.

"You'd better come downstairs at once," the housekeeper said, and dared not say more. And as Angélique came down the stairs in her new red dress for their party, she saw three policemen in the hall, and one of them was a captain. He looked up at her expectantly with a serious expression.

"May I speak to you privately, ma'am?" he asked respectfully, and she led him into the library, where he took off his hat and stared at her regretfully. "It's your husband. I'm sorry . . . he was hit by a runaway carriage someone left unattended, leaving his office. He was struck down immediately, ma'am. He . . . I'm sorry," he said again.

"Is he in the hospital?" she asked, holding her breath, hoping that he was, no matter how badly injured, which was better than the alternative. The police captain shook his head.

"There were witnesses. One of them said he didn't look as he stepped off the curb, he was in a hurry and never saw the carriage coming. The lead horse hit him full on and struck him down. He hit his head on the pavement . . . he's at the morgue." She sat down in a nearby chair with a dazed look, unable to believe what he'd told her. It couldn't be. That couldn't happen. They loved each other so much. "I'm sorry, ma'am," the policeman said again, as she thought she was going to faint. "Would you like me to get someone? Do you need a glass of water?" She shook her head. She couldn't speak for a long moment, and then she started to cry. Who could she call for, except Andrew, who meant everything to her? How could she live without him? How would she wake up every morning for the rest of her life if he was gone? Thinking about it, she wanted to die. She couldn't imagine a life without him, just as she couldn't without her father eight years before.

The police captain stood there for a long time, not sure what to do, and then quietly left the room as she cried. He went to tell the housekeeper what had happened, and then they left. Mrs. Partridge went to find her in the library, and gently took her upstairs and helped her lie down on her bed, and left Claire with her.

Mrs. Partridge informed the head footman, and when the guests arrived, they were told at the door what had happened and sent away. The supper for the party they'd planned was given to the servants, and the rest sent to the poor, and a black wreath was placed on the door. Mrs. Partridge had asked the captain if they had advised Mr. Hanson's father, and he said they were going there next, but had wanted to notify his wife first. Funeral arrangements would have to be made, and he assumed Mrs. Hanson would send someone to deal with it in the morning.

Angélique lay on her bed, looking shocked and frozen as Claire sat with her that night as she sobbed. There was no one Angélique wanted to see, no friend who could comfort her. Since the day they met, Andrew had been her whole life.

Andrew's funeral was a somber affair attended by hundreds of people who had been his friends, gone to school with him, or known him in politics and business. All of his clients were there. His father and Angélique sat in separate pews, and never spoke to each other, although they filed out of their pews at the same time and nearly collided. She was holding little Phillip by the hand, who didn't fully understand where his father was and why he was never coming back.

John Hanson and Angélique stood at the burial on opposite sides of the casket, avoiding each other's eyes, and Phillip nearly ripped her heart out, when he asked her if Daddy was in the box, and she nodded. His grandfather had stolen several glances at him, but didn't address her or the child.

And Angélique never came downstairs when friends came to the house after the funeral. She couldn't. The only life she had ever wanted was over, and the man she loved more than life itself was gone. She had no desire to go on without him, although she knew she had to for their child.

The house was like a tomb for the next several months, she rarely went out, and saw no one, although she spent time with her son.

She spoke to none of their friends and she had no idea what to do now. Andrew had left her everything he had, their house, his investments, his very considerable fortune, but there was nothing she wanted to do with it, except pass it on to her son one day. Thanks to Andrew, she had become a very, very rich woman, but as far as she was concerned, her life was meaningless without him.

And in May she got a letter from Mrs. White that woke her up. Tristan had admitted that he was ruined. He had nothing left, after Elizabeth's extravagances and his own, and his arrogant and wanton mismanagement of the estate. Her eyes almost fell out of her head when she read that he had put Belgrave and the London house up for sale. Mrs. White said that Elizabeth was furious with him, and they were barely speaking. He said they were going to move to a small house in London, when both homes were sold, unless the new owners of the estate let them stay on at the Cottage, and rent it. They had nowhere to go, and no money left, and needed every penny from the sale of both properties just to pay their enormous debts. Mrs. White said she hoped the new owners were going to let her stay on—she had been there since she was a girl. And Hobson was going to retire once Belgrave was sold—he said he was too old to adapt to new owners, who didn't belong there. The title would inevitably go to Phillip by law, but not the estate if it was sold.

Angélique read the letter again, dressed immediately in one of her black mourning gowns, and went to see Andrew's lawyer the same day. He had another appointment, but saw her at once when she sent him a message that it was extremely urgent. He hadn't seen her since the reading of Andrew's will in January, and had been told she'd been in seclusion ever since, in terrible shape. And he thought she looked very thin when he saw her, but her eyes were bright. She told him what she'd learned in the housekeeper's letter from Belgrave.

"I'm going over as soon as I can, and I'll need a solicitor in London. Will you help me find one?" She was suddenly energized and nervous and very concerned.

"What are you trying to do?" he asked her, looking sympathetic. "Help your brother with his debts before he sells?" He had no idea of the history between them, and had no reason to. Only Andrew had known. He had told no one else, although his attorney had been made aware that Phillip was the heir to the title and estate, and had sent the letter announcing his birth to Tristan, Duke of Westerfield.

"Certainly not," Angélique said about helping her brother, looking outraged, and more like her old self. "I intend to buy it, without his knowing I did, if possible. I don't want him to know until the sale is complete." Patrick Murphy, the attorney, was startled by the unusual request, but he assumed it would be feasible, if a competent lawyer handled the purchase discreetly.

"Will you be buying the Grosvenor Square house too?"

"No," she said thoughtfully. "I don't need a house in London, and my father never really liked it. But I want my son to know the estate he will inherit one day, and learn to run it long before he does. I can maintain its ownership until he grows up," since she would be purchasing it from Tristan now. And her father had schooled her well in the running of the estate while she was growing up. She was far more competent than her brother. "I'd like him to live there," she said quietly of her son, "just as I did as a child. It's a wonderful place."

"Will you be giving up the house in New York?" Murphy looked surprised.

"I don't know," she said honestly. "I haven't thought that far. All I know is that I want to buy Belgrave Castle before someone else does." He nodded. And as she thought about it, she knew that the house she and Andrew had bought together was too painful to live in without him, and that their life in New York was equally so now that he was gone. She had never thought it would be possible, but now that it was, she wanted to go home. "Please see to it that no one buys it before I get there. Explain all that to the solicitor you hire in London. Whatever another purchaser offers, I will outbid them. I don't intend to lose my home again." He didn't know what she was referring to, and didn't ask. He assured her that he'd take care of it and give her the name of the lawyer he found in London.

She went home then and sent for Claire and Mrs. Partridge, and told them both that she was leaving for England as soon as possible with her son, and she wanted Claire to go with her, if she was willing, which she said she was. She had been happy in New York, but she was young and had formed no strong attachments there in six years, and she liked the idea of going to England and being closer to her relatives in France.

"And when will you be coming back, ma'am?" the housekeeper asked her, looking worried. The staff liked working for her and had been heartbroken to see her so bereft after her husband's death. They wondered what she would do, if she would go back to Europe, or stay in New York. There had been no sign of change till then. She had barely left the house in five months.

"I don't know," she said sadly. "I have some family business to conclude in England. It might take some time." She wasn't ready to tell them she was moving yet. She wasn't sure herself. The housekeeper nodded, and she and Claire both left the room. Angélique

called for the carriage after that and went to the office of the Black
Ball Line.

She discovered that the packet boat *North America* was sailing to
Liverpool in four days, and she intended to be on it. She didn't want
to waste any time. She didn't want Tristan selling Belgrave to the
first offer out of desperation. It was a property that people had cov-
eted for years, and until Tristan took over, it had been in perfect
condition and impeccably run by her father. She had no idea what
the situation was there now, other than that her brother had run out
of funds.

She booked passage for herself, Claire, her son, and his nanny.
She got a stateroom next to hers for Phillip and the nanny, and another small cabin for Claire, as she had before. And when she got
back to the house, she informed the nanny, told her to pack for him,
and told Claire to start packing her trunks.

"What sort of clothes will we be taking?" Claire asked her, wondering. Her mistress had seen no one in five months, nor worn any
of her elegant dresses. She was still in deep mourning for Andrew,
and wore only her plainest black dresses.

"I'm still in mourning," Angélique reminded her, "and I intend to
be all year. But I'll need some other clothes for afterward, and maybe
some decent gowns."

"Will we be staying that long, ma'am?" Claire looked at her, surprised, and Angélique was honest with her, more so than with
Mrs. Partridge.

"Probably. I hope so. We're going back to the house where I grew
up," she told her, and realized that this time what she had claimed
last time on the ship was true. She had said she was a widow, which
had been a lie then, and now she was. And she realized, as she took

things out of her closets and laid them on the bed, how long Claire had known her, all the way back to Le Boudoir, and she had never said a word about it to the other staff. Angélique knew she could trust her, and always had.

She had the nanny pack for Phillip, and for the next three days the house was a furor of packing and sorting, and making decisions about what to take and what to leave, but at least she was no longer languishing on her bed. She had a plan, and she sensed that Andrew would have been pleased to see her up and busy again, and he would have approved of her trying to save Belgrave for their son. It was his birthright.

Patrick Murphy came to tell her that he had written to a solicitor in London, who had been highly recommended, and he hoped his letter would reach him before she did. She would be in London herself in three weeks.

She was adding a few last things to one of her trunks the next day, and had just packed all her jewelry, when Mrs. Partridge came to tell her that she had a guest downstairs.

"Who is it?" Angélique was distracted. She had no idea who it was, and didn't want to see anyone before she left. It was too painful listening to people tell her how sorry they were, when in truth they had no concept of the enormity of her loss when Andrew died. He and their son were all she had.

"I'm not sure who the gentleman is," Mrs. Partridge said, looking puzzled. "I believe it's Mr. Hanson's father, ma'am. He said he was John Hanson. I've never seen him here before." Angélique was startled and hesitated before she went downstairs. Why was he coming to see her now? He hadn't even spoken to her at the funeral, and had never seen Phillip until then. He hadn't even acknowledged the boy at his father's funeral. She almost decided not to go down, and then smoothing her hair and dress, she went.

She found him in the library, looking around the home that they'd lived in for six years and that he'd never seen. He had been no part of their life, only Andrew's, since they married. And she was sure that the loss of his only son had been hard on him as well. She was shocked by how much he had aged in the six and a half years since she'd known him. She had noticed it at the funeral too, but thought he was just grief stricken. He had suddenly become an old man. He was sixty-seven.

"Good afternoon," she said quietly as she walked in. He turned to look at her, and was shaken the minute he did. She was just as beautiful as before, although her eyes were deeply sad, and she was very thin. She didn't want to be rude and ask him why he was there. "I hope you're well."

"Patrick Murphy tells me you're leaving New York." Other than her servants, he was the only one who knew.

"Yes, I am." She was still standing, and didn't invite him to sit down.

"I wanted to say goodbye before you go. I wanted to talk to you a long time ago, but there was never a right time. I'm sorry for the way I behaved when Andrew wanted to marry you. I didn't realize until he died that my fury wasn't because you had been the madam of a brothel in Paris, but because you turned down my proposal and accepted his. I never wanted to face that before." He sat down in a chair then, and looked bereft. "I wanted to marry you desperately and thought you were the love of my life after all those lonely years. And then you married Andrew, and I could see how much you loved each other. I was jealous of my own son." There were tears in his eyes as he said it, and Angélique was stunned. It was an enormous admission, and she didn't know how to respond. She hoped he wasn't going to repeat his offer now that his son was gone. She held her breath, and her tongue. "The reason I wanted to speak to you before you left," he went on, "was to thank you for never exposing me to Andrew. You never told him that you had met me at the brothel in Paris. He told me that you said you'd never met me before. I was very grateful to you for that. You were very generous to allow my son to keep his illusions about me, more than I deserved. You were honest with him, I wasn't. And I'm deeply ashamed of that now. It proved to me that you were a good woman, and an honorable one, and I never admitted that to him. You were more honest with him than I. And I wasted so many years being angry at you for being with him and not me. We could have been together for all this time. And now he's gone, and you and the boy are leaving."

"But you were right that I destroyed his political career," she said regretfully.

"I don't think he minded," John Hanson said honestly. "He never seemed unhappy to me, not for an instant, while he was married to you. And the political ambitions were more my idea than his."

"Thank you for that," she said softly. They had cleaned the slate and settled old scores. It was a good way for her to leave. The war was over.

"Will you be coming back from Europe?" he asked, worried, and she wanted to be straightforward with him and not lie.

"Probably not. I want to see how Phillip likes it there. But I'd rather he grew up in my old home. It's a wonderful place for a child. Better than New York."

"But can you go back after all this time?" He didn't think she could—from what Andrew had said. And the lawyer had only said they were leaving—he didn't say why.

"I'm trying to buy the estate from my brother," she explained, and he nodded. And then he looked at her with pleading eyes.

"May I see the boy? He's the image of his father at that age." She hesitated and then nodded, and left the room to go and find him. He was in the nursery packing his favorite toys with his nanny. He was excited about going on the ship, and Angélique had been telling him all about it.

"There's someone I'd like you to meet," she said quietly as she walked into the nursery and sat down on a small chair next to her son, who was so exactly like his father, just as his grandfather said. It comforted her now to look at him and know that Andrew would live on through their child. And she could look at him every day and see the man she loved.

"Who is it?" Phillip asked her, curious about their guest.

"He's downstairs, and he'd like to see you. Your grandfather, Daddy's father." The child looked surprised. He had no grandparents he knew. Three were dead and one had refused to see him all his life, which he didn't know and had never been told. Andrew's father was simply never mentioned. He didn't exist in their life. Until now.

"Have I ever seen him before?" Phillip asked.

"He was at Daddy's funeral."

"Why didn't he talk to me then?" the child inquired.

"He was probably too sad, just like we were. But he'd like to see you now, and I want you to come downstairs with me to meet him." She held out her hand, and he took it and followed her out the door of the nursery. They went down the stairs together, and Phillip walked into the library ahead of her, and stopped when he saw John Hanson.

"Hello, young man." John smiled at him and reached out to him, so Phillip would approach. "I hear you're going to be taking a trip on a big boat."

"I am." His grandson smiled at him, and told him all about it.

"That sounds like a lot of fun to me. And you're going to England."

Phillip nodded as they chatted. "I'm going to see my other grandfather's house. One day it's going to belong to me, and I'm going to be a duke," he told him conversationally, as though that were entirely normal. His grandfather smiled.

"That's very impressive. Do you think you'll wear a crown?" his grandfather teased him, and Phillip laughed.

"I don't know. My mama didn't tell me that." And then he turned to her. "Will I, Mama?"

"No." All three of them laughed.

"But I'll get to ride horses and go fishing in a lake."

"That sounds very nice. Do you suppose I could visit you there one day? Or maybe you could come back here and visit me."

"If you come to see me, you'll have to take a boat too."

"I do that sometimes. Or maybe you and your mama could come to London sometime to see me when I work there."

Phillip nodded. It all sounded a little complicated to him. "I think I have to go and finish packing now. I'm taking a lot of toys."

His grandfather held out his hand again, and Phillip shook it, did a little bow, and then scampered out of the room and up the stairs.

"He's a wonderful boy," he said to Angélique, and then with sad eyes, "I've been such a fool, and missed so many years."

"You came to see him now. That's a start," she said, touched by the meeting and that he'd come to see them and humbled himself to her.

"May I contact you when I come to London? I'd like to see the boy." She nodded. It would be good for Phillip to have at least one grandparent, and John had just been nice to him. She knew Andrew would have been pleased. It had taken a long time to come around. Five and a half years.

"You're welcome to come and see him," she said carefully, not wanting to encourage him otherwise. His admissions had explained many things, but had also been overwhelming. It had never occurred to her that he'd been in love with her for all those years. She thought that he had forgotten her, except as an object of hatred and fury.

He stood up then, and she walked him to the door. "Thank you for coming and laying old ghosts to rest. It will make everything easier now," she said, smiling at him.

"For me too," he said, and looked relieved. "Take care of yourself, Angélique," he said softly, kissed her on the forehead, and walked out the door remembering the girl he had known and had wanted so desperately in Paris years before. He had finally let her go. And all he felt for her now was respect.

Chapter 22

The crossing from New York to England was very quiet. Angélique had no desire to socialize with anyone, unlike the trip where she'd met Andrew six years before. She ate her meals in her cabin, played with Phillip, and walked around the deck to get some air, and spoke to none of the passengers. All she wanted was to arrive in England and take care of business. She was terrified someone else would beat her to it and her brother would sell Belgrave for a song. She prayed that that wouldn't happen before she arrived.

As soon as they got to London after landing in Liverpool, she checked them into Mivart's Hotel on Brook Street in Mayfair and went straight to the solicitor that afternoon. He had received Patrick Murphy's letter two days before, and had been expecting her. The mission she was giving him was clear.

"I understand that you want to buy the estate and you don't want the duke to know who the purchaser is." He had checked around, and it was evident that the duke was in a great deal of financial trouble, and in debt up to his ears. "Do you want him never to know, or only at the time of the transaction?"

"Until the purchase of the estate is complete," she said simply. "After that I don't care."

"May I ask why?" He was curious but didn't need to know. She told him anyway.

"Because I'm afraid if he knows it's me, he'll block the sale, and sell it to someone else, even if it's for less money." She believed Tristan capable of doing anything to hurt her. His hatred of her was limitless and would be more so now.

"He'd be foolish to do that. He can't afford to. From what Mr. Murphy said in his letter, you're willing to pay almost any price to obtain it. And frankly, he needs the money. Do you know how much he's asking?"

"No, I don't. But simply put, he hates me, and sent me away years ago. He has no idea what's become of me, or that I could buy it."

"He's very lucky you're able to buy it. From what I understand, his many creditors are getting impatient. They could foreclose on the estate. He had liens against it, gambling debts, and it's been mortgaged to the hilt."

"We'll pay all the debts to clear it," she said quietly.

"So I understand. That will be a hard offer to refuse."

"Not if he knows it's me. It will kill him to have me get the estate in the end. Our father would have left it to me if he could have. My brother got Belgrave only because it was entailed to him. And he threw me out the next day."

"So I'm to tell him that it's an American purchaser who wishes to remain discreet and in the shadows, and always does business that way. Do you think he'll balk at that?" the solicitor asked her. Like everyone else, he was fascinated by her beauty, and determination.

"He'd sell it to a gorilla if it had the money." She smiled at him.

"And you're sure you don't want to make a deal for the London house as well?" She shook her head in answer. "He needs to sell that too. You could probably get a good deal for both."

"I want to live in the country. I don't need a house in London. I can stay at a hotel when I come, or buy a smaller house one day if I want to spend time here. One very large old house, with an army of servants to run it, is enough for me. And I still have a house in New York." She was thinking about selling it, but was in no hurry. She'd thought about it on the way over on the boat, trying to make up her mind. She wanted to see how Belgrave felt to her first, after all these years.

"I know who his solicitor is, and will contact him first thing tomorrow. Where can I reach you?"

"At Mivart's Hotel. I'll be waiting to hear what they say. What are you going to do?"

"Find out what they're asking, and make him a flat offer he can't resist. I won't play games with him," he said seriously.

"I want to conclude this quickly," she said firmly with a will of iron in her eyes, which took him by surprise too. She was a woman who knew what she wanted and in this case would stop at nothing to get it.

"I understand. We'll do all we can to make that happen," the lawyer said firmly.

"Thank you." They shook hands, and she left and went back to the hotel.

She walked around London a little bit that afternoon, admiring the shops, and went to bed early. And she was on pins and needles the next day until noon. And at five minutes after twelve, a clerk from the front desk brought her a note to tell her that Mr. Barclay-Squires was downstairs, and she told him to send the lawyer up to her suite. She let him into the room, and led him into the parlor of the suite. She had several bedrooms for Claire, the nanny, herself, and Phillip, and a parlor for just this purpose.

The lawyer was quick to reassure her. "It went very well. The solicitor was quite direct with me, probably more than your brother would have liked. He says they are desperate for a fast sale. He wants thirty thousand pounds, all inclusive, which would cover the debts and give him a small profit he needs to live on, and apparently there's a cottage on the estate that he wants to rent from you for a small amount."

"Absolutely not," she said with ice in her eyes.

"I thought as much, and already told the solicitor it wasn't possible."

"Thank you," she said, relieved. "So what did we offer?"

"Twenty-eight. I would have gone lower, but I know you want to do this quickly. They'll hold at thirty and we'll agree."

"Are you sure that's wise? Should we have just agreed to his price?"

"I think we're fine the way it is," the solicitor said calmly. "He said he'd go down to Hertfordshire today, and come back to me tomorrow when he returns. Your brother is as anxious to conclude this deal quickly as you are. I think we'll have an answer very soon."

"Are there any other offers?" she asked, worried.

"None, the debts will frighten everyone off, except you." She smiled at what he said, and he promised to contact her the next day as soon as he heard anything from Tristan's lawyer.

She didn't have long to wait, although it felt like an eternity to her. The following afternoon, Barclay-Squires was back, seated in her private parlor across from her.

"What did they say?" she asked anxiously.

"Thirty. He says he can't afford to take twenty-eight. I agreed, and said they could have the money as soon as the papers are signed. I don't think it will be long. He did ask who the purchaser was, in strict confidence, and I said I was under equally strict confidence not to reveal it. I don't think he really cares, just so he gets the money. I said it was a rich American who wants a castle, and rolled my eyes in disgust." He smiled at her. "And the solicitor specified that the purchase does not include the title, but he said he would sell that for another ten, which I said wasn't of interest."

"You're quite right," Angélique confirmed. "My son will inherit it when my brother dies. We can wait till then." It disgusted her to know that her brother would even have sold the title.

"Quite so," the lawyer said, realizing that she was a force to be reckoned with. She hadn't been able to inherit the estate, but now she was going to buy it, and fortunately she could. And as she thought about it that night, she realized that the money her father had given her was more than covering the purchase of his estate, which Tristan could never have suspected. In fact, long after he died, her father was buying her their ancestral home, which her brother was only too happy to sell, "with the title." It was revolting. But luckily for her he was in debt.

Two days later the papers were delivered to the solicitor's office signed by Tristan, Duke of Westerfield, with his seal. The solicitor had made it clear to the other attorney that the purchase was to include all the furniture, art, and contents of the estate, which Tristan had agreed to. His only question was how long he was to be given before he had to move out himself.

"Ten minutes," Angélique said, smiling. She was thrilled. "Forty-eight hours," she said more reasonably, but with no mercy in her eyes. She was a kind, compassionate woman, but not where her brother was concerned. He didn't deserve it after what he had done to her.

"He might balk at that," the lawyer said.

"He gave me one night nine years ago when I was eighteen and he cast me out into the world, only days after my father died."

"I'll tell them," Mr. Barclay-Squires said quietly.

And the next morning, everyone was distracted by the fact that King William had succumbed to heart failure, at the age of seventy-one. And with no legitimate children, he was to be succeeded by his niece, Victoria, who had reached her eighteenth birthday only weeks before. It seemed oddly fitting to Angélique that a woman should be taking the throne as she herself was returning triumphantly to Belgrave. And not in a million years had Tristan expected her to do that, and still didn't. He had no idea who had bought his home, and probably didn't care.

Angélique signed the papers with her married name, and only her first initial, not her first name, to preserve her anonymity. She returned them to Mr. Barclay-Squires, and he duly returned a set to Tristan's lawyer and informed him that the duke had to remove himself from the property in forty-eight hours.

"That is not going to go over well," the lawyer said unhappily.

"It's a condition of the sale, and he signed it. If he wants the money deposited at his bank, he'll be out on time," Barclay-Squires said in an iron tone.

"I'll convey the message." He returned to Belgrave for the third time in as many days, and Elizabeth shrieked when her husband told her that night.

"Are you insane? How am I supposed to pack and leave in two days?"

"If we want the money, we have no choice. I wasn't going to argue with them. This is the best possible deal we could have gotten. It's unfortunate they wouldn't let us stay at the Cottage. But we still have Grosvenor Square for now," he tried to reassure her, but diplomatic relations had broken down between them ever since she had understood the magnitude of his debts.

"Until your creditors throw us out." She glared at him. "You're lucky the American bought this house. Did they tell you who it is?"

"No, and I don't give a damn. We got what we needed out of it, Elizabeth, so stop complaining and go pack."

They had all of their belongings, heaped in mountains of trunks, in the front hall in two days, and the servants were scurrying everywhere, loading boxes and bags onto carriages. The staff were very nervous about the mysterious person who had bought the estate, but the departure of the duke and duchess was proving to be so challenging that no one had time to think about it.

Elizabeth left for London at sunset, and Tristan decided that he didn't care what they said, he was spending the night in his own bed, and would leave the next morning. And if the new owner didn't like it, they could be damned. They probably wouldn't show up for a few days anyway. He went upstairs to his bedroom, and the servants went downstairs to talk about the sudden changes at Belgrave, and guess at what would come next.

Angélique left Mivart's before dawn in a hired carriage. She wanted to get to the castle first, to look around, see the condition the place was in, and make sure there were comfortable bedrooms in good order. Her son, his nanny, and Claire would be arriving later in the day. And thanks to Mrs. White, her remarkable staff, and even Hobson, she was sure the place would at least be clean. She had no idea what changes her brother and his wife had made—but she knew there had been many while they had still had money to do them.

As of that morning, Belgrave Castle, its forests and lands, tenant farms, the Cottage, and the Dower House belonged to her, to pass on to her son one day, just as it was meant to be. And if an eighteen-year-old girl could become queen of England, Angélique was sure that she could run the estate. She was only sad that Andrew wasn't there to see it, and hoped that he was watching over them. She always felt him near her, just as she did her father, wishing her well.

The ride to Belgrave was longer than she remembered, and she was anxious to arrive. The carriage rolled through the main gates at noon, as she stared up at the familiar building, and tears rolled down her cheeks. She had never expected to see it again, and had thought it was lost to her forever for the past nine years.

At the sound of the carriage approaching, the staff filed out of the house in orderly fashion, and stood at the front door, waiting to greet the new master. The coachman let down the steps, and Angélique gathered her skirt around her. She had worn a simple black linen dress with a matching bonnet, and she lightly stepped down and looked at the many familiar faces that were still there. Mrs. White's hand flew to her mouth, and Hobson's eyes grew huge as they recognized her, and some of the maids who'd been mere girls were women now, and even some of the footmen were still familiar, as one of the older maids picked up her apron and wiped her eyes. Angélique was crying too as she ran the last few steps to embrace them.

"Oh, my dear child," Mrs. White kept saying as she hugged her, and Hobson threw his arms around her too. And just like the staff she had grown up with, she was a woman now, no different, but more mature, no longer the terrified young girl her brother had banished when she was only eighteen. She had survived it all and come back, like a swallow in spring to find her home again. And she couldn't wait for them to meet her son, and for him to see his new home, where she had lived at his age.

They were a melee of crying, laughing, smiling people, as Hobson opened the front door for her, and she was relieved to see that there at least, very little had changed. It was like traveling back through time to where she'd started, and hoped to never leave again.

She wandered from room to room on the main floor, thinking of her father, and feeling him beside her, as she heard footsteps on the stairs, and emerged from the library with her hair soft around her face and her bonnet in her hand. As Mrs. White had said to Hobson, she still looked like a young girl.

He reminded her that she was barely more than that.

And as she walked into the hall, to their mutual astonishment, Angélique found herself facing her brother, who was finally getting ready to leave.

"What are you doing here?" he said angrily, unable to understand why she was standing there like a ghost. She had come back to haunt him at the final hour, and neither of them was a welcome sight to the other, despite the blood they shared and the passage of time.

"You weren't supposed to be here," she said in a strong, firm voice.

"And why is that? What brings you back here, and on this particular day? Neither of us belongs here now. I just sold it to an American," he said, gloating over the fact that he had deprived her of her home yet again. But the final joke was on him.

"So I understand," she said quietly. "I came back to have a look."

"Well, you'd better get out before he arrives."

"The new owner won't be here till this afternoon." She was referring to her son. She had bought it for him, and the children he would have one day.

"And what would you know about all that?" He had told no one but the lawyer and the staff. "I see you still have your spies here. It won't do you any good." She was only listening to him with half an ear—she was so happy to be home again, and sorry that he was still there. But even he couldn't spoil it for her. The victory was hers, more than he knew. "I heard about your exploits in Paris," he said to her scathingly, as he walked over to her. "It doesn't surprise me that you wound up in a brothel. I always knew you would." She wondered how he had heard of it, but didn't ask. She didn't care. "Just like your mother, the French whore who seduced my father. He was besotted with her, just as he was with you." Tristan oozed poison from every pore.

"Will you miss all this?" she said, smiling coolly at him, ignoring what he'd said, not dignifying it with a response. "It's a shame you couldn't sell the title too. The person who owns it now doesn't need your title. He has his own." As she said it, Tristan looked at her with hatred in his eyes, longing to put his hands around her throat to throttle her, but she wasn't afraid of him anymore. She was taunting him, and suddenly he realized what had happened. For the first time, he knew why she was there.

"Did you . . . are you . . ." He understood everything now. He had no idea how she had bought it, but he was suddenly sure she had. It had never dawned on him that the secretive American was a woman, and even more shockingly, his sister. For him, it was like seeing her rise from the grave.

"I bought it for my son. I believe you're trespassing now. You were supposed to be gone by last night."

"I'll go when I damn well please," he said with his usual arrogance.

"No, Tristan, actually you won't. Get out of my house now, or I'll have someone fetch the constable. You don't belong here anymore. You never did." He looked as though he were going to slap her, but he didn't dare. "And if you want your money, stay away from me, and away from here. Belgrave no longer belongs to you." He stormed past her then and strode to the front door. He turned one last time to look at her with hatred in his eyes. He was bereft of speech for the first time in his life. He had thought he had gotten rid of her forever, and instead she had come back and won in the end. He turned on his heel then and walked out and slammed the enormous heavy door behind him, as Angélique heaved a sigh of relief. The nightmare was finally over, nine years after it had begun. Tristan had tried to take her home from her, and banish her forever, and despite all his evil machinations, justice had been served. He was gone. And she had won.

She spent the rest of the day looking around the house, at the changes they had made. Some of them were pretty and others weren't and could be undone. She wasn't sure what room she wanted to sleep in. Surely not her father's. She finally decided on her old suite of rooms near his, and a sunny one near her for Phillip and his nanny. She didn't want him in the nursery far away from her, especially in a new house. And she saw that the staff were slim.

"They let a lot of them go when the money ran out," the house-keeper explained, and then Angélique looked at her thoughtfully.

"You know, if you hadn't written to tell me when they put the house up for sale, I would never have known to buy it, and someone else would have. Thank God you did." The housekeeper smiled at her, still amazed by everything that had happened, and that Angé-lique was back again. It was like a dream.

"I'm sorry about your husband," Mrs. White said to her gently.

"He was a wonderful man. You would have loved him," Angé-lique assured her. "And he would have loved it here. I can't wait to show it to my son. Are there still horses in the stables?" she thought to ask then.

"A few. They sold all the fine ones, but there are still some good mounts left." Angélique wanted to teach Phillip how to ride, and show him all their land. He had a lot to learn before he grew up, about running the estate, and so did she while she held it for him. She still remembered everything her father had taught her about the estate before he died.

They went outside when they heard the carriage pull up, and Hobson came too. When the coachman opened the door, Hobson lifted Phillip out and set him on his feet.

"Good afternoon, my lord," he said formally. "Welcome to Bel-grave." He smiled at the boy then, and Phillip smiled cautiously at him, and then gave his mother a hug.

"Am I a duke yet, Mama?" he asked his mother, and she laughed.

"No, not yet. And probably not for a long time."

She took him through the front door then, with the others following, to show him his new home. It looked big and daunting to him. And she told him stories as they went through, about her own childhood, and his grandfather, of riding, and fishing in the lake, and all the things they were going to do, and then she took him upstairs to his room next to hers, and he stood on tiptoe, looking out the window, to see the view.

"Look, Mama, there's the lake!" he said happily as she stood next to him. "Does all of that belong to us?"

"Yes," she said softly. She had never thought this moment would come. "And one day it will belong to you." And to his children, and their children, just as it had belonged to their ancestors for hundreds of years. And hopefully would remain in their family for years and years. They were part of a chain, linking the centuries, their ancestors behind them, the children to come ahead of them, each of them contributing what they could before passing it on to the next generation. And now, through an extraordinary stroke of luck, it had come to her, and one day she would give it all to him.

"I like it here," Phillip said, as he turned to smile at her, and she could already imagine the man he would become one day, when he stepped into her father's shoes. She was the bridge between the two, the past and the present, as she leaned down to kiss him, and put an arm around him.

"I'm glad you do," she said softly. "So do I." Things were just as they were meant to be. Her destiny had brought her back to Belgrave, where she belonged. And as they looked out the window together, they both knew they were home.

About the Author

DANIELLE STEEL has been hailed as one of the world's most popular authors, with over 650 million copies of her novels sold. Her many international best sellers include *Against All Odds, Dangerous Games, The Mistress, The Award, Rushing Waters, Magic, The Apartment, Property of a Noblewoman,* and other highly acclaimed novels. She is also the author of *His Bright Light,* the story of her son Nick Traina's life and death; *A Gift of Hope,* a memoir of her work with the homeless; *Pure Joy,* a tribute to the many dogs her family has loved; and the children's books *Pretty Minnie in Paris* and *Pretty Minnie in Hollywood.*

daniellesteel.com
Facebook.com/DanielleSteelOfficial
@daniellesteel